Foul Wind

Foul Wind

Kathy McIntosh

A Havoc in Hancock Humorous Suspense

Dogged Kat Press
ISBN: 978-0692525692

For Mark, for every season, for every reason

Also by Kathy McIntosh

Mustard's Last Stand, A Havoc in Hancock Humorous Suspense

Praise for Mustard's Last Stand

An endearingly quirky cast of characters and a humorous voice that's sure to captivate, combined with a mission that both nature lovers and Don Quixote would celebrate, make *Mustard's Last Stand* an absolute charmer! *Don't miss this fun debut.* -

Kris Neri, award-winning author of *Revenge on Route 6* and *Magical Alienation*

One

When Surrounded by Wolves ... Never Turn Your Back

Charlene Sullivan, forest name Feather, strode up the brick path to the imposing home of Brad and Kristin Ganborena, tonight's objectives her only focus. First, find Brad, then find Jared. She walked through the open door, and ran smack into Kristin, the woman who despised Feather above all others.

Kristin waited to greet those invited to her party. Fortunately, the melee in the street distracted Kristin's attention long enough for Feather to pass. Thank heaven for Roadkill and his merry band of miscreants. Cries of "Come in out of the wind," "Not in my bat yard," and "Money for causes, not parties," accounted for Kristin's pained rather than welcoming expression. No doubt she and Brad had hoped to avoid the activists' picketing when they planned their party as a fundraiser for local conservation groups. As Feather eased into the mélange of costumed party guests, she heard Roadkill's unmistakable baritone shouting, "Turbines kill, oil spills."

Huh? Sometimes even Feather, now a semi-retired activist, wondered if Roadkill wished the world to live as lightly as he did, something not possible for most. Perish the thought of enough road kill to clothe the populace of Hancock, Idaho, let alone the world.

Neither an invited guest nor a welcome one, Feather was grateful for the protesters and for her costume, which included a large, far too warm but effective face mask that covered nearly everything except her mouth. With the food the Ganborenas offered, an unrestricted mouth was essential. She sent Kristin a vague nod of her striped, furred head and walked into the throng of festively costumed partiers.

She edged near a wall and pulled her costume down from where it threatened to give her a wedgie. Essentially a one piece swimming suit with fur and a tail, it was a tad short for her longish torso. Dark gray tights covered her legs. She surveyed the gathering, hoping to find her sister and elude her mother. Her mother was one of several investors in Windfall Works, the new wind farm that spurred the activists' protest.

Arguments sparked by the protesters competed with discussions of the party's menu. Go figure. Some folks got more excited by Basque food than by wind energy. Too bad no one could harness all of tonight's hot air.

Near her a tall guest, dressed as a pine tree, waved his branches with too much vigor for the conditions. "We have to find some way to decrease our dependence on coal-fired energy. You'd think those freaks outside would *love* wind energy." His voice rose in mockery. "But no, it hurts the little bats and the raptors."

His companion nodded. "There's hydro-electric. Idaho has plenty of water."

"But not plenty of salmon," his companion opined.

Feather wanted to argue the importance of locating wind turbines where they did the least harm to the wildlife. But she had to remain silent and inconspicuous, out of Kristin's radar.

She edged toward the food, alert to anyone who might recognize her and finger her to Kristin.

Before she reached her target, she was surrounded by wolves, alert but distracted by their surroundings and sluggish after their recent feast.

The badger, Feather, chose not to back away. She would stand and fight the wolf pack, if necessary.

"Bad choice of costumes, hon," said one of the nearest wolves. "Badgers have short legs and yours go on for friggin' ever." The man in the wolf costume leaned close and patted her fanny.

Feather curled her lip, a gesture she hoped conveyed contempt and disgust in both worlds—badger and human. She'd chosen her costume to discourage friendly chit-chat. Also because it was the only one in her favorite thrift store that came close to fitting her and her budget.

The men who circled her were, alas, appropriately costumed. Fanny patting, leering and drooling at the sight of a halfway comely female came easily to them.

"Badgers have been known to scare off grizzlies," she growled, disguising her voice. "No touching the badger's butt."

"But such a lovely butt," said a different wolf. "May I get you a drink?"

She shook her head and meandered off as if she simply chose to mingle elsewhere.

Where was her sister?

Roxanne's choice to come as a fluffy, innocent, pampered Persian cat to a party where most came dressed as wild animals suited her little sister. A wish fulfillment fantasy to be coddled and spoiled? And yet, still a predator, so beware, pine siskins, robins, and mini-fauna. The striking costume Roxanne wore should stand out, but other women had chosen to come as snow leopards—*in Idaho? Why?*—and Feather caught sight of several patches of white.

Feather accepted a glass of white wine from a member of the catering staff. She had to find Brad before she was recognized, but she might as well fortify herself first. She had to speak with Brad before she undertook the second half of her mission, despite her desire to simply dash up the stairs.

Without warning someone grabbed Feather's shoulders in a powerful grip. Her wine splashed on the hardwood floor. "Ah hah. Found you again."

She twisted her neck to see who held her. Her captor chuckled. "Not so fast, wee badger." His phony Scots accent rankled. "I claim my victor's prize." The man was muscular but not exceptionally tall, standing even with Feather's five feet, nine inches.

Keeping her firmly captive, to the point where Feather figured she'd have bruises to remind her, the man moved in front of her and leaned toward her. He flipped back the expensive wolf mask he wore. Jonathan Flynn. Another investor in the wind farm, who managed its day to day business. If he recognized Feather, he might tell Brad or Kristin and then where would she be? Out the door of the luxurious Ganborena home.

"Such a pretty badger," he crooned.

Feather's reaction came almost without thought. Old instincts rose to guide her. A man spurned would remember his prey. A man who felt he'd won would forget this conquest and move on to the next. Particularly a competitive, financial risk-taker like Jonathan. He counted coup.

Relying on her mask to conceal her identity, Feather stood on tiptoe and planted a vigorous kiss on Jonathan's lips. Startled, he released her arms. She grasped his face between her hands—paws tonight—and continued the kiss until she sensed his surprise morphing to arousal. She backed away and smiled.

"You are without a doubt the alpha wolf," she crooned, hoping throatiness masked her voice. With a mysterious, badger-like smile, she strutted away. Although she had little experience of smiling badgers.

She lost herself among the guests stalking the table where the caterers had provided, not only Basque snacks, but offerings suited to less adventurous palates. Feather loaded a plate with various pintxos, the Basque equivalent of tapas.

A voice came from her right. A too-familiar voice. "If I hadn't seen your plate, I might have thought I mistook that sexy voice."

Too soon. She wasn't ready. Feather gasped and looked into the eyes of her former lover Brad Ganborena. She switched her focus back to the food.

"I'm not going to ask why the hell you're here, or even how you got in without Kristin noticing, but it might be a good idea to eat and run. We don't need a scene tonight. Enough of that outside."

"God forbid I scare away potential investors."

"Of course. Rules of the game." Brad added a generous slice of Basque tortilla, similar to a frittata, to Feather's plate. "Tuna. Yellowfin's not endangered. With local eggs, even. You'll love it. Now eat up and scoot that gorgeous badger body out of here as fast as you can."

Feather looked up at Brad. Her pulse increased. To hide any expression she might reveal, she popped a pepper into her mouth. Chewing, good. Speaking, bad. Choosing one of the hottest peppers on the table, exceedingly bad. Her face flushed. She wished the mask covered her ears, which by now blazed bright red with heat.

Brad leaned across her and grabbed a napkin. He held it in front of her mouth and she spat the remains of the pepper into it. Then he scooped some yogurt from a bowl artfully displayed on a bed of greens onto her plate. He picked up a spoon and offered her a large bite of the cooling balm.

She realized that this man, the adulterer she had tried hard to hate—and yes, she knew she was the woman whom he'd strayed with, making her, in olden terms, a fornicatress—did indeed possess a few virtues. Like kindness and consideration and the grace to allow her to leave without being exposed to his jealous, spiteful—albeit beautiful and talented and highly educated—wife.

"Actually, I came to talk to you. I need to talk to you."

"Tonight? Couldn't you make an appointment?"

"Are you kidding? If I'm seen with you, Kristin will blow a gasket."

"No reason she should." Brad sighed. "But you're right. Come on. I can spare a few minutes."

He led her through the kitchen to the back porch, but switched directions when he saw the numerous smokers huddled in the cool evening. Back through the kitchen and down the stairs to the wine cellar.

"Okay." Brad waited, arms crossed in front of his chest, expression guarded.

Feather removed her mask. No pretense. No stalling. "I need a loan. Charlie West offered his time and his construction crew before the snow flies to get the B&B started. But I don't have enough cash for the supplies, and ... Mom won't loan it to me. She calls the idea *feather*-brained." Jeanette Sullivan despised her daughter's choice of forest names. "I don't have time to apply for a bank loan." Sweat dripped down the back of her neck. Her chest tightened.

"Not sure your credit report would get you much, anyway. Activist, waitress, unwed mother."

Feather's jaw clenched. "College graduate holding down two jobs. Already have the land, free and clear." Thanks to good friends.

Brad took a few steps to the left, then right. Dancing or a mini-pace for the crowded space? "I sunk a lot of money into Windfall

Works. The wind farm is taking longer to get going than we expected."

"Feather's Beds is a good investment. It will be a great place for potential investors, inspectors, whoever, to stay. Hancock has only one B&B, and if you don't count The Tidy Scot—and no one in his or her right mind would—nowhere else for investors or tourists to stay. Spokane's too far; Sandpoint's too pricey. If we can start immediately, I'll be open in the spring."

Brad raised his eyebrows. "Ambitious schedule."

"Exactly why I can't take time to find other loans." Begging was awful, worse than biting into that pepper. Why couldn't her mother have cooperated? Feather regretted her naïve refusal of any payment when she gave up Jared for adoption by Brad and Kristin, a decision that came after months of painful internal debate. But Brad was the father and Jared would be adored and coddled, his life stable and comfortable with the Ganborenas as his parents.

Not to mention the guilt Feather felt about her affair with Brad. She had asked for and received nothing from Brad and Kristin. Nothing, she thought with bitter regret, but a promise to comply with the terms of the open adoption. She'd not even received that.

She said nothing, only gazed at her former lover.

Moments passed. Feather held her breath.

Brad fiddled with a bottle in the wine rack. "How much do you need?"

Feather released her breath. "Thirty thousand. I'll pay interest, of course."

"I don't have that much to spare, Feather. Windfall's a cash drain."

Feather tried to keep her face from revealing her despair, but Brad could read it. "I'll talk to Kristin."

Oh, sure, Kristin would jump for joy at loaning Feather fifty cents, much less thirty thousand dollars. Since it was the best she could hope for from Brad, there was no point getting snotty. "Thank you. You know I wouldn't ask if I weren't desperate."

"I wish I could just give you the money. In a few years...."

"I need it now, Brad. Please talk to Kristin soon. Winter could arrive sooner than usual."

"Promise."

Feather knew he would keep that promise, just as she knew what Kristin's response would be.

Her shoulders sagged as she headed for the door.

"Now you really ought to leave before Kristin sees you. Even in that costume, you're distinctive."

"Uh huh." But despite her disappointment and the fear of exposure, she knew she would make her way to the second floor nursery. Nothing could stop her, not when she was so close to her objective.

Two

Seek and Ye Shall Find ... Trouble

Was it the costumes, or the beer and wine that flowed as fast as the Lochsa River after snow melt? Something had stripped away the inhibitions of the party-goers, despite the fact the costumes did little to hide the identities of most. It paid to be visible at parties, especially fund-raising parties. These events were all about networking.

When had fun and communion morphed into networking, one more method to get ahead? When would these people decide enough was enough, and let her get upstairs unseen?

Guests munched, drank, and launched desperate quests to find important people who could help their cause, loan them money, or employ them. From her shadowy corner Feather observed many attempted ascents on the peaks of power fail, the hopefuls walking away with downcast eyes and slumped postures. She definitely related to their feelings.

Politicians from Idaho and Washington state and their aides smoothly cut through the chaff of the everyday voter to the desirable wealthy patrons, presumably without offending the less powerful or wealthy. More likely just not caring, since re-election depended on money.

Eventually the party crowds thinned and Feather knew it was her time. She backed in the direction of the stairs, confident no one noticed. *At last,* she thought. *This evening couldn't have gone slower.*

A tall, lean woman, bearing a tray burdened with a mixture of tiny croquetas and shot glasses filled with creamy potato soup, walked past Feather. A female guest, costumed as a skunk and possibly as drunk as, hurried in front of the staircase from the great room, focused on the cell phone she held. She collided with the server.

For scant seconds it seemed possible that the server would recover and be able to rebalance her tray. Then one after another the shot glasses toppled over and the tray tilted to one side, soup and fried rolls falling to the hardwood floor along with a few shot glasses that bounced rather than broke when they hit the floor.

The server regained control of her tray by dropping to a crouch in the mess. Feather ran to her and took the tray from her so she could rise.

The "skunk," now streaked with white goop, yelled, "Idiot. You crashed into me. Ever heard of 'watch where you're going?'" She peered down at herself. "Look at me. You've ruined my costume. Where's your supervisor?"

Feather recognized the skunk, one of Brad's partners in Windfall Works. In Feather's experience banker Sophia Patton was neither rude nor nasty, but she was doing a good imitation of both tonight.

"I am so sorry, ma'am. I didn't see you."

"But —" Feather protested. Anyone who saw the collision knew the fault wasn't the server's.

"Thank you for your help." The server reached for the tray with a warning look at Feather. *Now shut up*, her eyes begged. To the woman she said, "Let me return this to the kitchen and find my supervisor."

Soon a man arrived, holding a small notebook and extending a glass of champagne to Sophia. He was a slight redhead whose freckled, porcelain skin and innocent blue eyes assured his being carded at every nightclub.

Rage exuded from Sophia like an ugly aura. "I wanted to see a *supervisor*, not a child. Must I search out our hosts?"

With a charming smile, the redhead assured the woman of his title, his maturity and his competence, took her name and address, gave her his card, and convinced her to take the champagne. A different server offered her a cloth to wipe her tights while the original "culprit" returned to clean up the mess. Feather knelt to help her. "She ran right into you. Texting, no doubt."

The woman smiled. "But the customer is always right."

A waitress herself, Feather knew that the woman was correct, even if Feather chafed against the statement. She pondered what kind of a burr Sophia had up her slinky costume tonight to be so rude.

Feather returned to the shadows near the stairs but before she did, she threw a comment over her shoulder to the supervisor. "That guest was texting, ran right into your server."

She refocused on tonight's quest. She edged farther into the shadows and waited for the opportunity to slip upstairs.

Upstairs, Feather turned right and opened the third door, a hard grip on the handle, breath caught against the tiniest creak. She'd made it this far. She couldn't be caught, couldn't be stopped this close to her goal. She closed the door behind her without a sound.

The cozy glow of a night light revealed the shape of an infant sleeping in the crib. She bit her lip, fighting to keep herself from cooing his name, from touching him.

Her son. Her beloved baby.

Nine months earlier, Feather gave birth to the child whose tiny snores now reminded her of a dreaming kitten. Then, giving him up for adoption by Brad and Kristin had seemed a good decision, reasonable and best for her baby. An open adoption—Jared would be Kristin's and Brad's son, and Feather would be kept updated on his progress and allowed scheduled, supervised visits.

That was then. She should have known better. Within a few months, Kristin's commitment to openness shrank faster than Feather's now-empty uterus. Kristin, a lawyer in Spokane, just over the Idaho border, used her legal expertise to interpret the adoption agreement so Feather's written updates were now without accompanying photos and her last visit with her son had been a long seven weeks earlier. Her last *official* visit.

Now, barely daring to breathe, she inched closer to the crib. The room had a baby monitor that the nanny, Brad and Kristin checked often. Feather's unauthorized party-crashing visit to Jared's room was messed up, but in *her* opinion, Kristin's behavior was unfair and unreasonable.

Jared's sturdy arms splayed out to both sides, his head turned away from Feather. He rolled over to his side, facing her, drooling a little, making tiny farting sounds. Absolutely adorable. She removed her costume mask she'd used to slip through the party unnoticed. What would it do to Jared's psyche to waken to the sight of a giant badger beside his crib?

Seeing the baby in his home environment was worth the risk of being caught.

Once Feather realized Kristin didn't intend to honor her promises, she convinced her younger sister to apply for the job of nanny when Kristin returned to work. Roxanne had been a nanny for another couple and had a genuine and obvious love for children. Getting the job wasn't easy. Everyone in their small community knew Roxanne and Feather were sisters, but everyone also knew they didn't spend much time together. Roxanne convinced Kristin, who was becoming desperate to find a good caretaker before heading back to work, that she had not approved of Feather's giving her son up for adoption. Told her that as Jared's aunt, she would be the ideal nanny. Kristin and Brad believed her. Roxanne should put talented, convincing liar on her resumé. A skill Feather knew she could never claim.

Unable to stop herself, Feather reached out and touched the baby's hand. He immediately grabbed hold of her finger. The little guy had quite a grip. Feather relished it.

She stood content beside the crib watching the baby sleep for some 10 minutes, minutes that seemed only an instant. Staying longer increased the odds she'd be caught. "This is where you belong, little guy," she whispered, her voice a mere puff from her lips. "They love you and you'll grow up in a good family." Except for her insane jealousy of Feather, Kristin was an adequate mother. Okay, an excellent, doting mother.

Jared's face contorted into a grimace and he let out a series of grunts. He produced a huge plopping bowel movement, noisy and runny and redolent of squash, possibly artfully mixed with turkey. Feather wrinkled her nose. Jared released her finger but his face again scrunched up. He apparently shared Feather's opinion of his recent discharge because his wail might easily have been heard 500 miles south in Boise. No need for an electronic monitor.

"Time for Mommy to say bye-bye, sweetheart," she murmured under his screeching. "Nanny will be here to take care of you soon."

Certain the yowling, either direct or via the baby monitor, would summon Kristin, or more likely, Roxanne, Feather leaned over the crib and blew a kiss at her son. The wide awake child didn't seem to recognize Feather, not surprising since she hadn't been allowed to see him for nearly two months, save for a couple of brief, unauthorized visits at a coffee house where she and Roxanne met up.

Feather backed away from the crib instead of picking the infant up to relieve his discomfort. Jared's wails increased in volume and possibly with surprise. The little guy wasn't accustomed to being left in misery. A giant was there. A giant should help him.

Feather reached for the door handle and the door opened, smashing against her wrist. She bit her lip to stifle the yelp of pain and melted against the wall, hoping the new arrival wouldn't notice her, silent and still.

Kristin bent over the crib, cooing to the baby. "What's the fuss? Did our big boy go poopy in his diaper? Hush now, we'll take care of this. Where do you suppose Roxanne is? It's certain she heard you. Everyone did." Chatting, reassuring, Kristin scooped Jared into her arms and spun to face the diapering table.

Sadly, the table stood against the wall where Feather was trying to look like part of the zoo-themed paper.

She prayed Kristin didn't drop the baby in her shock at seeing someone else in the room.

Kristin inhaled a sharp breath when she realized she wasn't the only adult in the room. She clutched her son to her. In a few seconds, she placed Jared on the table and began to remove the diaper, cloth, of course. "Why didn't you help my son?"

"Just popped in to see the little one," she said in a squeaky, faked voice. "I'll be off then."

Kristin kept a hand on Jared to anchor him to the changing table but moved closer to Feather. "Oh, no. You won't be off anywhere until I damn well tell you to go."

Uh oh. From Kristin's cold tone, Feather deduced either her attempt to disguise her voice or her badger costume had failed her.

Ditto the uh oh. *No mask, doofus.* She gave a weak chuckle. "Guess the jig is up."

"I don't know how you got in here, but you've given me a great way to block future visits with *my* son." Kristin sucked in a breath. Feather wondered how she could with the stench in the nursery. "Did Roxanne sneak you in? No. Brad brought you here, didn't he? That *bastard.* He says I'm not being fair, not keeping to the damn adoption agreement. Were you two playing around before you came to visit the kiddo?"

"Don't be ridiculous. If you hadn't broken the agreement, kept me from even a glimpse of ... Jared, I wouldn't have been reduced to sneaking in." It had taken an effort to stop from referring to Jared as her son. Kristin was his mother now.

"That's patently absurd. I'm a lawyer. You're wrong and Brad is wrong. I stayed within the boundaries of our agreement."

Did anyone aside from lawyers use the phrase "patently absurd?"

Jared decided the attention needed to return to the king of the room. He wailed and flailed and rolled close to the edge of the table. It had a rim to prevent his rolling off, but Feather's heart moved her hand to stop him.

"You know all about reluctant compliance, don't you, Kristin?" She pulled her hands back, the effort strenuous and painful. "A few blurry photos, right at deadline. What's the problem? Jealous he might prefer me?" *Oh, great, why not simply dump a can of kerosene on the situation?*

"He? Jared? Or Brad?" Kristin sucked in a breath. "So that's why Roadkill was outside kicking up a fuss. You conniving witch. I'll bet you were down there flirting with my husband—or worse— while I entertained his damn guests."

Wrong. I was down there hearing Brad refuse me a loan for Feather's Beds while your guests sucked up your food and drinks. She hoped no one had noticed them talking. He'd said he'd talk to

Kristin. Wow. Fat chance this harpy would want to loan her money for the B&B. Maybe for a one-way ticket to Patagonia.

Somehow Kristin had managed to re-diaper the crying infant. She picked him up and snuggled him against her. Possibly realizing her anger was upsetting the baby, she reduced the volume but not the venom. "I hope you enjoyed your little adventure tonight. It will be the last time you see Jared for a very long time. Now get out of my home and stay away from my boys. Plural."

Feather couldn't leave it. She walked to the door and flipped on the light. "You're wrong, you know. I don't want Brad and I gave you Jared. I only want what we all agreed to. It's only just."

"Don't talk to me about justice. You fucked my husband while he was married to me. Leave."

Feather glared at Kristin, forcing herself not to flinch at Kristin's crude but too true accusation. "You made a promise. You *will* make it good, believe me. I don't give up, I promise you. And *I* keep my promises." Feather walked from the room, holding herself erect, not allowing herself to turn and stare at Kristin and Jared, not allowing them to see the tears streaking her face. Neither woman had raised her voice, only the level of spite in it. Given that, it still surprised her the only person in the hall was her sister, who stood near the door but wisely had not entered. Feather assumed the entire contingent of party-goers heard their argument and would be gathered around the door, placing bets on what violence would erupt.

She sent a bleak look to Roxanne. "Well, that went well."

Roxanne patted her shoulder. "Sorry I didn't beat her up the stairs."

"She would have come in anyway. Not your fault."

"I'll walk you out." Roxanne lowered her voice as they descended the stairs, and Feather had to duck her head to hear her shorter sister's words. "This nanny gig is too dull, anyway. I'll be out of here soon."

Meaning Feather would never see Jared. "But...." Feather wiped her nose on the sleeve of her costume, leaving an oh-so-alluring trail of snot.

In her guise as a fluffy kitten, Roxanne appeared innocent and cuddly. Life wasn't fair. "Don't worry. Kristin will come around and do what's right. If she doesn't, we'll have the cash to fight her." She opened the door.

"How could we? She's a lawyer and we're both broke." Was Kristin's craziness contagious?

Brad trotted up to join them. "What's going on?" Roxanne put a look of innocent ignorance on her kitten's face.

Feather closed the door on him and his life and his wife and their son and walked down the cement stairs into the cool dark night.

Three

Skulking Skunk

The one place Sophia Patton did not want to go after the debacle of a party was home. Home, where Aileen awaited news, news Sophia dreaded sharing.

Instead of home, she headed west, toward The Tank, an upscale bar not far from their home. The Tank took its name from the huge saltwater fish tank the owners swore contained only non-endangered species. While it might well be true, Sophia had read that so many exotics died during shipment, far more had to be captured than were expected to eventually be sold to enthusiasts. Only the fittest survived, she guessed. An analogy appropriate to many areas of life.

She turned into the lot of The Tank. As usual, it was crowded with high end SUVs, a few custom pickups and some hybrids purchased without thought to winters up here mere miles south of Canada.

She yanked open the heavy, carved wood door. She craved the solitude of the far corner of The Tank, behind the aquarium. There she could ponder her problems and observe the graceful, colorful fish transplanted from their ocean homes to a bar, albeit, an upscale bar, in Spokane, Washington. Even fish had problems.

Sophia, tall, slender and curvaceous, was accustomed to heads turning and eyes, either lascivious or envious, widening when she entered a room. She was not accustomed to snickers and heads turning to hide smiles. She strode across the room and slid into the booth. She slid faster than normal on the fake fur bottom and tights of the skunk costume. With her dark brown hair striped down the middle with white powder, her face half white, half black, her legs in black tights, a very long, very fluffy black and white tail attached to her rump, she looked absurd.

She blessed the make-up and the dark room for covering the blush stretching from head to toe. Even her black boots had a white strip of electrical tape up the back. With more than a month till Halloween, she had no excuse for her outfit.

A server arrived at her booth and did a poor job of hiding her sneer. *No tip for you, college girl.*

Sophia ordered a beer. With no intention of leaving the bar before it emptied of its peering patrons, a long night lay ahead. No one had better stop by her booth and express condolences that she was skunked tonight, unless they hankered for a beer bath.

Four

Love for Sale

Roxanne crept up the stairs to her small apartment over the Ganborena's garage, anticipation increasing her pace, making it harder to be silent. *Just like the fog, coming on little cat feet. Who wrote that? Probably somebody good, like Stephen King.*

Roxanne hoped she would soon be swept off her little cat feet. Nearly half an hour earlier Teddy had left the party, telling her he was heading to her apartment. It had taken forever for her to make her way past the guests, their tongues loose from liquor and good food, thinking themselves clever with their sly comments about the sweet little pussy. Too tiresome, especially after the sixth, or the twentieth, repetition.

She shook off her annoyance. Soon she'd be out of this costume. Was Teddy naked already, waiting for his personal, very hot pussycat? She was moist, ready for him. Working at the wind farm had toned his already supple, lean body, strengthened his muscles. She loved his body, loved what he did to hers. She shivered. It was past two, but they had the rest of the night together. She could nap alongside Jared tomorrow. Tonight was their time, hers and Teddy's.

She opened the door slowly, wondering what Teddy had in store for her. Rose petals? Champagne, licked from her flat belly? That delicious combination of ice cubes and a warm cloth? Whatever awaited, she knew it would be memorable.

Teddy stood in the middle of the garage apartment, facing Roxanne, his hands on his hips, impatience showing in the taut lines in his face and his erect stance. "Where have you been? I've been waiting forever." He still wore his costume for the party, a simple outfit of camouflage, an orange hunting vest and a bright orange hunting cap with ear flaps.

She strolled toward him, almost purring, careful not to trip on the Tabriz rug her mom had loaned her. It gave an upscale tone to the rest of her borrowed and begged furnishings. "Impatient? Eager?" She smiled. "Why are you still dressed?"

His mouth tightened. "You can't have forgotten what tonight is."

The annoyance in Teddy's expression repelled her and Roxanne moved no closer. It had been a crazy day, with preparations for the event, then Feather's presence at the party and the dressing-down Kristin had given Roxanne after she caught her sister with Jared. She had no doubt she would have been fired if Kristin had someone on tap to replace her. "It's been a long day, sweetheart." She wanted to be next to him, to inhale his scent, a mix of masculine sweat, expensive cologne, and essence of Teddy.

"And it looks to be longer. We have a lot to do, kitten o' mine."

He really means to go through with this plan. "I thought that was just pillow talk, Teddy. Dreaming, you know?"

"Dreaming gets you nothing, Rox. Believe me, I want a lot more than nothing out of this world." He circled the small room. "You said you were with me on this. Were you lying?"

"Of course not. I'm with you, always. We're soul mates." She worried that her expression belied her words. She had assumed his big plan was idle dreaming, not reality. Sure, Roxanne preferred having money and she hated the way her mother and Teddy's stepfather parceled out cash as rewards for behavior they approved, as if she and her lover were children. But her mom had her back, always, as Teddy's stepdad had Teddy's. "We're young. We have time to make money."

His beautiful face took on a scornful expression. Roxanne flinched, hoping she'd hidden it. She hated it when Teddy was angry with her. "You don't get it. The rich stay rich and the poor help them stay that way. You and me, we're the poor, unless we do something to change things up."

"We're not poor. We never go hungry. We have jobs." *Not that she would, for long.* "We have each other."

Teddy's laugh rang throughout the apartment, and Roxanne worried that it could be heard outside by those leaving the party late.

She frowned. It wasn't that she wanted to hide her relationship with Teddy, heaven knew. She simply valued her privacy.

"You want the best from life, sweetie. You're used to it. We both are. Unfortunately my dear old Pops thinks I need to 'carve out a niche' for myself. He doesn't understand that it isn't that easy nowadays." He walked to her sofa, picked up his backpack, and withdrew two shopping bags.

"Your plan is brilliant, of course." She closed in on Teddy, ran her finger under his chin and up to his ear. How could she talk him out of this idiocy? "It's dangerous. It scares me."

"No risk, no fun, no gain." Teddy flopped onto the sofa and grinned at her.

"Blackmail is serious stuff. People will be angry. Angry people aren't rational."

"I know it's serious, babe. Sure, they'll be angry. I've worked hard to dig up good information, info none of them wants to get out. They'll pay me—us to keep quiet. We'll take the money and go far, far away from these jerk-offs."

He held out his arms for her but Roxanne didn't fall into his lap. She crossed to the window looking out to the Ganborena's driveway. She had so many reservations about Teddy's plan. It was illegal and too easy for people to figure out who was behind it. "If we disappear, they'll know we were behind the extortion." Her neck tightened and a sharp pain stabbed at her behind her ears. "I have a bad feeling about this."

Teddy crossed his arms and glowered at her. "I don't know what your problem is, woman. Two days ago you were hot and wet for all the money we can rake in. It's still out there, but much closer. With or without you, I'm going ahead. So what if we blow town? Most everyone under 25 leaves North Idaho. No jobs, no future. I, for one, have no intention of coming back to this burg. But with the equipment I have here," he patted the bags beside him on the couch, "no one will know who's behind our little game. Voice distortion, burner phones. My plan is foolproof." He focused his golden brown eyes on her own blue ones. "Are you with me?"

"You're rushing things. We have plenty of time." She looked

around the tiny apartment. It smelled of old microwave pizzas and gas from the cars below, despite the candles she lit whenever she entered. Still, it was her place, her hideaway, and she and Teddy had spent good times here.

Teddy's face tightened with anger. "One of the investors wants an independent audit, wants to know where the money's going. Maybe someone's embezzling or maybe the wind farm is simply a money pit. Who knows what will happen after the audit? I've spent a long time digging up information on every one of them and now's the time to launch the attack. In or out, sweetheart. In or out?"

"In." She needed him and hated that she needed him. Ordinarily it was the guys who begged her, who fawned on her. She sat down next to him, ran her fingers up his forearm and resigned herself to a long night without sex. She wanted his muscled body above her, inside her. She loved how his light furring of chest hair tickled her breasts. Maybe if she helped him, they'd have time for a quickie before he had to leave for work. "How can I help?"

Five

What Granny Doesn't Know

Sophia staggered downstairs after a long, hot shower. She had no desire to face her spouse Aileen, hoping she had decided to go to Mass this particular Sunday, even though Aileen hadn't ventured into a church for years.

No luck. Aileen stood in the kitchen and handed her a large glass filled with something thick and unappealing. "I told you to take the milk thistle before you drank so much."

Sophia glared. "I had no intention of drinking that much. Just as I have no intention of drinking this slop. And do not roll your eyes."

Aileen stopped mid-roll and crossed her eyes. "Go back upstairs and change into your jogging clothes. We can walk and talk."

"Don't you have somewhere you should be that doesn't involve interrogating me?"

"Nope. Hurry up. I've been ready for ages." Aileen gestured at her attire, a pair of very short shorts and a top that displayed her perfect breasts and perfectly flat abdomen to perfection.

Despite an aching head and a queasy stomach, Sophia was aroused. "Ready for what?"

"A walk. A talk. Some decisions." She shrugged and grinned. "Then, who knows?"

Sophia placed the glass on the counter and turned to go upstairs. "Put the stupid smoothie in a plastic container."

"Tell me what happened. What did you learn?"

Aileen had been right. The late morning was pleasantly warm and the sun felt good. Their sneakers crunched fallen leaves as they walked.

Sophia breathed in the clean air and a faint essence of smoke.

Farmers in the valleys surrounding Spokane burned their crops every fall to get rid of weeds and add nutrients to the soil. "I learned that champagne chased by beer isn't good for the stomach or the head. I learned that I can be an awful bitch."

Aileen chuckled. "Neither of those is news. You told me you thought you'd find out about Windfall Works and the wind farm's progress. Or lack thereof. Drink your smoothie."

Sophia took a sip and discovered the banana and honey covered the sins of whatever herbs her health-freak partner had included. She glanced down at the diminutive woman. "You were right. I should have taken you. You could have snuck around, looking harmless, and ferreted out more information than I did."

"Ferreted? That would have been cute. Me, a skinny little ferret, accompanying you, a statuesque, stunning skunk."

Sophia let herself enjoy the compliment and then remembered what she'd done. She scrunched her face in despair. "I got skunked in more ways than one. I was so upset by what I overheard between a couple of the other partners that I crashed into one of the wait staff and chewed her out instead of apologizing."

"Okay, that's not good. But she's probably used to it, sadly. And *she's* probably forgotten your rudeness. What did you hear that upset you? Who did you hear it from?"

This was the part she hated to talk about. She finished her smoothie. "Let's go a little faster." She upped her pace. Every step hurt but since self-flagellation was out of style, walking would have to do. "Peter Brewer—at least I *think* it was Peter, his bear costume must have been unbearably hot—cornered Jon." The bear pun didn't even elicit a tiny smile from Aileen. Sophia slogged on, hating what she had to say. "Jon handles most of the operations at the wind farm. Peter asked why things were going so slow but costing so much. Jon, like he always does, gave him a flip answer. 'Progress proceeds at its own pace.' Something like that. Peter got angry and said the money was going too fast. Jon told him to talk to Brad Ganborena."

"Brad's the lobbyist?"

"De facto. As partners, we all agreed to help. But Jon and Peter are in charge of operations and expenditures. That Jon's trying to shift responsibility isn't good."

Aileen gusted out a breath. "Look, Soph, you were so sure this wind project was our ticket to wealth and glory. A way to help the environment and our nest egg. We sank most of our savings into it."

Sophia shot her a look. "You don't have to tell me."

Aileen found a low stone fence and sat on it. Slowing down was uncharacteristic for her. Stopping? Sophia shuddered at the depth of her partner's concern. "We need that money," Aileen said, "particularly if your grandmother finds out we're married. And she will, you know. She's old, not stupid."

Sophia opened her mouth to protest, but Aileen stopped her with a finger to her lips. "I know she loves you, else why cut us such a deal on the house? But people her age are shocked by our 'lifestyle.' Once she knows for certain you're gay, she'll cut you out of her will faster than the glaciers are melting over in Montana these days. She might even kick us out of the house."

Sophia shook her head. No way would Grandma Pat-Pat invalidate the lease-to-buy contract. Sophia and Aileen adored the beautiful little Craftsman, and hoped to raise their family beneath its gabled roof.

"She'd never cancel our lease. You don't know her."

"And why don't I know her? Because you banish me from our home whenever she visits. It's time to be honest with her and face the consequences. She's bound to find out we're married and it's far worse that we hid it than we were open."

"I think gradual is better. Once one of us is pregnant ... she'd be so tickled about a grandchild ...."

"Gradual, right." Aileen sniffed as if there was something foul in the air, and of course, there was. Guilt and anxiety were stinky emotions.

"You're right, I know you're right. I am not ashamed of you or our marriage. I simply want to be sure that everyone is happy and—"

"Everyone is happy," Aileen interrupted in a mocking tone. "What a load of ... carp. We can fight about *that* another time. Neither of us is getting any younger. We don't have time for 'gradual,' or any other kind of pussyfooting around. We need to know what's happening with our money."

Sophia had to hide her grin. "Pussyfooting?" She sounded like Gran. She cupped her hand over her mouth as if in thought. "I promise. I'll find out about Windfall. Whatever it takes." She squared her shoulders and realized that, physically, she felt better than she had all morning. If only the rest of her problems could be solved with a banana/honey smoothie. She had no idea what they would do if the money they'd invested had disappeared, and she was not certain how to find out.

Aileen gave her a long, sober look and rose to continue walking. "Good to hear that. Because even though I love you and swore my commitment to you, I need to be a mother. We need the money, soon. If we've lost it...." She shrugged. After a long pause, the silence broken only by the sound of leaves crunching, she added in a low voice, "A baby with you would be best. Without you, if I must."

Sophia's relief from the hangover was short-lived. Now her gut clenched with fear and anxiety. She had to figure out the problems at Windfall. Fast.

Six

Money Doesn't Grow on Houseplants

Peter Brewer shuffled from the hallway to his desk. As he passed the money tree plant, several elongated brown leaves fell to the floor. He stuck his finger into the potting soil. Dry. He shrugged. He settled heavily into his executive chair. From the desk he plucked a yellow note pad that perched crosswise atop scattered piles: mail, opened and unopened, spread sheets, annual reports, bills, all lay haphazardly, as random as fallen leaves.

He hated that as his dull brown hair thinned, his belly grew. Ten pounds a decade, right on schedule, a cliché of middle-aged manhood. At least his mind remained sharp. He needed every cell to drag himself from the current disaster.

He added "water plants" to the long, handwritten list of tasks on the yellow pad, recognizing that he could probably accomplish the task in the time it took to record it. He had no need to look at the list to see "Task One: Ensure that Windfall Works is profitable." Without the wind farm's successful launch, he and his clients who trusted him would soon be digging for any traces of gold in the tailing piles that spotted the hills outside Hancock. Was the tiny town so near—just thirty or so miles east of Spokane—yet so totally different than its urban neighbor, ready for success? He took a sip from a paper cup that lay on an open space on the credenza behind him. He shuddered, his lip curling in disgust. The coffee was cold, the fake creamer curdled. Would the dregs kill his plant or keep it alive one more day?

"Money tree, my Aunt Fannie's patootie," he muttered. "Not bearing much fruit. Guess I need to talk to it." He stepped close to the plant and spoke in a sing-song voice many use for children, the elderly, and the impaired. "Now, now, little guy, you need to live up to your name and bring me good luck, and prosperity. And since I find those terms vague and hard to define, let me be more clear: cash, you damn bush, cash. Then maybe I'll feed and water you."

The door opened, admitting Jeanette Sullivan. Peter stood quickly and sucked in his gut. Not that he could keep up the façade for long.

Jeanette wore a short black suit, which at first glance looked like any professional woman's working attire. Then Peter noticed she wore no blouse under the suit jacket, only some sort of lingerie thing that displayed inches of black lace beneath her fulsome breasts. He marveled at the courage of a woman her age revealing that much skin. But it was good skin. Good breasts. Great legs.

He forced himself to stop ogling Jeanette. She was another partner in Windfall and no doubt had questions for Peter. The rumors were spreading. *Oh, Lord, why did I choose that word? Spreading?* He could well imagine those incredible legs splayed beneath him. *No. Don't go there.*

"Jeanette. A pleasure to see you, as always," he said. He scurried around the desk to offer her a chair.

"Peter." Jeanette smiled. She patted his arm with a well-manicured hand. Some no-doubt expensive scent exuded from her, a mix of musk and spice. Peter fought not to lean toward her and inhale. She looked around the room, which seemed to become even tackier in her presence. She sniffed and Peter wondered if she could smell the dust, the despair, the lost hopes. Peter turned his head away and sniffed surreptitiously. Dust, for sure. And something sour. Maybe a sandwich that he'd neglected to excavate from the scree on his desk.

"Please. Have a seat," he said, wondering if he should dust the chair before she sat. "Coffee? Tea? Water? I might even have a wee nip of brandy." *Good babble, Brewer.*

Jeanette seated herself, turning her legs to the side. He noticed how the suit skirt crept above her knees and he envied the fabric. "Coffee would be lovely."

"Good, good." He made his way around his desk and around Jeanette. "Let me get it going." He made his way to the small, square closet he had converted to a kitchen by way of adding a couple of folding TV tables, putting a microwave on one and an egg crate plastic box on the other to hold coffee mugs, instant coffee, sugar, fake cream and some plastic utensils. In the corner stood a three-foot wine refrigerator that housed a fraction of Peter's treasured selection of Northwest wines. Atop it stood a few bottles of water. From one of those he poured water into two coffee mugs and put them in the microwave. Once they were hot, he stirred in some instant coffee crystals. He tucked the sugar and cream boxes under his armpit and headed back to his desk, where he proffered the mugs. "No donuts today," he said with an awkward chuckle.

A look of utter horror crossed Jeanette's face when she saw the instant coffee and fake creamer. She swallowed and accepted her cup with a smile. "No additives, please."

Once again settled behind his desk, Peter asked how he might be of service to Jeanette. "A shame we didn't get more opportunity to speak at the party. Quite a crush of people."

Jeanette picked up her mug but didn't let it reach her lips. Lovely red lips. She nodded. "A pity, yes. Actually I came to speak with you about things I heard at the party. Rumors, that I'm sure you can easily dispel, that there are problems at the wind farm."

Peter took a long gulp of his coffee. Wanted to spit it out. As weak as his will power.

"Windfall Works, yes," he said only to stall. "Oh, you know. People love gossip. I wouldn't let it concern you."

Jeanette's smile dimmed. "I am concerned. I have invested a good sum there and as far as I can tell no progress has been made. A good portion of my daughters' inheritance is at risk. I cannot leave Charlene—Feather, and Roxanne paupers. Even though they probably assume I'm busy spending their inheritance." She brought the cup to her lips, sniffed, and set it down again. "You advised me to invest."

Peter wished he knew the reasons for the delays, prayed they were political and would soon disappear. "I also advised you that it was alternative energy and entailed some risk. However, we both agreed it would be good for the environment to put some energy back into the grid. With success, Hancockians, maybe a huge chunk of North Idaho, can reduce their reliance on fossil fuels."

Jeanette looked toward the ceiling, no doubt spying spider webs and anything they'd trapped in the past months. "You're a partner and my investment advisor. You should have a handle on what's happening. If there are problems, you're the one who should be alerting me. And yet I overheard you asking Jon what was going on."

Peter debated the best approach. Jeanette had brains and wasn't afraid to use them. If she withdrew her investments with him, it would hurt, badly.

"They're behind on the launch. Just the one prototype turbine installed so far." He made an effort not to wrinkle his nose. When it was running, the turbine forced wind across the hog pens. No one had imagined how pungent Hancock would become in the downdraft. "Ordinary issues encountered with any start-up, exacerbated by the political externalities that accompany all alternative energy ventures, especially given the political environment in Idaho."

Jeanette waved a hand in front of her nose. "Oh, pooh, Peter, you should know better than to try to distract me. When I want to know something, I am tenacious. And if I fear my daughter's fiduciary interests are in danger, I find out what's up. At the party, I heard rumors of financial shenanigans. You know, misdoings? That the lack of progress may be intentional. That funds aren't being adequately accounted for. Is that clear? I even heard the E word being tossed around. And I don't mean E.D."

Peter recognized the need for a better tango. "People tend to exaggerate, especially at parties, where liquor makes tongues loose. But it is time I do some digging, get another accounting of the funds."

Jeanette leaned forward in her chair. "I'm glad you agree that further investigation is needed. As you'll recall, I was an accountant in my past."

"I promise a full investigation. However, my dear, please remember that I warned you of the risk in such ventures. We may simply have to employ that rare commodity, patience. I'll do my best, but I'm only one man."

Jeanette stood. "Exactly what I was thinking."

Peter stood. He knew Jeanette. Surely it couldn't be that easy to calm her.

"Let me take you for some coffee and scones at the Blind Chukar. I have a few ideas to discuss."

I should have known. Whatever she has in mind, it can only mean trouble for me. "Can't wait to hear them." He brushed his hand through his hair and down the front of his suit. He offered his arm to Jeanette. And was again nearly overcome by her exotic scent.

Roxanne read the text on Teddy's phone. *Problems at Windfall? At home? Grandma, what big ears you have. Keep the authorities out of it or granny will get an earful. Await my call.*

Roxanne dropped the small burn phone onto Teddy's outstretched palm, feeling as if she'd been infected.

Teddy smiled at her and at that moment he looked like a weasel, or possibly like one of those hogs out at Windfall, ready to snatch, grab and consume whatever came its way. "What do you think of my message? This one's for Sophia. I have more on the others."

"I'm sure you do." She didn't want to tell him how sleazy she felt taking part in this scheme. She looked around the coffee house, one of their favorite spots since they'd started dating. She hoped no one heard them, no one knew their plans, Teddy's plans, really. Was she part of this? Could she live with it?

Teddy rubbed his chin. When they'd first dated, he'd sported a soul patch until Roxanne had told him it looked silly. "I think I'll add something advising them to prepare the money. Think I should specify the amount?"

"I'm not sure—"

"No, you're right. Maybe I should come up with different amounts, depending on how deep their pockets are."

Roxanne shivered. Was it the thought of all that money, or fear? "This may not be—"

"The right time. Of course. We'll wait. In the meantime, I'll decide how much to squeeze out of each of them." He rubbed the non-existent soul patch. "Peter Brewer handles Dad's investments. He's probably got a bundle. We'll squeeze that fat grape for some juice."

Roxanne knew "that fat grape" loved Teddy, saw him as the son he didn't have. They'd spent so much time together. Roxanne put her hand up in a "stop" gesture. "Listen to me, Teddy. Please. We need to think hard about what we're doing. It's blackmail. A serious crime. What if someone figures out it's you? What if they talk to each other? What if Brad and Kristin think I'm behind it? They'll call the cops and they're not bumbling fools. Neither is Peter. He's been good to you."

"He's a nice guy, but he talks too much. Where do you think I got most of the dirt?" Teddy scowled at her. "You think we shouldn't do this."

She shook her head. "No. Yes. I'm not sure. I am sure we need to understand the downside, the risks. You work at Windfall. You'll be a prime suspect."

Teddy dismissed her fear with a wave of his hand. "Nah. Lots of people go in and out of the office and the farm. You were at the party. There were scads of people there who heard the partners whining about progress with the wind farm. It could be one of the partners, wanting to recoup part of his or her losses."

"But you and I are close to it and you and I both need money."

"Everybody needs money, honey. Those who ain't got, want. Those who've got, want more." He sighed. "We talked about this last night. You'll be at the Ganborena's, taking care of darling Jared, when the text arrives."

Roxanne didn't like his sarcasm toward the baby. After all, Jared was her nephew and she loved him. She jiggled the sleeping baby's stroller, as if to reassure him she meant him no harm. She ignored Teddy's remark. One battle at a time. "Everyone knows you can schedule texts. There are apps for that." Last night their crime seemed far away, almost unreal. She'd agreed to his ideas, adding some gossip about her mother and the Ganborenas, mostly to humor him, thinking she'd figure out a way to talk him out of it later. In truth she'd wanted him in a good mood last night so he could do what he was best at—make love with her.

Teddy stood, slapping his hands on the table. Roxanne watched her coffee slosh over the rim of her cup. "The worst risk we have is your attitude. If you look at Kristin like you're looking at me, it's all over. Pull yourself together. This is our way out of Podunk living, of begging our parents for what's our due." He leaned forward, looming over her. "Let the good times roll, dude."

Roxanne shivered again. She nodded her acquiescence. Adamant, Teddy couldn't be stopped. She joined him, or she lost him. She raised her head and forced a jaunty smile. "Roll on." She only hoped it wasn't their heads that would roll.

Seven

Honey, Do Not

Brad saw the tight muscles in Kristin's neck, and knew she tried to control her anger. He wondered if she'd let him massage her shoulders once they'd both calmed down. Otherwise she'd end up with one of her headaches and he didn't wish that on his wife.

They talked in the dining room, redolent with the smell of the air freshener their housecleaner had used to dispel reminders of the party the past weekend. If only there were a spritz to rid Kristin of her jealousy and anger.

"What I don't understand is how you spoke with that woman, under our roof, when you knew how I'd feel."

"Would you have felt better if I'd met her at some sleazy hotel to hear her request?" *Great, Brad, way to handle it. Put dexterity with feminine emotions at the top of your resumé skills.* Before Kristin could react, he added, "I already told you I didn't invite her. I don't know how she got in. Once she was here and asked for a few minutes of my time, I didn't see the harm. Better to talk with her than get into a shouting match that everyone at the party could hear." *Ah yes. No better way to soothe the wife's feelings than to attack her behavior.* He swallowed and held up his hands to stave off her words. "I thought it would be the quickest way to get rid of her."

"So she could run upstairs and do who knows what to our son."

Brad moved toward his wife. "Feather is his mother. She's not the devil. She just wanted to see him. She wouldn't harm him."

Kristin's calm, or at least her façade of calm, dissolved. "Oh, yes," she shouted. "Stand by her. I suppose you told her which room was his."

He put his finger to his lips and looked pointedly toward the family room, where Roxanne played with Jared. "No, I didn't." He rubbed his tight right shoulder with his left hand. "The point is, hon,

I didn't promise her a loan, I didn't promise her anything. *We* promised her she could see Jared when the adoption went through."

Silent tears coursed down Kristin's cheeks, cheeks that flamed scarlet. "I didn't realize how hard it would be to keep ties with the woman you had an affair with. It hurts and it never gets easier. We *can't* give her a loan; it would keep us linked to her as long as she owed us money."

"We are tied to Feather, through the adoption agreement, and through our moral obligation to honor our word. But sweetie, believe me, that is the only reason we are linked. If you don't want to loan her the money, I understand."

Kristin turned away from him, arms crossed, shoulders hunched. "It shames me, but I can't bear to have any connection to her. If we can't figure a way to sever her rights with Jared, I—I think I may have to take Jared and move somewhere far away. You need to help me get rid of her. It *was* all your fault. Seduction goes two ways."

Brad staggered backward, her accusation worse than gunshot to the gut. "You can't mean that. We talked this through months ago. You took me back, accepted my apology. We both agreed the adoption made sense."

"I was wrong. Having her near our son is like suffering the same recurring nightmare over and over."

Brad swallowed, unsure how to react, wishing Kristin would take back her words. He regretted his affair with Feather, but it meant he—they now had a son. No matter how painful, he would not lose his son. "You can't take my son away. I won't allow it."

His cell phone emitted a tone that announced a text message. He hoped to heck it wasn't from Feather, more fuel to Kristin's fire. He pulled his phone from his pocket and read the message: "Problems at Windfall? At home? Boise can be a refuge. Keep the media and authorities out of it or you'll lose big. Await my call. And count your cash. I'll need fifteen thousand."

Brad's mouth dried. He handed his phone to Kristin and pulled a chair from the table and sat.

He watched her scan the message, saw her pupils dilate. She scrolled up to see who the sender was. "Blocked." She laid the phone down on the table, sat beside him, took one hand in hers. "We know who it is," she said. "She's desperate."

No. Never. Feather would not do this to him. Would she? Could she? And what was that about Boise? Feather didn't know, but god forbid Kristin focus on that part of the message. "Feather wouldn't do this. Blackmail is illegal. For a damn motel?"

"Bed and breakfast, you told me. It's her dream. She was willing to give up her son for that dream. Why not this?"

Brad stared at the carpet, saw a stain that the cleaner hadn't been able to remove. "Because if she's caught, she'll go to jail. Never see her son, never own a B&B. It's insanity."

"Excuse me, but this is a woman who lived on a platform forty feet up a tree for weeks on end. Who chained herself to the Federal Building. In most people's minds, she's passed the insanity test."

"Feather. Would. Not. Do. This." *To me.*

Kristin tightened her grip of his hand. "You're doing it again. Standing up for her, against me."

"I am not against you. You and I, together, have to fight this blackmailer. It's about Windfall. I better call the others."

"No matter what, we need to assume it's Feather. I'll talk to her. I know how to suss out liars, since I work with so many of them."

"No! I don't want you to confront her. You could end up in a cat fight."

"Thanks for your confidence in me."

"I know a guy, a private investigator. Has a company with branches all over. He can send someone to check Feather out. Follow her. Investigate in ways we can't." Brad rose and paced the length of the room. He rubbed his forefinger sideways against his front teeth. "But I can't believe Feather would do this, especially before I've given her our answer on the loan."

Kristin smiled for the first time that day. "A spy. Good idea. Call him now." She waited for Brad to return to her side. "If Feather knew you were coming to me about the loan, she already knew the answer before she left the house Saturday night. Call the spy."

From the family room came the gurgle of an excited baby, the laughter of his nanny. What did the blackmailer know? *Was* something wrong at Windfall, other than the expected delays? Was one of his partners behind this? Because no matter what Kristin thought, Brad did not believe Feather would stoop this low. She was too brave, too proud, too kind. He hoped this was just some kind of bluff, because he had pinned his dreams on the success of this venture, not to mention nearly all his private capital. If it failed, he would be a kept man, living off Kristin. And if she followed through with her threat to run away with Jared? He'd be destroyed. He would be lost without Kristin and Jared.

He made the call from the land line, leaving his cell open for the blackmailer.

Sophia loved her elliptical trainer. She bought it when she grew bored being hit on by so many guys at the gym. Even the occasional foray by an attractive woman irked her. She was committed to someone else. She loved having the machine in the room they'd dedicated to exercise, watching the flat panel TV on the wall across from her, wearing wireless headphones so the machine's noise wouldn't interfere with the television soundtrack.

She'd arrived home after a frustrating, busy day at the bank. She'd vowed to Aileen that she'd find out whether the rumors about Windfall were true or mere gossip. At the bank could she access the databases that would give her privileged financial data. However, staying later than usual would draw attention she didn't want. For the past two days she had hoped to do the necessary research. Tomorrow she'd go in early and no one would notice: no staff meetings, no early morning service club would stymie her as they had.

When she heard the alert for a text message, she slowed her steps on the machine to pluck her phone from the table beside her. Maybe Aileen was coming home early, having canceled her class to get herself the night off. Or maybe she wanted to ask Sophia about their dinner plans.

She read the message. She stopped. The machine halted, silent. Television noise droned on in her ears but she didn't hear it.

Nothing drew her focus from the hideous, frightening words.

"Problems at Windfall? At home? Grandma, what big ears you have. Keep the authorities out of it or granny will get an earful. Await my call. And count your cash. I'll need ten thousand."

No. No. This can't be happening. Not only was this message validating the rumors she'd heard at the party, it demanded ten thousand dollars to stay silent. And what was that about problems at home? Did someone know about their marriage? About Aileen's ultimatum? Where the heck could she get ten thousand dollars? They'd invested most of their cash in Windfall Works, were saving the remainder for the costs of pregnancy and the baby. Could she borrow from the bank?

What the heck was she thinking? No way would she, could she, pay a blackmailer. Unless he threatened to tell Granny Pat-Pat about the marriage. Then what would she do?

She scrambled off the elliptical, grabbed her face towel and scrubbed the sweat off. Stabs of pain shot from her stomach, her ulcer reacting to the stress. *Was this a hoax? A prank?* She had to know and she had to know before Aileen got home. No way could she let Aileen find out about the blackmail. Unless, of course it wasn't a hoax and the second request delivered specifics Sophia couldn't ignore. Would the pressure cause Aileen to decide to leave her or would it help them band together, united against adversity?

Suddenly the house seemed hulking around her like an enormous mushroom, smothering, crushing her. She had to think, had to breathe, had to escape its claustrophobic atmosphere. She glanced out the window and saw that enough light remained for a walk. She trotted to the kitchen and threw together a casserole; popped it in the oven, not that she felt like a happy homemaker tonight.

She scribbled a quick note for Aileen in case she did indeed have an early night and strode out the door.

She moved from a walk to a trot to a jog to a lope, and then slowed on the way home to a leisurely stroll. She arrived at their house relaxed and steadier, determined to identify and confront the blackmailer. As she walked up the drive, she heard a bleating noise. She entered a smoke-filled kitchen, alarms blaring. The casserole was crisp. Maybe her relaxing walk had stretched a bit long.

* * *

When Haley West, the administrative support person at Windfall Works, received a text from Jon Flynn—her boss at the wind farm— she was speed walking on a treadmill in the Sandpoint Gym. He had forwarded the blackmail text to her, asking in his note, "Any chance u sent this?"

Haley stumbled and fell off the side of the treadmill, taking her water bottle down with her. She hadn't flipped the top shut after her last sip, so it spilled: on the floor, on her exercise tee and shorts. Two buff men training nearby rushed to help her up. One brought a towel and wiped up the floor.

Haley realized she had two problems. First, why was Jon ready to doubt her? For god's sake, she slept with him several times a week. She figured she could regain Jon's confidence without much trouble, possibly something creative in the sack. Second, however, and far worse, was how she'd tell Chaz, her *real* boss up in Canada? Jon had a bad temper, but Chaz never got angry. He simply got rid of you, often permanently.

She thanked the guys who helped her and stood to the side of the gym. She texted Jon. "R U nuts? Of course not. I'll come up soon."

Jon texted back. "Sooner."

Haley hurried to the women's locker room.

Peter Brewer decided he'd open the bottle of Bitner's 2006 Cabernet at 5 p.m. He could wait forty-five minutes. Surely he could wait that long. He leaned back in his chair and it groaned under his weight. Why he'd thought advising people on investments was a good idea, he couldn't remember at the moment. Most clients were docile, it was true, but holy crud, Sophia Patton was a firecracker ready to ignite and Jeanette Sullivan's solutions to boredom threatened to create more chaos at an already stressed Windfall Works.

Sophia had phoned shortly after Jeanette left, screeching about embezzlement and auditors and sleazy advice. He had not calmed her much, only postponed her rage for a few days.

His phone announced that a text had arrived. He read it and wanted to smash his phone, the innocent bearer of rotten news. He wanted to vomit at the cute reference to "someone's been sleeping in my bed ... or is that my bank account?" He swallowed, decided this merited an early opening of the Cabernet. Whoever the blackmailer was, they had no clue as to Peter's financial status. In the long run, a good thing. The fewer people who knew Peter was cash-strapped and dipping into client accounts to pay other clients, the better. Who could have found out? Not that many candidates. But twenty thousand dollars was a joke. Maybe he could bargain the bastard down to two, or better one thousand.

Should he tell the cops? First thing they would do was audit Windfall and the partners. So not a good idea. Should he call together the partners? They, too, would barge in and try to find out if the blackmailer told the truth. Maybe that would be good. Shoot. The only thing he knew for sure was that he hoped the blackmailer took lots of time to get back to him. Although a week or two wouldn't help him as far as cash flow. He had to find out who was behind this and stop him or her.

His door flew open and Jeanette Sullivan marched in. "I told you something bad was going down. I got a threatening text message today about Windfall Works. We have a sleazy blackmailer in our midst. Today her outfit was linen slacks and a silky black shirt. Efficient yet attractive.

Peter knew he remained pale and shaken from reading his recent text. No way would he share the contents. However ... "I received a text, as well. Nasty thing. But we can't react too hastily. Calling the cops, for ex—"

"We can't call the cops or the blackmailer will spill his—or her—guts. We need to find the slimy rat and we need to find out what's going on at Windfall. That's where it all began. I'm going in, just like I said yesterday. For heaven's sake, blackmail? What next? Pay up or he'll slaughter the hogs?"

Peter nodded. Much as he hated to admit it, what he'd thought of yesterday as a harebrained scheme, today appeared to be a reasonable approach. "You'll have to be careful. For all we know, Jon is the blackmailer, or the one creating the problems there."

"I'm glad you've conceded my plan is worth a try. My money is on that little tramp, Haley, his so-called assistant. He took her to Brad's party, and she dressed like a slut." She frowned, her finger to her lip. "Maybe we can convince him to fire her and hire me. Do you have enough clout with him?"

Peter shrugged. "He's a partner, I'm a partner, you're a partner. Equal clout."

"Then I'll simply have to deal with little Haley. She seems lazy, so she'll probably welcome my help, particularly since I'm a volunteer she'll think she can boss around."

Peter kept his smile to himself. Fat chance of anyone bossing Jeanette Sullivan. "You'll need to let her hold on to that delusion."

Jeanette sat in Peter's guest chair. "I'm having trouble deciding who to believe. In fact, show me your text message."

Peter chose not to take offense at Jeanette's words. He himself was having trouble deciding who to suspect and would only place his faith in himself. "I could easily fake a text message and send it to myself. You're going to have to decide to trust me or not." He rubbed his fingers through his hair, trying to recall what was bothering him.

He grinned, even with precious little to grin about. "Maybe you sent the blackmail and I should worry about not trusting you."

Jeanette smiled. "You're learning, money guy. Actually, your pooh-poohing my idea yesterday annoyed me, so I'd been doing my own investigating, the low tech way. You'd be surprised what people, even shopkeepers like Darlene Belmont, know about the wind farm and its investors. And then I got that nastygram. Like I told you, I'm going in and it's now or never. If one of those two is the blackmailer, my speed may startle them."

Peter chuckled. It was hard to picture this elegant woman chatting up the dowdy owner of Belmont's General Store. "I'm sure you'll startle them, Jeanette. Some things are certain."

Eight

Order Up!

For an instant, Feather let herself wonder if her dream was really to start a B&B. How would getting up before dawn to prepare and serve breakfast for her guests differ from getting up at dawn and schlepping down to The Blind Chukar to serve breakfast to tourists and Hancockians? Wouldn't it be just as easy to let Walt, her boss at the Chukar, worry about making the mortgage and paying the staff and buying the supplies and the slew of other details running a business required?

No! A resounding no. I've been thinking and dreaming about owning my own business for years. Since I was camping in trees and chaining myself to brush cutters. I want to make the decisions, shed tears and sweat over my own business.

She took a breath before heading out to refill mugs of coffee for customers of The Blind Chukar. This was her chance. Gina was providing the land—well, courtesy of Emily Naismith, who'd donated it to Gina—, Ed Mustard said he'd help with marketing—and as a screenwriter, he'd be a genie with words—, and Charlie and his crew will do the work at dirt rate prices if she could get started within the month. Soon Feather's Beds will be open for business.

She pasted a smile on her face and swept back into the dining room, an orange-lidded pot in her left hand, a brown-lidded pot in the right. *My coffee will be better than this. I'll order fresh beans, and grind it fresh every day. People will flock to Feather's Beds just to drink my coffee and eat my omelets and muffins.*

"Refill?" "How you doing here? May I get you anything?" "Aren't those scones to die for?" She chatted and poured her way around the dining room, the smile resting easy on her face because she enjoyed customer service.

Thank the universe for friends. She'd known Gina for years, and then Gina and she had gone through their pregnancies together. Not the totally peaceful time Gina had imagined when she'd founded Rainbow's End, her shelter for indigent pregnant women, but they'd had fun together, despite Feather's difficult decision about the baby's fate. Roadkill, her old activist buddy, remained a loyal friend, and she'd grown fond of his more sedate brother Ed. She loved Hancock and knew her new business would contribute to the small community's growth and prosperity, even if only in a small way.

Gina had mentioned that Emily Naismith might be willing to provide a short-term loan until Feather could go through the SBA. She hated to do that. Emily had donated the land to Gina and they were partners in their new business venture. She trusted Emily but didn't want to become dependent on her. Darn her stubborn, stingy mother, and her refusal to help. "One bed and breakfast in Hancock is already one too many for that hick town," she'd said.

"Order up! Feather. Earth to Feather. Order up." Walt's voice from the kitchen grew in volume until Feather noticed and headed back to the pickup shelf. "Feather, hon, you're a thousand miles away this morning. Late night?" Walt asked from where he presided over the grill.

Feather stacked the plates up her left arm and paused to reply. "I wish. Most exciting thing for me late at night would be the darn squirrels rustling in their cage." Feather had joined the growing cadre of Hancockians who helped Mayor Myrna in her squirrel rescue project. She sent Walt a weak smile. "Stuff on my mind. I promise I'll get with it now."

"Mind you do. I count on you to do the work of ten." Walt let out one of his booming "ha's" that bounced against the kitchen walls.

Feather wished she had the income of ten. She dropped off the plates to some regulars and winked at Roadkill when she delivered his order to where he often presided over heated arguments with other Hancockians. "Ed joining you today?"

He shook his head. "He's fussing around at Camp Rainbow's End. Gina decided to mulch the garden patch. The man is whipped, I tell you." Roadkill laughed, throwing his head back against the booth. Despite all his pronouncements and preaching about the environment as if he were nearly as old as Mother Earth, Roadkill was only a few years older than Feather. He'd turned thirty-three earlier that year and Feather had baked him a cake in Gina's kitchen. He groused about the fuss, but she knew he loved it.

Feather ignored his slam against his brother, thinking instead that Gina might be mulching a bit early. She stood up straight as she moved to a booth across the room, where a truly fine-looking man sipped his coffee, observing the room and making occasional notes in a small notebook. When she got to his table, he scooped the notebook off and into a pocket of his jacket. "Here you go. Walt's Hancock Hippy omelet, with red peppers, avocado, zucchini and olives. Need some salsa? Ketchup? Cheese?" *A decent-looking woman in your lap?* She blushed and knew he saw her red face and probably wondered at its cause. "You're due an order of whole wheat toast, which I'll bring in two shakes." *Two shakes? Since when do I talk that way? I sound like my great-grandmother.*

He smiled, revealing even, white teeth between full lips. "Is the salsa from a jar or fresh?"

"Walt makes it fresh. You'll love it, I promise." She made a mental note that at Feather's Beds she'd serve Walt's salsa and several varieties of her own, made fresh from her garden. Could she grow the chilies up here?

"Then salsa it is. And more hot coffee, please."

When she returned, she asked Mr. Dreamy if he was in town for work or pleasure, a question she asked of many guests. *See? I'm treating him like I treat all my customers. Simple courtesy.*

"Combination of both, I hope. In fact, if you'd join me after your shift for a walk around your town, I'd be assured of the pleasure part."

Feather blushed again, and cursed her pale complexion. She knew she'd refuse his offer, she always declined to meet customers after her shift. Not a good policy to pick up the guys whose tips she picked up. "Sure. Sounds fun. I get off at one." *Whoa, girl, what is wrong with you?*

"Great. My name is Michael Bergmann. You're"—he looked at her breast where her nametag perched—"Feather, right? I look forward to it." He bent his attention to his meal.

As Feather bussed tables, delivered more meals, checked coffee levels and cashed out diners, she considered rescinding her acceptance of a "date" with the hot guy at Table 12. She eventually decided that cancelling would be more awkward than joining him for a brief tour of Hancock. It was a pleasant fall day and she could use the exercise and the sunlight. *Right. Good justifying, girl.*

When Michael left the café, Roadkill called Feather to his table, where he lingered over coffee and the Spokane, Sandpoint, and Coeur d'Alene newspapers that Walt provided his customers. "What's with the PI in Hancock? I might have joined him myself and asked, but I could see you two were far too occupied with each other."

Feather jerked the coffee pot away from Roadkill's mug, spilling a few hot drops on his wrist. "He's a private eye? How would you know?"

Roadkill put a backward palm to his forehead. "The all-knowing Roadkill sees all, knows all. Plus, I met him in Sandpoint a few months ago when he was new to his job." He picked up his mug and frowned at its emptiness. "Looked like he was setting up a date with you. Think he's investigating you?"

"Is it impossible for you to imagine a scenario where an attractive man is interested in me for my charm and other good qualities? Unlike someone who dresses in the skins of dead animals and lives in an ice cream truck, I clean up pretty good."

"Then you *do* have a date. Thought so. And by the way, *I* clean up good, too. Ask the numerous young women who swoon when I drive up in my elegant vehicle. And yes, I can imagine you with an attractive man, despite your insults to *my* charm and good qualities. But it is interesting that a private dick shows up in The Blind Chukar and wants to spend time with you. Wonder what's up." He pushed away the empty mug and the partially read newspapers. "Put it on my tab, okay?" He slid out of the booth and out the door, leaving Feather to wonder if it was her charm or her background that interested Michael Bergmann.

I'll find out later. "Count on it, Mr. Bergmann."

Foul Wind

Nine

PI on the Prowl

Michael Bergmann chewed the toothpick he'd snagged after paying for his meal at The Blind Chukar. He chewed on it, inhaling the scent of the mint flavoring. He considered how puzzling an Easterner might find the name of the little café. Not many people knew what a chukar was, a kind of partridge. Fewer knew how to pronounce it (chucker), and fewer still successfully hunted the wily bird.

He wondered if the sexy brunette who called herself Feather would show up to meet him after her shift or if she'd figured out a way to politely get out of it. Had she believed his interest? It was interest he'd intended to feign, but once he'd met his prey, his interest was truly piqued. If she met him, would she buy his lies?

Thinking of lies, Michael wasn't sure he could continue to play the game he was paid so well to play. Lying, spying, prying. At least as a soldier the rules had been clear. Now the lines were waving like a mirage on the Registan Desert and Michael often had no idea on which side of the line he stood.

He decided to walk around, scope out the town where the woman lived and worked. As he recalled, the projected site for Windfall Works wasn't far outside Hancock, on a farm taken over by the investment group. Kristin Ganborena worked in Spokane, she'd told him, and Brad spent a lot of time in Boise and in Olympia, talking to regulators and utility mucky-mucks. Brad had mentioned that the operations were under control of another partner, Jonathon Flynn. Although he wouldn't make his presence known at Windfall Works, it might be a good idea to scope out the location. Even though Kristin was certain Feather Sullivan was the blackmailer, he'd still check it out.

Speaking of tiny towns, he should have known the odds were high he'd meet up with Roadkill. What reason could he give the friendly and perceptive activist for his presence in Hancock? He'd instinctively ducked his head when he recognized Cliff Mustard, aka Roadkill, but he knew Roadkill recognized him. Probably wondered why Michael had avoided him.

Ah. There you go. Roadkill knew he was a private investigator. All he needed to tell him was that he was undercover. And imply that Feather was definitely not his target, simply a beautiful woman who'd aroused his interest. He'd assure Roadkill that it was a business thing, no danger at all. Would Mustard buy it? About as likely as Michael putting mayo on a hot dog.

More lies. More stories to keep track of. Wouldn't life be simpler if ... what? No lies in Afghanistan, at least at his level, just IEDs and Taliban and constant danger. Surely this was an improvement. Staying alive counted for a lot. Unlike many of his fellow soldiers, Michael had made it through with few injuries, none battle-related. The damn goat bite ... no need to dwell on that.

On the front lines of war, on those long night duties, what had he dreamed about doing once he returned stateside?

He shook his head. Reconnoiter now, meet up with the waitress, or server if he wanted to be PC. Maybe a quick visit to her trailer while he knew she was at work. Lordy, but he hated the invasion of her privacy, because really, something about her slender but erect frame, her alert blue-eyed gaze, her shiny brown hair told him ... "Sheez, Bergmann," he muttered, "are you thinking about a woman or a new dog? At least be honest with yourself. It is probably *not* her shiny brown hair that's causing your neck hair and other body parts to stand up and salute."

Across the street stood an old building, indistinguishable from most of the other wood-faced buildings but for a sign that identified it as Belmont's General Store. Ah. In most small towns, either the general store or the hardware store served as hubs where talkative folk got together to gossip and, if Michael were lucky, spill the beans about their neighbors to a newcomer with receptive ears and a friendly face.

He checked for traffic, unnecessary unless he worried about

being trampled by the town's one horse, and crossed to the general store.

The store appeared empty when he entered, so Michael grabbed a small basket and strolled up and down the broad, tidy aisles, choosing a few snacks to sustain a private eye on surveillance. A mini-pack of Oreos, barbecue chips, string cheese, and a bottle of Clamato. He headed for the produce section and found an apple that didn't look withered. The store didn't carry those cute mini-carrots that his mother assured him were a rip-off. His shoulders sagged in relief. Yay. He tried to be healthy but who could blame him if the store didn't carry them?

He'd about deduced, clever spy that he was, that this place was not Gossip Central for Hancock, given the lack of human (or other) chatter, when a short, buxom woman came around the corner of an aisle. She held a feather duster. They still made those? Her assessing gaze made him wonder if she'd had training in surveillance until he decided she was assuring herself he'd put all his potential purchases in the basket, not his pockets.

The woman made an obvious effort to change her expression from suspicion to welcome. That effort and the sturdy apron she wore told him she was a store employee. He shot her his standard, suspicion-melting, endear-the-ladies, grin.

It was possible one corner of her lip twitched. "Good morning. Looking for anything special I can help with?"

"Might be, ma'am." Michael chuckled. "You cottoned on right away that I'm a stranger here." *Cottoned?*

"We don't get many visitors in Hancock. You a hunter?" She glanced at his shoes and shook her head. "Not unless your boots are in your car." Taking in his khaki slacks and button down shirt, open, no tie, she revised her guess, shaking her head and pursing her lips. "Salesman. Can't think of a thing I need to stock here. Business is slow, slower than usual."

Realizing he was much more a hunter than a salesman, but glad the woman couldn't tell, Michael smiled. "I'm not selling a thing. Just picking up some snacks for the car. Well, for me to eat in the car, heh heh."

She didn't smile. Not much sense of humor here.

"Are you the owner?" Better to aim high and be wrong than to insult.

The smile she gave him seemed nearly genuine. "Oh, yes. I'm the only Belmont left to run Belmont's General Store. Darlene. What kind of help did you need?"

Arrgh. Was that an interested spark in her eye? Oh, dear, he'd have to tone down his grin. Or button down her sparkle. "I think I've found the supplies I need, Ms. Belmont. I was wondering, though, about a server back at The Blind Chukar. Slim brunette? Friendly? With an odd sort of name?"

Her expression soured. "You mean *Feather*." She sniffed. "Another offbeat name those environmental activists give themselves. She's fairly new to Hancock."

Michael set his basket on the old wood floor. What would make this woman spill? "So you don't know much about her?"

She toyed with the feathers at the end of the duster. "I didn't say that. What's your interest in her? She in trouble again?" She inhaled and looked at anything but Michael. "I hope not."

Michael realized that Darlene Belmont was struggling with her conscience. She sort of wanted Feather to be in trouble, yet knew that was not the right way to think. He waited a moment. "I hope not, too," he said, his sad expression implying it might be too late. "It's important that I talk to some of her friends."

"Then Darlene may not be the first person you'd want to talk to," said a deep, amused voice. Roadkill came around the corner of the aisle that Darlene had come from. Michael couldn't believe the activist, in his hiking boots and leather pants, could arrive so silently.

The store owner spun around, hands on her hips. "Clifford Mustard, you have been sneaking up on me since you were on your hands and knees."

Roadkill beamed. "And I'm still picking out slivers." He turned his eyes to Michael. "Ms. Belmont's not a big fan of Feather."

"Because she's an activist, like you?" Michael asked.

The big activist and the woman answered at the same time.

"Don't you go putting words or opinions in my mouth," Darlene said to Roadkill.

"Maybe because some of her actions got her in trouble," Roadkill said.

Darlene stalked toward Roadkill. "You shut your mouth or I'll find my duct tape. We can all change, every one of us. I had my issues with that young woman and her friends, but she did the right thing by her child, gave him up for adoption to an excellent family. I believe in charity toward all and malice toward none. As you should."

Letting slip that Feather had a baby out of wedlock didn't seem all that charitable to Michael, unless this small town was more progressive and understanding than many he'd visited over the years. He imagined Feather hadn't come out of the pregnancy unscathed in reputation or emotionally. But that didn't make her a blackmailer.

Roadkill's tolerant expression had vanished with Darlene Belmont's last words. Michael expected him to blow up at the woman, but he merely replied with a nod and a "Yes, ma'am." He took Michael's arm. "It's been a while since we last met up, my man. Finish your shopping and we can have a beer, or coffee if you think it's too early to imbibe."

Michael took a swig of the root beer both men had selected at the general store. Roadkill had led him to a patch of grass in the town center, where they found an empty bench.

After a few minutes of catching up, Roadkill pinned Michael with his brown eyes. "Feather's a good friend. Can't see any reason you'd need to be spying on her. Unless you've changed professions."

Michael shook his head. "For cripes' sake, since when can't a man express an interest in a good-looking woman?"

"And ask questions about her of her neighbors?"

"I was about to ask about her love life. I'm beginning to think you would have been the one to ask. Am I butting in on your territory?"

Roadkill raised his eyebrows. "She's a friend, period. No benefits.

But if you're still a private dick, I'm wondering what you're doing in Hancock. Feather's great, but I don't see you coming here from Spokane to meet up with her unless you're on a job."

Michael leaned back against the bench, stretching out his legs. "It's private investigator. And yes, that's still what I do. I'm here for another reason, one I can't talk about. I happened to meet up with Feather in the café and wanted to get to know her. I am a man, made of flesh and bones, you know."

Roadkill leered. "Don't give me opportunities like that, Bergmann." He lost the smile. "Feather's had a tough time lately and all of her friends are watching out for her."

Michael clenched his fists, an involuntary motion. "Like the innocent and well-meaning gossip in the general store?"

"Right." He swigged more root beer and contemplated the sparse grass in front of the bench. "The baby she had? She gave it up to the biological father and his wife. What seemed like a good idea has gone sour."

Michael had to ask and hated himself for being an investigator instead of a potential suitor. "Some women make a lot of money giving up their kids."

Roadkill's gaze turned up toward Michael. "Some women do."

Michael's head tilted. "Not this one?"

"Not this one. Against my advice, in case you're wondering. She could have used the money."

"So she was fooling around with a married man." Michael threw his hands up in a protective gesture. "I know that sounded damn judgmental and I've made my share of mistakes. But maybe she felt guilty?"

"You two deserve each other. Kindred spirits. Guilt is an emotion best left unexperienced."

Michael stood, pretty sure he wasn't going to get more out of the activist. "I won't bother to ask if you've never felt guilty."

Roadkill stood beside him. "Here's something for you to consider. Hurt Feather, you're not only going to feel guilty about lying to her and me, you're going to feel a lot of bruises and possibly some broken bones. She's a friend." He walked a few paces and turned. "If you're not lying, how come you haven't asked me about anything or anyone else in this town?"

That's why Michael hated his job. Lies and more lies. And fast thinking was as necessary as fast reflexes in the military. "You haven't given me much chance, given your obsession with Feather." He figured it wouldn't hurt to ask about the wind plant. Maybe see if anyone else could be the blackmailer besides the beautiful waitress. "Besides, I can pretty much foresee your response." He smiled. "Let's see if I'm right. My client, unnamed, of course, might be considering investing in some alternative energy projects in the Pacific Northwest. I heard tell there was a proposal for a wind plant near Hancock."

"Might as well be looking into slaughterhouses, my man. That's what wind turbines are. Kill the birds, the raptors, the bats, to run some rich bitch's hair dryer."

Michael's smile broadened. "Gotcha. I sort of predicted where you'd come from. Planning a big fight against it?"

"No comment. Seems a bit late to investigate Windfall. They already have a group of investors."

"No comment." Michael smiled.

Roadkill's smile slipped and he frowned. "So your client is measuring the community sentiment toward alternative energy."

Keep smiling. Always throws them off. "No comment."

Roadkill burst into raucous laughter. "As wily as ever, I see. At least you're smart enough for our Feather."

"So she's smart?"

Roadkill crossed his arms over his chest and grinned. "No comment."

Ten

Searching for Solutions

Roxanne stared at the screen of her cell phone, willing it to announce a reply to her text to Teddy. Why wasn't he responding?

When she'd heard Kristin and Brad arguing, she'd moved closer to the door and listened. It became clear that Kristin blamed Feather for the blackmail text that arrived during their fight. In truth, Kristin had begun to blame Feather for everything, including global warming, no doubt. Still, Feather had enough problems and Roxanne and Teddy shouldn't be adding to them. Sheez. They were going to sic a private eye on her sister.

She gave a gentle nudge with her foot to Jared's carriage. They were in the park, a hangout for moms, nannies, and their charges. "One of these days, you'll be climbing that jungle gym, Jared." Of course Roxanne wouldn't be there to see it and if things continued downhill, Feather would lose all chance to follow her son's progress. "Text me, Teddy. Now. What's going on?" He didn't reply. Jared let out a contented gurgle.

It was good she got him out of the house. Kristin's temper was toxic and Jared didn't need that much nasty acid around him.

How could Teddy's plan go so bad, so fast? Roxanne had worried, true, but Teddy had convinced her nothing could go wrong. And then, this. Feather didn't deserve it. Roxanne had to stop Teddy. A vision of stacks of cash floated through her mind and she wondered if there was a way to keep at least some of the blackmail booty. She shook her head and could almost see those stacks floating away from her.

She picked up Jared, who was fussing, wanting to be held, she guessed. She cuddled him against her chest and then bounced him gently on her knee. Both baby and nanny babbled sweet nothings. "Don't you worry, little guy. Your mommy won't get in trouble for this. She's straight up. Things will work out, you'll see. Nanny Roxanne will make sure they do."

* * *

Feather waited for Michael on the bench outside The Blind Chukar. Fat chance she could keep her "date" a secret from the rest of Hancock, but maybe she could slow the flow of gossip if she kept everyone in the café from watching her leave with the "handsome stranger." She chuckled. She liked Hancock. Folks kept an eye out for each other. If once in a while she was the focal point for their eyes and gossip, it was to be expected in a small town.

She wiped her palms on her black polished-cotton slacks. She'd fluffed her hair and checked her teeth for debris before she left the café, nothing more. Her blouse had the typical stains her work clothes always sported—coffee, syrup, jam. If Michael Bergmann was investigating her, he'd have some exciting data to share, such as the variety of jams served at The Blind Chukar. And if Michael was actually interested in Feather as a woman? What then? She took in a purposeful breath. The last man she'd dated had been Brad. She slapped her palms against her legs. Not the time for regrets or reminiscing.

A tall man strolled in Feather's direction. Michael.

He neared. And smiled. A smile she liked. "Feather." Her name sounded good in his voice. *Oh, for heaven's sake! Been celibate too long, have we?* If even his voice could turn her on, Feather was in trouble. Which made it even more important to find out if she was his official business or a side interest. She wondered briefly which she preferred.

"Michael." Feather cleared her throat. Had to get rid of that wavering in her voice somehow. She smiled and made a huge effort to toss her doubts into the gutter. She stepped toward him.

He took her hand in his for a brief squeeze. "I'm glad you decided to join me." He tilted his head in the direction of the Lutheran church at the end of the block. "I'm a nut for old architecture, even though I'm no expert. Shall we wander to that church?"

"Sure. There are a couple of old houses on the street beyond it that you might like. Queen Anne, and one that's sort of Craftsman style, not that I'm an architect."

"Sounds like you know more than I do. Lead on."

They crossed the street and walked south, their bodies occasionally nudging the other's as they negotiated the sidewalk. When they came to the building that would now become the sales outlet for Gina's latest project, Feather said, "This used to be called The Flat Italian. It was a pizza parlor."

"No town's complete without a pizza joint. Surprised it closed."

"Gina's folks decided to move to Italy. They left her the place but she didn't want to throw pizza dough forever." She told him how they'd all worked on the remodeling of the Flat Italian into a women's shelter and then a retail shop for the goods created by "Gina's girls" and those imported by Gina and Emily. Wealthy and independent, Emily traveled the world these days, seeking out talented entrepreneurial women to create products.

When they reached the old church, they discovered the door to the sanctuary was not locked. They wandered inside. High-backed wood pews faced the altar and a stained glass oval window behind it. At mid-afternoon, sunlight came mostly from overhead, so the window looked flat and dull, almost like those resin window decorations people buy at the dollar store. Michael moved closer to the altar and stared up at the window. "I bet that's spectacular when the morning sun shines through it," he said in the hushed tones people reserve for libraries and funeral homes.

"Uh-huh." Feather remembered being here, seeing the sunlight illuminate the images on the window, but couldn't recall the occasion.

"This your church?"

She started. "No. No. I didn't grow up here in Hancock. My mom lives in Sandpoint." She stared up at the window. "But I've been here before. Can't remember why or when."

"Sounds like the lyrics to a song."

Feather realized she was having too much fun with a man who might be investigating her. She moved to the door of the church. "Let's continue our tour outside."

Outdoors, she stopped and faced him. "Why are you in Hancock?"

"Can't I simply be interested in the architecture of North Idaho?"

"And you come to Hancock? On a weekday? Please. Either you work an odd schedule or you're independently wealthy."

He smiled. "Would you like me more if I were a wealthy man?" When she didn't respond, just waited, he continued. "I could be a fireman. But I'm not. I do research, market research."

She shook her head. "Again, I doubt that. Hancock?"

He walked ahead of her, and she wondered if he was coming up with a plausible lie. "Hancock is an interesting place. Someone's starting up a wind farm not far out of town. Buildings are being renovated. Beautiful women pour coffee and serve delicious scones."

She laughed. "Flatterer." *Yep. Roadkill was right. He's checking me out for someone.*

"Simply offering proof that many things interest me. Including you."

Something didn't ring true in his words. Feather sensed a discomfort in him. And a deeper sadness that she decided not to probe. She had no right. Still, why would a private investigator be interested in her? Might as well be blunt. "Look, Roadkill told me he knew you. Said you were a private investigator. Did Brad send you to check me out?"

Michael's face paled. He rolled his lips together. "I'll bet Roadkill used another term."

She smiled. "Duh. It's Roadkill. But you didn't answer my question. I honestly didn't think this would go any further. Brad said he'd have to ask Kristin and I knew then what the answer would be. But sending you ...." She began to have some hope.

"I ran into Roadkill earlier and I figured he had told you I was an investigator. It's not something I announce when I first meet people"—he gave her an assessing, slow look—"especially attractive women. It tends to make folks nervous." He rubbed his neck. "I do a lot of market and other research as part of my job, so I wasn't exactly lying to you. I'm investigating something, or someone, that I'm not free to discuss with you."

Feather's hopes dived. "So it's not for Brad. It's not me. I knew *she*"—she spit out the "she" with a venom that surprised even Feather—"would never agree to loan me money."

Michael leaned closer to Feather, looking into her eyes. "Why not? You two have a history?"

Feather reminded herself that this man, despite what he said, could be investigating her. She wanted to lie to him, but decided it made no difference. Her earlier conclusion held. No way would Kristin part with any of her precious funds for Feather, even if she knew she'd be repaid with interest. She nodded. "You could say that. Not a good history, and not Kristin's fault. Let's just say she's not my biggest fan or my best friend."

"You seem to have plenty of friends here in Hancock. Roadkill threatened my fertility if I 'done you wrong,' and even the charming proprietress of the Belmont General Store spoke well of you."

Feather grinned. "Roadkill's my buddy. We've known each other for donkey's years. But Darlene? Saying a nice thing about me? I'm stunned."

Michael laughed. His laugh was deep and disarming. "It was one of those back-handed compliments." He blushed. Despite herself, Feather was charmed by a man who blushed. Not a good trait for a PI.

"Ah. Told you I was a fallen woman, did she?" The man who more than likely peeped in motel room windows was embarrassed. "Not a big deal. She's come a long way, really. Especially since she approves of the fact that I gave my son to Brad and Kristin." At the surprised expression on Michael's face, she realized Darlene had kept some things secret. No matter. If he asked, he could find out. And if they saw each other again, she'd have told him about Jared. "Not like Darlene to be so circumspect."

"Roadkill interrupted, or she might have spilled a few more beans." He twisted his mouth in a rueful manner. "Then everyone in town knows you gave your son to the Ganborenas?"

Gotcha. This man wanted to know a lot about her, a lot more than a prospective suitor. She smiled. She was pretty sure she hadn't mentioned Brad's last name, one most people had trouble remembering. Michael would not have stopped the flow of Darlene's words had Roadkill not intervened. He was investigating her. But why? "Roadkill is almost as bad a gossip as Darlene. He probably filled you in on my oh-so-dull life."

He shook his head. "Mostly he warned me not to hurt you. Is he living in the 19th century? I'd wager you know how to take care of yourself."

"Friends have each other's backs." *And I fear you're not going to be my friend, despite your terrific smile and hunky body.* "Tell me about yourself. What do you do when you're not checking out the fascinating village of Hancock?" *And its residents?*

They walked and shared the typical information: hobbies, favorite movies, least favorite foods. Nothing Feather told Michael mattered, and she avoided telling him anything about herself except innocuous trivia.

She learned that Michael loved to read cozy mysteries, especially those where the sleuths had jobs he could learn about. He learned that she liked horror and thriller novels and loved to bake. They shared a love for *The Princess Bride* and Monty Python and *Chinatown*.

It was a shame, really. The man was friendly, the man was intelligent, the man seemed interested in her as a woman. Hadn't happened in way too long. Too bad she couldn't trust him. She couldn't fathom what he might find out that Brad, and hence Kristin, didn't already know about her. She'd shared everything with Brad.

Eleven

No, No, Nanny

Roxanne skulked through the back yard like a burglar, onto the deck and into the family room to gain access to the stairs up to Jared's room. She'd parked her car down the street behind their home so Kristin and Brad, who had taken the day off and remained home, would not notice her return. After she tucked Jared in for a nap, she made sure the baby monitor was on. The she ran softly to her room above the garage and packed her most precious belongings and favorite clothes into a large suitcase, hoping she could make it down the stairs without being heard or seen by the Ganborenas. She didn't need a scene. Kristin's volatile temper had already hit hot today. Who knew what it would hit with the news that the nanny was leaving without notice?

She had to leave, for so many reasons. Kristin hated and distrusted Feather, far more than was reasonable. She already suspected Roxanne of telling Feather where Jared slept. Once she found out Roxanne had lied about disapproving her sister, that she had arranged visits with Jared, she'd be out on her fanny faster than Roxanne's first boyfriend climaxed. And that was fast.

No future for Roxanne at the Ganborena's, then. Besides, taking care of Jared, terrific little guy that he was, had become boring, and Roxanne did not tolerate boring well. The pay was okay, but she knew she deserved more.

Out through the door, hauling her suitcase, clutching it against her body with one hand, gripping the rail with the other, she descended the stairs from her room and then from the deck to the yard. Her arms ached and she regretted the amount of clothing she'd stuffed into the case.

If Teddy wouldn't come to her to discuss his stupid, vicious scheme, then she would go to him. But she'd make certain they met in the open, not at his home. The guy used his sexiness like a weapon and when she was around him, Roxanne felt she needed a flak jacket. Of course Teddy would soon have it off. All her arguments against the blackmail would be forgotten under his ... well, under Teddy.

She made it to the alley behind the house and lowered the suitcase to the ground. She dragged it behind her, trying to ignore the effect of the gravel of the unpaved alley on the expensive case's wheels. She supposed they repaired those things. She'd have to ask her mother.

She staggered to her car and opened the door. While she caught her breath, she texted Teddy to meet her at a park not far from his house.

She wondered if Feather knew what was going on. Doubtful, since she wasn't an investor in the wind farm. Her sister made her opposition to the farm clear, despite Brad's and Peter's insistence that it was environmentally sound and a huge improvement over conventional power sources.

Roxanne had no issue with the wind farm, and she had little regard for the protesters who shouted, "Not in my bat yard." But family was family and Feather was *not* a blackmailer and didn't deserve to be investigated like a criminal. She wondered for an instant if she would suspect her sister if she didn't know Teddy was behind the blackmail. After all, Feather was desperate for cash for the stupid B&B. *No.* She couldn't see her sister doing something so blatantly illegal unless it was for someone or something else, like bats. The only answer was to get Teddy to stop.

She texted Feather, aware she was avoiding talking to her sister. It was likely the PI had tracked her down by now. "Don't worry about what's happening," she keyed. "I know what the problem is and I'll fix it." She added a happy face emoticon, knowing how much they irked her sister.

Roxanne waited in the park, pacing, hating the waiting. She texted Teddy yet another message, a repeat of her earlier ones, only shorter and this one in all caps. "MEET ME NOW. I'M AT CLARK PARK. URGENT!" No smiley faces, no x's or o's for Teddy. She'd tried calling but the phone went to voice mail time after time after time.

Nearby, mothers and grandmothers and nannies watched their charges play. Some chatted with others, some attended to their cell phones, and one actually read a book. All glanced up occasionally, mostly attuned to the children's sounds, alert only when the increased volume or pitch indicated a problem. *No more of that for you, Roxie.* Sure, Jared was cute and cheerful, but he demanded so much of his caretakers. Exhausting. Roxanne had better things in her future.

After another spate of unanswered texts and calls sent to voice mail, Roxanne phoned her sister. She'd have to go to Teddy's home and she couldn't go alone. Feather would be a good chaperone.

Feather's cell played Madonna's *Causing a Commotion*, the tune she'd assigned to Roxanne. Feather murmured, "Gotta get this one," and moved a few yards away from Michael. Roxanne was weeping, something she did without effort when she wanted to bend someone to her will. *Good grief, girl, you have become so cynical.*

"Meet me at Teddy's place." She gave Feather directions and promised to text the address to her. "He's gotten you, me, everyone, in way too much trouble. I have to stop him and I will, believe me, I will. He's gone way too far this time."

Feather steadied her breathing. "What do you mean, trouble? How? What could—"

All trace of tears gone from her voice, Roxanne said, "He told me it was a game. He was wrong. It's no game. And now they're blaming you." Feather heard a hitch in her voice that spoke of tension or suppressed anger. "You can be annoying, but no way will I let Teddy get you in trouble like this. I promise, this won't go any farther. But you need to meet me there. Please, Charlie-bear."

"I'll be there as soon as I can, Pox." Feather flipped her phone shut. She paced back to where Michael waited. "Gotta go. Nice meeting you." She extended her hand.

Michael took her hand in both of his. "You look troubled."

Feather retrieved her hand and gave him a steady look. "Not your problem." She turned and walked away, hoping no part of her body was trembling. She had no idea if he intended to follow her but it didn't matter. What mattered was getting to her sister.

Twelve

Chasing Shadows

Haley West despised Jonathon Flynn, considered him a worthless pest, but for now he signed the paycheck so she had to listen to him whine. She also had to at least make a pretense of doing what he wanted. His initial charm and her determination to keep him close got them in bed together, but the charm soured into demands for sex whenever the mood struck him with no regard for Haley's needs. She hated how he got off on sneaking a blow job in the office or fondling her to the point of arousal when others were near. It made her feel weirdly ashamed, and that irritated her, because Haley prided herself on never being ashamed.

Haley's assignment was to stay close to the manager of Windfall Works and report back to Chaz. Why the boss had to send her to a wind farm being set up on a hog farm in God-forsaken Hogs Wallow, Idaho, escaped her. Had she annoyed him? She assured herself she was probably the only woman Chaz trusted enough to do the job.

When the first text arrived about "problems at Windfall Works," Jon had gone into a tailspin and hadn't escaped it yet, more than twenty-four hours later. Between being certain he had to hide the news from Chaz and deciding he had to inform the Canadian right away, you'd think he was a hockey puck on ice fresh from the Zamboni. Of course Chaz knew within an hour because Haley's job was to keep her boss fully informed. Secrets made Chaz nervous and she definitely didn't want to see Chaz nervous.

This end of the Canadian operation was her responsibility, according to Chaz. So she always kept him informed.

Haley's father, a man she'd left behind with no regret, had trained her not to bring up problems unless she had a solution. Otherwise he'd wallop her. She'd learned early on to make her own solutions. So. Blackmail was a problem. Jon upset, a problem. Therefore, when she'd emailed Chaz about the text that arrived, she added that she would resolve it.

When the second text came with instructions for the payoff drop, she convinced Jon to make the drop, even though he'd wanted her to. She would hide and spot the blackmailer so they could get the money back and solve the problem.

She told Jon she needed to get in place long before the drop, so left early. That way she'd have time to stop at the art museum at Gonzaga University in Spokane and take in the photography on exhibit. She thought about the shots she'd been taking at the farm, the hogs, of course, and the blades of the lone turbine they'd erected.

Now Haley waited, not far from the drop site. She wore black chinos and an innocuous white polo shirt, holding a lunch bucket and her camera case, her long blond hair stuffed under a baseball cap. She hoped she wouldn't have to wait much longer; her butt already had a good impression of the metal park bench.

Across the green, an overweight man shuffled along, his head doing the tourist rubberneck thing. Peter Brewer? Or just another fat tourist? Too far to tell. She used the telephoto lens on her camera to shoot a quick pic of the man, thinking she might be able to identify him better later with some Photoshopping. Jon had been gabbing on the phone ever since he received the text. He might have told all the investors, for all Haley knew. Could make for quite a crowd if they all decided to track the blackmailer.

Speaking of a crowd, Haley noticed a woman cross not five yards in front of her. Sophia Patton, the investor who'd been bugging Jon, with increasingly frantic pleas, for a refund of her investment. She was a banker here in downtown Spokane and maybe it was a coincidence she, too, was in the park.

Maybe the blackmailer had sent out several texts at the same time, hoping to score fast and disappear. Was Sophia leaving her payoff, or following the person who picked up Jon's cash or her own payoff? Or ... maybe the Patton woman was the blackmailer, brazen enough to come for the payoff in person.

Haley wondered who had the balls to do the crime. After all the rumors flying at Brad's little gala, any of the investors could have been worried enough to put the squeeze on the others. She'd circulated that night, trying to find the source of the rumors, but never found out.

Thirteen

Easy, Peasy?

Teddy strolled east on Main. He passed the Mobius Science Center and grinned at the thought of meeting his "transfer agent" there rather than in the huge mall. His mother had to drag him to the science museum on his first visit, with promise of ice cream for good behavior. After that first marvelous adventure, he did the dragging of his by then bored mother until he could go by himself. Puzzles, mysteries revealed, thrilled him more than ice cream.

And now he had created a puzzle, one he knew those greedy investors who fooled themselves into believing their project would save the environment, could never untangle. He would pick up the cash and he would disappear. If Roxanne wanted to join him, great, but he knew rich, attractive men never lacked companionship. He entered the theater complex from the street and exited into the huge mall. He strutted past upscale stores he'd soon be able to afford and took a seat a few stores down from where he'd instructed his "mule" to transport the bag of money. When he saw him, he beckoned to a young teenager who'd just entered the line for free sample pretzel pieces for the second time.

"I'll give you five bucks to pick something up for me from that guy in the red shirt down the hall."

The kid looked Teddy up and down. "You lame or what?"

"Tired."

"Ten bucks."

"When you bring the bag. Fifteen if you're fast. Give him this." He handed the kid a playing card, the Ace of Hearts.

The teen raced off and returned in moments, the gym bag over his shoulder. He stood to take the bag and slapped a twenty in the kid's outstretched palm. "Sorry, no change," Teddy told him. The teen gave him a huge smile and strolled to the pretzel counter.

Already the wealth headed the right direction.

A quick glance in the bag confirmed it contained cash. Time once he got home to count it. He looked around but didn't see any cops. Good. Jon of all the investors wouldn't want to bring the cops in, with the secrets Teddy threatened to reveal.

Teddy's cell phone vibrated in his pocket. He glanced at it, saw it announced a call from Roxanne, and ignored it. She could wait. She deserved to wait. Her nervousness had almost infected Teddy, came close to making him stop this whole project. He chuckled. "Told you nothing could go wrong," he said to no one.

He strolled through the mall and exited on the side with bus stops. He occasionally glanced behind and around him, but saw no one suspicious.

Teddy got off the bus a few blocks before his home, so he could watch for a tail. Again he saw nothing. He strolled toward home, enjoying the crisp fall air and thinking he'd relocate somewhere he never had to use a snow shovel again. Roxanne said her father had traveled to South America for years. She'd always wanted to accompany him when winter took hold in Sandpoint, sometimes freezing parts of the lake and always freezing her tush.

They'd both enjoy sipping margaritas year-round. He turned onto a concrete sidewalk that led to the tiny porch of his beat-up abode. He pivoted to look up and down the street and saw someone pulling weeds. He snorted a laugh. Why bother for these crap places?

He unlocked the door and tossed the gym bag onto the sofa. One quick pit stop and he could count his first deposit on a life of luxury. He'd have to remember to make a checkmark by Jon's name on the grid he'd made of blackmail clients. He'd decided to refer to them as clients instead of victims. This was a business transaction.

He'd just settled onto the sofa, making sure to avoid the loose spring, when someone knocked on the door. Had to be Roxanne. Probably forgot her key, the little ditz. The door was thinner than a Reuben sandwich. He called through it. "Hey, babe, forgive me already?" He threw the door wide. His mouth gaped open when he saw the gun pointing at his chest.

"Teddy. I'm disappointed in you. Blackmail is such a nasty crime.

One that apparently requires a better mind than yours."

Teddy backed away, hands in the air, supplicating. "Wait. Let's talk. There's plenty to share."

Teddy's confronter closed and locked the front door. "Generous thought. A little late. Back away from the door."

"You can have it all," he said, hating the way his voice wobbled. "No one needs to know." He continued to back up until he ran into the living room wall. "Don't, don't shoot me. I'm a thief, sure, but killing me makes you a murderer."

"We all take chances."

He stared into merciless eyes, begging for mercy, looking for some way out. He saw no pity and no weakness, only the gun. For a moment, the gun wobbled and the shooter's face shadowed with sorrow. Then the gun steadied. Teddy had an instant for regret before the pistol fired, three times into his chest.

Teddy slumped to the floor, all life gone from his eyes.

His killer re-holstered the gun and backed away from Teddy. All that remained now was to find the text messages and the cash. Ideally, Teddy's notes on each victim. Then the blackmail could continue, with a more deserving recipient, and one who couldn't be traced.

Disagreeable, but best to get done with the body first. A pat-down of Teddy's cargo pants revealed a hard shape in the right lower pocket. Awkwardly straddling the body and working to avoid touching it, the killer unbuttoned the pocket and extracted a simple phone. Had to be the burner, because Teddy's personal phone had every extra including a fancy case this one did not.

Next came the gym bag on the couch. A quick check revealed it held the cash. The killer hurried to the bedroom. The tidy student desk opposite the bed held a burgundy leather 8 1/2 x 11 inch portfolio, with a yellow note pad inside. Neat lines across the page horizontally, divided it into five equal rows. Jon, Brad, Sophia, Jeanette, Peter, were written at the beginning of each row. Across the top were columns, labeled Reason(s), Est., Text 1, Text 2, Drop, Paid. No check marks yet in the Paid column. Under Reason(s), he'd made sketchy notes on each victim. The pad joined the cash in the gym bag.

Teddy had packed up most of his belongings in cardboard boxes now stacked in the closet. These were useless to both of them, so they'd remain in place. The killer took a fast survey of the bedroom and then returned to the hallway. In the bathroom Teddy's cell phone lay by the sink. That went into the gym bag, as well.

A quick glance into the back bedroom revealed more boxes, older, dusty ones, an expensive bicycle, and a couple of leather suitcases. Nothing but the best for Teddy. Except of course the house he rented, obviously with furniture supplied by the owner. Both crap.

The murderer's head ached. Teddy should have realized the danger in his latest project, but still. Shooting him had not come easy. Wanting to avoid passing Teddy's body, the killer decided the open street out front posed too much risk. Through the backyard, into the alley seemed the chosen exit strategy.

The decision firmed up when someone pounded on the front door and the key turned. "Teddy. Teddy! Are you in there? It's me, Roxanne."

The murderer waited, breath too loud, heart pounding; considered going for the gun and discarded the thought. *No. No one else could die.* Especially not someone innocent. Unless ... was Roxanne party to Teddy's little scheme?

"Teddy. I'm coming in. We need to talk."

Good luck with that. Bile surged upward and the killer's stomach cramped. What would Roxanne do when she found Teddy?

Roxanne would scream. The shriek came loud and long.

The bereaved lover's cries rivaled those of the turbine's blades in a high wind—piercing, painful, ceaseless.

Knocking over two metal kitchen chairs, clutching the gym bag in one hand and the gun in the other, the shooter ran out the back door, relieved that it unlocked from the inside with just a twist. Hurdled down the back stairs, stumbled on the tattered coco mat at the bottom, back up in a moment to head for the back gate, not looking back, not pausing.

Fourteen

No Body But You

Propelled by anger, Roxanne considered the promise she and Teddy had made to only use the key when invited by the occupant. By ignoring her text and voice mail pleas, Teddy broke their commitment. Early in their relationship, she walked in on Teddy so deep in a computer game, he'd forgotten to eat, let alone answer his new lover's text messages. *This* game, however, was real life and more dangerous. It was arrogant and selfish to ignore her.

She slammed the door open, leaving the key in the lock. Fussing with a key, neatly replacing it in her purse, would distract from the image of girlfriend spurned she was going for. The door bounced back from the wall and hit her foot. "Teddy?" she called again, this time more tentative. "You home?"

She moved into the house, scanning the room. Teddy sat against the far wall of the living room, slumped against it. For an instant she wondered at his odd choice of a place to sit. Then she noticed the blood and the stillness of his form.

She froze then screamed, long, and so loud it bounced inside her brain, and ran to him. She threw herself to the floor and across his chest, heedless of the blood. She smelled not the metallic trademark of blood, but rather Teddy's scent, spicy, almost fresh. Too like her vibrant Teddy to be dead. "Teddy. Stay alive. I'll get help." She reached into her purse for her cell phone. He remained still, inert. She pounded on his chest. "I told you not to do this! Dammit, Teddy, you can't die on me. I need you." She sobbed, punched the 9 of 911, and noticed her bloody fingers as if they might be attached to someone else's hand.

A crash sounded elsewhere in the house, followed by another, quieter sound. Her hands stilled and her breath stopped. Teddy's killer? Still here? She should run straight back out the front door.

Keep punching for help. Instead she crept toward rather than away from the noise. The compulsion to discover overcame her desire to escape. Even as she went forward, Roxanne knew she should not. The noise came from the kitchen. Nothing could have made that much racket on the carpeted floors of the rest of the house. She edged to the corner of the wall and peeked around to see the back door close. Whoever shot Teddy was escaping.

Roxanne ran to the kitchen and stumbled over the first obstacle, an overturned kitchen chair. "Ow. Damn. Shit. Hell." Had she broken or merely bruised her shin? Tears poured from her eyes. She righted herself, slammed the chair aside and hurdled the second one. She thrust the door open and ran outside. Why hadn't she worn something besides her ridiculously high platform wedges?

Across the yard the back gate slammed shut, flapping against the fence support. She ran to the alley and saw a figure some three or four houses away, running headlong, not pausing to look back. Thank goodness, because standing in the middle of the alley Roxanne presented a perfect target. No doubt the murderer heard her screaming in the living room. She almost smiled. Her scream had been labeled a deadly weapon in high school. By now Teddy's attacker was too far away even to identify the sex or the size of the person.

Teddy! I have to get help. She ran back into the house. Teddy remained slumped against the wall, his face now pale. She moved closer to him, watched for any sign he lived. Too much blood, so much. She knelt and crawled to his side, staying out of his blood even though the front of her shirt was drenched with it. She felt for a pulse she knew she would not find. Backed away, wanting to close his eyes.

She fell onto the couch, knowing she was spreading Teddy's blood, messing up the crime scene, not caring. She should call the police, but Teddy was beyond help and what would she tell them? "My boyfriend was a blackmailer and one of his victims got angry. Well, yes, I knew about the blackmail, but he was the one sending the messages. And yes, the killer identified me and could at any time return to get rid of the witness."

How had Teddy's plan gone so wrong, so fast? Who figured out his identity? Or had the killer followed him from the place the money was supposed to be dropped? If Teddy had already picked up the money, maybe it was still in the house. She took shallow breaths in and out, to avoid inhaling any scent of death from nearby and in a vain attempt to calm herself. She had to think. She was in danger. She had to disappear. She remembered her frantic call to Feather. Remembered Feather always saved Roxanne from the trouble she got into.

"Not Feather. No way." But ... Feather cared about her family and her friends and Teddy was a threat. Their own mother was a partner in the wind farm and had no doubt received a blackmail text. Brad and Kristin suspected Feather of the blackmail. Feather's temper spewed forth like a geyser, not always for good reasons. But no. No way. For one thing, she didn't believe in guns. But what if it had been Teddy's gun, something he got for protection when he launched this crazy, deadly game of his?

Could they have gotten into an argument, fought and ... Feather shot him? Ran away? A totally unlikely scenario, for a number of reasons. Feather disapproved of violence, had been a non-violent protestor à la Gandhi. Despite her "rebel" image, Feather did the right thing, and encouraged others, to the point of nagging, to do the same.

Roxanne took a breath. She had to escape. Hide. But first. She headed for Teddy's bedroom and spent a few frantic moments searching for the money, finding nothing but some bills tucked into his top drawer. She took them. Hiding out would take cash. She searched the pockets of his clothing in his closet, even dislodged the mattress. Nothing. In the bedside table drawer, she found a well-worn copy of the swimsuit edition of *Sports Illustrated*.

She dropped the magazine. Her fingerprints would be on everything she touched. Well, duh. She was Teddy's girlfriend. They would think it odd if her prints weren't there.

She didn't find Teddy's cellphone or a burner phone like he had used for the scam. The killer must have had enough time to shoot Teddy and search the place. It *couldn't* have been Feather. Far too calculating. Roxanne looked at her watch. Where was her sister? She'd said she would come right away and Hancock was only forty minutes from Spokane. If she'd driven, she might have beaten Roxanne here. Roxanne had left her car at the park, to give Feather time to meet her, so she wouldn't have to face Teddy alone. If only she had waited for Feather. Instead she had to barge in and play the rejected lover. If she'd arrived sooner, could she have prevented Teddy's death? Or would they have both been killed? She sobbed. She couldn't think straight.

Feather had to be here soon. Oh, Lord. Feather would think Roxanne had killed her lover, trying to stop his crazy plan.

She had to get out of here, hide, think, and figure out what to do. She'd go out the same way Teddy's killer had. But first ... She moved to the living room and stood above the body of Teddy Fitzpatrick. She whispered the Lord's Prayer, the only one she could remember. "Teddy, you didn't deserve this," she added. "No one does, even when they do stupid, stupid stuff."

Maybe not nice or religious to blame Teddy for his actions, but she simply voiced her first thoughts.

Out, now. If Feather came, it confirmed she hadn't killed Teddy, and Roxanne prayed it was true. However, her sister's first reaction would be to call the cops and Roxanne didn't want to spend all day explaining. If the killer recognized Roxanne, she might be next on the hit list.

She moved to the back door and down the porch steps. She crossed the yard slowly, looking for footprints, maybe cowboy boots with the owner's initial embossed on them, so all she need do was read backwards. No footprints, no initials. It was fall in a dry year.

She could not go to her mother and ask for sanctuary. Mom would know she was hiding something, and tell her to "make a clean breast of it, get it off your chest." Would she loan Roxanne money? No. She'd want to know why Roxanne left her position as Jared's nanny, when he needed a calm person.

She thought about hiding out in Feather's trailer. Her nose wrinkled. The trailer was old and emitted a faint aroma of mold. Every time she visited her sister, Roxanne's nose ran. How many times had she lectured her sister on the dangers of mold? Feather's place was out. What could she do? Text her sister and say, "I didn't kill Teddy. Did you?" Maybe not.

Any of her friends here in Spokane knew Roxanne as Teddy's other half and when his body was discovered, they would either suspect her and turn her in or run from her in terror. No good either way. Where then, could she run?

Suddenly the image of the ultimate bad boy, the man frequently bonded out of jail by his long-suffering brother, popped into Roxanne's mind. Why not Roadkill? The old ice cream truck he called home had undergone serious restoration and cleaning earlier in the year, so it wouldn't be too disgusting. And Roadkill would never turn her in, even if she still held a smoking gun. Well, maybe then. He was a non-violent kind of guy, despite his fiery words.

Other than opposing the wind farm for ecological reasons, Roadkill had little stake in it.

She strolled to where she'd parked her car, a young woman on a walk. Never mind the bloody shirt and bleeding shin. She'd head for Hancock and track down Roadkill. Cool. A savior wearing the skins of squished animals.

Roxanne drove sedately toward Hancock. A stop by state or local cops would not be a good thing. She tried to concentrate on the road, on the roadside attractions, on anything but the image of poor dead Teddy, an image seared forever into her mind and heart. Her entire body continued to shake from the shock and her stomach roiled and growled at the same time.

She shook her head. *Unthinkable. Do not think about it.*

She turned the CD player on, choosing an Enya disc; soothing and relaxing.

Unless Roadkill was off on a "quest," hiking, camping or simply hanging out with some of his weirder friends outside Hancock, finding his truck wouldn't be hard in the tiny hamlet of Hancock. She hoped she could find it fast, because she didn't want her little red Mazda to be noticed.

As she neared the south end of town, she recalled Roadkill mentioning he'd been parking Rosinante at a campground off the east-west road that cut off from Highway 54 toward Bayview. She slowed, drove onto the shoulder and hung a U-turn. For watching the campground, keeping the restrooms tidy, assuring that the trash stayed in the trash bins and out of the grounds, and reporting any issues to the Forest Service, he was allowed to stay at the campground for free.

Of course, if the activist needed to go to town for supplies, like a turtle he took his home with him, sometimes leaving a tent to mark his spot, sometimes not.

She slowed for a car turning out of a local bar, burger and pool joint, Potter's Felt. Her eyes automatically scanned the lot. Under the pines beside Potter's, Roadkill's recently restored turtle shell sparkled in the sunlight. She pulled onto the little side road that led back to the Potter's small home and the three cabins they rented out, following it past the cabins to the ancient old barn that moldered there. She parked on the far side of the barn, invisible to anyone except the most avid enthusiast of old barns.

Not a good idea to leave a trail of suitcase wheels leading between her car and Rosinante, the absurd name Roadkill had given his truck. She opened the hatchback and rummaged in her case until she found her sneakers and a pair of socks. She changed out of her Lilly Pulitzer wedges and repacked the case. Then she wrapped the strap of her purse around her neck and hefted the case from the rear trunk. It weighed too much to carry far. She hefted it back into the trunk, where she offloaded four novels and three pairs of shoes. Attire Chez Rosinante would be très casual. If Roadkill didn't toss her back out on her rear.

Carrying the now manageable suitcase, Roxanne headed for the ice cream truck. She'd forgotten that while completing the repairs to Roadkill's totaled truck, they had installed sliding door windows replacing the formerly open doorway. She hoped to find a way inside.

Not a problem. Roadkill had left the side door pulled back into its pocket, in a so-far-unsuccessful attempt to air out the smell of cabbage and who-knew-what-else.

"Who cares?" She staggered inside and took her case to the back of the vehicle, where a new queen bed beckoned to her. She stuffed the case under the bed, stripped her clothes off and fell on top of the bed, pulling the plush comforter around her. She doubted she could sleep, what with the horror of her day, but she needed to rest and the comforter's warmth, well, comforted her.

She fell asleep in moments.

Fifteen

... And She's Still There

Roadkill left Potter's after a late, too-liquid lunch. But he'd again won his lunch and a few beers, even using the house cue. Marv had accused him of being a hustler, but they'd all laughed at the accusation. You don't hustle for burgers, even if they're above average. Of course, if the regulars at Potter's compared notes and counted up the number of beers and burgers Roadkill had won, they might change their minds and their accusations.

Naah, they'd never do that. Would they?

But if so, he might have to find a job that paid more than space for Rosinante to park. Ugh. Back to bouncing? He'd better be sure he stayed in shape. Maybe a hike later today.

He stumbled only once on the way to his truck. Figured that meant he could drive, no problem. Should he take a nap first or simply head home? Or stop at Belmont's and see if Darlene would extend him credit?

He chuckled at that thought, the chuckle turning into a belch.

He used his key to open the driver's door even though he knew the pocket door remained unlocked. Easier to get a key in a keyhole than to maneuver across to the driver's seat without giving himself a concussion.

Okay. Home, nap, hike, maybe stop in at his brother's place for some dinner. Ed lived in the bunkhouse at the former Camp Destiny, but Roadkill suspected he spent a lot of nights at Gina's, in the main ranch house. It would be good to see Ed, and important to check in on the baby and Gina. Had to see how little Pia was doing, after all. And if he happened to drop in just before dinner, well ... He salivated at the thought of Gina's cooking. She'd been trying recipes her mom had sent back from Italy.

He started Rosinante and pulled forward, glad he'd had the

foresight to park where he didn't have to back up to exit. Of course he had forgotten the rugged, homemade berm that Kenny Potter and his sons had installed near the entrance to the parking lot. It was made to slow the cars of teenagers who found the parking lot of Potter's Felt an ideal spot to round the oval of the Hancock circuit: one end of town to the other. A short circuit.

The front wheels made it over the berm but something underneath Rosinante hung up on it, as if he was teetering on the top of a dunce cap. Which, to some extent, he was.

He threw the truck into reverse and gunned the motor, hoping the hang-up was small.

It took another three tries, teeth rattling events each one, to extract Rosinante from the berm. He headed out of the lot, swinging a hard right and heading south. "Home, Rosinante!"

Just before the stop sign at the corner of Main and Forest, two cats sped across the street a few yards in front of the truck. Roadkill smiled. Then he slammed on the brakes and swerved to the right to avoid the small black and tan beagle that raced after the cats, heedless of traffic.

Rosinante bumped over the curb with the right front tire before Roadkill brought the truck under control. Once it reached the shoulder, the engine stalled. He leaned forward onto the steering wheel. He flashed on another similar event, when his truck was forced from the road. That time, it didn't swerve to the shoulder and stall. It tumbled down a canyon, propelled by a fool in a pickup, and nearly killed him.

Roadkill heard a thump at the back of the truck. He hoped to hell he hadn't dislodged the muffler or the bumper or some other vital organ of his vehicle.

"What in the name of everything holy are you doing?"

At the sound of a woman's voice, Roadkill jerked his head up. He spun around in his seat, the seat belt tightening and threatening to choke him. Roxanne Sullivan staggered from his bed. "Anyone else with you?" he asked. It was an effort to keep his voice steady, but he had to maintain his reputation for cool.

Roxanne broke into tears and scurried toward him. The tears

appeared false to him, but his experience with weeping, near-naked women in Rosinante—or for that matter, elsewhere—was admittedly limited. He did a double take. Near naked said it. Roxanne wore a bra and a thong and nothing else but those damn tears. Her face looked like it had been hit by a chocolate cream pie. Dark streaks ran down her white face.

Rosinante reeked of lavender. How had he missed her scent when he staggered into the truck?

"Roadkill. Clifford. I need your help. You have to hide me."

"Hide you?" *Great repartee, buddy. Keep the smooth coming.* He couldn't help the tour his eyes took of her healthy, curvy body. Incredible smooth skin, lots of it.

Roxanne looked down at her nearly bare form and headed back to his bed. Yep, thong. "Oh, sorry." Her voice seemed tiny, but again something in it rang untrue. He knew he was biased; Roxanne never told the truth when a lie helped her cause. She grabbed the blanket from the bed and wrapped it around herself with a grace that some women had, some didn't. Definitely Roxanne did.

She looked out the side window, then the back and flung herself to the floor. "Please, can't we go somewhere less ... public? More private?"

"Do you have designs on me, young woman?"

She looked up at him from the truck's floor. Her tongue protruded from the side of her mouth, exploring her lips. After a moment, she said, "No. No. I need your help. I trust you. You're the only one I can." She paused. "But I *could* go for you. You're not all that much older than Feather, so don't 'young woman' me."

Oh, please. Quit the drama, sweetheart. Still, not often did women throw themselves on the floor in front of him, weeping. He decided to go with the flow, something he prided himself on doing well. He started the stalled engine, hoping Rosinante would cooperate.

Rosinante apparently favored romance and drama. The engine roared and revved and Roadkill pulled back onto the highway and headed for the campground he called home.

Once they were outside town, Roxanne climbed into the

passenger seat at Roadkill's request. "Seatbelt," he said.

Roxanne giggled, an unattractive mix of her earlier tears and an attempt at humor. "The rebel believes in rules like wearing seatbelts?"

"You may not recall, but this rebel barely escaped with his life not long ago. Saved by a belt. He found the sacrament of the seatbelt. Strap yourself in."

Roxanne complied, pouting.

Roadkill wished his lunch had included fewer offerings from liquid food groups. Fuzz dominated his brain and shaking his head hadn't cleared it so far. Still, he gave it another vigorous shake. "What's up, pumpkin?"

Roxanne told her story, accompanied by tears and hysteria, poorly controlled. Roadkill had met Teddy and found the blackmail plan believable and about as poorly executed as he'd expect from the spoiled young man. He sensed that Roxanne's grief was real but exaggerated, played to her audience and to make herself look less culpable. That effort failed. When she said that the person she saw dashing down the alley could possibly have been Feather, he burst into laughter.

"What a crock. Feather shoot Teddy? If she got really p.o.'d, she might deck the bugger, but no way would she kill anyone. She escorts spiders out the door of her trailer."

Roxanne snorted up snot and blew her nose on a rag he handed to her. "You're right, I know you are. It was just so...terrifying. And she didn't show up and—"

"And you left, leaving her to pick up the pieces and call the cops." Some sisterly love.

Roxanne burst into a round of mea culpas, ending with an impassioned plea that Roadkill hide her, help her figure out who the killer might be and somehow let Feather know Roxanne herself had not killed her lover. "You know Feather would tell me to turn myself in and I can't do that. A night in jail would be death."

Roadkill sighed. "You can stay with me for a few days." *If I can stand you that long.* "But even I gotta admit you should talk to the cops. You're a likely suspect." His conventional advice surprised him. *Getting soft.*

As soon as he said them, he regretted his words, because the girl burst into another aria of tears, guilt, and fear of "the horror" of being jailed.

"Jail food's usually better than my fare, but it's up to you, sweet cheeks."

Sixteen

Sister's Keeper

Feather walked away from Michael Bergmann, her pace steady. She hoped he couldn't see the shakes that shattered her attempt to walk steadily. Once she turned the corner at the end of Hancock's main drag, she ran full out. The urgency and the anger in Roxanne's voice had gone straight to her gut. She hoped her old Nissan had enough gas to get her to Spokane. She had no time for a pit stop.

At her trailer, she ran inside long enough to throw some food in the squirrel cages, in case she was late returning, and to grab a sweatshirt.

She called goodbye to the squirrels and locked the trailer door behind her. In the truck, she rejoiced that she had enough gas for a trip to Spokane and her return home. She checked her phone to assure herself Roxanne had texted Teddy's address. She was pretty sure she knew the neighborhood from earlier conversations with her sister, but she checked the glove box for a map of Spokane. Kind of old, but still, a map. She knew everyone else would use their smart phone to guide them, but hers hadn't gone past fourth grade.

She headed south. Her fear for her sister stretched the time to hours, but in reality it took just over half an hour to reach her destination.

Teddy's house was easy to find. Feather didn't see Roxanne's car in front, but she guessed it might be in back. She glanced down the street, although why her sister would park away from her boyfriend's home, she didn't know.

A barren street, an empty sidewalk. Feather followed a concrete walk that bisected what could only with generosity be called a lawn on its path to the small home.

A key was in the door's lock, a colorful braided string hanging from it. Feather knocked on the cheap door. A couple of good huffs might topple it.

She waited. No answer. She knocked again, louder, and looked for the bell. It was a tarnished brass affair, the push button jammed at the halfway point. That it was broken seemed confirmed by the silence in Teddy's home.

After another set of raps and a short wait, she pushed the door open.

She hoped she didn't catch her sister and Teddy in the sack. Too embarrassing. Given Roxanne's earlier anger, the most likely offense she'd catch them in would be a raging argument. She knew some people used rage to fuel the passion in their relationships, and hoped it wasn't true of her sister and Teddy. And what had Roxanne meant by "Now they're blaming you?"

"One way to find out," she announced to the front room and herself. She entered the room. What kind of place does the son of a rich guy like Lane Fitzpatrick rent? Outside sure wasn't much. One step into the room and she tripped on a hole in the hideous shag carpet. Tacky. Cheap. Obviously not underwritten by dear old Daddy Fitzpatrick.

A rusty, musty smell emanated from the room. Teddy didn't spend any more time cleaning than he did gardening.

After several steps into the room she knew something was seriously wrong chez Teddy. A heavy silence hung in the air along with that same metallic smell. If she were the fanciful type, Feather would think she smelled sorrow. "Roxanne? Teddy? Anybody home?"

Her eyes focused on the wall opposite the front door. Teddy Fitzpatrick slumped against it. Feather's stomach pulled taut against her diaphragm, knocking the breath out of her lungs. She knew without doubt he was dead and wondered how she knew. Her head seemed to buzz and she shook it to clear the fuzziness. *Don't be a moron. Check his pulse. You might be able to save him.*

"No way," she said aloud. But she crossed the room and crouched beside him. Why was he still called Teddy, like a little boy? Would the minister at his funeral call him Teddy or Ted or Theodore? She extended her hand to his neck, feeling for the pulse she knew had stopped some time ago. None. Somehow the vindication echoed empty.

Teddy's shirt stuck to his blood-covered chest, as if someone had tried to stem the flow of blood or employ CPR. But why was there no ambulance here? And where was her sister?

Feather's heart pounded as if to make up for the lack of a functioning one in Teddy. Her eyes filled with tears and she blinked them back. Wouldn't her tears contaminate the crime scene? It *was* the scene of a crime. There was no gun beside the young man. Thoughts and emotions collided in her brain. She ached for Teddy, for Roxanne, for his family. Who would have such disregard for life that they could shoot him? Could it possibly be—no, not possible. Not Roxanne. She had loved or at the very least liked and lusted after this man.

Which of course brought back the main question. "Roxanne?" She raised her voice. "Sis? Pox? You here?" Roxanne had commanded Feather to meet her at Teddy's, sent his address, told her ... what? That Teddy had gotten Roxanne and Feather in trouble. She swallowed. And that she would stop him. That Teddy had gone too far.

Teddy wouldn't be going any farther now. Feather realized she was breathing shallowly, panting, almost. It couldn't be. Not Roxanne. She forced herself to think logically. Teddy had been shot, point blank, in the chest. No way could Feather imagine her sister shooting a gun. In a mad rage, she might have slapped Teddy, shoved him, even thrown something—a dish, a lamp—at him. Maybe even connected. But shoot him? Even if it were Teddy's gun? Wait. Maybe in self-defense, she could have shot him. But why would Teddy have tried to kill Roxanne?

Nothing made sense. Not with her thoughts bouncing around faster than one of Myrna's squirrels. *Back to logical thinking.*

Roxanne had said she would stop Teddy. Said he had gotten Feather in trouble. Now Feather realized why a private investigator had been at The Blind Chukar today. Roxanne had said that Feather, Roxanne, Teddy were all in trouble. Said she was going to stop Teddy. Feather's thoughts rode a carousel, spinning round and round, getting nowhere. The only thing she knew for sure was that someone had indeed stopped Teddy. Shot him.

A black fog settled over Feather. Her eyes closed, once, again. Her head jerked up and back. Pushing off from the wall, she stood. Breathed, even though the scent of Teddy's blood mixed with his after-shave and a lingering hint of what she guessed was her sister's favorite Donna Karan perfume filled her nose.

Feather refused to believe her sister had shot Teddy, despite what seemed like the truth trying to kick her in the teeth. If Roxanne was not the killer, and she was not, then what had happened to her? Had the killer found her there? Had she found the killer? She gasped at that thought. Was her sister's body somewhere in this house? Outside?

She had to look. She forced herself to search the small home, moving from the living room down the hall to the bathroom and the bedrooms. At each door, her hands trembled so hard she could barely grip the knob.

The house turned out as empty as it felt.

Feather extended the search to the backyard and the ramshackle garage on the alley behind. A nondescript KIA sedan from the early 2000s was parked in front of the structure, adding support to Feather's thought that the door looked as if it hadn't been opened in years. Still she peered through the filthy, cobwebbed panes of glass on the door, but saw nothing but gloom and a few boxes stacked toward the front. She rattled the knob of the side door. The door swung inward. To the right of the door was a greasy light switch, which Feather flipped. A bare bulb hung from the center of the ceiling illuminated a dirt floor barren save for a few oil spots and dust bunnies.

She searched the alley for signs that a body had been dragged across it, recognizing her idiocy as she did, but found nothing. No sign of Roxanne or anyone else. However, someone had shot Teddy. She shook her head to deny the unbidden thought that Roxanne was Teddy's killer.

"Okay, time to call the cops," she said aloud.

Outside, away from the body, she found more courage to press

911. The dispatcher's steady demeanor also calmed her. She knew she'd have to wait and tell the police what she had done, touched, why she was there. Maybe she could do it without falling into shock. She clenched her jaw. She *would* do it without getting hysterical or going into shock.

The dispatcher told her to remain on the line and stay in the yard. Instantly she had the impulse to search the house again. If she could learn what Teddy was up to, why he'd been killed, she might have a clue as to who killed him. Because it was not her sister. In Feather's long years as an activist, she'd known good cops and bad cops. She trusted Byron Warnock, the sheriff in Hancock. But experience told her that police sought the most logical perpetrator. The cops would lay the blame on Roxanne or on Feather herself. She had to know more.

Obviously Teddy had done or said something that incriminated Feather. Hence, the PI on her tail. Rats. The first decent man to express an interest in her in a long time had been paid to do so.

After a few minutes of conversation with the calm dispatcher, her phone gave the beep that indicated her battery was low. If she went to her truck and plugged it in, she'd miss the opportunity to search Teddy's house. "My phone's battery is dying ..."

"Go to your car. You can recharge—"

"I told you the address. I told you there's a dead man inside." Feather turned her phone off. She might miss Roxanne's call, if her dratted sister bothered to let her know what was going on. But she had to do this, before the cops arrived and the crime scene tape went up.

She braced herself and returned to the kitchen, searching for ... what? Drugs, probably. She saw a cookie jar on the sink, incongruous in the messy kitchen. She looked inside and found a package of sugar cookies. The cheap store brand, yuk. She grabbed a dish towel hanging from the stove handle and wiped her fingerprints from the jar lid.

Using the towel, she checked the freezer, a place she thought people often hid guns and drugs. Box after box of diet meals, some thick with ice. *Yuk again.* Nothing wrapped suspiciously in plastic wrap and shaped like a pistol. No vacuum sealed baggies of weed.

Where else did people hide incriminating evidence? Ah, yes, the toilet! She trotted to the bathroom. She could now hear sirens, faint, distant. Were they coming here or responding to another urgent call? Just the thought of an urgent call spoke to her bladder. She checked behind the toilet tank, inside it, and in the built-in metal vanity. Nothing hidden in the toilet and only pain killers and OTC allergy tablets in the cupboard.

What could she tell the cops? How to explain her presence? She needed to use Teddy's bathroom? Really, only the truth would work, and even that, with Feather's background, would still arouse their suspicions.

Concentrate on the goal. A reminder from her activist days, when people threw things at them, heckled them. *Roxanne is the goal. Be safe, little sis. Be good.*

She hoped the police wouldn't hold her too long. She considered a quick exit, but for sure then they would hold her responsible, a former environmental activist who leaves the murder scene. Former? Or merely currently inactive? The *former* bothered her, and brought up thoughts she hadn't had since being pregnant with Jared. What does a *former* activist do? Is there a joke somewhere in there? Old activists don't die, they merely hang up their banners? So not funny.

But really … what could she do to continue the fight? She wasn't up to climbing trees anymore, but the bed and breakfast? What would it mean? Do? Help? Sure, she would be nurturing people, feeding them healthy food, maybe organic stuff she could grow in the garden, but would it be enough? Where was the truth, the statement, the battle cry?

She shook her head. She told herself she didn't miss it, couldn't afford to be in jail when she was a parent, even if she'd given her son up for adoption.

"Super. I try to stay on a narrow path and my darn sister throws me off it and into huge trouble. Thank you, Roxanne."

Nothing for it. She had to use the toilet. If she was found here, so what? It was the best excuse ever for going back inside when the dispatcher told her to stay outdoors.

The cops announced their presence when they entered the house. Feather flushed, walked out of the bathroom, and found two cops aiming their weapons at her.

Seventeen

I am the Watchbird

Michael had to find a new career. He hated that he'd followed Feather to Spokane, hated that he stood two houses away in the alley, watching her. Hated the deception, hated that he couldn't offer help.

He also hated that he'd been instantly drawn to the woman, sensing her innate goodness. But his brain, his sense of duty, prevailed. Never rely on emotions, rely on facts. He'd run to his vehicle and followed her back to her trailer. Accompanied by guilt, because the look of terror on her face told him she craved speed. He could have offered her a lift.

Sure, bozo. "Since we both know I'm going to follow you, you might as well let me drive. Save time, gas, the environment." And into his front seat she would have leapt.

Not.

When Feather parked her small pickup outside the small house and walked to the door, Michael cruised around to the alley and parked in an open area a few doors down from the decrepit garage and ancient KIA, then positioned himself where his binoculars got a view of the back and south sides of the house and the front yard and Feather's truck.

When his target stepped out the back door of the house, Michael had to squelch his urge to run to her aide. Her already pale complexion had faded to oyster gray. She looked ready to faint. Or lose her lunch. Definitely ready to cut and run on shapely but shaky legs.

Instead she went to the alley, peered into the side window of the garage and then disappeared from his view for way too long.

Michael was looking for a better vantage point when Feather returned to the back yard and pulled out her cell phone. She spoke for a few moments, walking in a seemingly aimless pattern around the yard. Then she moved the phone away from her ear and stood staring at the back door. In moments she had pocketed her phone and re-entered the house.

Who had Feather called? Was she meeting someone here?

He used his smartphone and reverse white pages to discover that the house was occupied by Teddy Fitzpatrick. Employee at the wind farm, son of a wealthy entrepreneur, according to his research.

He shook his head. All Michael's instincts told him Feather was an innocent involved in something ugly. Maybe not totally innocent, but definitely not a blackmailer, the slimiest of criminals in his opinion. Murder committed in a rage or even for vengeance, he understood. But premeditated threats to expose people's secrets? So low rent, so sleazy.

Glad for the contacts he and his superiors at the agency had developed in Spokane, Michael phoned Jerome at the downtown station and asked if he knew anything about the address on Grace. When Jerome came back on he was chuckling. "Jesus, Mary and Joseph. How do you get yourself into these situations? We had a possible dead body reported at that address. I'm gonna hope you're not the cause of the DB."

"First I kill someone, then I call to ask if anybody found it yet? Not likely."

"Stranger things have happened. However, a female called it in, then her phone 'died.' You need to talk to the guys who pick up this assignment."

"Of course I do. But I haven't been inside. Simple surveillance."

He ended the call. If Feather had talked to a dispatcher, she'd been instructed to stay on the line and stay outside. She'd done neither.

Now what? Go inside? See if he could offer Feather some help? *Great idea. If you've developed a yen for pain.*

Given Feather's doubts about his motives, he'd better hang around outside and see what happened. Given the imminent police presence it wouldn't be a great idea to head back through Teddy's yard or to climb a fence in a neighbor's yard.

He returned to his Ford Ranger and eased it out of the alley. He drove a couple of blocks east and took a few rights to return to Grace Street. He pulled in a few houses down the block. And watched and waited.

The police rolled in soon, sirens silenced, just in case the dead man was not alone and the living were not friendly.

He watched two police officers knock on the front door, wait and enter, some moments later, guns drawn. He wondered where the hell Feather was and regretted leaving his lookout point from the back alley. If she tried to escape ... nah, that wasn't her style, so far as he could tell in their short acquaintance. But if the cops were trigger happy .... With fewer than a dozen homicides each year in Spokane, they might get excited about this one.

He waited. Almost simultaneously, an ambulance and an unmarked vehicle that was obviously owned by the Spokane PD, pulled up. A female detective opened the driver's door and spoke to the ambulance driver. Together they walked to the door, trailed by another EMT. One of the beat cops emerged and stood on the porch, arms crossed, scowling.

The EMTs came out, went to the ambulance, and drove off.

He had to do something. He couldn't just leave Feather in there to deal with the cops alone. He exited the truck and walked toward the officer on the porch in a slow, easy stride. When he got near, he stopped, raised his arms and called out to the young cop. "Officer, I may have information you need. May I approach?"

The young man's hand went to his gun and Michael wondered if he'd made a grave mistake. Then the cop moved a few paces toward him, his hand near his side holster but not drawing his gun. "This is a crime scene, sir. Don't come any closer."

Michael lowered his head, attempting to appear docile and unaggressive. "I saw a detective arrive. I need to talk to her."

The cop shook his head. "Maybe later. Right now I'm going to have to ask you to move along."

Michael returned to his truck and again phoned Jerome. "How many female detectives are there in Spokane?"

"Just Hopper. She's solid."

"How's about you let her know someone outside has information she might need?"

"She inside? ME arrive yet?"

Michael heard a siren. "On its way."

"Keep those panties untwisted. I call her, she'll be pissed you interrupted."

Michael took a breath. "They've got someone inside. Someone who could not have caused the DB."

"They'll bring that *someone* out soon. Won't want too many people in their crime scene."

"But ...."

Jerome chuckled. "Like I said, don't get your knickers in a knot. Spokane isn't a hot spot for police brutality. Your girlfriend will be okay."

"So much for trying to be a good citizen." Michael ended the call.

Within ten minutes Detective Hopper exited the home, ushering Feather beside her. She spoke to the beat cop, who then escorted Feather to his car and locked her in the back seat. He noticed her hands were bagged. He also noticed that Feather did not look pleased to see him.

He smiled at the police detective. It was apparent she expected him. So Jerome had followed through, despite giving attitude to Michael.

The detective introduced herself. After displaying his identification, Michael quickly explained that he'd been hired to follow Feather. "I've been with her or trailing her since 1:30." The detective, a solid woman in her forties who looked like she could take Michael down if she got a notion, asked, "Why are you investigating her?"

Uh-oh. Brad had hired him to avoid calling the cops. "Background?" he said, the lie obvious in his expression and his voice. "She's no killer."

"Hired to investigate her today, but you know she's not a killer?" The woman smiled. "How do you know we have a victim?" She shook her head. "That darn Jerome and his mouth. Do you know the victim? Were *you* inside, too?"

"No, no." Michael had to backtrack fast. His boss wouldn't like it if he were arrested. "I'm assuming the dead person is the owner of the home?" He made his statement a question, but got no confirmation from Hopper. "Is it a male?"

Hopper gave him an amused look. "Jerome told me to watch my step with you."

"Are you arresting Ms. Sullivan? I can swear to you she only arrived here at," he glanced at his notebook, "15:15."

"I'll have to wait for the medical examiner to make the call, but I'd say our victim died quite recently. Maybe before Ms. Sullivan arrived, maybe after."

"I didn't hear a gunshot. Of course maybe he was killed by knife or beaten to death? I saw her leave the back door looking very ill. Not unlike someone who just saw a dead person."

"Not unlike someone reacting from killing another human being." She continued to stare at Michael, and then apparently relented. "She was instructed by the 911 dispatcher to stay outside. My officers found her inside, exiting the bathroom, having thoroughly scrubbed her hands. Not a smart move." She shrugged. "Not that most criminals are smart."

"She's not a criminal. Like I said, she looked ill. Maybe she was puking," Michael said.

"Whatever. She should have stayed outside. Just as an FYI, she does have a record. We're taking her downtown."

"No record of violence. Could you be over-reacting?" *Way to go, Michael. Piss off the cops. Sure way to help Feather.*

The detective's expression became as stiff as her hairdo. "I'll be the judge of my actions. A lot of these eco-freaks engage in activity most of us think of as violent. Tree spiking, arson, you know, your average acts of sabotage." She turned toward the house, and then pivoted to face Michael again. "I'd appreciate your providing a statement downtown, as well. Right away." She entered the little house.

By the time Feather was released by the Spokane police, it was 11 p.m. and counting. Her stomach had given up in despair that she'd ever eat again, letting out an occasional mewl accompanied by a stabbing pain in her side. The pain could have been anxiety related, since the Lord knew, she was anxious. She feared the internal battle raging in her brain would take over her tongue. Did Roxanne shoot Teddy? Impossible. Then where was her sister? Did the real shooter have her?

Feather's activist training and her initial reaction to Detective Hopper's hostility was silence. Hopper told her she was in trouble and could be arrested for going back into the house after the 911 dispatcher instructed her to stay outside the home. She had told Hopper she needed to pee and that she'd decided the safer locale was inside. Then she simply told the detective she didn't recall what had happened or why she was there. "Possibly the shock of seeing poor Teddy dead?"

They took her downtown for questioning, where she waited for the detective for several hours. When Hopper arrived, Feather had stayed silent, except when Hopper told her that a Michael Bergmann had vouched for her. "He told me you arrived just before you called in the man down and couldn't possibly have been the shooter." The detective smirked. "But you could have used a silencer and the man had not been dead long. In my opinion, you're a suspect until we find a better one."

The fact that Hopper gave more credibility to Michael Bergmann's statement of her innocence than her own irked Feather. Okay, more than irked … enraged her. "I barely know the man. He doesn't know me. I could be the killer. I'm fast and I believe in vengeance. He spoke too soon."

"Where'd you hide the gun?"

"I went outside. Maybe I threw it in the dumpster." Feather crossed her arms. "I'm not going to tell you. I would like to call my attorney."

Hopper shot her some venom. "Vengeance for what? How do you know the victim?"

Feather realized her annoyance with Michael was causing her to speak when she should stay mum. She made a zipping motion across her lips. "Either you let me call my lawyer or you release me."

Hopper smiled. "Ms. Sullivan, you have been free to go at any time. I deeply appreciate your cooperation and the fact that you told us about Teddy Fitzpatrick's death. Good Lord only knows how long that body might have rotted there otherwise."

Feather wanted to wretch but wouldn't allow the detective the pleasure. She stood and attempted to walk regally to the door. Wobbly knees and an errant table leg prevented regal. She caught herself on the door jamb. "You have my number."

"Oh, indeed I do. After all, this would not be the first time the perpetrator called in about a dead body. I know you'll be heading back home to Idaho, but stick around Hancock, okay?"

"It's where I work." True, even if Feather had no intention of sticking around Hancock. She had to find her sister, and she'd go anywhere necessary to do it.

She stopped in the bathroom long enough to splash her face and relieve her bladder and headed to the lobby. She hoped the desk sergeant would call her a cab so she could retrieve her truck and get home. She felt as if the day's horrors were stuck to her skin, embedded in her clothing, and nothing appealed more than a shower, except perhaps a meal. She'd last grabbed a cup of soup at The Blind Chukar, hours that seemed like days ago. The police had offered her a soda and a snack bar, but she had no desire to owe them anything, even the value of a crappy little snack bar and a wannabe Coke.

She entered the waiting room and Michael Bergmann stood and smiled at her. Nervy booger. First he vouches for her innocence and then he comes to rescue her, expecting her to grovel at his feet in gratitude.

"Need a ride?" he asked.

"I can call a cab." She walked to the person at the front counter. "I need a taxi. Could you call for me?"

The clerk shook his head. "I can give you a number but I can't call for you. Don't you have a cell phone?"

Feather flushed. "Battery died." Payment for lying about it to the dispatcher earlier. Karma always bit her in the ass. "I'll find a pay phone."

The man laughed. "Good luck with that. There's one inside"—he pointed toward the jail—"if you're really desperate. 'Course then you wouldn't need a cab."

A joker. She needed a joker at this minute like she needed a ferret chewing on her leg. "The squirrels." *Great going. Worry about the stupid squirrels. Keeps the mind off the important stuff.*

The man at the desk gave her a strange look. She ignored him and looked at the clock on the wall, a clock eerily imitating the one in her high school. She shook her head to avoid the launch of memories. She swallowed. *Think about it. Roxanne needs you. The squirrels need you. You need your car. Do not let pride stop pragmatism.* She smiled despite herself. Pride before pragmatism sounded cool, but wasn't. She turned to Michael, quietly waiting during her conversations with the desk clerk and her internal one.

"Yes. I need a ride."

The silence in Michael's truck reminded Feather of the hours she spent in The Blind Chukar, long past the time anyone, even the dishwasher had gone. Walt provided free wireless service and she often remained there, completing the online courses in management she was taking to prepare her as the owner of a bed and breakfast. That dream seemed ephemeral at this moment. And unimportant. She had to find Roxanne. She wondered if she'd been a fool to omit telling the cops that Roxanne was Teddy's girlfriend and Feather's sister, that Roxanne had instructed Feather to meet her at Teddy's. But her old activist ethic had kicked in: tell the authorities as little as possible.

Michael cleared his throat.

Ha! I knew I could outlast him. But should I trust him?

"I guess you're angry with me for following you."

She glanced at him. "For one."

"What else? I told Detective Hopper you didn't have time to kill Teddy."

"You have no idea what I might be capable of."

He chuckled. "I'd like to find out."

"Oh, please. Take me to my truck and leave me alone. Or will you follow me home, too?"

"I'm still on Brad's payroll. I'd like to go with you, check your trailer. You could be in danger. Someone killed Teddy and someone sent a blackmail note to the Ganborenas. And to others, I've since learned."

"Blackmail?" Brad thought she'd tried to blackmail them? "Others?" So that's what Teddy was up to. That's why Roxanne vowed to stop him. "I have no idea what you're talking about. But I do believe Teddy Fitzpatrick capable of blackmail."

Roxanne could be hiding in Feather's trailer. She did not want Michael to go with her. "I have been taking care of myself, all by myself, for a number of years. I don't need you."

He smiled. "My loss."

She'd think about that statement later. "If you don't think I'm a murderer and you don't think I'm a blackmailer, staying on Brad's payroll seems a tad shady."

"My company charges for a full day. It's been a long one, but remember, we met this morning."

"How could I forget? What I think might be a nice chat with an attractive stranger turns into what I'd agree was a long day. Not one I care to repeat."

"Attractive, eh?"

"Oh, for heaven's sake. Did you forget that a young man is dead?"

Michael immediately dropped the attitude. "No, I did not. And I know how bad it is to see, believe me, from all-too-personal experience. I was trying to distract you from thinking about it, but maybe it wasn't appropriate. I apologize."

Great. Really, truly great. Now he apologizes, the man Feather had hoped to focus her rage on, the way she hoped to escape her fear and worry about her sister. Okay. She would simply stop talking to him, ignore him until they got to her truck. Couldn't be that far. She aimed her gaze out the window. Couldn't do it. Jeanette had instilled manners into Feather that she couldn't let loose of. "Apology accepted." Said in a begrudging tone, but said, nonetheless.

"Thank you. I'm really not as bad as you might think. Even Roadkill would tell you that."

Her head jerked around. "He told me you were a PI."

"Bet he didn't tell you that I was also one hell of a ping-pong player. That I liked dogs and cats and uh, small children, and often help elderly women cross the street."

She stifled her laugh. "No, he didn't mention any of those virtues. Remiss of him." Could she believe him? Should she?

Michael's cell phone let out a ring like an old-time phone. He snared it from its dashboard carrier and pulled to the side of the road. "Sorry. This is one I have to take. I assign that ring to my clients."

Feather wondered if he would leave the vehicle to take the call, and thought it would reveal his level of trust in her. He didn't. "Bergmann."

"I see." He paused and said, "Yes, I agree it's short notice. But I think we should do it. I'll be there and stay on them. Forward the text to me, please." Another pause. "Anything else going on? Anything out of the ordinary?"

Michael glanced over at Feather while the caller spoke. "Yes, that's the kind of thing I meant. It might be important. Is important. Have you tried to reach her?" Another fairly long pause. "Name and contact information?" He wrote while the caller spoke.

He ended the call with the assurance that he would be in touch in the morning.

Feather hugged herself, almost huddled back into the car seat. "Brad? Kristin?" she asked.

He nodded. "They received another blackmail note, not 15 minutes ago. They're supposed to leave $10,000 in Spokane tomorrow afternoon at 2:00. Not much time."

Feather's eyes filled with tears, from relief or terror, she had no idea. "Now you have proof I'm not your culprit. My phone is dead."

He half-smiled. "They use burner phones, cheap ones they toss after using."

She started to sit up with outrage. "But you've been with me—"

"You're no blackmailer. Thing is, I thought the blackmailer was the dead kid, Teddy. Too coincidental that he died the day after the blackmail texts were sent. But now ..."

Now it looked even worse for her sister. "They told you something else."

"Yeah. Their nanny left today. Took her stuff. Left a note that the kid was asleep in his room, no other explanation."

A chill crept up Feather's neck and she shuddered. "I really need to get to my car. Can you drive and talk?"

"And chew gum." He started the engine and pulled onto the street. "Too many coincidences. You know their nanny?"

Everything was unraveling. The truth about Roxanne would come out soon. She couldn't have killed Teddy. But the pain of the possibility cut into Feather like a chain saw. Silent tears streamed from her eyes and she wiped them away, hoping Michael wouldn't notice.

"What is it? Feather, I want to help you. Sounds strange since we just met, but isn't."

Feather forced herself to breathe, in, out, deep, steady breaths. She had to rely on someone. Sure, Ed Mustard or his brother Roadkill would help her. So would Gina. But this guy had the cops in his pocket and a research network handy. This guy knew about burner phones and blackmail and murder and other nasty stuff. This guy had seen dead bodies. She took a final cleansing breath and rubbed her neck. "My sister is—was—their nanny. Only way I got to see my baby boy. Teddy was her boyfriend of a few months. And," she took in another breath, "she phoned me today."

The truck slowed, and Feather sensed it wasn't intentional. "I see."

"No, you don't. You can't. You don't know her. She wouldn't—couldn't—kill Teddy. Kill anyone."

"She called you from his house?" His voice was steady, the truck accelerating again.

"No. But she told me to meet her there. I never saw her. I'm afraid that the real killer, took her, or even ..." She couldn't go on. But she didn't cry. She had to focus on finding Roxanne and finding Teddy's killer.

"Did you tell the police she phoned you? Did you find anything in Teddy's house to make you think Roxanne had been there?"

"No, I didn't tell them she called. No, I didn't find anything of hers, but the police must have dusted for fingerprints. She's been there before, of course. You know, I thought the interrogation ended at the police station." Feather's voice quavered.

Michael sighed, blowing out through his lips. His voice remained calm. "Have you tried to reach her?"

"Of course I have! Why do you think my poor phone's battery died? I've texted her, called her. Nothing. It's as if she's … disappeared."

"It's as if she turned off her phone."

"Or someone did it for her." She sighed. "I … need to trust someone. And … I need help to prove my sister is innocent. To prove we're both innocent. Please," she nearly gagged on the word, "follow me home. Check the trailer. If Roxanne is there, we can get her to explain everything."

"Why did she want you to meet her at Teddy's? What did she say?"

You knew he'd ask. Knew it. Question is, are you ready to tell the truth? "She … she apologized for the trouble I was in. She knew about the blackmail and Kristin's accusations that I was behind it. She didn't tell me about it, just that I'd been unjustly accused. I had no idea what she meant."

"And?"

How did he know Roxanne had said more, said much worse? "She said Teddy had gone too far … and that she would stop him, somehow. But she didn't mean she'd kill him. She doesn't even have a gun, let alone know how to fire one."

Michael slowed, and stopped behind Feather's junker. "I'll follow you home and then find somewhere to spend the night in Hancock. We can finish this discussion there." He opened the driver's door and trotted around to open hers. "Don't go inside until I'm with you. Promise?"

Eighteen

Trust Me

Feather wondered just how huge a mistake she was making, putting her faith, and possibly her sister's life, in his hands. No, in *their* hands. Four hands, two brains, had to be better than hers alone. "Do you have a gun?"

He chuckled. "And a license to kill. As dangerous as they come."

"Stick close or I may decide to lose you. Your sense of humor could kill me faster than your bullets."

It took under an hour to reach Feather's trailer, time in which her mind raced from one awful possibility to worse ones. Roxanne would be in her trailer, bleeding, near death, from facing down Teddy's killer. Roxanne would not be in her trailer. The real killer would be waiting for Feather, after dispatching first Teddy, then Roxanne, why she had no clue. Finally she turned on her radio to a conservative talk show to focus her anger on an impersonal target.

Michael had stayed right behind, not much of a challenge since her little truck's maximum speed was 60 and the roads were barren approaching midnight. Without street or building lights, the stars shone brilliant and profuse in a near-cloudless sky. The waning crescent moon lifted her spirits.

She unlocked the trailer to the chitter of her hungry and annoyed squirrels. Michael alerted at the noise, like a canine on the hunt. She swore his nose twitched. He placed a hand on her arm before she could push the door open. "What's that sound?"

She chuckled. "Relax. That is the welcome song of the squirrel. They missed me."

"Can I say you have weird taste in pets? If a stranger were in there, they'd probably stay quiet, right?" He raised the handgun he carried.

"Yes, and believe me, my sister is a stranger to this trailer. She thinks it smells. And she's right, no matter how much I clean it. I hope it's not mold." She realized she was chittering as much as her squirrels. She rolled her lips together.

Michael thrust the door of the trailer open with his foot and then used his right shoulder to push it as far open as possible. He entered, gun first, the now-silent trailer. Feather worried about its tidiness and about the odor that assured her sister would choose another hideout. *Oh, please. He's not here on behalf of Good Housekeeping.*

Michael did a 360 degree turn from where he stood in the doorway and then took a few steps to throw open the door to Feather's miniscule bathroom. "Clear," he called back to her. Then he moved to the bed at the rear of the trailer and peeked around the cabinet ends. He backed away and stood in front of the squirrel cages that covered half of the table. "Hey, little guys, I'm here with the food woman. You're in luck."

Feather hurried to his side. "They look cute but they bite, especially strangers." She quickly filled the empty tubes that filled cups inside the cages.

"Odd choice of companion."

"No choice, not with Mayor Myrna's rescue program. These three will never go back to the wild, so she stuck them on me."

Michael frowned. "You don't seem like a pushover."

Feather laughed, feeling the release that came with it. "You don't know Myrna."

He cocked an eyebrow. "Maybe I don't want to."

Feather brewed tea and toasted bread that she slathered with Gina's pumpkin butter. After they'd eaten, Michael sighed again. "Look, I know you love your sister, but the fact is, you two aren't living together. You have no way of knowing if she has a gun or can fire it. You grew up in Idaho, didn't you? Doesn't everyone in the state have a gun and target shoot once a week?"

"Stop it. You know that isn't true. That's Texas!" Feather couldn't believe she was teasing him about something so serious. Maybe it was her relief at being home, at being safe in her little tin can, even if she hated it with vigor. "You have a point. There's a lot about

Roxanne I don't know. However, I simply cannot picture her as a killer. But I still need to find her and figure out what's happening."

"We're on the same path. I gather Roxanne thought Teddy was behind the blackmail."

Feather shuddered again, remembering Teddy's body. "I guess. So if any of the people he blackmailed suspected it was him, they could have killed him." She hated the hope in her voice.

"Or he had a partner and the partner is carrying on the blackmail."

"You think it's Roxanne." Her voice broke but she refused to weep.

"Someone told Brad where to leave the blackmail money tomorrow. I intend to follow that someone."

"I'm going with you. Two pairs of eyes." *It won't be Roxanne. It can't be her.*

"This isn't a partnership, Feather. I'm a professional." He yawned. "A professional who needs to find a motel." He pulled his smart phone from his pocket. His gun lay on the table near the cages.

She couldn't let him leave. If she had more time, she knew she could convince Michael to let her join him in following the blackmailer. She glanced at his handgun. He might not be convinced if she held him at gunpoint. "The only place around here is the Tidy Scot, and for sure it is not tidy. It serves as a model for what I don't want my Bed and Breakfast to be. My little tin can is a palace compared to their rooms." She paused. "Of course, you wouldn't have to sleep alone. There's mice, roaches, bed bugs and the occasional drunk who stumbles into the office and swipes whatever key he can find."

"Sounds great. Guess I'll go home."

"There's an alternative." Feather turned back to the stove and fiddled with the tea kettle to hide her blush. "We can bundle."

"Bundle?"

"Sure. Roadkill and I did it often when we were on actions together. We sleep, underwear on, a blanket rolled between us on the bed. We are, after all, adults."

"Sounds good to me." No leer, no smirk, not even a glimpse at Feather's chest. "I'm beat."

Maybe he wanted to stick close because he didn't believe her. Wanted to follow her when she sought out her sister. *Can't have it both ways, girl. Trust him or not?* "I trust him." When Michael glanced up, she realized she'd spoken aloud. *Great.* "You can use the bathroom while I make up the bed."

Nineteen

Momma Meddles

Jeanette Sullivan paused before striding up the steps of the old farmhouse that served as the site office for Windfall Works. The turbine was set on a hill beyond the back barn, more than 200 yards distant, but she could hear its whirr and recalled one of the other partners telling her the loudest noise came from the blade on its downturn. She'd been out to the farm before and rather enjoyed the sound. She told herself it was the sound of money being churned. Money for her. Less for the power companies. And yet her daughter opposed it, at least, opposed it being here. Feather had no idea that part of the reason Jeanette had invested in the wind farm was to please her daughter. Of course, like so many of her overtures to her oldest daughter, it backfired.

Then she recalled the reason for her presence: someone wanted her to pay to keep quiet about the wind farm and its concerns. And about ... she shuddered, squared her shoulders and moved on up the wooden stairs to the home's broad porch. With luck, no one would find that out. No one else.

Now her job was to discover if the blackmailer's hints had been based in reality, and what might be done about the problems at the business. She looked down at her Eileen Fisher linen slacks and the black silk blouse and knew she looked ready to work. She allowed herself a small smile. Everyone thought of her as "that lonely but wealthy widow," "Roxanne's or Feather's mother," or maybe someone who "looked good for her age." Not many people knew she'd begun her life poor as a woodchuck, one of six children of a lumberjack, and that she'd met her daughters' father when she was a bookkeeper for a logging company. She knew figures and figures rarely lied unless someone manipulated them.

She stood up straight and tucked her tummy in, confident she still had "It." At 58, "It" was getting harder to summon each day.

The living/dining room combination that crossed the front of the house had been made into a reception area, with a desk that faced the front door. The space opposite the desk served as a waiting room and an occasional board room. In it squatted a few second-hand chairs and a coffee table with a glass top covering recycled egg and milk crates and some other "found" items Jeanette couldn't identify.

A tall man, dressed in chinos and a middle of the line sports coat, stood facing the desk. Beside him a sturdy woman of about five-five or five-six, wearing sensible shoes and pants the same color as Jeanette's, turned and took in the new entrant to the office, even before the little bell attached to it jingled. The only thing their slacks had in common was the color. The woman's polyester-blend pants bunched at her substantial thighs. Her appearance was criminal. Did she shop in the same thrift stores as Charlene-I-mean-Feather— as Jeanette often thought of her eldest daughter?

Jeanette knew the young woman who sat facing the man and woman. Haley something looked more disconcerted than Jeanette had ever seen her.

Behind Haley, Jeanette saw Jonathan Flynn, bent over a filing cabinet drawer. Something Jeanette would have considered Haley's job. *What was going on?*

"Oh, my," Jeanette said with a bright and false smile, "I hope I'm not interrupting. I'm here to help."

Jon jerked away from the filing cabinet, in the process dropping the files he was retrieving. He clutched the one he hadn't dropped to his chest. "Then you've heard."

Haley stood, abruptly and with none of the grace Jeanette associated with the athletic girl. "Ms. Sullivan. These are police detectives."

Jeanette's smile froze. "Police? Why ever for?" Someone must have reported the blackmail. Now everything would come out.

The police peered at her with curiosity. Haley smiled, possibly glad someone else was there to share the heat.

Jonathan bustled over to Jeanette and gripped her arm in an unwelcome and firm clutch. "Perhaps you should sit down." He edged her back toward the waiting room chairs.

Jeanette ripped her arm from his grasp. "I am not here to be coddled, Jonathan. I am here to help. However, I am confused about why you brought the police in. I thought this was a *private* matter." She recalled the warning in her blackmail text, forbidding the involvement of the police.

The woman with the bulging pants peered at her tiny notebook, flipping pages. She turned to Jeanette. "Jeanette Sullivan? Here to help? Wait a few and I'll have some questions for you."

Jeanette stepped back and when her knees hit the chair seat, she collapsed into its lumpiness. What would Officer Frumpy ask her? What would, could she tell them?

Jonathan sat down beside her, his normally pale face white with red mottles. Not a good look for the man, who seemed to attract women despite what Jeanette considered his smarminess. He seemed to always be on stage, smiling what she considered a phony smile, but what others saw as openness. The smile was absent at the moment. "You don't know. I thought not."

"Of course I know about—"

He put his hand on her lips. "Teddy is dead."

Jeanette's heart pounded in her ears. Roxanne was dating Teddy. "How? When?" Her throat and tongue were so dry she could barely get the words out.

Jon's hand flew to his chest and his face filled with emotion. Regret? Sorrow? Shame? Jeanette didn't know. Jon spoke, keeping his voice low. "Homicide. In his home. They won't tell us any more than the bare details. But he was alone. I forgot he was dating your daughter." He immediately gazed over at the police, who were taking in their conversation with interest. Haley, too, stared at her with an interest Jeanette read as over-avid.

She let out a long, slow breath. The poor boy was dead. More than likely it was related to the blackmail. Which meant that ... She shrank away from Jon. He could have killed Teddy. Any of the partners could be a stone killer. And Roxanne. Who would tell her baby that her boyfriend had been killed? And where was her daughter? Jeanette had texted her, tried to phone her, last night once she'd decided to investigate Windfall Works. But Roxanne had not replied, and Jeanette's calls went to voicemail. Was she all right?

The female detective neared. "Mr. Flynn, did you find the employment application?"

Jonathan began to rise, but Jeanette stopped him with a hand on his arm and spoke in a low voice, even though she realized the police could probably still hear her. "Wait. Do they know about the blackmail? We have to tell them."

Jonathan looked at her, his face clouded. "Yes, they know. Apparently Brad and Kristin hired a detective to shadow your daughter."

"Roxanne?"

"Your other daughter. Feather. She called in Teddy's ... body."

Jeanette glanced at the cops, who appeared calm, patient. Behind them Haley sat, grim, unsmiling, a lot like she looked the few other times Jeanette had seen her. A lesser woman might have jumped to her feet but Jeanette rose with studied grace. "Feather a blackmailer? Impossible. Let me talk to these people."

She stomped to the female detective, remembering as she completed the last few stomps to do it with grace. "Show me your identification. Then take my statement."

Haley watched Jeanette Sullivan take the stage and dominate the room, moments after she entered. What a diva.

Her lips twisted into a smile. So the older sister, Feather, had called in the body. Little Miss Priss Roxanne no doubt in hysterics, too upset to talk to the cops. Maybe Feather had covered for her. Teddy had complained that Feather was way too protective of Roxanne.

At least Jeanette's theatrics had drawn attention away from Haley. Yes, she was sad that Teddy was dead; he'd been a nice enough kid, if spoiled and full of himself. Too bad he put himself in a position to get killed. Haley needed to appear willing to help with the investigation, but somehow get the cops away from the farm as soon as possible.

She wished she could figure out a way to be alone. She had to let Chaz know what was going on. How much should she share with her boss? She opened a link to the site that allowed her to send emails under a fake name to her boss. She looked around to see what Jon was up to, but he had disappeared somewhere. She sent a quick note to Chaz letting him know of Teddy's death and that the cops were investigating. She added that it was probably connected to the blackmail. She'd sworn to Chaz that she would solve the blackmail problem. He might well think she had killed Teddy. She wasn't sure if he would approve or disapprove of that kind of initiative.

Jon bustled in from the kitchen, bearing a large tray with mugs of coffee. As he passed her he muttered, "You could have done this, you know."

"You could have asked, you know." Haley rarely took shit from her boss. She also rarely served coffee to him or his guests. This might have been a good time, allowing her to get closer to eavesdrop on the cops' conversation with Roxanne's dear mother. Jeanette and the two detectives had settled into the room across from her but she could make out only parts of their conversation.

She grabbed a box of tissues from her desk drawer, rose and crossed to Jon and the others. "Let me help," she said, placing the tissues in front of the weeping Jeanette.

After a delicate blow into a Kleenex, Jeanette said, "I told you, I can't reach either of my girls on their cell phones. And now you tell me Roxanne walked out on the Ganborenas. I would go to them, but I'm needed here. I sense it."

The old lady retained her looks, and she knew how to dress, and had the bucks to pay for obviously good stuff. Haley smiled to herself. "Sugar? Jon brought the fake creamer but I can probably find milk."

Jon shot her a curious glance at the rare exhibition of courtesy. Just because she rarely bothered didn't mean she didn't know that stuff. She smiled back, basking in her plan for Jeanette.

Both detectives declined, but Jeanette, always happy to be waited on, said, "That would be lovely, dear."

Dear. My butt, lady. Haley stomped to the kitchen and returned in record time and plopped the carton of half and half onto the coffee table. The milk was Teddy's. He'd have no need for it. Guess she'd better not mention that to Jeanette, who was blabbing about her blackmail note. Ten grand. These people must bathe in bucks.

Twenty

All Kinds of Help

Roadkill watched Roxanne Sullivan walk the length of Rosinante, spin on her bare heels and return. "Feather will fix it, if you'd just let me text her."

Roadkill sat in the passenger seat, reversed so he could face his guest, better called stowaway. "You're not a prisoner here, sweet cheeks."

"Don't call me sweet cheeks. You said they could trace me if I use my cell phone. Let me use yours."

"How about you go online on my laptop and send her a message through one of those anonymous services? I have links to a couple."

"A laptop? Roadkill, the great rebel, has an instrument of the great, consuming society?"

"Cute. I find it easier than heading to the library. Librarians are snoops. Even activists need to do research and communicate with each other."

She strode to his chair. "Okay. Let's do it." Her eyes filled. "I miss her. I miss Teddy. I even, almost, miss my mother, who always drives me crazy. I'm obviously falling apart."

He rose and pulled her into a comforting hug. "You're gonna be fine, sweet cheeks. Roadkill's on the job." He knew she hated the moniker sweet cheeks almost as much as she hated when he spoke of himself in the third person. But what's a man to do? He had to do something to jolt her out of her funk.

When Jon had passed on the news to Haley that Jeanette would be working at Windfall, Haley smiled. The smile, allegedly one of gratitude, Jeanette pegged as envious and spiteful. She'd seen it in the eyes of women at cocktail parties, on the boards of charities she served. Didn't the young fool recognize that she had what every woman Jeanette's age yearned for? Youth. Vitality. A neck without wrinkles.

"It's awfully kind of you to step in and help us out. Especially now that Teddy is ... well, no longer with us."

Haley did solemn better than grateful but Jeanette thought that too was an act. The brat was delighted she could boss around one of the partners, someone who probably paid more for her shoes than Haley earned in a month. But Jeanette would not back down. She returned the girl's solemn look with her own sad smile and a nod.

"Teddy worked outside a lot," Haley continued. "In fact, every morning his first task was to clean up after the ... swine. They go outside practically on their own once someone opens the gate."

Jeanette tried to hold her ground, but stepped back. *Only a pace or two, darn it.* But who wouldn't? She'd thought she would be answering the phones, maybe, or helping with the books. Office work, yes. Not mucking out some evil-tempered, vicious, stinking hogs.

The young woman's sly smile said that she expected Jeanette to run home as fast as her Donald Pliner loafers could take her. *Ha.* Jeanette Sullivan had seen more manure of various varieties in her lifetime than Haley and all the pigs outside could manufacture.

Jeanette smiled right back. "Where do you keep the barn clothes and gum boots?"

Haley widened her eyes. "I guess Teddy took his home. I really don't know."

Jeanette widened her eyes right back at Haley and said she had to run a brief errand. "I'll be back soon."

Darlene Belmont at the Belmont General Store might have been in cahoots with Haley, given her attitude when Jeanette arrived in search of coveralls and boots. Darlene emerged from the storeroom after several minutes, bearing overalls fit for Shrek or some other fictional giant and another pair so small they restricted Jeanette's movement and threatened to cut her in half vertically.

"You don't have anything closer to my size?" she asked after a painful session in the tiny, makeshift dressing room.

Darlene smirked. "Maybe some sweat pants."

Great. Get those puppies soaked in hog excretions and they'd drag their wearer down into the muck. Jeanette bought the ginormous overalls along with a box of safety pins. And a T-shirt that proclaimed loggers know all about big woods.

The only gum boots Darlene claimed to have in stock were made for the same giant. Jeanette added a couple of pairs of wool socks to her shopping spree.

Back at the barn, Jeanette changed her clothes, hanging her linen slacks and silk blouse on a hook inside the room that once held tack and now held hog feed. She tightened the shoulder straps as far as possible, finally bunching the strap together and pinning it. She used the remaining pins to hem the overalls. She grabbed the huge shovel and wished she'd remembered work gloves.

She'd always told her daughters to count their blessings but she saw few here. Maybe the urea in the "product" would be good for her skin?

She was glad the hogs were outside and she was inside the barn. At least they weren't snorting around her legs, or stepping on her. Was it hogs or goats that ate everything they saw? She hoped it was goats. Hogs terrified her, and she worried that one might slip back into the barn and go for her.

The stench in the barn chewed into her skin, her nasal passages, inside her mouth. Jeanette had thought the odor blown into Hancock by the trial wind turbine nauseating. *Ha. Mild.* Now she knew what nauseating was. Her hair would reek for weeks, at least in her mind. Once she'd rid herself of her good clothes, she let loose the first of several bouts of puking. Not her preferred weight loss method.

After nearly an hour, the pile of hog excrement appeared slightly smaller. She figured she'd set a record by postponing hurling for a full fifteen minutes after puke number three. Or was it four? Tying her silk scarf around her mouth and nose, bad guy fashion, helped some. Of course that transferred some pig mess and straw from her hands to her hair.

The worst thing, and she believed herself saintly to have this thought, was that she was stuck out here with the hogs where she could learn nothing about the problems at Windfall Works.

A door thumped behind her. From outside the indoor pen, Haley called out a greeting. Jeanette heard the chuckle underlying the young fiend's voice. "Oh my goodness. It is rather a bog in here." She grinned. "I see you found a change of clothes."

Jeanette slogged through the mess and leaned against the fence. She'd seen the way Haley eyed her expensive clothing earlier that morning. She would not attempt to become the young woman's pal, but maybe she could get in a little sleuthing. "I've seen worse. I find it hard to imagine Teddy mucking this out every day, but we all do what we must. Poor Teddy, such a tragedy. Do you think he's the one who sent those nasty blackmail texts we all got?" She eyed Haley expectantly.

"I didn't get one, if that's what you're asking. Blackmailers go for people with money." Her sly grin confirmed Jeanette's suspicions. She'd need to be careful around this spiteful, jealous, young woman.

"The text I got said there were problems at Windfall. Of course, that was the rumor going around at Saturday night's party. When I went to his office, Peter claimed to know nothing." Jeanette wondered if flattery would work with Haley. "You know a lot about the operation here. Possibly more than Jon or Peter. Definitely more than Teddy."

That got Haley's attention. She switched from sullen to outraged. "Are you accusing me of blackmail? It could have been any of you partners. You rich folks are always running out of money. It was probably Teddy, though." She sighed. "Why else would he be dead?"

"I wasn't accusing you of blackmail. I meant that you are very knowledgeable. I'd like to know if the problems are real or imagined." She drew as close as she could to Haley, hoping to gauge her reaction. Isn't that what detectives did?

Haley's expression switched to guarded. She shook her head and her nose wrinkled in reaction to the odors emanating from Jeanette. "They're real, all right. The problems started with the clause in the sales agreement that the hogs remain. Folks complain about the stench, and we're just in testing phase." She stared at the muck covered barn floor, then looked up at Jeanette. "I suppose there are other problems, but you partners know more than I do, or Teddy."

"So you liked him? Teddy?"

Haley smiled, and for an instant her face was ravaged by pain. If Jeanette hadn't been doing her detective thing, she doubted she'd have noticed. "Teddy was ... Teddy. Spoiled, funny, witty, lazy. He was okay." She shrugged. "You knew him. He hung with your daughter. I need to get back to work. Looks like you have enough to chew on."

Jeanette made a face. "No chewing, thanks."

Haley looked at her watch to establish who the boss was. "We both need to get back to work. You've made some progress," she added begrudgingly. She left the barn.

Progress on shoveling shit, but not on digging dirt. Jeanette realized she'd actually not known Teddy well at all. She rarely bothered with her daughters' boyfriends. All were fleeting. She picked up the shovel. *Maybe the exercise will increase blood flow to my brain.*

After what seemed like half a lifetime but was probably less than an hour, Jeanette's arms and shoulders ached. She'd become immune to the foul odor, but her body needed a break. Plus she needed to use the facilities and wondered how rugged they'd be here, or if this barn even hosted a potty. Without thinking, she ran her hands through her streaky blond hair. And felt the muck she'd deposited on her head. "Rats."

She heard a rustling in the tack room and hoped her statement hadn't proven an omen. Rodents would cap a fine, fine day. That was it. She would rinse down at the faucet she'd seen outside the barn, change clothes and then snoop around the outbuildings. After all, she wasn't here to care for hogs. Maybe she'd find a clue. Maybe she'd find a bathroom.

She passed the tack room on her way to the faucet and trough. The rustling there grew louder. She tried to stomp her feet to make enough noise to frighten away the rodents, but they stuck in the muck. Her left foot pulled free from the oversized gum boot and she fell forward onto her hands and knees. "Eeew. Yuk." Her squeal was loud enough to frighten the intruder in the tack room. She heard what sounded like children giggling, a high pitched, fast, nyeh, nyeh, nyeh. Not children. An animal. A sheep?

"A goat." She crawled to the door and saw a goat about three feet high, standing on its hind legs, which were braced against her silk shirt on the floor, eating her linen pants. It bent its head to take an occasional snip of silk. A tasty cloth salad. She looked on the chair and saw her Donald Pliner loafers, intact and obviously next in line on the goat's menu.

Jeanette crawled to the wall and pulled herself to standing. She dashed as fast as a woman in one gum boot and one socked foot could dash and snatched up her shoes. "Ha. Got 'em. Stupid goat. I can buy another pair of pants but they don't make this style shoe anymore."

The goat nuzzled her shoes and tried to nibble one toe. Jeanette reached above its head and put the shoes on a high shelf. Something ran over her hand and scampered into her loafers.

Jeanette yelped and jumped back, nearly squishing the goat. A mouse. What else? She grabbed her shoes, gave them a thorough shaking and stuffed them down inside the overalls. They might get wet when she washed up but at least they wouldn't be decorated with mouse bites or poop.

Her stomach growled. Hunger seemed out of place, given the aromas that surrounded her. Hard work had its benefits. Since she was working for nothing, no reason to get Haley's permission to stop for a while.

She'd have to have her car detailed if she drove back to the Osprey's Nest B&B, where she'd decided to spend the night, in her mucking wet clothes but she refused to ask Haley for help. Feather lived in Hancock. She'd phone Feather. Nothing could hurt Feather's beat up old pickup.

Twenty-One
Dawn Breaks at Laughing Pines

Feather awoke to the sound of squirrels chomping their chow. She'd won the argument with Michael over who would sleep closest to the trailer's outside wall and who would get the inside bed closest to the bathroom. Michael said it was hard to guard her if he wasn't closest to the door, but she insisted that she often awoke in the night to use the bathroom and she'd be nervous he'd shoot her. The old weak female bladder trick. In reality she knew she might not sleep much at all. She didn't know if her sister had been taken away by a murderer or if, worse, her sister was a killer or dead, herself. Feather was a blackmail and murder suspect. She had surprised herself by drifting into a light, dream-filled sleep that left her less rested than when she'd gone to bed.

Sunlight filtered through the trailer's faded chintz curtains. Next to her, separated by the folded blanket, Michael slept on, one arm flung outside the sheets and over the blanket, resting on her hip. He smelled of toothpaste and very faintly of a cedary after-shave. Or was that the squirrels' cedar bedding?

She rose quietly. The squirrels immediately created an outcry, expressing their hopes for something better than chow for breakfast. She opened the upper cupboard and withdrew several shelled peanuts that she slipped through the cage wire. "Now, hush."

She extracted her laptop from beneath the bed and realized its cheerful opening tune would waken Michael. She did an eye roll. Far more convenient to live alone.

She booted up outdoors, sitting on an elegant wicker lawn chair gifted to her by Emily, the ex-wife of the former owner of Camp Destiny. It perched before her tacky trailer as if the new environment and new owner amused it.

She checked her email, hoping Roxanne had sent a message.

Nothing from FoxyRoxy. Her shoulders tightened. She'd so hoped to hear from her sister. She scanned the rest of the newly arrived messages, paused at one from Slimmer. Who was Slimmer? Seemed vaguely familiar. Then she remembered her little sister's taunt: *Slimmer'n you, slimmer'n you.* She clicked on the email. It said only, "Slimmer has sent you an email greeting. Click here to read. (Requires password.)"

Ordinarily Feather ignored messages like this one. So easy to catch a virus from some creep of a hacker. But the name nudged her to try it. Actually something *was* nudging her and it had a cold nose. "Pudding. What are you doing up so early?" She reached down to fondle the soft ears of the friendly Golden Retriever. "I suppose they let you out to do your business, with absolutely no intention of cleaning up after you. Not that a little dog doo could detract from the ambiance of this place." The Laughing Pines Trailer Court had seen better days. Long past better, it now boasted a few rusting heaps of rental trailers, a few travelers who paid for the honor of hooking up, and a few near-permanent tin tubes like hers. Nothing to boast of. Butterscotch Pudding was owned by a couple who lived a few rows away. The dog often dropped by to see Feather and she walked her home.

She put her hands on either side of the dog's soulful face. "Listen up, critter. I'm busy. You lie down and I'll walk you home soon as I'm through." Her fur felt damp, as if she'd been rolling in dew-soaked grass. She lay down beside Feather's chair and stared up at her with the attentive look she did so well.

Feather decided to go to the email site and read her greeting. She'd never been there, so had no idea of the password. If, big if, it was from Roxanne, what password would she choose? Probably one they both used often enough. She typed in ColdHardMomma and the message opened.

"Teddy is dead. I didn't kill him. Someone was there when I walked in. Lost him/her, but I think they saw me. No cops—they'll think I did it. I DIDN'T. Afraid real killer will track me down. I'm hiding. Help me. Please. Find out who killed him."

Feather rubbed absently at her lip. She'd chewed it raw in the time it took to read the short message. At least, praise the gods, her sister was alive. But where the heck was she? Did she know about the blackmail? Is it Roxanne who's still sending out Teddy's messages? She swiveled to peer into the trailer where Michael slept. Should she tell him? Really, whose side was he on? Brad and Kristin hired him and he owed them his loyalty.

For now, she'd keep quiet. She'd see what he did and decide where to place her confidence later. For now, she trusted herself.

Beside her, Pudding whined. "Oh, sweetie, I trust you, too. Are you hungry? Thirsty?" The sweats she'd slept in would do as clothes for now. She'd take the dog home. Again. "Sheez, dog. You're more reliable than your humans. And friendlier, too. But you belong with them."

She closed the program and shut down her laptop. She left it on the chair. If no one had yet stolen the expensive furniture, they probably wouldn't snatch it or her computer in the next fifteen minutes. She headed for Pudding's trailer, the dog at her side, tail wagging.

Returning a stray dog home was a lot easier than figuring out how to help her sister. And it gave her time to decide on her next steps.

Feather threw open the door to her trailer, Michael's beauty sleep now much lower on her priority list. She turned and spoke to the dog. "If you mess with the squirrels, I'll take you straight to the shelter. If you're good, you may get to stay a while."

The bathroom door opened and Michael spoke in a high, squeaky voice. "Please, please, don't send me to the shelter. I promise to be good to the squirrels."

Despite her worries, Feather chuckled. "I was talking to Pudding, not you."

Michael moved around the door. "Talking to pudding. That makes *much* more sense." He spied the golden retriever and froze. The dog's ruff raised and her lip curled over her teeth. She growled.

Michael stood silent. Feather looked from dog to man, wondering for an instant which was the greater threat. "Cool it, Pudding. This is Michael. Friend."

Michael extended his hand, knuckles first. Pudding sniffed. Michael smiled. Pudding's tail wagged. Michael said, "Good dog," at the same time Feather said, "Good dog."

The dog finished with Michael's hand and walked past him to the squirrel cage. The squirrels chittered and squealed their outrage. The dog stared at them for several moments. Then her tail wagged and she returned to Feather.

Feather relaxed.

Michael came all the way out of the bathroom. "Didn't know you had a dog."

"Don't. She's visiting. Her family moved out and left her."

Michael's expression, outrage combined with sympathy, gained him points. "Find them and I'll beat them up for you," he told the dog.

Feather walked to the cupboard and pulled out a pan. She filled it with water and placed it on the floor beneath the table. "I think I have enough eggs for all of us. I'll get dog food later." She busied herself in the kitchen, awkward at Michael's presence, especially knowing she had no intention of telling him about Roxanne's message.

"Can you scramble eggs?" she asked. "I need a shower."

She rescued her laptop, shut it down, and stored it, then left Michael to manage breakfast while he chatted with the dog. He didn't seem fussy about dog hair in his eggs, something she found oddly endearing.

Over breakfast, Feather told Michael she intended to ask for time off. "I need to find Roxanne and figure out what's going on." She sipped the strong coffee he had brewed.

"Leave it to the professionals."

"Thank you for your support and respect."

"Someone killed Teddy. They could kill again. Chasing after a murderer is not smart."

"And you are ...?"

He smiled. "Why yes, I am smart. And trained. So are the police."

"They think I killed him."

"At this point, most everyone's a suspect."

She so wanted to confide in him about Roxanne's message. But he'd tell the police and they'd take her computer and probably arrest her for withholding information. "Thanks for breakfast."

"Thanks for letting me stay here." He rose and held his plate. "Can Pudding get started on this?"

Feather nodded and laid his plate beside hers beneath the tacky trailer's table.

Liking the man made her decision to follow him even harder, but she had to help her sister. "I'm going to The Blind Chukar and talk to Walt. I'm not scheduled until later today. With someone like you on the job, maybe all will be solved by then."

"And maybe someone else will be dead. I don't want it to be you."

Michael's response annoyed the feminist in Feather. She'd never been a meek little woman seeking a man's protection. Neither did she consider herself an idiot, ready to put herself in danger. Anger was good, better than guilt at lying to him. However, now was not the time to be drawn into a political argument. "Hey, Pudding, want to take a trip to town?" She gathered up her things and waited for Michael to leave the trailer so she could lock up. They exchanged cell numbers with mutual promises to inform the other if something momentous occurred.

All seemed rosy between the two of them, yet Feather knew she'd already lied to Michael, if only through omission, by not telling him about Roxanne's message. She was equally certain she'd lie again, if she thought the lie would save her sister.

After the cops left, Jon went to town to update Peter on their visit, leaving Haley in charge. She was used to that. Jon didn't do much around the wind plant, spending most of his time schmoozing the partners or fishing in the St. Joe River. It gave her time to handle things for Chaz, keeping Jon vague on the details of the business that powered the wind farm. It definitely wasn't wind, nor was it Jon's hot air or the efforts of the idealistic Brad Ganborena.

She figured they'd both be shocked to know about Chaz and his connection to the wind farm, although Jon had to know more than he professed.

The arrival of snoopy Jeanette Sullivan could present a problem. Haley thought assigning her mucking-out duty would speed Jeanette home in her fancy clothes and high class car, but the stupid woman proved stubborn. She hoped she wasn't smart enough to make anything of the amount of stuff they had stored here. If she did ... she would have to figure out how to handle the snooty old broad.

She seized the time alone to phone Chaz directly, something she rarely did.

He answered immediately, not a good sign. "Haley, my dear, I expected your call earlier. We agreed you would phone me if problems arose." He paused. "I believe a dead employee and blackmail of the company principals add up to problems. For us. As I recall, you said you would handle things."

Haley knew Chaz hated excuses. Excuses could be fatal. "Someone got rid of Teddy, so I figured that would stop the blackmail. Unfortunately, it didn't." Haley hated to apologize but now was not the time to avoid things she disliked. "Sorry, boss. I should have acted faster."

"Did I hear right? Haley West said 'Sorry'? Things must be the bollocks down there."

Haley forced herself to chuckle. "Shouldn't last long. Trust me."

"I do trust you. For now," he reminded her. His tone chilled Haley. She knew what happened to those who lost Chaz's confidence. "What about Jon? Is he holding steady or falling apart?"

Haley wondered if ratting out Jon would be good or bad for her. She decided to support the idiot, for a while, at least. "He's okay. Shaky, but a dead employee can do that to some people."

Chaz chuckled. "I suppose it can. Keep an eye on him, and do keep me informed."

Twenty-Two
Chasing Tails

Michael headed toward Spokane, unsure of his destination. If he went into the office, the boss would want a full report. He wasn't sure how much to include in his report. Definitely not where he spent the night. No one would believe he and Feather had slept side by side and nothing sexual had happened. Of course, if you counted a non-stop hard-on as sexual, then sexual had happened. For a long time. He'd thought he might never get to sleep, but eventually the night sounds outside the trailer and Feather's breathing soothed rather than stimulated him and he slept.

The report could be postponed. Simon trusted him.

He phoned Brad Ganborena and verified where the drop was to take place and confirmed that neither Ganborena nor his wife would become involved in the process. Michael would drop the bag and Michael would tail it to the blackmailer. He relied on the plan.

At 9:15, he drove toward the drop site, again in Spokane, giving himself time to scope out the scene. That made sense, no matter where the blackmailer was headquartered. Hancock was a small town and people would recognize whoever picked up the money, and definitely notice if the person had say, a ski mask on to hide his or her identity. But if Michael was right, and Teddy had been the original blackmailer, who had carried on with the crime? Despite Feather's denials, his guts said Teddy's girlfriend Roxanne. It made sense. Teddy would have confided in her. She'd disappeared after Teddy's murder. Despite Feather's confidence in her sister's innocence, it was obvious Roxanne killed her lover.

The previous day Michael downloaded photos of all the partners from the Windfall Works website. Whoever created the copy for the site was a master at vague promises and high-minded, well, wind. If any of them showed up to collect the money, he would know. He had seen a photo of Roxanne and Feather and her mother in Feather's trailer and he'd recognize the younger sister anywhere.

As he walked the area where the blackmailer had directed Brad to drop the money, Michael realized it would be prudent to call in some of the other guys at Simon's Simple Security. It was a park along the river, directly across the street from several high rise buildings. Far too many places for the pick-up person to disappear.

He headed for the office and spent a frustrating hour updating his boss Simon Freeman and trying to convince him to allocate two assistants to be on hand for the pick-up. Generally Simon went along with Michael's plans, but he'd taken on the job as a favor to Brad and wasn't being paid their regular fees. Apparently that made him less eager to throw additional resources on the case.

"We can do it cheap and lose the blackmailer, or we can spot three of us and nail him. I would think our reputation is more important than saving a few bucks," Michael argued.

Simon glowered at him. "Thanks for your sage business advice. Problem with this one is timing. I have a lot of guys working the arrival of that group of CEOs for their annual retreat. Big coup to have it here. Big opportunity for the enviro-wackos to make a statement." He sighed. "I'll give you Parsons. She fits in anywhere and she's sharp."

Michael smiled. "I'll take her. Thanks, Simple." Simon should have predicted his nickname when he named his company.

Sara Beth Parsons blended in anywhere she was assigned, whether as a waitress or the hostess of an elegant fete. Pushing or possibly towing fifty behind her, she kept fit swimming and running and practicing an obscure martial art. Michael liked her, admired her, and feared her sharp wit and occasional bursts of temper.

They reviewed maps and discussed the assignment for half an hour and then Sara Beth told Michael to take a nap. "You look like poop, cutie," she told him. "Must have had one heck of a night."

"If you only knew." He crashed in the small room containing four single beds and an adjoining shower.

Twenty-Three
Burning Biscuits

Feather ran through her mental checklist for the day as she opened the little Nissan truck's door for the dog: find sister, find mother, track down blackmailer, absolve self from suspicion of murder, and walk dog. Oh, and take time off from work to do it all, meaning no pay, no tips, no savings. Pudding hopped into the backseat, panting her delight at the thought of an adventure. Oh, for the carefree outlook of a dog.

She dressed in a lightweight burgundy crew shirt and a cardigan over jeans and sneakers. She threw a bag with some snacks for herself, water for dog and self, her camera, a small pair of binoculars, and a black sweatshirt and ball cap that said "Save the bees" into the trunk.

She again called her mother's cell phone and left a voice message that revealed her frustration. Her mom, a partner in Windfall Works, no doubt received a blackmail text. Did she know both her daughters were suspects? Would she care? Feather snorted. Only if it affected Jeanette's well-being.

She shook her head. Mom wasn't *that* bad. Self-absorbed, but she loved her daughters. After all, good mothers loved their daughters; it was a rule. Thus, Jeanette loved Feather and Roxanne. She sometimes revealed her love in odd ways, however. Where the heck was she today?

Roxanne and Teddy had dysfunctional families in common, Feather guessed. Who didn't? Still, she found it fascinating that Roxanne considered Teddy's stepfather a potential suspect in his death. Family issues were one thing, but murder was more than a squabble over holiday dinners. Or in her family's case, who had Mom's favor that month. Roxanne won hands down lately, because she hadn't asked for a loan and she had a worthy job. Face it, she'd won since they'd entered their teens, when Feather turned rebellious and Roxanne, realizing how hard things became for the rebel, turned what she called realistic. What Feather often considered manipulative.

Feather found a shady spot behind The Blind Chukar to park and entered the kitchen door. Scheduled for the lunch shift, she wasn't due in until 11:00. She needed time off to track down Michael's place of business and follow him to the drop-off of the blackmail money. Would have been easier if he'd invited her to tag along instead of staging that macho scene.

When she walked into the Chukar, Walt's solemn expression told her he knew at least something about the events embroiling Windfall Works. No different than any small town, Hancock cultured its gossip in petri dishes of fact sprinkled with speculation, causing it to grow at pandemic speed, often with little accuracy.

She moved closer to Walt, smelled the cooking grease that permeated his body, the onions that he chopped each morning for the Chukar's famous hash browns. "You heard about poor Teddy."

He held up his hand in a stop gesture while he moved the hash browns to the cooler side of the grill. "Heard about Teddy. Heard that you called the cops." He paused and his eyes narrowed. "Heard you and your sister are prime suspects."

Her breath caught. "You can't believe that." She stared at Walt, a man she'd grown to count on. Someone she considered more friend than employer.

He shrugged and looked back at the grill. "Don't matter what I think. If customers are concerned I'm employing a murderer, they aren't about to flock in. 'Least that's what our attorney says."

Of course. "And it happens that your attorney is Kristin Ganborena." Feather's eyes threatened to tear up. She fisted her hands until the nails cut her palms. The only way Kristin could have found out so fast was through Michael. Michael, that rotten traitor.

Walt broke two eggs, one-handed, on the grill. "Once you get it all straightened out, you can come back. It's nothing personal, Feather. Business."

Don't burn your bridges or your friends. She could almost hear

Gina's calm voice and tried to emulate it. "I understand. Believe me, I *will* straighten it out and I will be back. Promise. Meanwhile, I'm due a paycheck tomorrow. Think I could get it sooner?" She'd put in a lot of hours recently and she figured the check to be a couple of hundred.

Walt strode away from the grill, leaving the eggs to frazzle and the hash browns blackening. He headed into his office and jerked open the middle drawer of his desk, where he stowed his wallet and keys. He drew two twenties and a ten from his wallet and thrust them at Feather. "Ah, hell, Feather. We were advised to withhold your paycheck since you might be a flight risk. Bullshit, I know, but her daddy owns our building. You can gas up your truck."

Feather took the bills and left, fighting the urge to tear them to bits, biting her lip hard to keep from screaming at Walt, Kristin's blameless messenger.

At the truck, she slid beside Pudding on the front seat and buried her head in the dog's soft fur. "You're a lot better than those stupid, selfish squirrels, girl." The dog licked away Feather's tears. She wrinkled her nose. "But you need a bath. I'll add that to my list."

She wasn't sure what to tackle first. It was clear Kristin had smeared her reputation everywhere possible, or at least where it mattered to Feather. So much for gratitude to the mother of her child.

She slid out of the truck, leaving the door open. That Kristin hated her was clear. That she deserved her hatred, understood. Feather had an affair with her husband. But the affair stopped and Kristin and Brad had the baby now. Kristin would never forgive Feather, never stop trying to make Feather's life hell.

"Well, you've pretty much succeeded." She stomped her feet. "Darn it, Kristin. Dang, darn, *damn*." Her voice rose and she pounded her fists on the roof.

Pudding yelped and scooted out of the front seat and past Feather in an instant. Instead of heading into the alley or across it, where traffic would be non-existent on the residential streets, Pudding darted around the corner of the restaurant and toward Hancock's main drag.

Feather ran after the dog, shouting and crying. "Pudding, no! Stop. Sit. Pudding."

As she dashed around the building corner, she heard a car horn and brakes squealing. "No. No, no, no."

She stopped, watching the Golden Retriever speed across the road, watching a sedan and a pickup that were able to swerve and miss hitting her. Watching the compact pickup tilt forward as the driver slammed the brakes on and hit Pudding with its far front wheel. The dog's body bounced forward, careening off the tires and landing at the side of the road. The driver came to a stop, still on the road, threw open the door and ran to where Pudding lay, panting rapidly, her rear leg bleeding as she thrashed about trying to stand up and flee.

"She just ran straight into the truck," the young woman protested.

"You'd better move your truck so no one hits it," Feather said from where she knelt next to Pudding. "And grab a blanket if you have one. Please." Her calm voice amazed her. Inside she shook, berating herself. She pulled off her sweater and wound it around her right hand, knowing the injured dog was likely to snap at her.

The pickup driver returned with a puffy coat. "No blanket. Take this."

"There's a lot of blood," Feather warned.

"That's the least of my worries. Is she yours?"

"I'm watching her."

"Not doing much of a job of it," said a woman who had stopped her vehicle.

"I know." Feather swiped at the tears streaking her face. She moved slowly to Pudding and laid the jacket over her. Pudding growled weakly but did not object when Feather wrapped a sleeve of her sweater around her muzzle.

The driver helped Feather scoop the dog from the ground and into her arms. "I can drive you to the clinic."

"Great. Thanks." Feather walked to the pickup bed. Across the street, she saw Walt and Angel, the morning shift waitress, watching. She turned away.

On the short drive to the veterinary clinic on the outskirts of Hancock, Feather sat in the bed of the truck, cradling Pudding in her arms. "Pudding, sweetheart, I am so, so sorry. You deserve a better owner, but I'm yours if you want me. We'll figure out a way to pay for this, I know we will." She continued to croon, nonsense talk mixed with apologies, until they arrived.

After the person who had struck Pudding dropped off Feather, Pudding, and a hundred apologies at the vet's, Feather realized she'd need a ride back to her truck. She hated to bother Gina, who was absorbed with running the shelter and its subsidiary business while raising her new daughter, Pia. But she called her anyway, trying hard to stifle her tears during the call. "Can you come get me? I need a ride."

Gina didn't hesitate. "Where are you?" When Feather told her, she didn't stop to ask questions, simply said, "I'll be there inside of ten minutes."

Gina arrived and hugged Feather. Feather clutched at her friend. "I'm so sorry to bother you, but I didn't know who else to call—"

"Hush. Of *course* you should call me. Whenever. Now let's talk to Dr. Bhatti." Gina held Feather's hand while Dr. Bhatti reported that Pudding had a compound fracture in her leg that would heal in time, probably without worse than arthritis in the dog's old age. Unfortunately, Pudding's previous owners had not been clients of Hancock's only veterinary clinic, so they had to assume the dog needed her vaccinations in addition to the x-rays, surgery to re-join the broken bone and cast the leg, antibiotics and follow-up care.

Feather swallowed at the doctor's estimate of the cost. She had the money in her savings account, but its loss would seriously delay the start of work on the B&B. She shoved that worry aside for later. She owed Pudding the best care. "If I hadn't made such a racket, she'd still be resting happily in the seat of the pickup," she said.

Gina gave a soft punch to Feather's upper arm. "If you didn't have such a big heart, the dog would be wandering around the trailer park, or in the forest or already be dinner for a hungry cougar."

"It doesn't seem right to try to find another home for her now," Feather said.

Gina smiled. "Did you really think you'd go through with that?"

"I won't be taking good care of her if I wind up in jail," Feather said. "Thanks for coming. I needed a friend ... and a hug."

Pudding would spend the night at the clinic, to be observed after her surgery, and Feather promised to pick her up the next day.

Twenty-Four
More Maternal Meddling

When Jeanette couldn't bring herself to leave yet one more phone message to be ignored by Feather, she texted her daughter to meet her at Windfall Works, adding an *urgent* to it. No way would Jeanette get in her car to drive to the B&B when her daughter had a perfectly awful yet serviceable vehicle that hog muck couldn't harm. She refused to ask Haley for assistance. The woman would get too much satisfaction.

She squared her shoulders. Might as well get a little detecting in. Feather would come, she was confident. No matter her faults, her stubbornness, Feather could be relied on. In the meantime, Jeanette could start what she came to Windfall Works to do.

But first ... no reason to give Haley an excuse to replace her with a more diligent worker. She picked up her shovel and finished mucking out the barn. She couldn't get any dirtier but her gloveless hands definitely developed more blisters.

Once she'd done the hard stuff, and a lot of stuff there was, Jeanette considered her options. On the way to the barn, she'd counted three other outbuildings, along with a foreman's cottage, where Jon now put up the occasional guest. Jeanette had not asked to stay there, preferring to keep her snooping headquarters in town. Now she wished she'd commandeered the cottage, yearning for a bath and clean clothes.

The tack room where she'd changed held nothing but her ruined clothes, hog feed and an ancient wooden table with four mismatched legs so ugly it bordered on chic.

The rest of the barn stood empty. She saw several stalls, with a few tired tools hanging on the outside walls, but little else. A teetery ladder led to an opening to the hay loft. Jeanette would leave climbing that ladder as the last stop in her snooping.

She stepped through the barn's side door and went to the closest of the other outbuildings. It was a long building some twenty feet wide with one window at the side and high, wide double doors. A power line stretched to the upper outside corner of the building. Like the barn, it had power. It was padlocked, but Jeanette grabbed the lock and wriggled it.

That accomplished nothing, but she realized that although the lock was new, the hasps on either side of the latch were the originals. It should be a snap to pry those loose from the rotting wood if she could find a suitable tool. Preferably one that would allow her to replace the hasp and hide her intrusion.

Where she stood allowed anyone looking out of the farm office to see her. She hoped Haley didn't notice. She took a few steps so she could see the drive beside the house and let out a breath. Haley's little car was gone.

Alone, at least for a while. She ran back to the barn. All she could find to use as a pry bar was an old-fashioned steel sheep shear. A pity to ruin something with antique value, but needs must when the devil drives. "Lord, now I'm thinking like Grandmother Taylor." The shear was two long, pointed blades at the ends of two handles curved into Cs joined together so they looked like a heart shape. She returned to the double doors and wedged the point of the shear beneath the right hasp. The screws pulled out easily and fell to the ground and the lock and shackle tilted sideways so it was dangling on the left door. Jeanette squatted to retrieve the screws.

The ground where the screws lay was smooth and flat. Several tire tracks led into the building. Jeanette pulled on the lock, using it as a handle to open the door. The door opened without a creak or a grumble. Jeanette's mouth gaped and again she heard Grandmother Taylor spit out a warning about catching flies.

The large interior lay in shadows save for sunlight that filtered through the side window. The light cast a pattern of spider webs and leaves on the car in front of her. That she noticed at all surprised her, because her attention was on the car, a classic no doubt of considerable value. It was a Chevrolet or a Ford, sixties vintage. Okay, maybe fifties. Jeanette knew antique furniture, not antique cars. She knew, however, that she'd no doubt spent time in the rear seat of similar vehicles, so that meant it was most likely from the fifties. Definitely a classic and the body seemed, to her unskilled eye, to be in pretty good shape. She wondered what it was doing out here, on a wind and hog farm?

But she was on a mission. She was Harriet the Spy, Nancy Drew, V. I. Warshawski, Sue Grafton—no, wait, that's the author's name. *Who is her character?* She moved past the car, noticing another beside it, also of classic vintage. She headed for the side wall, a wall lined with shelves. She realized she still held the sheep shear and clutched it close to her body. Wouldn't do to scratch either car.

The shelves held tools she assumed were for working on the cars but that may well have been useful for people working on wind turbines. She had no idea. Wrenches of various sizes, screwdrivers, bottles of nuts, bolts and screws. A large workbench spanned part of the rear wall. It held a large vise and more tools. She grabbed a screwdriver to help her replace the padlock and cover the sins of her entry.

At the end of the bench was a door into a storage area. She peered through the window at stacks of equipment. Several turbine blades were obviously for future growth, but the rest of the equipment was foreign to Jeanette, who didn't pretend to understand the wind generation technology.

The fictional detective's name came to her. "Kinsey Something."

"Milhone," said a man's voice behind her. "And you're trespassing."

Jeanette yelped, sucked in air and spun around, her back to the workbench. She extended the screwdriver in the direction of the voice. A man's frame was silhouetted in the sunlight streaming through the half of the double door.

Jeanette squinted at the silhouette. "I'm an owner here. Who are you?" She was proud that her voice didn't shake.

The man came forward. "You need to leave. The outbuildings are private property."

"Stay away from me." She waved the screwdriver, a fairly puny one, at the interloper.

"Jeanette, calm down. It's Jonathan Flynn."

She put her left hand to her eyes to shade them and realized she still held the shears. She was armed in both fists. She laid the shears on the bench behind her. "Doggone it, Jon, I almost peed my pants." She moved to where she could see him.

"Doubt anyone would notice." His lip twitched at the corner, as if he were trying to hold back laughter. Jeanette shot him an as-if-anyone-cares-about-your-opinion look. He cleared his throat. "Really. You shouldn't be here. You need to leave."

"Then you fix the door. Here's a screwdriver." She paraded by him, as regally as someone in gum boots and filthy overalls could appear. She handed him the tool as she passed. "I was simply becoming acquainted with my new workplace. There's a lot you didn't show us on that partner tour."

"The outbuildings are off limits. Besides, the farm has little to do with wind technology."

"Except for the delicious odor it brews up for the turbines to send out."

Jon stiffened. "Stick to the barn in future. Now, I have work to do. Do you know where Haley is?"

Jeanette shrugged. "I assume she ran into town on her lunch hour. I'm not her keeper ... or anything else." It was obvious to Jeanette, if not to the other partners, that Haley and Jon were lovers. Or, more correctly, sex partners.

Jon flushed. He was an easy target. "Please clean up before you come into the office." He wrinkled his nose. "You definitely get into your work."

Jeanette smiled. "Of course. I'm intense about everything I do. I'll see you later."

She strolled back to the barn, as if out for a pre-lunch amble. It was hard to keep up the casual façade, because as soon as her focus on snooping waned, her discomfort surged. Her skin itched up to the top of her head, her nose wrinkled in disgust at eau de hog, and every muscle in her body protested the morning's intense workout. Why hadn't either of her daughters answered her pleas? She didn't deserve this. She'd give Feather another call.

* * *

Feather drove home. The quiet in the back seat disturbed her. Before she picked up Pudding the following day, she'd stop and buy dog food and a bowl. She could pick up something to serve as a dog bed at a thrift shop. Maybe they'd have a collar and a leash, as well. She knew how costly dog ownership was, a reason she'd stayed pet-less save for the stupid squirrels Myrna forced on her.

Someone had placed a rolled up yellow flier in the screen door handle of her trailer. No doubt someone wanted her to hire maid service for her castle, or spend a day being pampered at a spa in Sandpoint. If only that "someone" wanted to pay for it. And if only Feather had time to be pampered.

Before she put it in the recycling pile, Feather glanced at the flier.

Three Day Notice to Terminate Tenancy

This is to serve as your final notice to quit the premises at Laughing Pines Trailer Park. You must deliver up possession of the same to McLaughlin Enterprises. Anything left on the premises will be considered the property of McLaughlin Enterprises.

Failure to vacate the premises will result in forfeiture of the lease agreement and of any deposit you rendered and will institute legal proceedings against you to ensure vacation of said premises.

All tenants and occupants have previously been notified that the premises, Laughing Pines Trailer Park, will be demolished. This is your final notice to quit the premises.

Feather reached into her tiny fridge for the bottle of wine. She sank into the banquette. Using her free hand, she pulled the stopper from the vacuum sealed bottle and gulped down a long swig. The wine was too old, all life and flavor gone from it, bitter as well. She hoped it retained some alcohol content.

"Too much," she said. "Overkill." She snorted out a giggle that deepened into a laugh. The laugh continued until her breath came in gasps and snot ran from her nose, but she couldn't stop.

Where could she go? She must have received an earlier eviction notice, but perhaps it was hidden in stacks of junk mail, or perhaps it had blown away. The Laughing Pines was the last resort for most who ended here. Nothing in Hancock came so cheap because nothing else was this tacky, this ancient, this ready for demolition, really. Maybe the Tidy Scot, but she refused to share her bed with insects. She considered the worn, faded linoleum floor, the permanently spotted and shadowed windows that she'd covered with cheap but colorful curtains. One good shove to the outside of her tin can would do it in. But it was her home. Here she could make a home for stray rodents and a loving, injured dog.

Feather sipped the cheap wine and grimaced. Way past its time. She looked around the trailer. It, too, had passed its expiration date years ago. Long before the problems Teddy, and possibly her sister, had catapulted her into, Feather had marooned herself at the Laughing Pines, wishin' and hopin' like that old song. Hopin' that Kristin would let her get a moment with her son, wishin' her mother would loan her money for the B&B. Heck, even the idea for the inn had been Gina's, probably a ploy to prod Feather from her despondency after giving Jared up for adoption.

She walked to the sink and dumped the wine in her glass, then clutched the bottle and dumped out the dregs at the bottom. With no job and nowhere cheap to live, her hopes for opening the B&B next spring were dimming. Time to re-assess those hopes and to shake out of the blues. She shimmied her entire body, stretched her finger tips to the trailer's ceiling and bent to touch her toes. Her mother might, grudgingly, let her stay for a while, but she wouldn't welcome a dog and three disabled squirrels. With the many unresolved issues between Feather and her mom, staying there was a last option. But she had other options. For one, winter had yet to arrive and the weather was fine. She owned a tent and knew how to camp.

If Feather could screw her head on right, she could figure out her life—where she could live, whether or not she truly wanted to operate a bed and breakfast, really, where her life was going. She shimmied again and forced a smile onto her face. "The sun is shining and the grass is green." Someone once told her saying that phrase made you smile. Later she learned it also started the Christmas carol, "I'm Dreaming of a White Christmas." Which made many people cry. Go figure. Oh, right. She was figuring out her life while smiling like a loon.

Her phone rang. She pulled it out and glanced at the ID. Mom. Might as well answer. Her day could do nothing but improve. She'd wallowed at the bottom long enough. Dragging herself out of this mire was up to her. She straightened.

"Hi, Mom, what's up?"

Feather pulled in front of the old farmhouse that served as offices to Windfall Works. In the distance she heard the whine of the test tower blade. How many raptors must be killed to run humanity's blenders?

Her mother sat huddled on a bench on the porch, in an outfit far worse than anything Feather had seen her mother in. Ever. If she took a photograph, could Feather blackmail her mother into stopping this "investigation" of Windfall Works? For that had to be why she was here, dressed in filthy overalls, begging her daughter to rescue her. None of those things were in character for Jeanette Sullivan. Feather was determined that her mother share anything she'd learned. Sounded easy, but Mom personified stubborn. Of course, she'd passed that trait on to her oldest daughter.

As a partner in the wind farm, Jeanette might know something that would help Feather discover who killed Teddy. She might even, if she knew, tell Feather where Roxanne was hiding. She had to. Both her daughters faced big trouble.

Feather stepped out of her truck and grabbed her sweats and a couple of towels from the back seat. She struggled to keep a straight face. She lost the battle. "Do they have a shower here?"

Her mother descended the porch stairs and walked to the side of the house. "They have a hose. It will do." She sat on the grass and removed a huge pair of gum boots and a couple of pairs of heavy socks. Then she stripped to the buff and turned the hose on herself. The icy water raised goose bumps all over her body.

Eew. Feather was used to seeing other people naked from rafting and swimming with her friends. But her own mother? "That's enough, Mom. You'll freeze." Feather threw her mother a towel once she'd stopped drenching herself.

Feather held the sweats in the air. "Tell me what in the hell you're doing here and promise you'll stop and I might give you these."

"I'm freezing. I could catch my death here if you don't give me those sweats."

Feather backed away. "Plus you never know when someone might come. That towel's pretty skimpy."

Her mother's eyes widened. "What kind of daughter are you?"

Feather smiled. "Yours."

Her mother growled, low and mean and bared her teeth. As if that scared Feather. Jeanette tossed her wet, formerly sleek and streaked blond hair back. "I'm investigating. Your sister's boyfriend was murdered and someone is blackmailing the partners in Windfall Works."

Feather stepped closer and waved the clothes at her mother. "What did your blackmail note say? Did every investor get one?"

"None of your business. To both questions."

Feather tried to stare Jeanette down, but looking at her practically naked mother made her want to either weep or laugh hysterically. "So you're investigating. What have you found besides a lot of hog poop?"

"Nothing but some old cars before Jon kicked me out. The nerve of him. I have as much right here as he does." She shivered. "The sweats. Now. You'll get nothing from a frozen corpse."

Feather's mind went to the sight of Teddy's body and she barely heard her mother's response. She handed her the clothes. "I might have a garbage bag in the back for your clothes."

"I will never wear them again. The goat can have them for dinner," her mother added.

Goat? "You should never have come here. Why in hell did you end up mucking out the hogs? And you didn't find anything Teddy could have considered blackmail material?" Great. Mom put herself in danger and Jon and Haley on the alert. Plus she didn't find anything of value.

"Spare me your preaching. Right now, I need a ride to The Osprey's Nest. But I'm not stopping my investigation. I will *not* tolerate a lecture. As if you never put yourself at risk for your convictions."

Feather shuddered. "Don't use the word convict or any form of it right now."

On the way into town, Feather and her mother caught up on their versions of the horror of the past two days. Feather didn't bother to share the news of her suspension from The Blind Chukar and expulsion from the trailer. She knew her mother would offer up some excuse for Kristin's vengeful nature. Jeanette had already provided her own condemnation of the trailer park months earlier. No one, especially not a daughter of hers, should live there.

Feather decided it wouldn't hurt and would definitely help calm her mother, so after extracting a promise of silence, she told her she'd heard from Roxanne and that her youngest daughter swore she had not harmed Teddy. Her mother burst into tears. "I thought she was dead, too. Or worse, a murderer."

"Excuse me? Being an accused murderer is worse than being dead?"

"The good Lord knows I didn't raise you two to be violent. What would people think?" Her mother hiccupped and blew her nose. "You're both okay. That's what's important. But where *is* she?"

"Good you care, Mom. As I said, she didn't tell me where she was, just that she was safe. I thought she might be at your place."

"No, of course not. I wouldn't harbor a wanted criminal. Both of you know that. We need to find her and have her turn herself in. If she didn't kill Teddy, she'll be fine."

"She'll be in jail until they find whoever really killed him, or put me in there instead."

"That's absurd. The police do not jail innocent people."

Feather slowed so she could stare at her mother. She wasn't that ignorant. She couldn't be. "Tell me you didn't say that."

Her mother shot her a prim glance. "Possibly they do in other countries, maybe in big cities. Not in the Pacific Northwest."

"And besides, we're the wrong color," Feather muttered. As usual, it was pointless to argue with Jeanette Sullivan. Neither was it a good idea for Feather to share her plans with her mother. She could only hope Jeanette would be safe working and snooping at Windfall Works, because no way could Feather stop her.

But she had to try. After Jeanette left the vehicle, Feather called to her, "Is there any way I can get you to stop with the snooping?"

Her mother leaned into the window, "About as easily as I can get you to stop or Roxanne to turn herself in. We're a stubborn bunch. I'll be careful. You do the same." She grabbed Feather's head between her still cold hands and planted a big kiss on Feather's mouth, then her forehead.

Feather's breath caught. Her mother worried about her? That had to be a first. She watched her mother enter the lovely bed and breakfast where, as she'd told Feather, she'd set up temporary spy headquarters, elegant and poised in the oversized sweats.

Her mother loved the Osprey's Nest. It didn't surprise Feather that she'd elected to stay there. She expected the sight of the established B&B to elicit the usual pang of jealousy. It didn't arrive, perhaps because her emotional system ran on overload about the murder and blackmail.

Feather headed to Sandpoint for a quick check of her mother's house. Roxanne could have waited until Jeanette left to enter. Both girls knew where she hid her house key. She looked at her watch. If she skipped lunch, she should still have time to track down Michael Bergmann and trail him to the drop point where Brad had been told to leave his payment.

Twenty-Five

The Rugged Life of a PI

Feather found her mother's home as immaculate as always, and empty. She checked each room and the decks and patio outside. Nothing, no one, no sign of anyone having dropped in. If Roxanne had considered hiding out here, she'd changed her mind.

She wondered why the thought of moving back home, even for a short time, disturbed her. Her mom lived northeast of downtown Sandpoint on Lake Pend Oreille in a home that definitely classified as upper. The neighborhood, typical in resort communities, boasted homes like Jeanette's, upscale, super-sized and professionally decorated, interwoven with tiny old homes many thought tacky but Feather preferred. These were originals, their battered paint and tired brickwork the kind the faux specialists worked to imitate.

She loved her mother, but their personalities were too similar for peaceful co-habitation. If her mother offered to house her—fat chance of that—she'd expect Feather to live by her house rules. Camping appealed more.

Time to find Michael.

By the time Feather reached Spokane, about a ninety minute drive, she was starving, but it was nearly time for the blackmail drop. She drove directly to Michael's downtown office and hoped she could catch him as he left. If he hadn't gone into the office, she was up the creek without anyone to shadow, but at least she'd have time to eat. She parked her truck down the street, hoping to see him.

"We've got a tail. Beat up mini-pickup."

Michael glanced at Sara Parsons. "I know. She's not very good at it." He continued driving, keeping pace with the traffic on the busy street.

Parsons smiled. "Ah. You know her? She stalking you?"

He chuckled. "In my dreams." He cleared his throat. "She wants to help on this job. Her sister is somehow involved."

"Her sister's the dead guy's girlfriend, right?"

He should have known. He briefed Sara before his nap and left her his notes. She wouldn't have wasted her time or his. "Yeah. I don't want her involved. Could be some risk and she's a civilian."

"Of course." He shot her a glance and noticed a skeptical raised eyebrow.

Michael hung a right at the next red light and then made a series of maneuvers designed to lose a skilled tail. He lost Feather a quarter of the way through, but kept it up to be certain he had lost her. Now why did he feel a pang of regret?

Twenty-Six
Really Chasing Tails

Until this afternoon, Michael had been fond of Spokane's Riverfront Park, even proud of it. Something for everyone. A carousel and a memorial to Vietnam Vets, a tour train and even a gondola over Spokane Falls that was impressive in the spring. Places to eat, places to walk, places to run. Places to pick up a money drop and way too many places to disappear afterward. The Ganborenas had been told to leave a laundry sack filled with the cash at the base of the Clock Tower. Brad insisted on being the one to leave the sack but had agreed to leave right away and not try any heroics. Michael assured him he and his team had it covered. He didn't mention that his team consisted of Sara and him.

Sara was good and so was he. They had placed themselves so their view of the tower was complete. Now they had to wait and appear inconspicuous. Sara was on a hillock west of the tower and he covered the east side. They both saw Brad make the drop and stroll away, glancing over his shoulder so often he was going to have a stiff neck. Not the picture of subtle.

That's about the time Michael began to worry. A teenage boy on a skateboard darted past the tower and scooped up the bag, barely slowing his ride. He headed toward town, down one of the many walking paths, an easy target. When the path became congested, he got off his board and continued walking. Pretty sure he wasn't their suspect, but a go-between, Michael followed. So did Brad, ignoring their agreement. Michael cursed under his breath.

When they passed the carousel, two preteens, a boy and a girl, flanked their target. Each of them carried a laundry bag, but Michael kept his eyes focused on the drop bag. He caught up to Brad and nudged him. "Back off. We've got it." Brad yelped and backed away, shaking his head.

The kids separated. Michael stayed with his original target, who by now was jogging across Spokane Falls Boulevard, toward city center. He entered an office building. Michael ran to catch up, dodging honking, braking vehicles on the boulevard. Inside he saw his target, but the youth carried nothing and walked out the door. Michael took a quick photo of him with his cell phone, then grabbed him around the body. No one else was in the building but it had a side entrance. Sara dashed inside and Michael instructed her to question the skater.

He ran outside and saw a teenage girl across the street walking rapidly with what he hoped was the drop bag, heading south. She turned into an alley and he lost sight of her. He sprinted across the street, again risking death and arousing the ire of drivers stomping their brakes. He ran into the alley. Nothing. Empty. Several doors led off the alley, which crossed to the next street, another one busy with pedestrians, cafés, and office buildings. She couldn't have gone far, so he tried the first door. It led into a long passage with multiple doors along it. If he tried each one and they didn't pan out, he was sunk. Although he guessed he might already be sunk. He shrugged. Never say die, at least not while the body is warm.

He ran back to the alley and tried the next door, back entrance to a Chinese restaurant. A woman who stood outside, smoking, shook her head when he asked if she'd seen a teenage girl. "Just came out. Didn't see nothing."

He trotted on, not ready to give up, but acknowledging he'd lost the girl. His painstaking search down the alley earned him a few locked doors, an entrance to a high rise office building and a lobby to another that led back to the Spokane Falls Boulevard. Nothing.

This blackmailer was sharp. The body was cool, so Michael returned to Sara and the teen.

The teenager who'd picked up the original drop knew nothing. A little kid had passed him a note and two twenties, with promise of three more if he picked up the bag and passed it on in this building. The girl who took the bag handed him an envelope, which he'd given to Sara while begging her not to turn him in. "I thought it was some kind of scavenger hunt. I didn't know."

She held him until Michael returned and interviewed him. They agreed the teen knew nothing more and after making a note of his name and address, they released him. He was either too naïve or too nervous to ask for their identification. They gave him cash to replace that which they confiscated. Simon or the police could check for fingerprints or DNA.

"Damn. Damn. Damn. That kid did a better job of earning his pay than I did," Michael said on their way back to his vehicle.

Parsons patted his arm. "It happens. It's a big park next to a boulevard. Someone's a better planner than we predicted."

"It's no amateur. I was wrong." Michael gnawed at his lip. "I'm no better than a rookie."

Parsons smiled. "Rookie mistake doesn't make you a rookie. Temper tantrum about it? Maybe." She shook her head. "Maybe we should have let your friend help out. The blackmailer obviously used several intermediaries."

"Maybe. That first pick-up by a teenager should have clued me in that it was a string."

"And what could we have done? We tagged it through two hand-offs, probably three. Someone is nervous. And smart."

"Wait until I tell Simon, and the client. The cash was marked, so we can hope it starts to circulate, but anyone this clever will hold onto it or find a way to launder it." He pulled out his cell phone. "Might as well get it over. Want me to drop you at the office?"

Haley pulled beside the farmhouse next to Jon's car at Windfall Works at a sedate, measured pace. Before Haley left her car, she smoothed her hair and freshened her lipstick. Jon was back, and probably wondering where she was. She rarely left Windfall over the lunch hour, but she'd needed time away from the farm and from Jon's nerves. If he asked, she'd gone to the gym to work off some anxiety, but she wouldn't volunteer any information. She'd learned that from Chaz.

She climbed the porch stairs. God, how she needed to get away from all this. Months of deadly boredom and now big time drama.

Jeanette Sullivan's fancy-schmancy car was still in place in front of the office. Who would have thought the old snoop would last that long? She probably knew exactly how long Haley had been gone from Windfall Works. She fantasized eliminating "Her Nosiness." Old woman has heart attack and falls in hog pen. Disappears.

She opened the door. Put on her happy-to-see-you face for Jon and ran into Chaz Stedman.

"Chaz! What a surprise." Lord, she hoped her voice hid the dismay. He'd come to see what the hell was happening. He would have questions for her, so many questions.

From the look on Jon's face, relief mixed with gray exhaustion—or was it terror—he'd already been grilled by the boss. Chaz never threatened his minions, but the threat remained, subtle and mysterious.

She neared Chaz. He kissed each of her cheeks, gently. He gripped both her forearms. He exerted no pressure but somehow she recognized his strength and his willingness to squeeze the truth from her. He smiled, his eyes alert, focused totally on Haley. "Jon's been telling me about the problems you've experienced. Quite the dust-up." Haley wondered if he could somehow see inside her brain, see her thoughts zipping around a tiny racetrack, one bumping into another as they sped, collided and began again.

She swallowed, hoping the dryness would fade. "The dust is settling."

Jon spat out a laugh. "Settling like nuclear fallout. Brad Ganborena phoned. They just paid out $10,000 to a dead drop. Clever one. Their money is lost."

Haley walked into the kitchen area for coffee, intentionally not offering to fetch more coffee for either man. She was so tired of being their slave. When she rejoined the men, she said, "I hadn't heard. Maybe not under control. But the cops came and left, none the wiser."

Chaz raised a patrician, groomed eyebrow. "So Jon said. I gather one of the partners decided to help us out." His average height and slender frame were always clothed beautifully, always right for whatever occasion. Today he wore designer jeans, pale chamois leather boots and matching jacket and a wool shirt.

Haley chuckled. "I doubt she'll be around much longer. In fact," she went to the window, "I thought she'd be gone by now."

"She is." Jon joined her at the window. "She left a note. Says she'll be back tomorrow." He cleared his throat. "No more mucking. These are investors in our business."

"You had a partner cleaning the barn?" Chaz giggled his trademark high-pitched giggle. "Give me twenty thousand dollars and here's your shovel."

Haley flushed and turned to Chaz. "She volunteered to do anything. That was one of Teddy's jobs."

"She was snooping," Jon said. "Shouldn't have let her stay." As if it were Haley's fault. He was there this morning, too.

"I thought the smell would chase her home. She's tougher than I thought. Nosier, too."

"She didn't find anything. Really, nothing to find." Jon looked nervous, as if the woman had found something and he was trying to cover it up.

Chaz noticed Jon's nervousness, Haley gathered from his raised eyebrow, even though he said nothing. He took Haley's coffee mug from her hands, as if by accident. She saw it as it was meant, a gesture symbolizing his absolute power over her. "Seems to me the poop may be getting a bit deep around here." He drank the hot brew and placed the empty mug on Haley's desk.

Chaz leaned against the back door, the picture of a relaxed businessman. "I'm sure both of you are aware that all this fuss over goings-on at Windfall could have a negative impact on our business. In fact," he added as if struck by a new thought, "it could mean we'll have to shut things down." He rubbed his chin. "That's how I see it from here. We've had a good thing going, but murder, particularly when the body is found so quickly, is messy. I don't like messy, as you know."

He looked from one to the other of his employees. "The number of people who wanted this Teddy dead are few. I suggest you figure out who it is and resolve the problem, one way or another. I'm spending the night in town and plan to go to Coeur d'Alene tomorrow to take a look at a '64 Chevrolet Impala. If I decide to purchase it, I'll have it shipped here. If there is a here. If you two can't resolve the controversy around Windfall, we'll need to shut it down."

He smiled and Haley suppressed a shiver. The smile chilled her. She knew better than to speak, to argue with Chaz. She stayed silent.

Jon forgot that piece of wisdom and opened his mouth. "But Chaz, that's less than 24 hours. The police have had days and haven't—"

"Need I remind you we are not the police? If they continue to investigate, they may make unfortunate discoveries, unfortunate connections could be found. We do not want that. I expect a report tomorrow afternoon that tells me things are calm, once again. Or I shall be forced to calm them myself."

Haley knew from experience exactly what Chaz meant by calming things himself. It was time, past time, for her to make a getaway. When Chaz made a decision to shut down an operation, he left no loose ends. And the bodies were rarely found. She wondered if Jon knew exactly what the ultimatum set by Chaz meant to the two of them, the loose ends of this operation. She glanced at him, and concluded from his gray face and shallow breathing, that he, too, knew the hidden message Chaz was sending.

"Which of you wants to give me a lift to town? I'll need to rent a car, so Spokane?"

Haley knew Chaz wanted to spend time alone with her. "I can do it." She hated having to volunteer, but it was how she earned the big bucks. It was her job and Chaz expected her to deliver.

Jon stepped in front of her. "Seems to me you've been gone way too long already. I'm sure you have work to do. I'll run Chaz into town."

Chaz raised an eyebrow but said only, "Excellent. I shall see both of you tomorrow afternoon."

Since Jon had no idea that Haley was Chaz's ears at the operation, he had no idea he had just saved her from a grilling. Possibly worse. She rarely felt grateful to Jon the wimp, but she wanted to give him a blow job for serving as her inadvertent savior.

* * *

Feather slammed her hands on the steering wheel. "Dang it. Ratfarts. Hell." Michael Bergmann had spotted her tailing him and had lost her in minutes. She took a breath. She shouldn't berate herself. He claimed to be a pro and at losing a tail, he was. If only he hadn't refused to let her join him. She considered calling Brad on his cell to find out where the drop was to be. Fat chance he would tell her. If Kristin answered, she would find a way to twist Feather's question into a confession.

Kristin wouldn't be with Brad. She must be at home, keeping an eye on Jared while Brad made the drop. She imagined he'd come home and wait with his wife to hear from his private investigator.

She pulled to the side of the street and parked, because tears blocked her vision. Images paraded through her mind. Kristin, Brad and Jared, together, in their lovely home. Feather, alone, nowhere to live, not even a crappy trailer. No job, no prospects. Three stinking squirrels and an abandoned dog whose care she could scarce afford her only companions. She let the tears pour forth. Sheez, she couldn't even tail someone without losing them.

A horn blared behind her. Her head jerked up and she realized she had parked in a delivery zone. As she pulled out, the delivery person sent her off with a cheery Bon Voyage of his middle finger.

"Chin up, Feather," she said. Things could be worse. Teddy's lifeless face flashed in front of her. A lot worse. She needed to think. She needed to eat something. Michael might be a better PI, and the cops might have more resources, but Feather knew her sister better than they did. Her sister had worked in a boutique in Coeur d'Alene during school and afterwards. The owner had become a good friend, one who might hide her sister. She might also have other ideas about Roxanne's whereabouts.

She headed south to catch I-90 east.

Heartthrob was not a great word play on Coeur d'Alene, but it had worked for its owner Pamela Hart, whose boutique had thrived for more than a decade. Coeur d'Alene actually means heart of the awl, a name given to the resident Native Americans by French fur traders for the tribe's sharp trading skills.

She dropped into a small café for lunch before heading to Heartthrob. Her head ached, most likely from lack of food, and she needed to plan her next steps. While she waited to be served, she decided to make a list of Roxanne's friends. It ended up quite short, making her realize she didn't know her sister all that well. She held out hope for Pamela Hart. If not, she would try to search her room at the Ganborena's. Maybe she'd left a clue.

When she entered the boutique, a beautiful black woman not much younger than Roxanne greeted her. Feather tried to hide her dismay and simply asked to see Pamela. "She's working in the back. Is there nothing I might help you with?"

You never know which path leads to the center of the maze. "Actually, I'm trying to locate my sister. We have something of a family emergency and ..." Feather gave her an innocent look.

"And your sister is ..."

Uh, yes, that would help. Feather blushed. "Sorry. Stressful day. Her name is Roxanne Sullivan and she used to work here."

The girl smiled. "I know Roxanne. She drops by often. But not for the last week or so. Let me ask Pamela." She parted a curtain leading to the back of the store.

She returned, accompanied by a muscular, fit woman with short cropped, stylish dark brown hair. Her cropped pants were a garish orange shade that was echoed in her multi-colored silk wash blouse. She rushed to Feather and engulfed her in an embrace. "Feather, darling, I heard about Teddy. How horrendous for Roxanne and for you. How is the poor thing holding up?"

Feather's hopes plummeted. "Actually, I'm trying to locate her. I thought perhaps she'd been in touch with you."

"No, no. Of course I have plenty of room and would welcome her, but she hasn't called or dropped in." She lowered her voice. "I heard that Teddy was shot. You don't think ... Roxanne ... no, that's not possible."

Feather managed to smile. "Thank you for that vote of confidence. I believe she's in hiding for fear the killer will come after her."

"Or the cops," the young woman interjected. "They always blame the wife or the lover."

Pamela frowned at her assistant. "For shame, Tiana. Roxanne is a true innocent." To Feather, she said, "I wish I could help. Do give me your number in case I hear from her."

Feather did so, promising to keep Pamela informed as events unfolded. She wondered how Pamela could consider her sister a true innocent. Innocent of murder, for sure, but not so in everything. Neither Pamela nor Tiana could offer any thoughts on other people who might offer shelter to Roxanne.

Time for the next step. She hoped to find Brad alone, workaholic Kristin returned to work. She knew she could convince Brad to let her search Roxanne's old room above the garage. If Kristin was there, she'd have to take a stealth approach and hope they didn't press charges if she got caught.

Feather had little regard for their choice of homes. True, it was in a good location between Hancock, where Brad spent a good deal of time, and downtown Spokane, where Kristin's law firm occupied prime real estate in a high rise. But really? A McMansion for someone who called himself an environmentalist?

She drove slowly past the house, trying to peek past drawn curtains and see who was there. Then she realized she could look through the garage windows, see whose car was there. She parked a few houses up and walked back.

Since the garage was situated perpendicular to the house on the west end, the car access doors were some distance from the pedestrian entrance. Windows on the side of the garage mimicked those on the house, extending the line, as the architect would have said. Feather could reach those windows without fear of being seen from any of the home's windows. Of course, she would be in plain view of anyone arriving on foot or if Brad or Kristin chose that moment to drive in or out of the garage. But the odds of that were low. A brick paver sidewalk led beneath the windows, fronted by a row of rose bushes, their blooms dying.

Because of the contrast between the bright daylight and the dark interior of the garage, she had to lean against the window, cupping her palms around her eyes to block out the sunlight. "Rats," she whispered. Brad's car was gone, Kristin's there. She was pleased to notice spider webs on the inside of the windows, a tiny blot on the home's perfection.

Feather sighed. If Michael had seen the Ganborena's blackmail threat, he didn't share with Feather. She liked him better for that, but wanted to know what Teddy might have had on the Ganborenas that they didn't want the world to know. Her mother had clammed up when she asked about her threat.

It wasn't hard to imagine that everyone had secrets. It *was* hard to imagine how Teddy had learned them all. Way too much pillow talk with Roxanne?

She pulled away from the window. She ought to postpone contemplating her problems to somewhere and sometime safer, and get to work on her objective.

She picked up a heavy stone at the base of the stairs behind the garage and then took the stairs to Roxanne's apartment. If Roxanne left in a hurry, she must have abandoned belongings, because she didn't travel light. On the landing, she peered through the window beside the door. Enough remained that Feather had hopes she'd discover a clue to Roxanne's current location.

She took a breath, wrapped the stone with the stretched bottom of her sweatshirt, and broke the window. She pushed the shards of glass through onto the floor and reached through to unbolt the door, expecting at any moment that Kristin would charge up the stairs and accost her.

Once inside, she caught her breath and tried to make a systematic, methodical search of the small dwelling. Roxanne must have been in a dreadful hurry, because not only did she leave clothes on the hangers, she left several pairs of shoes. Her baby sister loved shoes.

After the bedroom and bath, she entered the tiny kitchen area. The cupboards held virtually nothing. She concentrated her search on the tiny desk area adjacent to the kitchen. A small cork bulletin board above the desk had several items tacked to it. None proved to be a list of Roxanne's friends and acquaintances. In fact she found no phone numbers, only a reminder of a doctor's appointment and a bill. Smart phones eliminated the need for address books and Rolodexes. She found no matchbook from a friendly neighborhood bar, but she did uncover a ruler with the name of an insurance agent.

In other words, her venture in breaking and entering had earned Feather no information. She was no closer to finding her sister, no closer to discovering who shot Teddy.

The building shuddered and Feather heard a car engine in the driveway. Most likely Brad returning.

She waited a few minutes and decided it was safe to leave. She quietly descended the stairs and turned onto the rose-lined brick path.

Angry voices came from the direction of the house's back door. "Come on, babe, that's not fair. Let's talk." Brad.

"Enough talk. I need a walk and Jared needs some fresh air."

"I'll join you."

Feather threw herself to the ground and rolled under the rose bushes. Fortunately, the baby squalled, covering any noise she made. "Thanks, Jared," she whispered.

"There's a blanket in the car," Kristin said. "I'll get it."

Kristin trotted toward Feather. Feather scooched as close to the rose bushes as she could. Thank heavens they had been pruned into a hedge-like shape, leaving no branches extending outward below a foot or so above the ground. No one had pruned away the thorns, however. Feather bit her lip against the painful punctures.

Feather heard the crunch of Kristin's shoes on the walkway. Then she saw those running shoes stop, no more than ten inches away, facing the garage. She'd seen her. Still, Feather refused to budge. They'd have to pry her out. Given the nature of the bushes she was hiding under, that was not an impossibility. What if Kristin didn't see her and Feather remained there, impaled on who knew how many rose thorns, until someone discovered her cold dead body?

The shoes turned around. "You know what? It's pretty warm," Kristin called. "No need for a blanket. If it gets chilly, I'll give him my sweatshirt." The shoes walked toward the house. "He'll need to get used to rags as swaddling clothes, now that we've lost our last cent."

"It's not that bad, Kris. Michael still might get the money back."

"You're an idiotic optimist. The wind farm is a bust. You can bet at least one of those rumors will get out, and true or not, you'll lose all chance of investment and permits. You put all your money and a lot of mine into this pipe dream."

"It's not a dream."

"Plus, I'll be too embarrassed to stay here." There was a pause and a squeak of what was probably the baby carriage tires and Feather feared she wouldn't be able to hear the rest. Kristin continued, her voice growing fainter. "I've been offered a transfer to the firm's offices in Charlotte, North Carolina, and I accepted it this afternoon. I'll be leaving with Jared before the end of the month."

"You don't mean it. Things will work out, we can save Windfall."

"I want Jared far, far away from that woman. You can join us or not. Let me know your decision. Right now, I'm going for a walk. I need to burn off some steam."

"Let me go with you. On the walk, sweetheart. I know we can work this out. We always have." The begging tone in Brad's voice startled Feather. He sounded so wimpy. Who in his right mind would want to go on a nice little walk with his wife right after such an ultimatum?

The voices and the squeak of the carriage wheels grew fainter.

After a few minutes, Feather dared to inhale, wondering if she cared enough to breathe. The wind farm stopped, good. Brad's marriage over, a shame. Her baby transported to North Carolina, a disaster. Tears poured down her face. She wriggled herself from beneath the bushes. Thorns clutched at her cardigan sweater, threatening to strip it from her body. She rolled onto the sidewalk, still working to free the sweater from a stubborn thorn. She needed to get away before they returned. They'd headed the opposite direction from her truck, but if they walked around the block, they would see it. Its decrepit appearance and the bumper stickers that held it together would give her away.

She hurried to her pickup while a thorn buried in her left sock poked at her foot. She welcomed the pain. It distracted her thoughts.

She drove several blocks away and parked before she allowed the meltdown. She had no idea how to save Brad's marriage and keep Kristin, and the baby, in Spokane. But since it had all started with the death of Teddy Fitzpatrick, she might as well start there.

Feather needed to check out every partner in the wind farm. Sophia had been upset by something at the party. Not too big a leap to think she'd heard the rumors, as well. But had she, too, been a victim of blackmail? Her mother had told her that all the partners had received texts. Sophia was a banker, a solid citizen of Spokane. Feather had known her for several years. Nothing could go wrong with her next encounter.

Twenty-Seven
Going 'Round in Circles

Sophia said she could meet Feather at 4:30. "Do not come to the bank. I don't want them to know anything about this." No doubt. Bankers who were blackmail subjects were prime to embezzle from their employers. Not a good piece of information to share at work. Good thing Feather had asked to discuss the situation at Windfall Works rather than blurting out, "Hey. You get one of those blackmail texts, too?" Maybe Feather was becoming a discreet, subtle investigator.

They agreed to meet by the carousel in Riverfront Park, across from the high rise where Sophia worked. Feather arrived early. While she waited, Feather decided to ride the carousel. The sign showed prices and hours for the Looff Carrousel. She wondered at the spelling and reminded herself to look it up when she got home. That of course reminded her that she would soon have no home, nowhere to hook up her laptop, nowhere to shelter her recuperating dog.

"Ack." She glanced at her watch. Time for a phone call *and* a carousel ride. She phoned the vet clinic and enquired about Pudding's condition—woozy but with good vital signs. She smiled. At her best, the Golden Retriever appeared goofy, if not woozy. Good to know she was getting back to normal.

Carousel rides had been under a buck when Feather was a child. She disregarded the cost, however and bought three tickets. For the first round, Feather rode a prancing horse. She moved then to an ostrich. On her third time around, she chose a frog. She did not think about the symbolism of her choices, but let the music and the movement calm her pulsing nerves.

Moments after Feather began her third time around, she caught a glimpse of Sophia striding toward the carousel. She squinted and twisted around to see more clearly. Could she have been mistaken Saturday? Surely this sophisticated, sleek woman looked nothing like the angry, insufferable, drunken skunk who'd ripped into that server she'd collided with. Of course, Saturday she'd been wearing tights and a fluffy tail and today her severe black pencil skirt, burgundy shirt and heels screeched sophisticated banking executive.

On the next circuit, Feather waved to Sophia, but Sophia didn't respond—not expecting Feather to ride a frog to their appointment. However, Feather noticed an elderly woman some 20 yards behind Sophia, her focus on the young woman. Odd.

Next time around, Sophia had seated herself on a bench by the carousel. She glowered and pointed to her watch when Feather waved. Her appearance had changed from Saturday, but her cranky mood seemed the same. Feather scrambled from the frog and off the still rotating platform as soon as the carousel slowed, earning a glare from the attendant.

The old woman she'd noticed trailing Sophia was seated on a bench ten yards or so back from Sophia, not visible to the seated banker. The elderly spy wore a felt hat as old as she was, the crown kept low on her forehead. Bad hair day? Feather shrugged. She was probably imagining conspiracies and spies where none existed and the poor old lady was just out for an afternoon stroll in the park.

Slightly dizzy from her circuits on the carousel, Feather joined Sophia on the bench. "Thanks for coming."

Sophia took another pointed look at her watch. "Some of us have no time to ride frogs. I'll give you ten minutes, and then I have to get back to the bank. I need to be there for closing."

Feather smiled at Sophia's mention of riding frogs, but her smile died when she realized the woman was dead serious. Where had her fun sense of humor gone? She'd known Sophia and Aileen for several years and they'd always enjoyed trading bad jokes. "Then I'll get to it. My mother and the other partners at Windfall Works are being blackmailed. Are you?"

"None of your business."

Feather inhaled at the abrupt words and Sophia's cold, angry manner. "Teddy Fitzpatrick was killed yesterday. I found his body."

Sophia stared straight ahead, her gaze on the now immobile carousel. "So I heard. You kill him?"

"No. I didn't. Had I known all the trouble he had caused, I might have wanted to kill him. Now the cops suspect me and they're looking for my sister. She was Teddy's ...."

"Yeah, they played hide the sausage together. She kill him? He deserved it."

"No. She didn't. But why do you think he deserved to be killed?"

"If she's missing, how do you know Roxanne didn't kill him?"

"If you have only ten minutes, let me ask my questions. Even with Teddy dead, the blackmail continued."

"So?"

"As I heard it, the blackmail texts didn't stop at the problems at Windfall. They got uglier. Did yours?"

Sophia crossed her arms. "Again, not your business."

Feather extended a tentative hand to Sophia's arm, but Sophia jerked away. "You were in a foul mood Saturday night. I saw you tongue lash that server. It's not like you. Is it the wind farm, or something else? I'm trying to help."

Sophia stood up. "What you are trying to do is pry into things that are none of your concern. You already know I invested a bundle in that stinking wind farm. Now it appears I'll lose it. Aileen and I had plans for that money, plans that now may never happen." Her face looked haggard, beaten, far older than the mid-30-year-old Feather knew her to be. Sophia inhaled through her nose. "You can't understand. You gave *your* baby away. We ... Aileen ... if the truth came out ..." Tears rolled from her eyes. "Everything's over."

Feather stood and put her hand on Sophia's arm. "If we work together, we can still stop this."

"Talk about naïve. You cap it. Everything is falling apart. Here's one piece of news: I'd be delighted if Peter Brewer ended up dead. He's the one who convinced me that damn wind farm was a great investment. And of course your precious Brad, all shiny surface but no depth, no delivery."

"Brad got a second blackmail note. Did you? Will you pay?"

Sophia's pale face flushed. "Must I repeat myself? None of your business. I'm sorry you found Teddy, and whether or not you or your self-absorbed sister killed him, it's time for you to butt out of this. I can't help you." She turned and strode back toward town.

Feather wanted to follow her, convince her, but instead she sank back down on the bench. Roxanne, self-absorbed? Not only was Sophia adept at blocking inquiries, she had Feather's sister's personality absolutely right. When did they get to know each other? "This is hopeless."

"There's always hope, my dear. Don't despair."

Feather yelped and jerked around, startled even though the words were gentle and the voice frail and feminine. The old woman who had been tailing Sophia slid beside Feather onto the bench and gave her a sweet smile from under the grey fedora. Her green eyes looked from Feather's face to her dark and admittedly sloppy outfit. Then she patted Feather's hand. Her hand was pale and well-manicured with prominent blue veins that stretched from her wrist to the tips of her fingers. Feather jerked her hand away.

"How do you know my granddaughter?" The elderly woman nodded in the direction Sophia had taken. Her voice was soft but her words were clear and unslurred.

You won't catch me that easily. "Who?"

The woman smiled, a tolerant, understanding smile. "Sophia Patton. She lives in Spokane, works at the town's largest bank."

She might know that much and more, if she were an excellent stalker. But if she really were Sophia's grandmother, she might know something that would help Feather. And she had Sophia's lovely complexion, even past seventy, and the same green cat's eyes. "I've known Sophia for years. We met at an event for the environment."

The woman's smile broadened. "Oh, yes. She used to sit in those trees. Did you join her?"

"We helped each other."

"I understand. Someone has to bring the sitter food and a honey bucket. I can't imagine doing any of that. I haven't the courage and I'm afraid of heights. It made her happy, however." Her eyes darkened. "She isn't happy these days. She's been avoiding me." She stared at Feather. "Would you know why?"

"Recently, there have been a few troubles that I'm sure bother Sophia." Good. Vague but may lead her on.

"I heard the word murder. And I heard her say you killed someone." Instead of edging away, the woman moved closer to Feather. "But I don't believe it, now that we've had a chance to chat. It's a shame I phoned the police."

"You called the police?" Stunned, Feather echoed the woman's words.

"I was worried for my granddaughter. These days one must be cautious."

"But then you sat down beside me. How cautious was that?" Why she continued this inane conversation, Feather had no idea. It was time to make tracks. Vamoose. Scat. Scram. She stood. Her knees wobbled. Her mouth dried up and she feared she couldn't protest her innocence to this woman or the cops. She licked her lips.

"You're not a killer. Neither is little Sophie. I'll stall the fuzz when they get here. Pretend to be senile." She winked at me. "It always works. They'll take me home and you'll have time to get away. But you have to promise to help Sophia. Let her know I love her, no matter what, no matter how strangely she's been acting." She extracted a pink card with her name, Victoria Douglas, and her address on it. "I tell the cops my daughter had these made for me in case I get lost or confused. Of course my daughter lives in France and has nothing to do with me. I don't know what's going on, but if it's upsetting Sophia, you must fix it. I love my granddaughter. I want to know what is wrong, no matter what it is." She licked her lips. "Even if *she* were the killer, I would love her."

She remained sitting on the bench and Feather turned to leave. She considered thanking the woman, but she was the one who called the cops. She turned back. "I'll be in touch."

"Remember this. Money is important to Sophia. Far too important. I don't know why she worries. She'll get mine and that's considerable."

Button pushed, Feather couldn't keep quiet. "It always irked me that people wait until they die to give away their money. It makes their heirs feel guilty—should they wish the old girl dead?"

Victoria Douglas laughed, a boisterous laugh out of place coming from her frail form. "I do so like your spunk. However, my granddaughter has a good job and has no need to worry about money. I blame her mother for her fixation on money." She sighed. "Now get out of here. I'd hate to see you go to jail."

Feather smiled back. "You'd better be a great actor. You don't look at all crazy to me."

She walked away, a woman on a stroll after a lovely afternoon at the carousel.

Nervous sweat soaked Feather by the time she reached her truck. Her shoulders, long since stiffened from her attempt at a casual walk from the carousel and her battle not to peer over those shoulders for pursuing police, cried out for a massage or a long, hot shower. She couldn't afford the former and the water heater in her trailer was miniscule. Her showers were short and often cool.

Besides, she couldn't give up and head home. She checked her phone again, and again found no messages from her runaway sister. Rats. She drove slowly and purposefully to the outskirts of town, trying to decide next steps while evading the police in case Victoria's ploy failed. She wished she'd brought her computer, so she could send her sister an email at the new, secret address.

Her mother had announced her intention to return to Windfall Works tomorrow, because "that's where the trouble started and where it will end." Her mother often spoke such pronouncements and that one hadn't registered with Feather when she taxied Jeanette to her B&B. It made sense, however. She didn't want her mother back at the farm, snooping around. Since Jeanette was an unstoppable force, the only way to prevent her return to the farm was to find out Windfall's secrets fast, before her mother headed out there again.

She had to know more about what was going on at the wind farm, today. The only person she trusted was Brad. Trusted a little. Okay, she didn't *think* he'd lie to her, but then she hadn't dreamed he would sic a private investigator on her.

Now that she'd been grilled by the cops and slept with the enemy—and you could call the bundling with Michael last night sleeping with him since they'd both eventually fallen asleep despite the weirdness of being near—Brad might feel some remorse for siccing a private eye on her. She could trade his guilt for information.

She had stopped corresponding with Brad by phone or text once their relationship ended. He'd wanted to "stay friends," but she found it too painful. Besides, Kristin, the jealous witch, was apt to check Brad's phone. However, Brad might be her last hope for information. She sent him a text requesting they meet.

Brad texted her back that he couldn't be gone long from the house but would meet her at the coffee bar. The same place where she used to meet up with Roxanne and Jared. It was too much to hope that Brad would bring Jared.

Brad arrived alone, ten long minutes late. He slid in across from her with his iced mocha and an apologetic expression. "Kristin's mother just arrived to watch Jared. But she needs help changing him." He raised an eyebrow. "Not used to boy parts."

Feather wanted to smile but all she could think about was Kristin's threat to move away. She took a long slow sip of her iced chai to focus. She found herself staring at Brad and remembering good times together. She shook her head. Not the place to go. "I heard you got another note."

Brad nodded. "Text from the same phone. We decided to pay it and try to catch the blackmailer." His lip curled to one side. "Bad idea. Michael and his team lost the money and the person behind the play. Caught a minnow."

"Minnow?"

"One of several runners they hired to pick up the drop." He stared at his drink and then looked up at Feather. "Look, I'm sorry about putting Michael on your case. Kristin insisted."

"And you went along with her. How could you?"

"I don't have much clout these days."

As if he ever did. "It's not important. What is, is finding the killer and the blackmailer. The cops not only suspect me, they're looking for Roxanne. If I can find out more about the wind farm, maybe I can figure this out."

"Right. When no one else can. Teddy worked at the farm and it probably wasn't hard to dig up information on each of the investors. It was obvious he felt entitled and resented having to work, at his father's insistence. I can picture him as the blackmailer. Not so easy to think Roxanne would join him."

"She didn't. She wouldn't. And neither of us would have killed Teddy." Feather could see suspicion on Brad's face and it hurt. She shook her head. Not important. "Tell me about the trouble at Windfall. What do you think Teddy discovered?"

Brad's smile came tight and his eyes filled with sorrow. "Ah, Teddy. Such a loss. Irrepressible. And witty."

"What did Teddy find out? How?"

"Teddy could be annoying but he was a good listener. If there was something to be discovered, he'd be the one to find it. Clever, and curious."

"And willing to break the law."

"That, too," Brad admitted. "He didn't take life too seriously."

"Apparently neither did someone else." She swallowed. "What did he know about the problems at the farm? Sophia didn't have anything kind to say about you when I spoke with her."

Brad shrugged. "None of the other partners, save for your dear mother, would have much good to say about me, I'm afraid." He picked up his mocha, an obvious stall.

Feather leaned forward and poked Brad's arm. "Tell me. Please. You know how urgent this is." Later she would regret stopping him from draining his drink.

Brad set his drink down. "I've been having some problems getting the permits to expand the number of turbines. We got the test one approved, but you know what that did to Hancock's air quality. One would think the atmosphere in Hancock could only get better, but ..."

"One would be wrong. Okay. No one likes the smell. But you can get rid of the hogs, right?"

"Not easily. Covenants with the seller. We're working on them. There are more problems. The Idaho legislature is slow to make a decision, even if it means less pressure on the grid." He looked up. "You know, our power will mean the utilities won't have to generate as much power from non-renewable resources. And now we have protesters. You know about those. 'Not in my bat yard.'"

"We both know protesters rarely have an impact. Even if saving bats is good for the environment, for farmers, for everyone. I do like the slogan."

"Protestors, well-organized, do have an impact. There have been a few up around Hancock, but the majority of them are working in Boise, going to committee meetings, talking to political staffers. It's having an effect."

"Yes, but that began long ago, before the legislature got out this year. You're smart. You will eventually get around all those political hurdles. The partners know it. Something else is happening that Teddy found out."

"I hate that Sophia's mad at me. Peter's the one who convinced her to invest, she should be pissed at him."

Was Brad whining? He always wanted people to like him, a trait that could impede a person's success. "Sophia thought Peter should have been the victim. What about the problems? Financial? Technical?"

"Peter is the victim, in a sense. He thought of Teddy like a son. He's hurting. I'd also bet he's regretting some of those confidences he shared." Brad's expression turned smug. "I told him to play it closer to the vest."

"They were close?" Feather leaned in, put her hand on Brad's arm. "Why won't you tell me about the finances? What aren't you saying?"

Someone grabbed Brad's other arm and jerked him to standing. Kristin Ganborena shouted at both of them. "That cuts it. I am definitely moving to Charlotte and taking our baby away from this woman." She snatched up Brad's mocha and threw it at Feather. It struck her in the chest, burst open and spilled down her shirt. She jumped to her feet. Kristin continued to rant, and every customer and barista in the store stared at them. "Stay away from my man. Stay away from my baby."

Feather and Brad both tried reason, something the legal mind in Kristin should have responded to. Feather stammered, "I needed to know about Windfall Works."

Brad said, "Honey, please, it's not what you think. We're talking about Teddy. Feather's trying to help."

Kristin backed away from the table, her face red and blotchy. She pointed at Feather. "Ask your mother. Ask your sister. She's no doubt the one behind the blackmail, if you aren't." She turned her finger and her angry gaze to her husband. "I don't know why I trusted you to stay away from her. You're worse than she is. You two-timing scumbag. I take back my invitation. I'm moving to Charlotte, taking the baby and leaving you to your little tootsie." She ran from the store.

Brad ran behind Kristin, trying to stop her, calling to her, not glancing back at Feather.

"Tootsie?" Feather sat back down, ignoring the mess dripping down her bosom and legs. She giggled, and the giggle turned into a laugh and the laugh turned into an uproarious hooting, complete with snorts of chai from her nose.

One of the baristas ventured to her table, bearing a damp rag and sympathy. "What a bitch," she said of Kristin.

"She has a point." Feather stood and swabbed herself with the rag. "I just need to prove to her how wrong she is. I definitely do not want her husband."

Twenty-Eight

Midnight Marauders

Hancock lay silent. It generally did past six p.m., except on weekends when Barney's had karaoke or the Shriners staged one of their you-solve-it mystery dinners. One reason why Roxanne preferred Spokane or even Sandpoint to this hick town. Tonight's barrenness, however, provided the ideal surroundings for their evening's activity.

Despite, or possibly because of the danger, Roxanne's body thrummed with anticipation. Hiding out in Roadkill's claustrophobic and rustic ice cream truck had been safe, and deadly dull, although it did give her a start at healing her immense sorrow over Teddy's death. She had cried so much, she feared she'd become dehydrated. Teddy had been a good choice in partners. She hadn't expected their relationship to be a forever one, had assumed they would part at some point, and both move on. But not this. Never the horror of him dying at such a young age, shot by someone who had no soul. Teddy had brought excitement to her life, always changing things up. Teddy would never again be Roxanne's fun, experimental lover, never again make her laugh in the midst of an orgasm or giggle over the boring headlines in the papers. She missed him terribly. Being with Roadkill had soothed her pain but had also been boring and frustrating. How could she read or play a board game when Teddy's killer remained free and the police were hunting her to blame her for his murder?

Roadkill had succumbed to her pleas that they leave Rosinante and do some investigating. He believed her when she said she didn't kill Teddy and he believed her when she said she imagined the police thought she had.

"Why else would you run?" he asked, speaking as he believed the cops would think.

She shuddered and banished the memory of the gory scene at Teddy's house. Tonight she needed her best thinking.

Roadkill had learned over a beer with his brother that Roxanne's mother had spent the day at the wind farm. Darlene Belmont had spread the tale of Jeanette's time with the hogs with jealous glee and obvious envy of Jeanette's wealth. "Your sister, on the other hand, is keeping company with a PI hired by Brad and Kristin. That ought to be interesting."

Since Roxanne needed to remain underground for a while, they decided to search someplace close. The offices of Peter Brewer, investment counselor and partner in Windfall Works, were in "downtown" Hancock and should provide some clues to the energy company's finances.

Roadkill parked behind the building and the two of them walked to the front to scope out the traffic on the street, and found it ideal for burglars. "I wish I'd paid more attention to Teddy and his plans," Roxanne said. "I never thought he'd actually go through with the blackmail. I assumed he was bragging about all he knew. He really did have a knack for getting people to talk about themselves. He learned more about my family than I've told anyone else." She gasped. "Which is probably what he used for Mom's blackmail text. That rat. That weasel. That douche bag."

"The weasel-slash-douche bag is dead. Nobody deserved that."

"Nooo, but I bet Mom's figured out where he got the dirt. She'll never forgive me."

Roadkill hugged her. "She'll forgive you. That's what moms do."

Behind the ancient pine siding of Peter Brewer's office lurked a typical strip mall kind of office building. Peter had upgraded to a wood door instead of the glass ones that opened to the barber shop and the beauty shop down the street, but a large plate glass window still fronted onto the street. The top third of the window was backed by a stained glass panel of the Rathdrum prairie. Beneath the stained glass were wood shutters to help block the heat of the afternoon sun. The shutters now were opened wide, unfortunately for the wannabe intruders.

Whatever the problems at the wind farm and with the partners' finances, at some point Peter had felt flush enough to upgrade his office shell.

They returned to the back door and the parking lot that lay empty save for Rosinante. The ice cream truck was familiar to most Hancockians so wouldn't draw attention.

The back door was of cheap aluminum painted brown to match the pine siding.

Roadkill pulled a set of lock picks from a pocket. He also carried a small steel pry bar in his backpack. Roxanne had been disappointed to learn that her credit card probably wouldn't do the trick. Roadkill had told her he'd tried it when he was a teenager and few locks cooperated.

"Picking locks is also tricky," Roadkill warned as he knelt in front of the door. "Keep an eye out."

Roxanne faced the parking lot, trying hard not to breathe her anxious breaths down Roadkill's neck. After a bit, the anxiety built up enough to force her to pace, back and forth, the width of the building. About seven feet from the back door, a fire escape hung down from a platform outside the upstairs window. Roxanne couldn't remember if Peter's offices held an upstairs, but she jumped up and grabbed hold of the bottom rung of the ladder, about seven feet up. It lowered with a resounding metallic clang and rattle.

"Holy crap," Roadkill hissed at her. "If this were a cemetery, you'd wake the dead."

Roxanne looked around at the still empty parking lot. "Might as well be a cemetery." She began the climb up the ladder. Even lowered, the bottom rung was about four feet from the ground, so she had to pull herself up by the arms until she found a rung with her foot. Her arms objected but at least they were quiet about it.

The platform rested only ten feet above the ground, so the climb was brief. The ladder hung from a hole in the platform. The weight of Roxanne's body on the metal grate caused it to creak and groan and wobble. She doubted the fire department came frequently to assess the sturdiness of the fire escape. It was there and would serve the purpose of allowing people inside to exit and descend, although in its current condition, their descent might be faster than anticipated. She huddled as close to the building as she could, waiting for the old metal to stop moaning and her heart rate to slow. After a moment, she edged over to the window. It was open a few inches at the bottom.

Because it is a rule that nothing is easy, the window did not respond to Roxanne's first efforts to open it. She wished she had Roadkill's pry bar but she didn't want to share this news with him. She searched around the platform, glad for the light from the nearby streetlamp. Nothing. She needed a lever. Leverage. She remembered that she carried a penlight in her backpack. By inserting the penlight under the window and stepping down on the penlight, she was able to nudge the window open wider. She grabbed it with both hands but it didn't budge. She turned around, facing the street and grabbed the window with her palms facing backward, fingers curled around the filthy bottom and stood as near as she dared to the window. Bent her knees and lifted, careful not to break the glass with her protruding butt.

It opened. Yes. Yes. Yes. She rolled into the window and landed on a carpeted floor in a room filled with cardboard boxes, stacked high.

Grinning, she clicked on her slightly bent but still functioning flashlight and headed downstairs to let Roadkill in.

When she turned the knob, she heard him say, "Yes."

Roxanne opened the door. "Hi."

He jerked back and fell on his butt, and stood, a pissed-off expression on his face. She grinned wider and pointed upstairs. "Window."

Roadkill closed the door behind him and turned on his flashlight. "Showoff."

They split up as they'd planned: Roadkill to search the files, Roxanne to tackle Peter's desk. Their objective, to find anything that appeared out of place for an investment counselor, anything that indicated he might know and be hiding something about the wind farm. Everyone in Hancock and nearby communities knew Peter had been and remained a big proponent of Windfall Works, even after people began to complain of its stalled development and the disgusting smells coming from it.

Roxanne began the search in Peter's overflowing inbox, her pulse beating at intruder, could-be-caught-at-any-moment rate. As she thumbed through the stack, wearing latex gloves Roadkill had picked up that afternoon, she realized that she couldn't open any of Peter's mail. They'd decided to try to leave his office looking normal, not to arouse his suspicion with a pseudo burglary. Looking around his office she knew that was a good choice. No one would covet anything in this office, from the half-dead money tree plant in the corner, to the ancient, if real wood desk where she sat.

She decided to steal any promising mail and steam it open back in Rosinante. Peter wouldn't notice something missing from this chaos. Bills, one stamped past due on the envelope —hadn't they stopped that rude behavior?—dominated the inbox. One envelope from Canada. Several catalogs, including one for guns and shooting products that touted its low prices. A postcard reminder of a dental appointment. She considered stealing that, assuming Peter would be delighted to miss an appointment with pain.

The top drawer held the usual paraphernalia, nothing of interest. Then, when she reached the bottom drawer, separated for file storage, she decided to remove the files. That's when she noticed the manila envelope lying at the bottom of the drawer. She pulled it out and was pleased to notice it wasn't sealed. She pulled out the documents within.

The documents were a Deed of Trust for a property transferring title from George Wringold to Peter Brewer. It was dated two years earlier. Another dated shortly after that one transferred title to someone named Chaz Stedman, a Canadian citizen. She decided to make a copy of the papers so she and Roadkill could consider them later.

She laid them aside and looked through the file folders. This year's Invoice file was thin for three-fourths of the way through the year. Peter's laptop sat on his desk, dark. She wished she were a computer wizard, able to break in and steal all his files for perusal later. But she wasn't and neither was Roadkill. Hard copy it must be.

The current year's letter file held very little, probably because most of Peter's correspondence was by email. She scanned the letters but found nothing of interest, except to learn that he received fairly frequent updates on someone in a long term care facility in Southern California. She jotted down a few notes on the facility and the patient's name.

Once finished with the desk, Roxanne wandered to where Roadkill had pulled a chair to the file cabinets. "Find anything?"

He jerked away from the file drawer he was investigating and rolled the chair back, almost toppling Roxanne. "Watch out," he hissed.

She giggled. "You're the one who flushed like a quail in a sagebrush."

He snorted. "We're supposed to be partners in this crime. No sneaking up on me." He sighed. "I found the files on each of the investors for the wind farm. Turns out he's found quite a few smaller investors down in California, gathered them into a sort of syndicate. That place should have enough money to plant a hundred turbines. Bad news for bats and raptors."

"Give me the paperwork. I'll make copies." She turned the copy machine on.

Roadkill shuffled through the files and handed Roxanne several sheets of paper. Then he walked to the window and pulled on the cord that would lower the ancient venetian blinds. The blinds and their mounting crashed to his feet. He cursed.

"Good to keep things quiet," Roxanne said, not making an attempt to hide her amusement.

"If we get caught, you're not going to think it's so funny."

"Nobody's around. It's after dusk in Hancock."

"Huh." He returned to the files. "Hurry up. I'm getting a bad feeling about this."

She returned to the copier, remembering what had sparked all this. Teddy was dead and someone had shot him. She had no business being amused and she wished Roadkill would stop with his "bad feelings." It unsettled her.

The copier was a cheap older one without a bin feeder, meaning Roxanne had to place each piece of paper on the glass and press the copy button. Time-consuming and annoying. After she'd made the copies, Roxanne carefully returned the ones she'd filched to the desk files and helped Roadkill file those he'd found.

Her flashlight rolled off the bookcase shelf where she'd left it to cast some light on her task. When she picked it up, it didn't work, so she used the flashlight app on her phone.

"Geez, you might as well turn on the lights," Roadkill said. "That sucker is bright."

"I know. I love it," she said. She finished returning the papers and cast the beam on the bookcases. "Think there's anything here, or upstairs in all those boxes?"

"I think it's time to go home," Roadkill said. "We're pushing our luck."

"I forgot to pull up the fire escape. He'll know for sure someone was here."

"He may notice the blinds fell down."

"He might think that just happened. The fire escape, not so much." Roxanne stepped to the window, holding the stack of papers she'd copied. And saw the sheriff's car pull around the corner and stop. It wasn't funny at all, but something made her want to holler, "Cheese it, the cops!" She didn't. Instead she ran to the desk, rolling the papers into a tube as she ran and opened the top drawer, where she'd seen a pile of rubber bands. She wrapped one around the papers and said, "We're screwed. The sheriff is here."

"Not funny," Roadkill said from the doorway. "C'mon."

"Not kidding. I saw the car park out back."

"Then let's go out the front door." Roadkill trotted toward the front.

Roxanne paused at the bookcase and pulled a tall, thick book out, stuffing her roll of papers behind it before returning it to the shelf. She shone her light on the book's title: *Bulfinch's Mythology*. Unexpected reading for an investment adviser, but nobody said Peter did the expected.

"I'll try the back door," she said. "Maybe one of us will escape."

She opened the back door and realized she wouldn't be escaping. Byron Warnock's newest deputy, Lacy Ponder, stood a few feet from the door, her hand poised near her side arm. "Well, well. Quite a few people have been wondering where you are. Glad to be able to tell them you'll be safe and sound, in jail. What the hell were you thinking?"

Roxanne inhaled a breath and strived to keep her voice steady. "I was trying to figure out who shot Teddy."

"It wasn't you?"

Roxanne stamped her foot. "Of course not. The only reason I ran was to escape being gunned down like him."

"Do I have to cuff you or will you come willingly? I'm sure Byron will want to discuss all this once you're in custody." Lacy didn't seem terrifically upset about Roxanne's new burglary career.

"What-how did you find u—me? There isn't a soul out tonight."

Lacy burst into an unprofessional burst of laughter. "You don't know Sarah Mae Ickles?" At least once a week Ms. Ickles phones us at the office and warns us of evil spirits haunting one building or another downtown." She snickered and pointed across the parking lot. "She lives across the street beyond there, in a tall Victorian. She has a telescope up there that she swears can recognize non-virtual souls. Like you, I guess. She has a view of most of Hancock and she keeps tabs on it. Tonight she saw weird lights flickering in Peter Brewer's office building. So here we are. She'll be disappointed to learn it was mere mortal intruders." She stared at Roxanne. "Did you have company? Feather, maybe? Your family's been keeping busy."

Maybe they won't catch Roadkill. "My family? You're looking for *Feather*? She wouldn't hurt anyone, she won't even hairspray spiders, for God's sake."

"No Sullivans in our jail tonight. Or anyone, for that matter. We hear a lot about what's going on and ... No matter. Let's haul you into jail and see what Peter has to say."

"Peter? I didn't hurt anything."

Lacy took her arm and led her to the sheriff's vehicle. Before placing her in the back, Lacy read Roxanne her rights. She also placed her backpack in the front seat, just in case it contained a weapon, Roxanne assumed. The deputy had become much more formal and Roxanne realized the trouble she was in, despite Lacy's somewhat casual arrest process. She decided to keep quiet until she had an attorney, even though she had no idea who to call.

Since they heard no commotion from the front of the building, Roxanne assumed Roadkill had escaped. If he'd been apprehended, there would have been a commotion, that was certain. Roadkill knew commotions.

Relief washed through Roxanne like a warm enema but without the same results. Her cohort in crime had escaped. Roadkill had provided refuge for her without a lot of fuss. He didn't deserve to be locked up. Because she was on a quest for truth and justice, she believed she too deserved freedom, but she doubted Sheriff Warnock would agree. Her heartbeat increased to even think about time in the slammer, so she thought about how she could retrieve those papers before Peter found them. If only she'd told Roadkill before they separated.

Since she was no longer in hiding, she could use her own cell phone to call her sister and her mother for bail and assistance in retrieving the papers. "When do I get my one phone call?" she shouted to Deputy Ponder.

"That's a myth. We lock you up and throw away the key until you confess."

"You're kidding, right? You've got to be kidding."

"You may call an attorney and a family member. Hancock's a small town. We're not that big on formal rules. Be polite and you'll probably get some of Myrna's carrot cake. And that problem with bedbugs seems to be under control now."

Roxanne froze. Rosinante had been rustic, but bedbugs? What had she gotten herself into?

"Kidding, Roxanne. It won't be half as bad as you imagine."

Was this woman never serious? It was hard to remain terrified in the presence of the deputy's sardonic humor. If indeed that was her intention, it worked. Roxanne had told Roadkill she would die if she had to do jail time, but maybe it wouldn't be as bad as she'd feared. At least in the Hancock jail. Of course, Hancock could be the first step to a life in prison or the death penalty. Idaho had one, did

Washington?

The car turned into the lot behind the sheriff's office. Once she'd parked, Deputy Ponder turned to Roxanne. "Hasn't Roadkill ever mentioned his times in jail?"

Was this a trick? Did they know she'd been hiding with Roadkill? "I don't see him that often, he's more a friend of my sister. Besides, only an idiot believes most of what Roadkill says."

"True."

The only problem with the phone calls was that they had to be made in the presence of the deputy. Roxanne sat at Lacy Ponder's desk. No secret messages. Also, no answers at the other end. She tried her mother's home and left a message on the land line. She tried her sister's cell and left a message. She tried her sister's work and was told she no longer worked at The Blind Chukar. What happened to Feather? Where was she? She tried her mother's cell phone and left yet another message.

Frustrated, Roxanne gnawed at her fingernails. Her manicure had gone south somewhere in Rosinante, that beastly truck. She'd sent Feather that message declaring herself safe, telling Feather to check into Lane. Is that what she was doing?

Not one to dwell in the land of regret, Roxanne realized she'd already arrived. If only she had never dated Teddy, never allowed him to carry on for a single minute about that ridiculous, foolproof scheme to make a bundle.

She turned to Deputy Ponder. "Guess I ought to look into a lawyer. Can't get hold of any family. Any law offices in Hancock? Or do I have to wait for someone to drive from Sandpoint or Bonners Ferry?"

Lacy Ponder smiled. "We have one lawyer, part-time, in Hancock. Melvin Belkin. He calls himself a generalist. There are others in Bonners Ferry and Sandpoint. I can loan you the phonebook." She opened a drawer. "You might reach your mother at The Osprey's Nest. I heard she was staying there."

It made sense that her mom would stay in Hancock while she worked out at the wind farm. She still had a hard time picturing her mother mucking out the hogs. She shook her head but said nothing.

Ponder cut her a grin. "In fact, she was seen being dropped off by your sister, wearing sweats."

"Feather."

"Your mother. And her hair was wet."

"Someone's pulling your leg. My mother wouldn't be caught dead in sweats. And wet hair? No way." But her sister was with Mom. Yet they hadn't answered their phones.

"Sheriff Warnock can be a real card, but I think he was giving the straight 'poop' this time."

Roxanne's mouth fell open. Her mother would accuse her of catching flies. "The sheriff saw her? No lie?"

"No lie. You can phone her room."

Neither her room nor a person within it answered, so Roxanne left yet another message, this one a humiliating one with the receptionist at the B&B's front desk. Deputy Ponder had informed her she wouldn't be able to receive calls on her cell phone, so all return calls had to come through the sheriff's office.

"So if Peter doesn't press charges, will you let me go?"

"You broke the law. Plus, you're a person of interest in a murder. By the way, how *did* you get in?"

Before she remembered she wasn't supposed to admit anything or say anything without an attorney present, Roxanne blurted out the truth. "Through an open upstairs window." She swallowed. "So if the window was open, that's not against the law, right?"

"Wrong. Unless Peter told you to enter through that window."

"I think I'll be quiet from now on. Except I have to use the restroom before you lock me up. I could *never* use a bucket."

"Obviously not as rugged as your older sister."

Roxanne grinned, amazed that she could smile while under arrest. "No one's as tough as Feather. I'm surprised she didn't give birth in a tree." Her smile vanished. "How is Jared? Have you heard from Brad and Kristin?"

"Nope." Lacy frowned. "It doesn't look good, you disappearing after Teddy was killed."

"I ran because I thought I'd be killed, too."

"Uh huh. Still, you have a lot of questions to answer. Better take that bathroom visit. No telling when Byron will be back."

Twenty-Nine

Saving Sister

Feather dragged herself into her trailer, pulling her mocha-slathered clothes off on the way to the shower. The typical puny trickle turned cold in the first minute and then trailed off. Had the dratted landlord shut off the water?

She went to the kitchen sink, and discovered that there, at least, cold water poured forth. She shampooed her hair and sponged off her body. Three days and no more cold, crap showers. Possibly no showers at all, if she was forced to camp. Maybe Roadkill would let her visit. His outdoor shower was better than this one. Someday her B&B would have wonderful, powerful and energy efficient showers. Feather's Beds: A Place to Roost, was what she'd call it, a name she awoke with one morning after weeks of struggling for a clever name for her B&B.

That reminded her. No one would be roosting in Feather's inn if she couldn't get the money to the contractors by the end of the month. That was when the incredible deal Charlie West had cut her would disappear. Construction slowed to near nothing when the snow flew and next spring he was already booked to build a large hotel near Sandpoint.

Once clean, and changed into jeans, she fed the squirrels, adding some lettuce she'd harvested from the pots outside the trailer. She pulled some carrots from another pot, a turnip and a rutabaga from a third and some cabbage from the half wine barrel. She wondered if Roadkill and Ed would help her move, once she figured out her destination. Gina would keep her pots of vegetables for a while.

She scrubbed the veggies free of dirt. She'd make a stir fry, adding herbs from pots inside the window. Her stomach growled at the thought. She'd serve it over quinoa. Might as well eat as much as possible from her cupboards. Less to pack. The thought discouraged her. How to find a new home, one that would welcome the squirrels and a recuperating dog, pack her admittedly meager belongings and clear herself and her sister of suspicion of blackmail and murder? She could probably Google her problems and find several answers, maybe even the question of who was the murderer. After all, Google had all the answers.

She found a bottle of white wine in the cupboard over her table and poured a large glass over some ice cubes. She needed a break from today's drama. She noticed that a call had come in from an unknown number. She had voice messages waiting. She'd muted her cell phone while she met with Brad and forgotten, in the messy aftermath, to restore the sound.

"Later. I need this wine."

Feather hadn't taken more than three long, slow sips of the wine when someone pounded on the trailer door. Before she could go to the door, it opened, revealing Roadkill, looking grubbier than usual, standing on her tiny metal porch. "Come with me. We have to get her out of there."

Feather closed her eyes and put the glass against her forehead. Get who out of where? "Now what?" She struggled to find energy to speak.

"You're sitting there enjoying a nice glass of wine and your sister's probably hanging herself from her belt in the Hancock jail cell."

She jerked the glass down to the table, its contents sloshing over the side. "Oh for pity's sake. She hid with you. In Rosinante. I don't believe it."

"Let's go. The fuzz have her. I couldn't stop it."

"Oh, sit down and have a glass of wine. You're as dramatic as Roxanne. She won't hang herself, she's far too self-centered." She took another swig. "Besides, I need to know what's happened."

Roadkill shook his head. "You're awfully cavalier about your little sister's life. This is urgent." Still, he moved to the cupboard, grabbed a wine glass and filled it and then stood, looming over Feather. He sipped his wine and said, "This is hot. Gross."

"You know where the ice is. I lived through 16 years of Roxanne's theatrics. She'll wait, and she'll probably enjoy being the focus of the cops' attention. It's been a day for me, too."

Roadkill got some ice and resumed his stance above Feather. "She's been terrified since she found Teddy. Begged me to hide her. She feared for her life."

"When we were little, she feared for her life on the swing. Mom coddled her. But now she should be afraid. She's not answering Mom's calls."

He glared at her. "Not to mention that her boyfriend was murdered. Are you drunk?"

"Tipsy. Relaxed, maybe. Haven't eaten since ... oh, who knows? Okay, maybe this time Roxanne has good cause for her fear. But they can't have arrested her for murder. She simply could not have shot him. Maybe poison, but ..." She shuddered, remembering the crime scene, not quite so tipsy nor relaxed. And possibly not so ready to judge her sister a coward. If she saw Teddy's body ...."

"Not for murder. For ... breaking and entering. I feel like scum. She's terrified of being jailed."

"Doh. Who isn't? She'll survive while you explain. Besides, Mom will bail her out. Always does. If they don't keep her for the murder thing." The wine didn't taste as good to Feather.

"Then call Jeanette. Somebody's gotta save her."

She shot him a grin. "Clifford Mustard. Are you sweet on my sister?"

"Good Lord, no. But I feel sort of responsible."

"Was the break-in your idea?"

Roadkill explained their night's adventure, closing with his opinion that Roxanne had left the papers she copied inside Peter's office. "So if we go see her, and I raise a ruckus, maybe she'll be able to tell you where to look. Why the hell would Peter buy that land and turn around and deed it to some Canadian? And why recruit more investors than the damn wind farm needs?"

"Brad wouldn't tell me about the finances, just said they were having problems at the farm. If Peter's dug up even more investors, what's happened to the money? Time to be asking Peter Brewer a few questions," Feather said. She stood and stretched. "I had some phone calls. Maybe Roxanne called me." She listened to her messages, nodding at the sound of Roxanne's frightened, suddenly humble voice. She was clicking out of voice mail when another call came in. She answered it.

"Michael Bergmann here. Can you meet me at The Osprey's Nest for a drink? I'd like to catch you up on a few things."

"Not a good time. Why the sudden cooperation, Mr. Wile E. Coyote?"

Roadkill poured himself the last of the wine and gave her a puzzled stare. Then, his face cleared. "Is that my man Michael, eyes on the world?" he shouted.

"Your mother's staying here, too," Michael said.

"Believe it or not, I knew that."

"She's having dinner with an interesting character. Wonder if you would recognize him."

Feather wondered what her mother was up to, and wondered what Michael had to catch her up on. But she needed to see Roxanne, reassure her sister, and find out what she knew. Michael didn't realize that her mother would eat dinner with almost anyone.

"Not a good time now. Take a picture. I'm sure your resources can identify him." She paused, giving him time to tell her he'd lost the money and the trail of the blackmailer. "I could meet you for breakfast there. Your treat."

"I'm hanging out in the Aerie, the Osprey's cutesy name for their bar, in case you decide to help." He paused and sighed audibly. "I need your help, Feather. The clock's ticking and I don't know what will happen next. Things haven't been going my way, and I don't see them changing." He hung up.

Feather closed her phone, thinking that might be the closest to an apology she'd ever get from Michael. She wondered if his concerns were valid. "I was hoping for an early night. Now the offers keep rolling in."

Roadkill cocked a brow in query.

"If I tell you that Michael got tired of tailing me and now has his eye on my mother, you wouldn't believe me. He wants my help." Who was Mom with? Could she take care of herself or was Feather just kidding herself?

"Jesus, the guy's an idiot if he thinks your mother is a blackmailer. I'll go with you after we see Roxanne."

"And he wasn't when he believed I was?" She finished her wine in a quick gulp. "I'll handle Michael. Let's go see Roxanne. Shall I dress for B&E?"

"Not funny."

She grabbed a dark sweater for the autumn chill and a couple of carrots that would have tasted a lot better stir-fried for her empty stomach. A fine dinner.

Feather and Roadkill paused at the bottom of the steps leading to the sheriff's office. He threw an arm around her. "Buck up. This is just like old times."

She looked to the heavens, although she knew his attention was focused on the office door and the disturbance he planned. "Those *were* old times. We were younger. Wait. I was younger. You haven't grown up yet."

"Don't plan to. You grow up, you die."

"Some of us died young for our beliefs." Feather recalled their fellow activist who'd fallen from a tree during an action, another who'd died from a reaction to tear gas. Roadkill's expressive face stilled and darkened and Feather knew his thoughts followed hers. She immediately regretted her dampening words. "But you will live forever, my friend. Now go do your thing. It might even work."

He chuckled. "Problem is, Byron knows me too well. Lacy, not so much, but ooh, do I wish she knew me better."

"Maybe we should have brought a lawyer."

Roadkill hooked his arm in hers and they marched together up the stairs. "We know more about rights than old man Belchin' ever dreamed of."

He was probably right, but Feather refused to agree with him in his disparagement of Melvin Belkin, the town's only practicing attorney. Melvin had a good heart. Still she marched up the stairs beside her leather-clad friend.

When they entered the office, Lacy Ponder looked up from where she sat alone at her desk. She smiled broadly at both of them. "My prayers have been answered. And possibly those of someone else. What can I do for you two?"

"I want to see my sister," Feather said.

At the same moment, Roadkill bellowed, "Set my people free."

He strutted behind the counter to Lacy's desk. "Woman, it pains me to see you, a woman of beauty and discernment, here amongst the jack-booted enforcers of the rule of law."

The deputy smiled. "What's wrong with the rule of law?"

"It caused you to lock up that poor, innocent creature, the younger sister of my dear friend, Feather."

"Yeah. And the rule of law will cause me to let her out after she explains her activities this evening."

"I need to see her," Feather said, surprised at how easily the throatiness of tears came into her voice. "I insist."

"Okay." Lacy stood. "Just as soon as the sheriff says so."

Roadkill crossed his arms. "And when might that come to pass? Christmas is coming, too."

"Sooner than that."

Feather joined Roadkill. "What's going on? Roxanne called me and begged me to come, but she didn't say why. If it's about what happened in Spokane, I'm sure she'll cooperate."

"You know nothing of the kind," Roadkill said. "She has no reason to cooperate with the machine. They could be trying to force her to confess."

"Confess? You idiot. We're talking about murder. My sister is *not* a killer."

Ponder, who'd been looking back and forth between the two former activists as if at a tennis match, moved between them. "Look, you two. I caught your sweet little sister trying to escape from some offices here in Hancock, where she had broken in."

Feather tried to appear shocked. "She must have had a good reason. My sister is not a crook. She's under stress, of course, with her boyfriend being killed this week. Maybe she's cracking. Maybe she needs medical care." Feather rather liked that touch. "I must talk to her. I can probably find out what she was up to. I promise I'll tell you."

Without warning, Roadkill burst into song. "Let my people go." He couldn't remember any of the other words in the song so he sang the phrase again. "Let my people go." He made an attempt to sound like Louis Armstrong. The attempt failed.

Lacy moved closer to Roadkill and raised her hand to silence him. "Please. Be. Quiet. Or I'll arrest you for disturbing my peace."

"Police brutality. I can see it now. Headlines, video."

"For heaven's sake, you two, I give up. You can see your sister, Feather. For just a few minutes." She pointed through a door where a hallway led to the cell.

Roadkill hooked his arm through the deputy's. "I would so dearly love to disturb your peace, Ms. Ponder."

She snorted a laugh. "Deputy Ponder to you. I'm on duty."

"Regardless. Let me buy you a cup of coffee." He led her down the hall to the kitchen.

Feather went to the room that held the two cells and found her sister, standing at the bars, alert and smiling. "Thank God. I heard you two out there. You're both safe. I have to get out of here. Now."

Feather grabbed hold of her sister's hands that clutched the cell bars. "Ain't gonna happen tonight, little one. You play the game, sometimes you pay the price. I can bet they'll keep you at least until the cops from Spokane can come and have a chat. They might even take you to Spokane. No fun, that." She lowered her voice. "Quick. Roadkill told me you hid something in Peter's office. Tell me, fast."

Roxanne leaned forward. "Bookcase. Behind somebody's mythology. Big book." She began to cry, little hiccups turning to sobs. "You need to get me a lawyer. Spring me. I was—we were"— she added sotto voce—"trying to help, trying to find his killer. Some logic in all this horror. You have to believe me, I didn't kill Teddy. I loved him. Well, I thought I loved him."

You thought you loved him? "Did Teddy spend time with Peter? Did he know anything about Peter's investments? His other work?"

"Teddy was a great listener. He dug up dirt on everyone."

Feather smiled. "Not me."

Roxanne shot her a grim smile. "Don't be so sure, sister o' mine."

Feather's shoulders slumped. What could her sister have blabbed to Teddy about her? Didn't matter. He'd never have tried to blackmail someone as poor as Feather. Then she wondered what he'd threatened her mother with. Something humiliating about one of her daughters, rather than about herself? "I'll do my best to get you out of here, but ... breaking and entering? And you thought tree-sits were trouble?"

"I couldn't just hide with Roadkill and do nothing. You need to get those papers and figure out who killed Teddy. What have you found out so far?"

"Not a lot, but I'm working on it. I'll retrieve the papers you hid, and see what Peter has to say. You holding up okay in here?"

Roxanne sighed. "So far, so good. It's dirty and it smells funny but I can stand it. Myrna's carrot cake is to die for." Her hand flew to her mouth at the poor choice of words. "Oops."

Feather smiled at her sister. "I know. But it tastes even better on this side of the bars. Once you get out, we'll talk more."

Thirty
The Problem Is Relative

Feather left Roadkill to flirt with the deputy sheriff. An odd couple, to be sure.

She and Roadkill had driven to town in Rosinante, leaving her without a ride home. It wouldn't be the first time she'd walked. But her first stop was The Osprey's Nest. She hoped Michael was wrong and that her mother was with a perfectly harmless friend. And maybe he'd offer her a ride.

She heard the Aerie's canned music from down the street and wondered if the noise from the bar, especially on live music nights, disturbed their paying, slumbering, guests.

Wouldn't affect their business, since the only competition for lodging in town was the Untidy Scot. Those who had reason to stay overnight and didn't want to drive forty-five minutes to a larger town, chose The Osprey's Nest. If they could afford it. "Wait until Feather's Beds opens. You'll lose customers faster than gray hair disappears in a beauty salon."

Michael's small pickup was bedded down in a row of larger vehicles. Feather walked past it to the entrance, glancing inside to see if Michael was slumped down in the seat, hiding himself in a stakeout. The truck was empty. He'd said he'd be in the bar, so she headed there.

Would her mother be there, having a drink, as Michael reported, with a man? How could she be flirting with some stranger, when her daughters were under suspicion for blackmail and murder? She sighed. Her mother was totally capable of that. If a good-looking man, make that a barely passable humanoid with a penis, expressed interest in Jeanette Sullivan, she'd respond, sharing more information about her family, her issues with her daughters, than the poor man desired or deserved.

She squared her shoulders. Feather's mother had been on both girls about their posture since they were toddlers. No matter the perceived flaw, good posture would make it go away, in Jeanette Sullivan's philosophy. Feather's crooked nose? "People will think you a queen if you walk like one." Roxanne's thin hair? "A good haircut and great posture can solve any problem."

After Feather's disastrous day, good posture, sprinkled with a smidge of will power, was all she had left to carry her forward.

Michael sat in the bar. Feather slid into the booth opposite him. He jerked back at her unexpected arrival and then smiled. "Roadkill couldn't deliver?"

"None of your business. He sends his disregard, by the way."

"That's unexpected. He is usually the picture of graciousness."

"Speaking of which ...."

He signaled the waitress. "What would you like?"

Feather remembered her budget. "Who's paying?"

"I see you've been taking lessons from Clifford Mustard. It's on me, officially on your friend Brad."

"He's not my friend." She reflected on the scene at the coffee house. "He's a wimp."

Michael raised his eyebrows, but did not comment.

"Iron Goat Goatmeal Stout. And steak fries." After her beer arrived, she asked, "How did you recognize my mother?"

"First thing I do on an assignment is research all the related characters."

"You're calling my mother a character?" Feather chuckled. "Too true."

"The man she's with didn't show up in my research. Not a big deal. He could be a lingerie buyer."

"But?"

"Don't get me wrong. Your mother is a very attractive woman, it runs in the genes." Feather blushed and stared at her beer. "However," Michael continued, "when there's a murder, blackmail, and something not-quite-kosher at the wind farm, I am suspicious of anyone walking into your mother's life."

"Walking into her life? A drink? Maybe dinner together, for two people alone at an inn? I'm seeing a little paranoia."

Michael smiled. "You are no doubt correct. I'm probably over-reacting. I'd like you to take a look at the guy, see if you recognize him. They're in the dining room next door. They have to come out through here, so you will see them."

"Which means she'll see me, with you. I need to talk to her anyway. This works. Although she knows lots of people she'd never introduce to me, the bad seed child."

"You've got a better chance than I do. It's probably just an old friend, or even a new one." "Again I hear a but."

Michael looked puzzled, doubtful. Feather hadn't known him more than a few hours, but somehow she knew those expressions weren't frequent visitors to his admittedly attractive face. "I don't know. You're right that I am way too suspicious. Comes with the territory."

Feather's steak fries arrived and she concentrated on her food for a few moments. "Speaking of territory, we need to talk after I put eyes on this man. You lost me today, and then you lost Brad's money."

Michael took a drink of his ale and snatched one of Feather's fries. "Delicacy is not your middle name, woman."

She slapped his hand. "Neither is generosity."

"He who hesitates loses the fry."

"Apparently even he who doesn't hesitate loses the drop."

"Okay, okay. I was wrong. I should have let you help me. We didn't have enough people on this one. The blackmailer had some smarts."

Woo hoo. She got a real apology. Feather couldn't resist pouring on a little salt. "It would seem prudent to count on that and then be grateful if they become an easy target."

"Enough. We lost him or her. I didn't want you involved. You're not trained and these things can get dangerous."

"Uh huh. So what's next?"

"The money can be traced, but most criminals know that. For now, I need to look into each of the partners and their backgrounds. Someone took over from Teddy. You say it couldn't have been your sister, but she's high on the list. Her disappearing right after Teddy's murder says something to me."

Right, Feather realized. Michael didn't know about Roxanne's arrest. He didn't know where she'd been hiding. Why hadn't she asked Roadkill about Roxanne's and his whereabouts at the time of this last blackmail drop? She needed to decide, trust Michael and tell him all or shut him out, discover the answers on her own. Neither of them had much success on their own so far. She sighed. "You're wrong. She's trying to find out who killed him. Got arrested trying."

Michael's lips twitched. "She's surfaced, then. Care to share?"

"She allegedly broke into Peter Brewer's office earlier this evening. She's convinced he knows more about the blackmail and Teddy's murder."

"I'm sure the cops checked everyone's whereabouts at the time of Teddy's death."

"I believe she was looking for information, not a murder weapon. Peter was one of the windfarm's first investors and he was friends with Teddy."

"Have you seen her yet? Did she find anything worth getting arrested for?"

For some reason, Feather didn't want to share what Roxanne had found with Michael. Maybe she wanted to see for herself if the papers had any value, maybe she simply wanted to solve the whole thing on her own. *Sheez, Feather, share or don't share. Doling out tiny parcels of information?* Oh, wait. Isn't that exactly what Michael had been doing?

"I saw her and she's not pleased to be in jail. However, the Hancock jail is not exactly Alcatraz. She's enjoying the sheriff's wife's carrot cake."

"Do you know where she's been hiding out?"

She smiled. "Yes, I do."

"But if you tell me you'll have to kill me?"

Her smile broadened. "Let me think on it." She twisted around so she could peer into the dining room, beyond a row of booths. "Shall we move into the dining room and casually encounter my mother enjoying the company of some stranger?"

Michael smiled. "This is the only way out, unless they want to set off the fire alarm. I think we'll just wait 'em out. Once your mother sees you, she can stop and introduce us. I don't think it will matter if we meet the guy." He shrugged. "Of course, he might have to kill us."

Feather shuddered. "Don't kid around. And don't be certain Mom will introduce us. She has secrets from me, lots of them."

"Ah, families."

"Roxanne swears when she got to Teddy's house, he was already dead. She saw someone leaving and was afraid, so she ran. Roadkill told me she thought for a bit that *I* might have killed Teddy."

At Feather's inadvertent mention of Roadkill, Michael revealed a smug smile, but didn't comment on her slip. "Poor Feather. Kristin thinks you're a blackmailer, your sister's afraid you're a killer."

She gave him a level stare. "She knows I'm not a killer. Just as Kristin should know I'm not a blackmailer."

"And Roxanne suspected Peter Brewer because?"

"Peter handled a lot of the partnership's funds, and he did suggest most of the partners join. Besides, knowing Roxanne, she suspected him because he dresses badly." She paused. "But if she found anything, she didn't share with me."

He laughed. "So Roxanne is a fashionista. Not what I'd expect. Tell me more about your family. Looks like we'll be here awhile, waiting for the new friends to dine."

"Then you can feed me more while we wait."

Jeanette awoke in the early evening from the nap she'd taken after a long shower, where she scrubbed at least one layer of skin from her body. She vowed to return to the wind farm and she vowed to refuse to muck out the hogs. Ever. Again. Haley could find someone else or the hogs could live happily ever after in their slops, for all she cared.

She dressed carefully, hoping to overcome the shame she felt when she dragged past the Osprey's owners and up the stairs to her room. She should have invited Feather to join her for dinner. She hated to eat alone in a restaurant, but she'd be darned if she'd hide in her room. She wasn't even sure the B&B provided room service.

She marched downstairs in linen slacks—take that, goat, I have another pair!—and a brilliant turquoise print top with flattering, flowing sleeves, simple turquoise stud earrings and a few cheap bangles at her wrist. She gave her hostess a gracious smile and received one in return. No dummy her. You don't laugh at your guests' embarrassing moments or the guests don't return. Jeanette's pants were a size 10, her waist still narrow. Hard work for a woman in her late fifties but worth it. She decided a drink was in order and headed for the bar. She chose a table not far from the bar itself where she could observe the other customers but not feel too alone and conspicuous, two comfortable chairs, what Feather referred to as a "two-top."

Generally Jeanette stuck to wine, but tonight she ordered a Manhattan after her pig poop brown letter day.

She sipped her drink, resisting the urge to swig it down like a college freshman. She was a lady. She stifled a giggle. A lady who'd been slopping out hog muck hours earlier. She allowed herself a big swallow, then another. She'd earned it.

She felt awkward alone, but didn't want to pick up her menu and order right away. She needed time to wind down and figure out her next moves at the wind farm. Clearly Haley disliked her, but that might not have been the only reason she banished her to the barn. And Jon? What was he hiding in those outbuildings that caused the normally affable man to flare up at her? Why did they have old cars stored on a wind farm?

Her eyes scanned the room. Not much of a crowd, but this was Hancock, where crowds never occurred unless someone staged them, like the anti-wind energy activists or like the previous year when Darlene Belmont and her ridiculous friends marched against Gina. And Feather, of course. Feather and her adorable little boy, the baby she insisted on giving up for adoption. Jeanette would have helped her with him. They could have moved into her home in Sandpoint. But no, as usual, stubborn Feather made up her own mind.

And wasn't that how you raised your daughters? To be independent women?

She shook her head and concentrated on the menu. Thinking about Feather and the missing Roxanne gave her a headache. Although maybe it was the alcohol, or the lack of food today. She couldn't recall having any lunch, or any appetite for lunch.

She felt the intensity of a gaze on her and looked around the room. There. A slender man, a few years—okay, a decade or so—younger than Jeanette, smiled when her gaze rested on him. He raised his glass to her and stood. His brows wrinkled in a query, obviously asking if he minded if he joined her. She smiled her acceptance. An acceptable piece of arm candy, a distraction for the evening.

She liked the way he walked toward her, confident, alert, and watchful. His eyes scanned the room and she wondered for a moment if he was a cop, but discarded the notion. Nothing about him said law enforcement, and nothing about him said "too much." His haircut was tidy, longish but no ridiculous ponytail, his face looked freshly shaven, as if he'd taken time to freshen up before coming to eat. His khaki slacks fit well and his long-sleeved cotton shirt was crisp. He had a sweater tossed over his shoulder. He walked like a panther, silent, almost over-confident. And like a panther, he might have been looking for prey. Jeanette shivered and dismissed the fanciful thought.

He stood across the table from her and smiled. "Am I presuming far too much, or did you agree that I might join you?"

Jeanette nodded and smiled back. "Please."

He glanced at the neighboring tables and pulled a chair around so his back was to the wall and he faced the room. He seated himself. She liked his accent—British? Scottish? Australian?—She wasn't sure. She also liked that he had not brought anything but the cocktail glass that he still held, not presuming she would assent to his joining her.

He nodded his thanks to the server who had brought his menu and a place setting to him and poured a fresh glass of water. Then he turned to Jeanette. "I *am* presuming, but I find myself eating alone far too often. It is more pleasant to have company, when the company is good."

"That sounds almost like a quote."

He tilted his head back. "If so, I don't know the source, but I assure you it isn't a line."

She smiled. "If it is, it's an excellent one."

"Are you planning to eat dinner? Have you ordered?"

"Yes, and no. I'm relaxing from a long day before I think about eating."

He raised an eyebrow in query but Jeanette said nothing.

"Permit me to introduce myself: Chaz Stedman."

"Jeanette Sullivan." Jeanette did not offer her hand, merely nodded. They both sipped their drinks.

As they finished their first drinks—or at least Jeanette's first—they chatted about the town of Hancock and its surrounding beauty. Over the second, Jeanette learned that Chaz was from Canada, but had moved there from England. She revealed that she was visiting from Sandpoint, much closer than Vancouver. She bragged a bit about her two daughters, one a volleyball star in high school, the other a beauty queen and sometime model.

Over her third Manhattan, Jeanette told a sympathetic Chaz about her day. "Would you believe I spent my day shoveling hog shit?" she said, realizing that her enunciation had deteriorated. She knew that her judgment had not. She never lost that.

"Not something I can easily imagine."

"Nor I." She thought for a minute about what to divulge to this stranger. "I needed to get closer to a business of mine, find out a few things, and that seemed the best way at the time." She laughed easily and Chaz joined her.

"And did you find what you needed?"

"Far more than I expected. The place is in deep shit." She kept her expression serious.

"Really?"

"And so was I." She laughed again and shook her head. "I found out far more than I ever wanted to know about the art of shoveling hog manure, but nothing else." And if she had, why tell this man?

She picked up her menu. "Time for Jeanette to eat."

Chaz picked up his menu as well. After their server took their orders, Chaz asked for a bottle of Pend d'Oreille Cabernet Franc. Jeanette confessed it was a favorite of hers. She giggled. *Giggling, at my age?* "I hope you're not trying to get me drunk."

"Not at all. Whenever I visit Idaho, I like to have something from Pend d'Oreille Winery."

"So you visit often?" Time for her to do a little prying into the affairs of this man who had probed her life earlier.

"Not often enough, if there are many women like you."

She pouted. "I like to think of myself as unique."

"But of course. How tactless of me. I only meant it as a compliment."

She smiled prettily at him and pursued her question. "You said you have business here? Hard to imagine in Hancock, Idaho."

"And yet here we both are." He sipped his wine. He ate more quickly than Jeanette. And yet he didn't look like a hog. *No. Never will I use that metaphor again.* "Would you care for dessert? Cognac?"

Urbane and mysterious. And more interested in hearing about Jeanette than in talking about himself. Rare in a man. Yet she didn't know enough about him to trust him. She reflected that maybe the reason men spilled so much about themselves on a first encounter was to establish trust with a woman, the weaker sex. And wondered how much of what she'd heard from past dates had been lies, meant only to establish trustworthiness. Not reassuring. If that were true, then Chaz's reticence wasn't as suspect as she'd first thought.

She gazed at him, hoping her assessing look held for him only polite interest. Over his shoulder, across a booth that made up the dividing line to the bar, she saw her oldest daughter and a strange man. Not that strange, except that his normality made his appearance with Feather strange. His hair was not in dreads and was cut in a conventional style, his face was clear of brush and looked clean. When he smiled, he appeared to have all his teeth. In fact, he resembled Brad, Jared's father, the one Feather let slip away, back to his boring wife.

After an instant assessment, she drifted sideways enough to be out of her daughter's line of sight. She wasn't ready to make introductions. Intuition told her not to introduce Feather to Chaz, not to let this man know that someone she cherished sat no more than 20 feet away. Why? The man had been nothing but charming, if perhaps too discreet about his presence in Hancock.

She realized Chaz was waiting for an answer. "Dessert? I think not, and no more alcohol. My goodness, I could be tipsy." She smiled prettily. "I think it's time for me to toddle on up to bed." *Toddle? Really, Jeanette, maybe you are tipsy.* "Could you ask our server for our checks?"

"I'm taking care of that. No argument." He rose and extracted a number of bills from his wallet, which he deposited on the table. "Let me walk you to your room."

Again, a frisson of danger ran up Jeanette's neck. Did she want this man to know which room was hers? Then she gave a mental shrug. In Hancock, no one at the desk would hesitate to tell him or anyone else which room was hers. He might as well walk her up.

The only exit would take them directly past Feather's table, but Jeanette was determined not to talk to her daughter, not to let this curious Canadian find out her daughter was here. She stood and took his arm, looking up into his sable brown eyes, eyes she noted had enviably long lashes, and said, "I'd like that."

She found it harder to ignore her daughter than to slop hogs. As soon as they'd stood, Feather focused on them, but Jeanette kept her eyes on Chaz, only noticing Feather in her peripheral vision. She put on a starry-eyed expression and moved past their table, resisting the compulsion to stare at Feather's companion. And who knew, that she, Jeanette Sullivan the controlled, would experience that electrical connection with her daughter, one that threatened to drag her into the booth beside her beautiful offspring. Her grip on Chaz's arm tightened and he gave her a quizzical look in return for what she'd hoped was her passionate gaze.

She patted his arm. "I feel a bit dizzy. Too much of that lovely wine." She was simpering the inane words just as she passed Feather's table. Impossible that her daughter hadn't heard. What would she think? That her mother had lost her sanity or be in awe of her mother's speed in finding a man? Matched only by her daughter's speed in snaring the hottie at her table.

They made it past Feather's table without an incident, although she imagined she could feel her daughter's outraged glare on her back.

At her door, Chaz held out his hand for her key. Maybe her suspicions were wrong; the man appeared to be a true gentleman. Still, she wouldn't invite him into her room. If he were a gentleman, he wouldn't expect it, and if he weren't it was an even better decision.

She gave him the key and held out her hand for it after the door was unlocked. "I've had a lovely evening. So much more enjoyable than I'd imagined when I went downstairs. All thanks to you."

"My thoughts exactly. And the gratitude is all mine, Jeanette, my dear. You are a delightful surprise, and my evening was definitely better than I had hoped." He leaned in and pecked her cheek, a chaste, gentlemanly kiss. She noticed his scent—an enticing mix of cedar and possibly basil—distinctive and masculine, like Chaz. She chastised herself for being the least bit disappointed at his lack of passion. It was exactly what she wanted.

She closed the door behind him, hugging herself. As she removed her makeup and changed into her silk pajamas, she put the evening behind her and worked on her best approach tomorrow at Windfall Works. How could she find out what Jon was hiding without exposing herself to his scrutiny, really his paranoia that she'd ventured on forbidden ground? Her mind crept back, traitorously, to her delicious dinner, to Chaz and his fascinating accent and enigmatic background and she chuckled at the impression she'd probably made on her daughter. Not that one evening made much difference. Feather had long ago placed her mother on the shelf of ridiculously expensive and worthless trinkets that no activist in her right mind would hold dear. Enjoying a meal with a younger man fit Feather's stereotype of her mother, one that neither of them had tried to dispel.

She wondered if there were any way to close the chasm between her and her oldest daughter. She could loan her the money for the ridiculous B&B, but money wouldn't soothe Charlene's pain about her father's frequent, extended absences from their home and his unexpected and far-too-early death. Perhaps the truth would clear Jeanette, but she doubted the pain would be worth it to Feather to learn the truth.

She picked up a pill bottle. Her doctor had prescribed a mild sleeping pill and she wondered if she should take it after the cocktail and wine she'd consumed. She put it back. She'd probably wake up at two or three, unable to quiet her mind, but it seemed safer.

Feather wanted to trip her mother, wanted to see her fall flat on her over-made-up, snooty face. She knew Jeanette had seen her and was avoiding her. You'd think at the least she'd be interested in the eligible man her daughter was with. She gritted her teeth. Sure, she'd told Michael her mother might ignore her, but she hadn't really expected it. Triple darn.

"You were right. She ignored you." Michael reached out and touched her arm. "But you don't know why. Maybe she didn't see you, or maybe she didn't want to intrude. After all, you're with a pretty cool dude."

Her lip twitched. "Dude? Seriously?"

He put on a mock pout. "You better believe it. I'm surprised your mother didn't put a move on me. Happens all the time."

That earned him a full-on smile. "Okay, I'm restored to my normal self. You do have a great sense of humor." She paused a beat. "Unless you weren't kidding, and if that's so, you have some serious issues, *dude*."

"You'll never know." He got back to business. "Did you know the man?"

"Never saw him before in my life. Of course, Mom doesn't parade her cougar kills in front of us. But still ...."

"It looked like lust at first sight to me."

Feather wrinkled her nose. "She was hanging all over him. Which, come to think of it, is not Mom's chosen style. Do you think he drugged her wine?" Visions of her mother being the victim of date rape flashed into Feather's mind. "We need to find her, find out who he is, stop them." She slid out of the booth, bashing her knee on the table edge as she rose. "Ow. Ow, ow, triple ow." She rubbed her knee and danced around.

"Is that some kind of tribal dance to prevent ... let's call it intimacy?"

Feather stopped jumping. "With you?"

"That works. But I meant your mother and the handsome stranger." He slid gracefully from the booth, neither bashing his knee nor jiggling the table's contents. Pig.

"No. We need to find out her room number and his name and, and stop them."

"Your mother *is* a consenting adult. Nearing senior citizen status, but you didn't hear it from these lips." He put an arm out but Feather batted it away.

She limped toward the lobby. Over her shoulder she called to him, "Coming with?"

He caught up with no effort, given that Feather was limping and slower than a constipated porcupine.

"Watch my back. I don't want that fellow hearing me pry into his business."

"Thought you were convinced he was in your mother's room, taking dastardly advantage of her."

"Just in case, partner, just in case."

Feather recognized the woman at the desk, but couldn't recall her name. A glance at her name badge reminded her. "Marsha. It's been forever. How are you?"

The woman smiled. "Charlene Sullivan. You having some kind of family reunion?" Then her expression changed. "I'm so sorry. I heard about Teddy Fitzpatrick. He and Roxanne were dating, right?"

Feather nodded. "Yes. It's been a tough time. I gather you saw Mom? I'm supposed to meet her but I got held up."

Marsha looked over her shoulder at Michael. "He can hold me up anytime. You want me to phone your mother's room?"

Feather gave her a pleading look. "Could you just give me the room number? I want to surprise her. She's got a new friend and I want to see him before she shuffles him back to his room. You know, slim, good-looking guy in his forties?"

Marsha's eyes widened. "The Canadian with the killer accent and the steely eyes? He's with your *mother*?" Marsha blushed at her gaffe. "I mean, Mr. Stedman definitely has a different room, so you don't have to worry."

"No worries. Mom's an adult. But she's been keeping him a secret from me. I don't even know his first name."

"It's Chaz. So terribly British. Your mom's in Room Eleven." She jerked her head toward the back stairwell.

Feather pivoted to head toward the stairs. Her recently bashed knee gave out and she fell sideways. Michael was there, grabbing her side, holding her up, smiling. "You okay?"

"Perfectly. Let's go." She pulled herself erect again and limped stairward, wishing they had an elevator, regretting that so-not-green thought immediately.

The Osprey's Nest was not a grandiose hotel, not even a large motel. It was a Bed and Breakfast attached to a bar and restaurant. The building was old, remodeled with grace and art, with much of the original building retained. The upstairs hall floor was broad pine planks, refinished with a pale wash. A runner down the center preserved the wood and made walking quieter. Feather's exhaustion, however, blurred her vision and the floral pattern in the carpet seemed to move in and out, in and out. She wanted to lie down on it or escape its oscillations. Possibly lose the steak fries on it, along with the spinach salad she'd had for dinner.

The corridor seemed as long as those in a big city hotel, the kind you wander in for days before discovering the elevator is really around the corner from your room, if you had turned right instead of left out the door.

She forced her gaze to the doors to each room. Each was adorned with an image of a bird, and, Feather knew from an earlier visit, each room's décor continued with the bird from the door. One might have imagined that the birds would be native to North Idaho, but the owners hadn't restricted themselves. The closest door featured a carrier pigeon, the next, a pelican. She reflected that Idaho had two species of pelicans, which probably surprised visitors from the coast. She passed the ubiquitous Mountain Quail, a Mountain Bluebird and a Great Blue Heron in the long corridor leading to her mother's door. "She should be in the Loon Room," Feather whispered to Michael. "It would fit."

When they reached the door, Feather stifled a giggle. A Peacock in full display. "Someone at the desk knows Mom," she whispered again. "This is better than a Loon."

She realized she'd dashed upstairs before they had agreed on a plan. She backpedaled to stand in front of the Mountain Bluebird room. "Shall we just barge in? Knock? Mom won't like being warned about a gigolo, especially since we have no idea if he *is* a gigolo." She paused. "Maybe we should listen at the door, see if we hear signs of struggle."

"Unless he's killing her, I'm not sure we can tell the difference between cries of ecstasy and cries of fear or pain through the door."

A voice came from inside the Bluebird room. "Believe me, you can hear *everything* through these doors. And walls. And if I hear you again, I'll call the desk."

"Oops." Michael moved toward the Peacock Room.

Feather stretched to get close to his ear. "We still don't have a plan."

He grinned at her. "Blow in my ear and I'll follow you anywhere?"

She walloped him.

"Plans always need to be adjusted. Let's wing it."

Apparently he was getting his ideas from the avian motif. They flapped their wings back to number 11 and Feather laid her ear against the supposedly cardboard door. It seemed sturdy enough to her. She heard nothing.

She knocked gently on the door. Again, no response, no sounds. Had her mother gone to his room? She regretted not obtaining that information from Marsha, but it might have been too much even for an old high school buddy, well, acquaintance.

She knocked harder and called out. "Mom. Jeanette. It's me, Fea—Charlene." She glanced over at Michael, who wasn't working at hiding his smirk. "Nothing's wrong with Charlene," she growled.

He widened his eyes. "I could try my lock picks."

She stepped away from him. "Seriously? You have lock picks?" *How cool is that?*

"Nah. Just trying to impress you with my tools."

"Your non-existent tools." She knocked louder and repeatedly until someone across the hall yelled, "Pipe down," and added after a pause, "Please."

Feather and Michael exchanged a smile. "Only in Idaho."

Finally the door opened to reveal a sleepy, crumpled Jeanette, in silk pajamas with a sleeping mask dangling from her neck. The mask, of course, matched the deep purple pjs.

"Char—Feather? What's happened? Why are you here?" Then she stepped back and opened the door wide, crossing her arms. "You're checking up on me. Invading my privacy."

Feather entered the room, dragging Michael with her. No way would she take on Dragon-Mom alone. She took in the bed at a glance, covers pulled back but obviously only one person had been beneath the sheets. "We were worried when you whooshed past us in the restaurant without even a nod. Who was that man?"

Jeanette's lips formed a straight, angry line. "Do you have news for me about Roxanne or who killed Teddy or who's been blackmailing innocent people?"

Feather wouldn't let her mother cow her. "Are you alone?"

"No. He's hiding in the bathroom. It's a kinky sex game I enjoy."

Feather heard a soft snort from Michael but refused to look away from her mother. "You seemed intoxicated when you strolled past us. I worried that you didn't know the guy. And the way things are happening ...."

Her mother sighed. "I am alone. I am not drunk, although I did have a few cocktails and some wine. Idaho wine, if you care. Which is why I didn't take a sleeping pill. A pity, since I might have slept through your incessant pounding. I am not an idiot and would not invite a total stranger into my bed, even if he was attractive and had a British accent." She let out another long-suffering sigh. "Speaking of keeping company with strangers, who, might I ask, is this man?

Did you never consider I might have walked by your table in an attempt to honor *your* privacy?"

Ah, the attack defense. One of Mom's favorites. "That would definitely be a first." She took Michael's hand and drew him close to her mother. "Jeanette Sullivan, meet Michael Bergmann, PI. Hired by dear old Kristin to get the goods on your daughter."

Jeanette stepped back. "I should have known. He's far too civilized to be romantically interested in you." To Michael, she said, "What have you found about Roxanne?"

Neither Michael's tone nor his voice displayed any emotion. Yet Feather detected annoyance. "Actually, Ms. Sullivan, I started out investigating Feather."

Jeanette laughed. "You're kidding, of course. The only time Feather would break the law would be to save a tree or some animal or plant no one cares about."

"I'd call that admirable." Again, his tone was mild, yet Jeanette stepped back until her knees hit the bed. She sat. "Do you know anything about the man you ate with?" Michael continued.

Jeanette looked uncomfortable and Feather wondered why. What was she hiding? "His name is Chaz Stedman, I didn't ask for the correct spelling. He's from Canada. In Hancock on business. I'll admit he was a bit enigmatic about what his business was. I assumed it was boring."

Michael had pulled out his little notebook. "Probably. What town in Canada? Do you know how long he's been in Hancock?"

"For heaven's sake, it was merely a way for two lonely people to have company for dinner. Unlike you, I don't give people I've just met the third degree." Her face reddened and she fanned herself. "I need to go to the powder room. Then I would like some answers from the two of you." She stalked into the bathroom.

Michael looked at Feather. "Powder room?"

She smiled. "Hot flashes. She probably drank red wine with dinner."

They wandered around the room, both, presumably, looking for evidence that Chaz Stedman had been inside. Feather saw nothing. When she heard the toilet flush, she walked to the bathroom door.

"My turn," she told her mother when Jeanette came out.

"Make it fast. I need to catch some sleep before I head back to the wind farm tomorrow."

Feather returned, having found no evidence of another occupant or visitor in the bathroom. Jeanette was perched on the chair by the room's delicate desk and Michael leaned against the door. As far as Feather could tell, they had not spoken.

"I don't think you should go back to Windfall Works tomorrow, Mom. Things seem to be heating up. Plus, you'll probably want to visit Roxanne in jail."

Jeanette shot out of her chair. "Jail? Roxanne? Whyever for? Why didn't you tell me sooner? I must go to her." She ran to the closet.

"Chill, Mom." Feather moved to stand in front of the closet. "No one's going to let you see her tonight. And come to think of it, she may be tied up tomorrow. Seems she's a material witness to a murder."

Jeanette returned to her chair. "Oh, good grief. Now both my daughters are persons of interest."

"And both of them are innocent."

Michael cleared his throat. "At least one of them is."

Feather glared at him. He could have kept his opinion to himself.

Jeanette stood. "Leave now. Both of you. Since I doubt Feather is witless enough to hang out with someone who suspects her, you must suspect Roxanne of killing poor Teddy. That is ridiculous, purely ridiculous. Roxanne does not get into trouble."

Feather smiled. "Funny thing. She's in jail for breaking into Peter Brewer's office." Feather bit her lip. Dang. She hadn't intended to drop that one on her mother, but despite the fact that she was thirty years old, it still irked her that their mother thought of Roxanne as the good little girl and Feather as the wild one. The pleasure she felt at the look of worry on her mother's face was diluted by guilt. "She's fine. Eating meals cooked by the mayor, Myrna Warnock."

"I still intend to investigate the wind farm premises. Unless this so-called private investigator has been able to capture the blackmailer, I'm due for one of those beastly texts. And I have no intention of paying."

Feather glanced at Michael. *Now, that was interesting.* "Why not?"

"Because despite the temporary embarrassment it might cause, our family can weather it far better than I can weather the loss of $10,000. The nerve of that Teddy. I have the tiniest bit of sympathy for whoever killed him."

Feather sat on the bed, staggered. "Don't forget Michael isn't necessarily on our side. We're working together temporarily." *In other words, no need to share everything with him.*

Michael put on an innocent face. "Feather's understandably worried, Ms. Sullivan. But I like to think we're all in this together. What you tell me can only help us solve our mutual problem faster."

Feather thought that sounded like a load of hog poop. This man was paid by Kristin and Brad and he had to be on the side of his paycheck. Stood to reason. "Why don't you let me decide, Mom? He's paid by Brad and Kristin, and she's convinced I'm the blackmailer."

"Oh, piffle." Jeanette plopped herself on the bed beside Feather. "I like this one's cut. He's a keeper. Of course, my saying that will make you drop him like a hot Tater Tot."

Okay. Enough. Was Feather thirty or thirteen? She would not give her mother the satisfaction of a response, although she imagined her jutting chin and angry expression were enough. "I need to talk to Peter tomorrow. But it scares me to have you off at the farm all day. You said yourself you distrusted Haley."

"We're snooping. Our motto is 'Trust No One.'" Jeanette looked sideways at Michael. "I guess that includes you, dear boy."

Dear boy? "So you'll stay away from Windfall?"

Jeanette kept her eyes on Michael, possibly avoiding Feather's, possibly considering flirting with him. "First thing, I'll visit Roxy." She sighed. "I don't know how you two get yourselves in these positions. Especially Roxanne. She generally knows better. Where was she hiding?"

Feather stuffed back the grin, predicting her mother's reaction to her news. "With Roadkill."

Jeanette pushed herself off from the bed, as if she'd spied a tarantula on the fluffy comforter. "In his ice cream truck?" She might have been asking if her daughter had been living in a pit toilet with an anaconda for a companion.

"It's really quite nice once it was remodeled after the crash," Feather said.

Jeanette waved a hand. "But it's tiny. Cramped. With one bed." She closed her eyes. "A strange choice of protectors."

"She couldn't very well hide out with you or me. Besides, I thought you liked Roadkill. We ate lunch with him not that long ago."

"He's fine as a friend, and he's been your friend for years. But Roxanne is, I thought, a bit more ... refined."

Feather caught Michael's smirk. Her mother was such a snob. "She's safe, and that's what's important." She paused. "Of course, he helped her with the break-in."

Her mother frowned. "I'm sure Roadkill instigated it. But why? Did they find anything worth going to jail for?"

"I think it was Roxanne's idea." Despite her mother's opinion that Michael was a keeper, Feather didn't want to discuss what Roxanne had hidden in Peter's office in front of him. "I didn't get long to talk to her. Maybe she can tell you tomorrow." Feather rubbed her neck. "Mom, I think you know more about this Chaz guy than you told us. He's a stranger in Hancock. Does he know anything about Windfall?"

Jeanette chuckled. "He knows a lot more since dinner. I might have mentioned the hog-mucking incident." She moved around the room, idly picking up and putting down the staged photos of people having fun in North Idaho that populated every bare surface in the room. Feather vowed her B&B would not go for this cluttered, Victorian look. What a bother to dust it. It flashed through her mind that managing it might be a bother, as well. She flushed at the traitorous thought and turned her head away from her mother's perceptive gaze.

Jeanette stopped and faced Feather and Michael. "Unlike most men, Chaz didn't spend the evening droning on about himself. He expressed genuine interest in me." She shrugged. "I know that should have thrilled me, but instead it made me nervous. Honestly, he was smooth, charming, good-looking and intelligent. And he creeped me out, just a little. I have no idea why. Too much mystery? Too self-confident?"

Michael said, "Women's intuition. And I'm not being facetious. Do not knock your intuition. I want to check him out." He stood. "Ms. Sullivan, I'm staying here, Room Six. If you get nervous or need anything, knock or give me a ring. Feather, let me run you home."

Jeanette lifted a hand. "It may not be as bad as Roadkill's truck, but no one would call Feather's trailer *home*."

Feather rose and walked to her mother. "Except me. Give me a hug, Mom. And stay away from the wind farm. Call it my intuition, but there are bad vibes emanating from there."

Her mother turned her cheek for an air kiss. "That, my dear, is the smell of hog manure." She wrinkled her nose. "I think perhaps I need another bath."

Feather inhaled and smelled nothing. She patted her mother's shoulder. "I can barely notice anything, Mom."

Thirty-One
Break-In Breakdown

Peter's entire body thrummed with anxiety as he watched the sheriff examine the lowered fire escape. What could Roxanne have found? Had she come here alone? Had she told anyone what she'd found? He didn't know her well, but she'd accompanied Teddy on a few visits, when he ran errands for the team out at the wind farm. It was next to impossible to imagine that sweet young woman a criminal. But Peter had misjudged Teddy, to his eternal regret, and now he doubted his ability to judge anyone's character. Not to mention his own.

Sheriff Warnock turned from his examination of the fire escape. "I'll drop by tomorrow and check this some more, but I don't see anything that tells me if she was alone or with someone else. My bet's on Roadkill. How else could he have known so fast the girl had been caught by Lacy?"

"It's all beyond me. Why anyone would kill Teddy, why Roxanne would break into my office and then steal nothing, as far as I can tell." *Not that I would tell you.*

"If you're sure she took nothing, and my deputy caught her as she walked out the door, then the charges will be less severe. She's never been arrested for anything other than a drunk and disorderly at a party a couple of years ago. Pretty clean slate."

Peter exhaled, trying to control himself. "It's all been so grim. You know Teddy and the poor young woman were seeing each other." Peter sounded like a fussy old woman, but his nerves were shot.

Warnock nodded. "Yes. But losing a lover doesn't give you a free pass."

Peter knew about loss and its effect, and about no free pass. He felt sorry for Roxanne, but he had to know what she'd discovered.

And Teddy. He'd told Peter he was a better father to him than his own, all while he was gathering information for his scheme. Little rat fink. *Dead* little rat fink.

The sheriff clasped his arm. "You look done in, man. Better call it a night. If anything comes up missing in the morning, let me know. You'd better get the fire escape taken care of. It's pretty far gone. Roxanne is lucky it supported her."

"I'm surprised she didn't fall, and sue me, the way my luck's been going. First thing tomorrow, I'll get it fixed."

"I'll have a report for you tomorrow, if you need it for insurance. 'Night." The sheriff headed around the front of the building for his SUV.

Peter locked his office, thinking as he did how futile the effort was. Then he walked slowly to his hybrid SUV, parked haphazardly behind the building. He'd received the call from Deputy Ponder while he was at home, trying unsuccessfully, over a glass of wine, to figure out how he could extricate himself from the mess at Windfall.

Feather was tired enough to accept Michael's offer to drive her home. It only took a few minutes, but they utilized them well. They agreed Michael would research Chaz the next morning and Feather would track down Peter and see if he would share anything he'd let slip to Teddy. She told him she also hoped to see Roxanne again and find out if she recalled more that she'd seen at Peter's office.

Feather wondered if Michael knew she was hiding something from him.

Michael parked his truck and walked Feather to the door of her trailer. He stood on the second step as she stood on the wire doorstep. That made their lips level. He leaned in and gave her a gentle kiss. Feather warmed down to her toes. If he'd really laid a searing kiss on her, she figured she'd have melted. Michael backed down a step. "Wow."

"Wow back at you. Thanks for the ride. Oh, and for dinner. And the beer." Before she could start babbling or drag him bodily onto her bed, she unlocked the trailer and entered, tossing a quick "Good night," after her and spinning around to watch him drive off.

The squirrels commenced their loud chittering complaints that they faced starvation the moment the key turned in the door. She fed and watered them and cleaned their cages and then covered them for the night.

She sat at the table with a notepad to jot down her thoughts regarding Teddy's death and the blackmail. Not at all hungry, simply to distract herself, she went to the cupboard and grabbed a Weetabix to chew on. She might as well have stolen some squirrel chow. Not tasty.

"Who am I kidding?"

The squirrels rustled in their clean cedar shavings, as if her voice disturbed their sleep.

"I am so not a note-taking, record-keeping kind of person. I am a dig in the dirt, climb a tree, physical effort kind of person." She had to go back to town, find a way into Peter's office and find the documents her sister had hidden. Cogitating through the night was fine for Sherlock Holmes, possibly for Michael Bergmann. Feather had to take action. She was more like Roadkill, with his "Carpe the crap along with the day," motto than she admitted.

She grabbed her backpack and a jacket heavier than the one she'd worn to the Osprey's Nest and snatched her car keys from the hook. On the top shelf of the closet she found a navy blue watch cap. The jacket, the cap, jeans: burglary-perfect. "'Night, squirrels. Guard the place."

Feather drove around the block twice and parked a few blocks from Peter's office, on a residential street where her truck would not stand out. She grabbed a few supplies from behind the seat and stuffed them into her backpack. She walked to the end of the block and climbed the ancient, rotting staircase that led to the patio. In the last century, there had been an intimate restaurant in the building, with a romantic outside garden at the second floor. Roadkill's parents knew the owners, who closed the place in the 90s. Roadkill and his brother played there as children. Roadkill had told her he went up when Roxanne went down earlier that night and had climbed into the attic and out the skylight to the roof. It had taken him quite a while to find the stairs that led down to the outside patio from the roof and then those that led to street level.

With that knowledge, Feather knew where to go but wasn't sure which building was the one rented by Peter once she reached the rooftop. She was wary of using her flashlight, in case the sheriff was watching the place more closely since the earlier break-in. Although, she reflected, he had the culprit in a cell. What were the odds of another intruder the same night? She hoped the sheriff and his sharp-witted deputy thought along similar lines.

Cupping her hands around the beam of the flash, she aimed it at the rooftop. She figured Roadkill had been in a hurry and would have left signs of his exit. Yes! She found the skylight, still thrown open on the third rooftop. Hurry, indeed.

She stood at the opening and beamed her light down. And down. And down. She wondered how Roadkill had been able to get out. She moved the light in an expanding ring and saw the legs and bottom rung of a ladder. He must have kicked it over in his rush to escape. As her eyes adjusted, she realized it wasn't that far to the attic floor. Ten or twelve feet. She opened her pack and withdrew a sturdy rope. She shone the light around, looking for an anchor. A brick chimney jutted up about 10 to 12 feet away. She wrapped the rope around it and tied it off with a bowline knot.

She dropped softly into the attic. What would her mom say if both daughters ended up in jail for breaking and entering? She smiled but sobered when she realized that if she too were caught, she wouldn't be able to continue the investigation.

Roadkill had had the foresight to shut the attic access door so she pried it loose from the floor and dropped down to the room below. The noise she made on that descent would have awakened the gods of Mount Borah. She decided she ought to plan her escape in case someone was downstairs. She carefully lifted, moved and stacked several boxes beneath the access door so her ascent would be easy and quiet. Of course if anyone came upstairs, they would immediately know where the intruder had gone. With luck she would be long gone, with the papers Roxanne had hidden, and perhaps a few more of Peter Brewer's secrets.

She waited several minutes upstairs, listening, trying to sense whether or not the building was empty. When it seemed she was alone, she muffled the light to a tiny stream with her handkerchief and proceeded into the hallway and down the stairs to Peter's office space. When she passed the bathroom, she had an overwhelming urge to pee, but she struck it off to nerves and continued.

Downstairs was a mess. Black fingerprint powder covered the shelves and all other surfaces. She went to the bookshelf where Roxanne had hidden the papers. What the heck had she said? Myths? The bookcase stretched the length of the room. She began at the end nearest the front window, startled each time a vehicle passed. She quickly realized she couldn't remove every book, so she focused on those with the word myth in them. Who'd have thought Peter would have so many? He must be fascinated with myths of all kinds. *Overcoming Financial Myths, Legends and Myths of Northwest Native Americans, The Mythology of Fiction, Truth in Myth, Myths of Time.* These of course were interspersed with dozens of other books on the shelves. After finding these books, pulling them out and searching for hidden papers, Feather realized she needed more, needed to remember if Roxanne had said anything else. She imagined herself standing in front of her sister's jail cell. Imagined Roxanne telling her ... when someone came, she had to hide the papers, the papers she had just copied. So she might have been near the copier. What else did she say? It was a big book. So small paperbacks were out.

She moved to the copying machine. Put herself in her sister's position. Cocked her head. Did she hear something, or did Roadkill warn her?

So intent was she on re-enacting the scene with Roxanne and Roadkill, she incorporated the sounds she heard into her scene. Roadkill said her sister saw a car in the back lot and told him they had to leave, but she ran to the desk and grabbed a rubber band to put around some papers. He left before he saw what she did with them. But Roxanne had said ... behind the book. So she'd hidden them behind a big book with mythology in the title.

A clunky sound came from down the hall, but Feather was too focused on her search to take alarm. She returned to the bookshelves and scanned them with her light, focusing first on the ends of the shelves nearest the door. Roxanne probably started to leave, holding the tube and decided if she was caught she didn't want the papers to be found. So the ends nearest the door and at a level she could reach ... yes! There it was. *Bulfinch's Mythology.*

She dragged the large book from the shelf and snatched out the roll of papers hidden behind it. She spun around when she heard another clunk, one definitely not part of her re-enactment of Roxanne's arrest scene.

She stuffed the rolled papers into her backpack and searched for a hiding place. She sped to Peter's large desk and crouched beneath it. She heard footsteps and the sound of someone dragging something. Something big.

She took shallow breaths. It was dusty beneath Peter's desk, a combination of good old North Idaho dirt and the metallic smell of fingerprint powder. With her backpack beside her, it was crowded. She wondered who it was. Not Peter, because the lights were still off. He and the cops had no reason for secrecy.

Oh, shoot. Was it Roadkill, here to help Roxanne and her? She should have warned him, but she wanted to do this alone. Crouched as she was, her view was restricted to the outer corner of the back of the desk, and of course in front of her, where she hoped not to see anyone. She peered at the corner. The back of the desk extended only three-fourths of the way to the floor. Good for her in that she had a tiny view out, bad for her in that her butt and feet were clearly visible under the desk.

Footsteps neared and she saw shoes beneath the desk. Men's, but not Roadkill's. He always wore battered hiking boots—when did he batter them, since she'd never seen him in new ones—but might deign to don sneakers in a break-in such as this. These shoes, however, were leather trainers, and looked expensive. And much smaller than Roadkill's feet.

She had no idea who belonged to the shoes and hoped she wasn't about to find out. Nothing could be worse than for one intruder to be found by yet another.

She heard a gurgling noise, and then smelled gasoline. Something could be worse. Much worse. Should she reveal herself now?

If the arsonist was truly evil, he would knock her out and leave her here, senseless, to die. She'd rather try to escape the flames on her own, conscious. She remained crouched under the desk, terrified the liquid would reach her and soak her jeans.

The whoosh of the fire starting petrified Feather. She knew too well the power of flames, having helped with food service for firefighters. Even the burning of slash piles, meant to clear areas to prevent big burns, was frightening, and those fires were relatively small and controlled.

She had to escape before the fire grew huge and engulfed the building but the act of rolling out from under the desk's seeming protection was more than she could manage.

"No, I will not stay here like a terrified rabbit. I will survive." Immediately her mind flew to the song and she hummed it as she crawled from beneath the desk. Her legs cramped. Standing and slinging on her backpack took far too long in the fire's growing heat. Who sang that song? Gloria something.

Gas had been poured on the carpet and the linoleum floor and splashed over the desk and table before being ignited. Now more smoke than flames filled the room. If Feather opened the back window to escape, the oxygen might well cause an explosion. Better out the way she'd come. To the roof.

As she ran out the door, the ceiling sprinklers came on. They were sparse and issued little water, but she took a second to stand under the closest one, soaking her jacket and jeans, holding her backpack away so its precious contents were not wet. She dampened her handkerchief, her beloved and useful 104, called the 104 by Girl Scouts because of its 100 plus uses.

She ran down the hall, slowed by the wet linoleum. She paused near the bathroom. Could she survive the fire in the bathroom, with the porcelain fixtures, probably a tile floor in this old building? If she did make it through, she'd be caught, but if the fire grew, the entire building would collapse. Making her plan to exit via the roof dicier. And time more precious.

She ran faster and dashed up the stairs to the file room, already engulfed in flames. The arsonist had been up here, as well. Darn.

She glanced behind her. If she used the stairs, she could probably just leave through the front door. Then she heard the sirens from the volunteer fire department. Terrific. Feather would waltz out the door into the arms of either the fire marshal or with her luck, the sheriff or his deputy, and she'd join her sister in jail. Even though she could probably prove herself innocent of arson, explaining her presence in the building would not be a treat.

To the roof, then, through the attic, with only a moment's dash through the flames that grew larger as she debated options.

She paused to grab her watch cap from her backpack and yanked it down as far as possible. She wrapped her wet 104 around her face, nose to chin. Already it was so very hot. She looked into the room and realized that soon the flames would reach the outside walls of the wood frame building. The boxes she had arranged beneath the attic access door remained in place. The arsonist had either not noticed them or not recognized their significance. Unfortunately they were soggy and lopsided, wet from gasoline or sprinkler water, she didn't know which. But they were there and they were not in flames, her only piece of luck so far.

She dashed toward the boxes and they exploded into flames. Like a tiger jumping through a flaming hoop, she ignored the flames and continued, the heat scorching the soles of her shoes. Had she stacked them high enough for her to easily grasp the rim of the access door? She'd left it ajar. She slipped her pack off and used it to flip the door away and then shoved it into the attic. She had to leap and grab the edge. She'd planned to use her rope to get back up, but she didn't have time. She dangled from the edge, her fingers damp with sweat and water. Did she have the strength to pull herself up? She heard the wail of a siren, heard the flames beneath her, felt their heat. She fell back down. She couldn't do it that way.

Fortunately, she had stacked the boxes high. She crouched on the top one, trying to ignore how wobbly it was. She gave a mighty shove with her legs and jumped upward. This time her hands grasped a beam half a foot away from the edge of the access hole, so that her elbows were at the edge. Using strength she didn't know she had, from years of tree climbing, perhaps, she pulled herself through the hole and rolled to the side, gasping.

Heat and smoke from the fire below her came through the opening. She jammed the cover in place. Her arms and hands throbbed with the strain of pulling her body through the hole. Now she had to call on them again to climb to the roof via the rope she'd left there.

She hummed more of the song by Gloria something and ran to the rope. This time she had to wear her backpack, making the climb harder. "But it's short," she said aloud. "I think I can, I think I can," she chanted.

She grabbed her gloves from the backpack and put them on, remembering only then that she'd been downstairs without them. With luck her prints would be history just like the rest of the building. Luck?

Backpack on, she took a running leap for the rope, so her exhausted arms would need to haul her a shorter distance. The rope swung when she grabbed it and she hoped to goodness she'd tied a good knot around the rooftop chimney. When she began the hand over hand climb, the rope steadied. Soon she was kneeling beside the chimney, cutting the rope free with a knife from her faithful backpack.

At the end of the building, she descended the stairs, trying to be stealthy, knowing the fire had gathered a crowd of firefighters and looky-loos, hoping no one would notice her, because she did not look like a casual passerby. She removed her watch cap and gloves and fluffed her hair. She scrubbed at her face with the slightly damp, very smoky bandana.

She rounded the corner. Deputy Lacy Ponder walked toward her. Perfect. Feather looked like a shape-shifting monster dressed in black with flat hair and a filthy face. She smelled like smoke and sweat and her hands were bleeding. Probably nothing the sharp-eyed deputy would notice.

The deputy smiled broadly. "Feather. Wonderful to run into you. You're looking stunning this fine evening." She eyed her, top to toes. Her attention focused on the backpack.

Feather gulped. She noticed. But what could Ponder do? They were outside the building, and smelling and looking awful weren't crimes or the Hancock jail would be overflowing. She'd bluff her way through this. "Hi, Lacy. Guess I should call you Deputy Ponder when you're in uniform."

"I don't stand on formality and I don't think Byron does, either. However, you *will* need to call me deputy if I arrest you for arson."

"Arson? I was afraid of that. I heard the sirens and wasn't sleeping, so I came to see what was up. What happened?"

"Strange attire for a looky-loo." She leaned toward Feather and sniffed. "You smell like smoke."

"You know us trailer park dwellers. Campfires outside, smoking hot inside, always close to the action, wherever it is." She sniffed at herself, in broad parody. "I did visit with one of my neighbors earlier." Feather would have felt guilty at maligning a non-existent neighbor if her dominant emotion wasn't fear at the moment. She had to get away from Lacy.

"I know you. You're up to something."

"I confess to being curious. Not sure that's a chargeable offense."

"I'm curious, too. What's in your backpack?"

Feather smiled. Activism had taught her a lot about law and cause and justification for search. "This, that, and everything else. A girl can't be too prepared."

Lacy smiled back. "You and Roadkill know all the loopholes. I have a first-aid kit in my vehicle." She gave a pointed look at Feather's hands.

Feather gulped and clenched her fists. "Whatever for? Was someone injured in the fire?"

"No way to tell yet. With all the ruckus, it's odd that Peter Bergmann hasn't shown up yet."

Unless he's the one who set the fire. "Odd, yes. Such a shame."

"Arsonists know how to set timers so fires start hours after they break in. Your sister was here not that long ago. I suspect she wasn't alone and I suspect she knows more than she's told me."

"Really. Are you accusing my sister of arson?" She inhaled. She'd almost added "or Roadkill?"

Lacy puffed out a sigh. "I can't see Roxanne as an arsonist. Then again, who would have thought she'd break into Peter's office? Kill her boyfriend?"

Feather reared back. As she did, the papers in her backpack rustled, crackling, in Feather's mind, louder than the flames she'd just escaped. She raised her voice, both to express her indignation and to hide the paper noise. "She did *not* kill Teddy. No way. You're yanking my chain."

"Moi?" Lacy leaned against the building and crossed her arms. "You got a chain to yank? I would so love to see what's in that pack, but I doubt you're going to share."

Feather managed to keep her voice calm, her face relaxed, when every muscle in her neck and shoulders was taut with tension. "You are so right. I believe in my right to privacy."

Lacy's face tightened. "I believe in *all* your rights and I'm only trying to uphold them. It's my job. It is *your* job to tell the truth."

"My job is to protect my sister, my family, and myself. Not to mention our reputations, which you seem ready to shred." She stepped away from the deputy, feeling guilty for her harsh words and her lies. Lacy and her boss Sheriff Warnock were good cops. But they were, after all, cops. She yawned. "If you don't need me, I think I'll head home and catch a few hours' sleep."

"Since you're unwilling to share what I do need, the truth, you might as well go."

"G'night now." Feather strode off, hoping her pace displayed confidence and not the rushed speed of the guilty.

Back at her truck, Feather gulped down half a bottle of water. The roll of papers called to her from the backpack, but she headed home before she looked at them.

When she did, her tired eyes opened wide and her heart thrummed. The name Chaz Stedman might have been branded into the list of company directors on the corporate registration form. Feather hadn't known Windfall was registered in Canada, but there were the names: Chaz Stedman, Peter Bergmann, Jonathon Flynn, and a few others she didn't recognize. No mention of the other partners the firm had taken on—or perhaps taken in would be the better wording—Brad, her mother, Sophia. Another document included Peter, Jon, Brad, Jeanette, and Sophia, along with a few others with California addresses, as partners in the American incorporation of Windfall Works. Chaz Stedman's name was not mentioned.

Someone had used this information to blackmail the partners. Feather didn't know if everything in the blackmail texts was related to Windfall. Roxanne had said Teddy learned a lot from Peter, but only Peter knew what. Who became the blackmailer after killing Teddy? She ran her fingers through her hair. Really, even though she *had* to know, she didn't *want* to know. She liked these people, had known most of them for years. And yet, the only one of the partners she could eliminate with certainty was her mother. Her mother was many things, but she wasn't a sneak or a thief.

Hmm. You'd have thought it was required that a company registered in two countries provide complete information about shareholders. Feather knew little about such concepts. Her B&B would be an LLC, but she hadn't done much yet about setting it up with the state of Idaho.

She returned to the documents her sister had copied, realizing that the fire might have assured they were now the only proof that Chaz Stedman was linked to Windfall Works. Why was it a secret? Who was the suave gentleman who'd treated her mother to dinner? Was their meeting a coincidence or was he after information from Jeanette?

The next document was an invoice, marked paid, from a supplier of parts for wind turbines. The amount was huge and covered the cost of six nacelles, the central housing for the wind turbine and the blades. At the bottom was typed, "Hold for shipment when requested."

Feather marveled that her sister had the insight to seize this invoice. She must have wondered, as did Feather, why Peter would order and pay for products they weren't even sure the state of Idaho would allow them to install. It made little sense to her.

Peter had some 'splainin' to do and Feather saw no reason to wait. He hadn't shown up at the fire, unless those were his shoes she'd seen under the desk.

She yawned again, this time for real, not show. Exhaustion threatened to sideline her, but not until she figured out what was going on with Windfall Works. A cold shower should revive her and cold showers were the norm at the Laughing Pines Trailer Park.

Thirty-Two

Cleaning Up Another Mess

Haley didn't mind doing the dishes at the wind farm, because it kept her occupied somewhere Jon couldn't demand a blow job. When she'd started working at the wind farm, sex had seemed the easiest way to control Jon, but he had become a demanding prick. She couldn't wait to escape this place and his incessant humping. He reminded her of a little dog continually humping every bitch it encountered, simply to prove it was alpha. But Chaz was the alpha of this pack. When Chaz wanted to assert his authority, he didn't raise his voice or his penis. He needed only a raised eyebrow and she and Jon hopped. The man was seriously scary.

Her hands were deep in the warm, soothing water when she heard a car drive up and screech to a stop in front of the house. It wouldn't be Chaz. He never rushed, never squealed his brakes. She hoped it wasn't the return of wicked witch Sullivan. The woman was too snoopy. Jon had told her how he'd stopped the old broad just in time from entering the storage area for all the excess equipment. She'd have been surprised, but not for long. Hadn't the wretched woman told Jon she'd been an accountant at some time?

Haley shook her head. *Nah, it wouldn't be Jeanette. She had shoveled enough poop to wear out a person twice her size and half her age. She was no doubt sound asleep under her beauty mask by now.*

In moments she heard voices in the living room. Jon and another man. She hoped they'd come in the kitchen so she could find out what was causing all the excitement, because the other voice was high-pitched with anxiety.

Jon pushed through the swinging kitchen door. "Put the kettle on. Peter's here and he could use some tea."

Typical Jon, bossing Haley as if she were a kitchen maid. She twisted around to glare at him. "Do it yourself. I'm busy."

Jon heaved a sigh, but went to the large stove and turned it on beneath the kettle after shaking it to see how much water remained. "He's a total wreck. Major problems in Hancock."

Peter waddled through the door behind Jon, looking paler than normal and totally disheveled. Disheveled was normal for Peter Brewer, but tonight his shirt was buttoned crooked and hung open, some belly hair hanging out. Haley swiveled back to focus on the dishes. Sad, when dirty dishes were more appealing than the men you worked with. "I could use something stronger than tea, Jon. Whiskey? Wine? This is a total disaster." Peter pulled a stool out and plopped onto it, his oversize rump spreading over the edges. "Let's stay here and I'll catch you both up."

"You have to drive back to Hancock," Jon said. "Let's stick to tea. Herbal will calm you."

"Herbal will nauseate me, but I'm at your mercy. For heaven's sake, Haley, stop washing those dishes and dry your hands. You need to hear every dismal word."

After Peter told them what had happened, with dramatic embellishments, she realized he was the loosest link in the entire chain of partners. Hysterical to the max, and ready to blow to the authorities at the slightest provocation.

When Peter headed for the bathroom, Jon whispered to Haley. "We've got to handle this. He's falling apart. You heard the idiot. He's been keeping papers with Chaz's name on it and God knows what else. You keep him occupied. I'm going to town and make sure no one finds any of the moron's records."

Haley wondered what Jon was up to, but didn't much care as long as it got him out of her pants. But now she was supposed to entertain Peter? Sad-sack Peter? Please. Her stomach knotted. "How am I supposed to occupy him? Knock him over the head?"

Jon gave her a knowing leer. "You know how to domesticate any male, my dear."

"I am not a whore, Jon."

"Do whatever you want. Just keep him occupied for an hour or so."

Haley tightened her eyes. "Whatever."

When Peter returned, Jon threw his arm around his shoulder. It was an awkward stretch for the smaller, slighter man. "You're right, buddy. It is a FUBAR of a situation. What you need to do is chill. And let me tell you, no one is better at helping a man relax than our little Haley here. Me, I have to do a final check on the damn hogs and a few other things and then I'm for bed. You can bunk here with us, so you don't have to drive." He grinned. "What would you like to drink?"

Peter's desperate expression turned to bemused. "Relax? I wish. But I do welcome a drink. Bourbon?"

Jon beamed. "Coming right up. As I recall, we have some Crown Royal Reserve. From Canada." He winked. "I believe you will like it."

Haley decided she might as well play along. "Let's go into the living room, Peter. It's so much more comfortable in there." She hated her sultry tone and the alluring look she shot over her shoulder at Peter. She couldn't get out of this town too soon.

Surely Teddy never imagined what he set in motion with those beastly texts. In a way, he deserved to die, for his stupidity and his greed. Of course, if stupidity and greed led to an early death, the world would not have a population problem.

Now Peter, ready to blab all the details about the wind farm to the nearest cop. Had he already spilled his guts, his guilt, to the sheriff of Hancock? She figured discovering that was her first assignment while she *helped him relax.*

Jon brought Peter a stiff drink and a beer for Haley and took off. Haley turned on the stereo, figuring Peter was distraught, but not so upset he wouldn't hear Jon's car when he drove off. She fiddled with sound levels on some Celtic music for a few minutes, starting out way too loud for soothing tunes. As she walked back to the CD player, she raised her voice over its din and said, "I always do that. Some of these CDs are recorded louder than others, but I never remember which." She got to the machine and turned the volume up instead of down, spun around to return to her chair and then returned to the player, at last getting the volume right.

Peter had at some point covered his ears. Laughing, hoping he didn't realize how fake her laughter was, she went to him and placed her hands on his ears. She mouthed, "It's safe to come out," and leaned down and placed a gentle kiss on his lips. She immediately stood and backed away.

Peter's eyes widened with surprise. His mouth fell open, revealing stained teeth. This man was the poster boy for unkempt, aging bachelors going to seed. She figured it had been a while since he'd been kissed, let alone had sex with anyone he didn't pay. *Well, it ain't gonna happen tonight, despite Jon's hints.*

The liquor, the music, and possibly Haley's attentive presence all served to calm Peter while loosening his tongue.

It didn't take long for Haley to realize that Jon was right. Peter was a hurricane, ready to strike. No, he was the levee, ready to break. Whatever. He had managed to keep his trap shut while the sheriff viewed the site of the break-in, but one more conversation with the authorities and he would tell all. He had to be silenced.

Bile rose in her throat. How could she get away before it all broke bad? She needed more money. Peter was no option. He'd blubbered that he was broke, had stolen from Chaz—the idiot, signing his death warrant if Chaz found out—and the partners, had sent most of it to his disabled daughter in California. When he mentioned his daughter, he began to weep. "Angelica needs me. What will happen to her if I go to jail? I didn't mean any harm, but the assisted living center is dreadfully expensive."

Her only sources of money were Jeanette Sullivan and the bitch banker from Spokane.

"Peter, have you heard from Sophia? What does she think of this mess?" She forced a look of surprise to her face. "Say. She's from Spokane. You don't suppose ... no, not her. She's a banker, well-paid, why would she need money? I can't picture her killing anyone, let alone poor Teddy."

Peter giggled. "I can picture her and her lovely wife doing all sorts of things. And I can picture her little granny, with all the lovely money to leave to her favorite granddaughter, finding out her granddaughter is a lesbo, married to another pervert."

Maybe it wouldn't be *that* terrible if Peter were to become the next victim. "Did Teddy know this?"

Peter had the grace to look abashed. "I told Teddy way too much. Trusted him, the little creep." A tear rolled down his face and was joined by another, then another, until he was again sobbing, blubbering. "How could he do this to me? He was like a son to me." Once the blubbering slowed, a sly look took over his face. He stared at Haley. "You're right. Sophia does live in Spokane. She could have followed Teddy after the first payment and then taken over."

Haley chewed her thumb. "And I ... she called and Jon had just told me about the text Brad got and ... oh, my God. I told her where he had to make the payment."

"Jesus. Loose lips sink ships."

"Huh?"

"You're too young." He wobbled as he stood. "We need to tell the cops."

"When Jon gets back, we will. But right now, I want to show you something." She peered at him as if taking his measure. If she were in truth, measuring him, the man would fall far, far short. Or the measuring tape would be too short. "You seem like someone I can rely on. Should I?"

He leaned forward to pat her shoulder and staggered. "Of course you should, my dear. No secrets between us."

She smiled. "It's something Jon has been hiding from all of us. It's a bit of a walk, but I'll take a flashlight." A very heavy flashlight, along with a roll of duct tape. She needed to get Peter and his huge mouth out of circulation until she could leave town. His ever-so-common white SUV would be the perfect escape vehicle. All she had to do was hide it in one of the outbuildings, hide Peter in another, text Sophia to deliver her cash here at Windfall Works and Haley would be saying, "Hasta la vista, Hancock," before sundown, tomorrow.

"If we're going for a walk, I need to visit the little prince's room again," Peter said with a ridiculous simper.

While Peter was performing his princely duties, Haley went to the front closet to grab a jacket against the night's cold. Once there, she grabbed one of Jon's work coats and slipped it on.

"Did you bring a coat, Peter? Or shall we take your SUV? It's a bit of a walk to the outbuilding I want to show you."

Peter pulled out his car keys. "Left my coat in the SUV. I can walk, in fact, I should. It will sober me up. You know, liquor has a bad effect on a man's prowess." He giggled. "I must not be too drunk if I can say 'prowess.'" He leered at Haley. "Believe me, little lady, I have some serious prowess to show you when we return. Or maybe we could just skip the preliminaries. You can show me whatever it is you had in mind tomorrow."

Haley smiled back, hoping her revulsion didn't show. "Oh, no. You could use a little fresh air, and I want you to see this. I need your advice. First, I'll grab a flashlight from the kitchen."

Her purse, large enough to hold a handgun, flashlight and gloves in addition to the more usual wallet and makeup bag, was in the kitchen. She considered the gun and shook her head. Not necessary. She stuffed the flashlight and a roll of duct tape from the utility drawer into the capacious pockets of Jon's coat and slipped on her leather gloves so her fingerprints could not be found in Peter's SUV. She'd have to dump it at some point and it had to be pristine, or as pristine as anything belonging to Peter Brewer could claim. "Let's grab your coat from your car and walk." She held out her hand for the keys and Peter handed them to her without hesitation. Was the twinge that flashed across her shoulders guilt at Peter's naïve faith in her or disgust at the look on his pudgy face? Didn't matter.

Outside, Haley opened Peter's SUV, removed his coat and handed it to him. As he donned it, she put his car keys in her pocket, hoping he wouldn't notice. He didn't. She clutched his arm and they strolled toward the outbuildings. Haley chatted nervously as they walked, pointing out buildings Peter had already seen.

After the second such faux pas, Peter stopped. "What's up, Haley? You seem nervous."

Oh, crud. Maybe I should have shot him in the kitchen, said I thought he was an intruder. "Who wouldn't be, with all this going on? And now that I've found the stuff I want you to see, we'll be in deep doo doo if the cops nose around anymore. You know they came here right after Teddy's body was found, right?"

"Yes, Jon phoned me. He's nervous, too. Guess we all are." He threw his arm around Haley and resumed walking. Haley resumed breathing. "Let's see what Jon's been up to. Never did like the son of a bitch."

Haley was treading on shaky ground by showing Peter the hidden equipment. If he by chance escaped or was found before she could make her getaway, he would have ammunition, either to tell the cops or to hold over Jon and Chaz. Of course, if he tried anything with Chaz, it would be a mistake, but Jon? Who knew? She decided not to worry. She would simply make certain Peter didn't get away before she did. With all that body fat, he didn't have much chance of fading away in a few days. And she was going to be gone tomorrow, for sure. Sophias' extortion payment should keep her flush on the run, get her to a nice country in Central or South America.

They reached the farthest building. It was locked, but Haley had a key. She opened it while Peter held the flashlight, then stretched her hand out for the large implement. Peter merely strode into the building, using the light to guide him. *Now what?* Haley had planned to whomp him with the light, truss him up and leave him.

She reached around the corner and turned on the lights.

Peter stopped. "This building is huge. Look at the insulated walls. You'd never guess from the decrepit looks of the outside."

"Exactly."

Peter moved slowly into the building, making note of the concrete floor, peering at several stacked boxes bearing the names of suppliers of energy equipment. He used the flashlight to point toward the far wall. "Jon told me there was a waiting list at the suppliers. Shortage of materials for the gears, that kind of thing. He was lying. There's enough here to implement the entire plant, once the license is granted and we figure out how to get the longer blades here from the rail line. I don't get it."

"I'm not sure of the whole scheme. But I suspect he plans to sell it and keep the cash when everything goes wonky. You know the folks in Hancock won't let this go much further, with the smell from the hogs." His response to this comment would tell Haley whether Peter knew about the money laundering scheme, not, at this point, that it mattered.

"Butcher the damn hogs. We can start making money on this operation if we grease a few palms."

So he didn't know the real story. If Chaz focused on the DEA maybe he wouldn't worry about one missing female employee. If she let Peter in on the secret and then tied him up until tomorrow ... it might work. Jon would be satisfied with Peter out of the way, even if he assumed Peter had gone home, freshly laid.

She lowered her voice and touched Peter's arm. "Follow me. There's more you ought to know. I was okay with this until someone killed poor Teddy when he found out the truth."

"The truth, my ash—ass," Peter said. "He distorted the things he learned to scare people into giving him money. He deserved to die." He spat out the words with enough venom he could have been Teddy's killer.

Haley had one last chance to get the light from Peter. "Part true, but ... well, come with me." She moved to the center of the building, to the wall that divided the rectangular building in two. She grabbed the large handle and walked the twelve-foot high sliding door open. The ease with which it moved revealed the expensive construction. The adjoining room was dark. Haley strode to the front of the building and hit the electrical switch beside the outer sliding door. Those doors led to a gravel road that passed the building and ended where the first, experimental wind turbine stood. The doors were locked from the outside with a huge sliding bolt latch, the keys held again by Jon.

Peter stood, approaching sober and silent, facing the now well-lighted room. Six vintage cars, in varying but excellent condition, were parked in the room. All were raised on jacks, tires not touching the ground. The floor, a higher grade concrete than in the other half of the building, was carpeted, with moth balls scattered over it.

"I don't get it," he said.

Haley crossed the room to stand beside Peter. "Took me a while, too."

"Give me a hint. Why are these stored here, hidden away? Jon can't afford these."

"Few people can. Think, Peter. Where is Chaz from? Where does he get all the money to invest? And why in a dinky little wind farm in Nowhere, Idaho, which happens to be fewer than 100 miles from the Canadian border? You think Chaz Stedman is an environmentalist?"

Peter stared at Haley. "These belong to Chaz?"

Haley said nothing.

"Wait. Oh, my God. He said ... he wouldn't say much about his businesses, let me think he was in construction ...had a few big contracts from the government .... That's why he didn't want his name on the deed, why we formed the damn company. Windfall is laundering his drug money?"

"I suspect it's also a conduit for some of the drugs," Haley said, as if she were just figuring this out with Peter instead of being Chaz's key American operative.

Haley continued. "This explains the hogs and the stench. Jon and Chaz don't want the wind farm to succeed. If the permits go through, there will be lots of people here, more government inspections. The laundering would have to stop."

"And Teddy figured all this out? I knew the kid had a good mind." Peter lowered the flashlight to the ground, as if its weight were too much to bear along with the news of the scheme between Jon and Chaz. Haley picked it up, making it seem, she hoped, a casual gesture. "You can pay cash for a used car. The seller would probably like that. Vintage stuff like this doesn't lose value, probably gains."

Haley nodded. "Follow me. There's an office in the far corner with a filing cabinet. I think you should see it. I haven't had time to go through it." She took off toward the tiny office, hopeful that Peter would follow her. She stopped and turned to him, smiling. "I know there's water and a tiny fridge. Obviously the power is always on to keep the temperature in here stable. Knowing Jon, there's wine."

Peter followed her to the office, but stopped outside the open door. "Why did you decide to show me this? What's your involvement?"

Haley tried to look repentant. "I confess I've known about the money laundering for a few months. I didn't know how to get out.

Chaz scares me. So I went along, kept quiet, felt guilty." She sighed. "Then Teddy, who we know was always a snoop, must have found out about the hidden equipment, maybe the cars? I don't know. I had no idea what he was up to, believe me." She moved to the mini-fridge. "I'm having a glass of wine. Can I get you one? We'll have to use paper cups." She pulled a box of wine from the cooler.

Peter turned around to look back at the cars and then moved inside the little office and fell into the small fake leather sofa. It let out a squeak. "Sure. I still don't see why you're telling me. I'm flattered, but what can I do? Why not the cops?"

Haley moved behind the couch and rubbed Peter's shoulders. "I trust you. You're smart enough to figure a way we can stop the laundering but not be arrested for our involvement."

Peter, who had begun to slump down into the cushions, sat up. "Involvement? You're right. Lord, I need that wine." He bent forward, head in his hands. Haley's chance had come. She raised the flashlight high and brought it down in a sideways blow to Peter's head. He slumped farther down and fell to the left, unconscious.

Haley pulled the roll of duct tape from her pocket and quickly wrapped Peter's ankles. She dragged his body to the floor. He fell onto his face, his left arm under his large body. She wrapped tape around his right arm and managed, with some effort, to extract his left arm from beneath him. She wrapped the tape around both arms and between his legs, forcing them to bend backwards. Worried that he might figure out how to roll to the door and somehow kick the outer walls and gain attention, Haley then dragged his limp and incredibly heavy form to a metal support beam in the corner. Thank God for her gym workouts. She wound tape around the beam and around Peter until he was trussed and immobilized.

Peter moaned. Haley didn't know what she would do if he came to and saw her trussing him up like a roasting pheasant. She trotted to the huge room and found a cabinet with supplies, including polishing rags and towels. She tied one around Peter's eyes and used a small one to cover his mouth before she taped it shut. She started to walk out the door and then thought about what would happen if someone gagged her that way. She would either vomit and choke to death or be unable to breathe through her nose until she was rescued. So she took the gag off. It was not likely anyone would wander near the building anytime soon, and certainly not before Haley made her escape.

She should leave the gag in place, but Peter reminded her of an old dog she had taken in during the years she lived in Seattle: innocent yet beaten down. If Peter died, who'd send money to support his disabled daughter? She couldn't have that on her conscience, if she had one of those outdated things.

She walked back to Peter's SUV, parked askew in front of the office.

Lord, she was exhausted. It had to be past midnight. But she had to hide Peter's wheels and get her things packed and send off the blackmail text to Sophia before she could consider going to bed. She'd hide the SUV on an old dirt road that turned off to nowhere about a mile east.

The space for Jon's car was still empty. Relieved, but still pressured, she dashed inside and stuffed some clothes and a few cherished belongings into her second-hand, mildew-scented suitcase. She ran downstairs and stowed the case in the rear of Peter's SUV and drove off to hide it.

Tomorrow she'd take only her backpack so she could hike cross-country to the hidden SUV.

She hid the vehicle and locked it and decided to risk walking down the road back to the farmhouse. Better she risk being seen by a passing driver than arrive back at the house after Jon. While she walked, she let herself dream of her escape: freedom from poverty like she'd known in Seattle, freedom from the dominance of Chaz and the petty demands of Jon, freedom from the boredom of working at the wind farm. She worried she might be pressing her luck, sending the text to Sophia tomorrow, but she needed the money. After all, the woman was a banker, with access to lots of money, right? Asking her for ten thousand dollars shouldn't put a strain on a professional's budget, and keeping the secret of her marriage from her grandmother would be worth far more to her. And if Haley allowed the woman only a short time frame for the delivery, she'd have less time to get the police or anyone else involved.

Haley would pick up the drop and leave town, never to return to Idaho, or indeed to anywhere north of the U.S./Mexican border.

Back at Windfall, the lot in front held only her car. She checked the huge clock inside and realized Jon had been gone only a little more than an hour. It had seemed an eternity, lying to Peter, convincing him to join her on the trek to the outbuilding, and trussing up his ungainly, bulky and unconscious form.

Before she went to bed, she dug out a hidden burner phone, readied the text to Sophia and set her alarm. Four hours sleep should do it. She could rest once she got to Mexico.

Thirty-Three
Peter, Where Art Thou?

Feather headed east on the state forest road to Peter's home. A compact architectural and ecological wonder, his home was constructed from straw bales and sided with plaster. Peter had spent a lot of money: installing solar panels on the roof, passive solar lighting, plus lots of other energy-conserving concepts. Despite the skepticism of locals, so far Peter's home had stood the tests of winter's cold and summer's sun.

Would whoever torched Peter's office come next to his home? Chilling thought. Hot, actually, if it caught fire.

She tried Peter's cell phone again, but he'd apparently turned it off, along with every light inside and out. Wasted watts, weakened world.

She pulled into the drive in front of Peter's home. She needed answers that Peter likely had. According to Roxanne, much of Teddy's information used for blackmail came via gabby Peter. So he could gab again, this time to Feather. Maybe if she woke him, his defenses would be down and he'd reveal more.

Feather grabbed a flashlight from her backpack and trotted to Peter's front door. She rang the doorbell. She waited a few seconds, pressed again, then forced herself to give Peter time to wake and come to the door. She leaned her head against the ornately carved wood door, listening for sounds inside. Pounding on that door wouldn't do much good either, but she gave it a try. Maybe he had a dog that would bark and wake Peter. Maybe the dog was outside and would come around the house to confront the intruder. Maybe it was a pit bull or a Rottie, ready to protect Peter's home with its life— or its teeth.

"No more maybes or I'll scare myself witless."

Forcing herself to think logically at this time of night—make that morning—with as little sleep as Feather had in the past couple of days was an effort. If she could find Peter's bedroom window, she could probably get his attention. The back door was half glass. Feather peered through to the kitchen and the room beyond and saw no one. She climbed the back stairs to the second level balcony. She pounded on the French doors, yelling, hoping Peter would realize this was no burglar but a friend trying to get his attention.

Maybe Peter drugged himself or wore heavy ear protection when he slept. Or maybe he wasn't home. She decided to check the garage, something she should have done upon her arrival. She slapped the side of her head and trotted downstairs to the garage out back.

A side window revealed an empty garage through spider webs and dust. It was beginning to look like Peter had not returned home since meeting with Sheriff Warnock after the break-in at his office. Could it be that Peter himself was the arsonist, trying to hide evidence of his pyramid-like scheme of selling partnerships in a wind farm when it was already owned by a Canadian firm?

She rubbed a tired hand across a very tired chin, if indeed chins can register exhaustion. "Think, Feather."

Peter often spent time at the wind farm. Since Feather had nowhere else to look for him, Windfall Works it was. By the time she got to the wind farm, the early birds and early pigs should be stirring.

She ought not venture onto the wind farm in her current exhausted, sleep-deprived state. No telling what she might do or say, if she did find Peter, Jon or Haley, or God forbid, Chaz Stedman. But if she went home, she wouldn't wake up before dusk tomorrow. What if she tried a Goldilocks entry to Peter's home? His bed, any bed, called to sleep-deprived Feather. Arrgh! If he came home, neither of them would enjoy the surprise. She remembered a small campsite on the way to the farm where she could park the truck and nap.

On the way to the campsite, Feather drove with the windows open and sang loud, raucous songs to keep from falling asleep and driving into a Ponderosa.

At the campsite, Feather crawled into the covered bed of her pickup, where she always kept an old sleeping bag, and fell asleep instantly, despite the cold and the unforgiving metal truck bed.

* * *

Rustling noises atop her camper shell woke Feather. She scootched her head and shoulders out of the sleeping bag and onto the tailgate. Three curious squirrels darted from the new expanse they'd been exploring. Perhaps they had received psychic messages from her captive squirrels: "This human provides adequate, if not gourmet, food."

"No luck here, fellas."

She dug out her cell phone and realized it had shut down. Needed a charge as much as Feather had last night. She slid from the truck bed, stuffed her bag into a sack and secured the tailgate. Now for her morning toilette. She moved away from the truck, pulled down her jeans, squatted and peed. A splash of water from her water bottle to clean her hands, followed by another to face and eyes and she was done. She found a very wrinkled sweatshirt jammed in a corner of the truck bed, and gave it a sniff. When it passed, she pulled it on.

She turned on the truck and plugged her phone to its charger. Immediately it beeped and she saw she had three voice messages and a text.

Michael: Voice message, left at 5:03 a.m.: *Where are you? We need to talk, so call me. Sorry I called so early, but I've been looking into our friend and I need to get more information from the database at our office.*

Mom: Message 1, left at 6:37 a.m.: *Join me for breakfast at the Osprey's Nest? We can plan our investigation.* Message 2, left at 7:52 a.m.: *Breakfast was delightful, if lonely. I am heading to Windfall after a brief stop here in town. Meet me there.*

Michael: Text message left at 7:42 a.m. *Stedman dangerous, but not blackmailer. Others dangerous, too. DO NOT GO TO WIND FARM. DO NOT LET YOUR MOTHER GO THERE. I MUST FOLLOW HIM. HE'S HEADED SOUTH.*

How could she have slept so long? It was after 8. Her mom was headed into danger, Michael, the muscle, was unavailable and they still didn't know who the blackmailer was. Terrific. At least Stedman wasn't headed for the wind farm. What did Michael mean by "others dangerous, too"?

"Focus, Feather, focus." First, stop Mom. Second, find Peter. Surely Michael didn't mean scruffy Peter was dangerous. *Anyone can be dangerous, when provoked. Like wild animals, if they don't see an out, they attack.*

She pushed speed dial for her mother. Jeanette picked up. "Feather, darling, where have you been? I drove by your trailer, but your truck wasn't there. I went to the door and those nasty little creatures you keep were inside making a fuss."

Not the time to lobby for injured squirrels. "Mom, where are you? Do not go to the wind farm."

"Whyever not, darling? They took poor Roxanne to Spokane for questioning, so I decided it was time to find the truth. I've just arrived at Windfall—"

"Mom, no! Leave now. Walk out the door—"

"Nonsense. We'll have a little chat and I'll see what I can—Thank you, Haley, dear. This is lovely. Got to go, you." She hung up on her daughter.

"Shoot, hellfire, and damnation." Her mother was right in the middle of the trouble. Alone with people Michael had called dangerous. If Feather charged in, the two of them would be up against Jon and Haley and possibly Peter. She needed reinforcements and a distraction.

She phoned Roadkill.

Thirty-Four

For Whom the Wind Blows

Feather parked in a clearing off the road to the wind farm, pulling behind a stack of slash left by the road department. Her little truck wasn't completely hidden, but it wouldn't be noticeable to inattentive or hurried passersby. With luck today wouldn't be the day chosen to set fire to the slash. She grabbed her backpack and set off.

She crawled under an old wood fence and walked to the house by staying in the small grove of aspen trees that ran along one side of the entrance lane. Sage and buckbrush made the going a bit rough, but provided a screen against suspicious eyes.

Her mother's inappropriate little sports car was parked in the gravel yard. Feather's breath caught. She ached to race inside and grab her mother and forcibly haul her from the building. To drag her to safety, no matter her mother's wishes.

But she figured that gesture wouldn't go over well. If her mother was already held captive by one of the occupants of the wind farm, Feather was too late. If not, Mom was likely to raise an objection to being dragged away from the action.

Best to do a little scoping out before entering. Several outbuildings were scattered behind the main farmhouse, but since the wind plant's offices were in the house, she decided to check there first. The high-pitched whine of the prototype wind turbine located toward the back of the farm grew more intense as Feather neared the farmhouse. Even at several hundred yards, the sound assailed her ears. Her mother never complained about it, proof that a wild youth attending too many Rush concerts had dulled Mom's hearing. She shook her head, as if that was going to solve the problem.

A broad porch stretched the width of the house, making anyone who wished to peer through the front windows starkly visible. The entry lane continued along that side of the house to the outbuildings beyond. On Feather's side of the house the woods grew near. A narrow, old garden, its gate hanging askew in invitation to neighborhood deer, bordered the house. Any other day Feather's fingers would yearn to explore the garden's rich and fertile soil.

Next to the house a gigantic rhododendron stretched nearly eight feet high and four feet wide. It would provide cover for Feather to look inside the front rooms. The unskirted front porch meant she could crawl from the rhody to the porch, under it and around to the other side. She refused to consider what dwelt beneath the porch.

She strolled from trees to rhododendron. Since she had to be in the open, she strove to appear more casual than furtive.

She made it. No one called to her, no one shot at her, presumably no one noticed her arrival. There was a front room window behind the large shrub, the sill not far above Feather's waist. If someone looked from inside, they would no doubt see her and probably not confuse her with a grazing elk. She ducked to the side and peeked around the edge of the window, holding her breath.

The room was empty, no sign of Mom, not even a coffee mug. A desk, the chair rolled snugly against it, faced the front door. It held a few neat stacks of paper, stacks that called to Feather to be examined.

Feather duck-walked, thighs aching, to the next window along the side of the house. It led into the same entry area. Much of her view was blocked by a tall bookcase. The next room had only a high, narrow window, with no easy way for Feather to look inside. She guessed that was the bathroom window. The next room had another high window. Feather spotted an old plastic bucket in the garden. She upended it and clambered onto it, praying the ancient bottom would not give way. Over the kitchen sink she spied a table that held three coffee cups. No one sat enjoying their morning java. But, heck, no body lay slumped on the table or the floor.

Safely off the bucket, Feather hotfooted it back to the rhododendron at the front of the house and braced herself for a creepy crawl under the front porch. Grateful for her gloves and sweatshirt, she gritted her teeth, clamped her mouth shut and crawled. It smelled of old leaves, mold and something dead beneath the porch. She focused on the other side and didn't look for bodies.

Her exit from the crawlspace beneath the porch was blocked at the other side by an ancient rosebush, its trunk grown thick. She forced her way through the branches that snatched at her watch cap and clothing. She pulled her cap off and shook it free of leaves and uninvited guests.

The window above her head led to a sort of sitting room with a couch—empty—and a couple of high-backed chairs—also empty.

"That's it," she muttered. "I am so not into skulking. In we go." Direct action had always been Feather's m.o.

She hoped no one would notice the absence of her truck. Once Roadkill and his crew arrived, no one would.

She skirted the rose bush, and mounted the stairs to the porch, crossed to and opened the front door to Windfall Works. Feeling like a bad actor in a so-so play, she turned right and walked to the receptionist's desk—had to be Haley's—stood for a moment or two and called out, "Good morning. Anyone here?"

Her answer was silence, so she repeated herself, louder. Maybe she'd hear a responding thump from above or below.

Maybe not. The silence continued, heavy as swamp gas in the room. She leaned forward and thumbed through the stacks on Haley's desk. Nothing exciting: utility bills, a government form requesting it be re-filed with corrected information, a brochure on the Pimsleur Approach to learning Spanish.

Where was her mother? She'd vowed not to work outside again. Mom should be in this office or Jon's.

Feather walked down the hallway and into the kitchen, pausing before a rack of hooks on the wall that held several coats, her mother's jacket not among them. One coffee mug showed a smear of raspberry lipstick. Her mother's shade.

Where was her mother?

She opted to take a quick circuit of the upstairs. Maybe she'd find Mom, deep into some project Haley or Jon had assigned her. If not, and if the house remained as empty as it seemed to be, it gave Feather a chance to look for clues as to why Michael had warned her off, and what was going on at Windfall.

Upstairs revealed a typical farmhouse layout: three bedrooms and a shared bath. One bedroom held a plain double bed and barren dresser. The master bedroom clearly was Jon's. The jumbled chaos echoed that of his office downstairs. Most of one wall was taken up by an unmade, rumpled queen bed. Papers littered a corner table and dirty socks and shirts lay willy-nilly on the floor. She checked his closet, in case someone had stuffed Mom in there. Nothing but rows of clothes too nice for Hancock, Idaho.

Haley's bedroom, the smallest of the three, mirrored her desk. Tidy, painfully so. A double bed, blankets tucked in, ship shape, corners taut. Nothing on her bedside table but a guidebook to North Idaho. The drawer held a packet of condoms. Being prepared seemed reasonable for someone like Haley. Bare walls: no art, no photos, no indicator of who lived in this room. Sunlight coming through the window shone on the wall behind Haley's bed, and clearly revealed three widely spaced nails where pictures had hung. But the walls were bare. Someone as excessively tidy as Haley would have removed the nails.

The dresser top held nothing—no jewelry box, no doilies, no letters. She opened the top drawer. Empty, as were the rest. Someone had stripped the closet bare, as well. Haley was leaving, already packed, luggage gone. If the items left behind meant anything, she had no intention of staying in North Idaho and wasn't much interested in protected sex in the future.

Haley was leaving Windfall. Her timing? Not auspicious. Not damning, unless she had a lot of money hidden somewhere, but probably not in a room she had abandoned. Feather pulled back the bedcovers. No sheets. Haley planned to leave today.

Back downstairs in the empty farmhouse, Feather spent more time searching the office. She glanced at the large schoolroom clock on the wall. 9:30. She wanted to call Michael, but he'd already told her he followed Chaz. Until Roadkill got here, she flew solo. She had to find her mother above all else. But she also had to figure out who created the problems at Windfall.

In Haley's office, an unlocked file cabinet held little of interest.

More invoices than you'd think necessary for supplies for the prototype turbine, but she left that analysis to someone more experienced with the technology. Any startup had expenses.

Had Haley cleared out her desk as well as her room or was she leaving that until later? She sat down behind the desk, wondering as she did what excuse she would offer Haley if she walked in on her search. "I heard a phone ring and hated to leave it?" "I thought I saw a mouse on your desk?" "I've been taken over by the spirit of the former owner?"

Without a decent excuse, Feather angled the chair so she could bound out of it at the slightest sound.

Feather searched the drawers, finding nothing except a few paper clips, the obligatory fuzzy mints and aspirin. But no purse, not even in the "purse" drawer. Where was Haley's purse? She looked around. The coats on the hall rack could cover purses, packs. And right next to the coat rack she spied a small entry closet.

She opened the closet. No bodies fell out, no owls or bats flew at her. A couple of hangers, covered with tattered hand-crocheted padding, hung empty. A battered but once-elegant leather briefcase stood on the floor. Feather pulled it out into the light in the hall. She shook it and felt rather than heard the papers inside. The case was locked. She could have easily pried it open, but she found the brass plaque above the keyhole more interesting. Large ornate script, three letters. PAB. She knew it stood for Peter Aloysius Brewer.

Teddy often called Peter, Aloysius, or Saint Aloysius.

Peter had to be here. Feather hadn't seen his white SUV. Had he wanted to hide his arrival? Maybe he'd rushed back to town, briefcase forgotten, when news of the fire at his office came in. Or maybe he'd set his own office afire and come here to destroy any remaining evidence of his crimes.

She returned the case and checked the coats. Her mother's hung from the peg, along with three others. One barn coat, a waxed canvas, heavy duty number for mucking out the hogs. Jeanette could have used that yesterday. The others were unisex rain jackets, one red, the other army green. The red jacket concealed nothing, but a large shoulder purse hung behind the army green coat. It had to be Haley's. Feather took it off the hook and replaced the jacket.

Feather spun in a complete circle, even darting to the front door to glance out to the porch. No one, so far. The purse she held had some heft. She unzipped the first compartment and extracted a wallet. She flipped it open to reveal an Idaho driver's license for Haley West and opposite the license, one credit card. The wallet held a large number of bills. Feather thumbed through at least fifteen twenties and several fifties.

She knew some people carried more cash than she did, okay, most people carried more cash than she did. Tips at The Blind Chukar ran to coins, ones and the occasional five. Sometimes bulky or heavy, rarely high value.

An office manager for a small startup couldn't earn much. She bore a lot of responsibility, since Jon traveled frequently and most of the partners remained fairly silent. Silent until things went the wrong way. They'd howled nonstop since the rumors about trouble surfaced at the Ganborena's fundraising party.

Focus, Feather. Back to Haley and her wad of cash. Perhaps she'd been saving her money. Not many places to spend it on a wind farm outside pipsqueak Hancock, Idaho. If she stayed away from upscale Sandpoint and Spokane's bustle, she could save. But most people kept this much cash in a bank. Granted, many activists scorned banks as too "establishment," and boycotted them, but Haley had never shown any activist inclinations.

Thinking of activists, however, reminded Feather that many of them kept their cash very close: in hidden compartments in their purses, or sewn into their clothing. She went into the bathroom. If Haley returned, she might not go first for her purse, but she definitely would notice its contents scattered on her desk.

Once locked in the bathroom, Feather checked Haley's purse thoroughly and methodically. She removed everything and laid all on the small antique table opposite the bathtub. Save for the Swiss Army knife in the outside pocket, nothing unexpected. A cell phone. It required a password. After trying Windfall, Feather gave up. No checkbook. Maybe Haley's stash simply revealed her reliance on cash.

Empty, the leather bag still had considerable heft. Feather wondered why. She upended it and tugged at the lining to turn the bag inside out. Hello. Speak of a stash. The liner bottom felt much thicker than the usual crappy cardboard. Feather squeezed it and it seemed spongy. She held it to the window and saw tiny hand stitches. She used the tiniest blade on Haley's army knife to cut the stitches.

Her mouth opened. Fifty and hundred dollar bills lined the bottom of the bag to a depth of more than a couple of inches. Ordinarily Feather couldn't imagine how much money the bills represented. Today she figured she beheld the results of Teddy's avarice. Avarice that ended up with Teddy dead and Roxanne a murder suspect. Money talks, all right. She stretched a finger out and touched the top of the stacks. That cash could smooth the path to building Feather's Beds and—. Feather pulled her hand from the bills. When she closed her mouth, which she realized still gaped, a bitter taste remained. The taste of greed? Envy? Regret?

Poor Teddy. Haley had killed his plans. A traitorous partner in crime or an opportunistic thief? Maybe, like Feather, she entered Teddy's home after someone else shot him. Maybe her worst crime was stealing his blackmail loot. Feather doubted that; the timing didn't work.

Teddy comes back from picking up his first "drop," enters his home and is shot by the unknown killer. Haley enters, sees his body and steals his score. Roxanne enters, sees his body and then sees Haley as a blurry figure escaping with the money. Roxanne leaves. Feather enters, sees Teddy's body and calls the cops. Ludicrous to imagine someone arriving before Haley to shoot Teddy and leave without the cash. More ludicrous to imagine that parade of people through his small home.

Feather shuddered. Even more ludicrous to stand here, holding the purse of a known killer who could return at any moment and discover Feather snooping. A killer who at this moment accompanied Feather's mother.

Feather replaced the money and the items in Haley's purse, and the purse to its place on the coat rack, hoping the woman wouldn't notice Feather's tampering.

The blackmail texts continued. If Haley sent them, and she wouldn't send them from her own phone—no one could be that dumb—burner phones existed. Whoever retained the phones could be proven a blackmailer, if not a killer. And since the cops hadn't found a gun at the scene of the crime, maybe she still had that piece of evidence. Her stomach knotted. Her mom, with her tendency to mouth off, hanging out with an armed killer. And what about Jon? And Peter?

She wanted nothing more than to find Mom and get her off the property and away from danger. Her mother would not go without a fuss. With one daughter jailed and the other under suspicion, Jeanette sought the real killer, with no thought to danger. Feather blew out a long, slow breath. She had to postpone worry and find proof of Haley's guilt. Were Jon and Peter co-conspirators or victims, as well? She told herself her mom could survive a few more minutes. Of course if Feather heard a gunshot, she knew the remorse would kill her almost as fast as a gun could kill her mother.

She moved to Jon's office and sat in Jon's desk chair to observe his desktop as he did. She smiled. Whispered, "Got it." The stacks to her right held catalogs. A red manila file folder with a label neatly printed that read, "Signature Needed" sat atop a closed laptop in the middle of the desk. Had to be Haley's work. A smaller stack on the left held opened correspondence. She thumbed through it, conscious every second that outside, her mother danced with criminals.

One letter on slightly heavier stock had a name and address embossed at the top. Sophia Patton. The letter, dated three weeks earlier, stated, in legalese, that Sophia withdrew as a partner and demanded the return of her initial investment.

Across the bottom, written by hand, "I'm not asking for interest on money you've held over eighteen months. I need it now, Jon. It's urgent." She had underscored urgent several times.

Had Sophia resorted to an illegal way to get that urgently needed money when Jon ignored her?

Her scan of the remaining correspondence revealed nothing of interest.

Feather left Jon's office and exited the front door. Still no sign of Roadkill or Michael or anyone else. Her mother and the others must be out back, but where? She texted Michael, knowing he'd be ticked that she and her mother came here. "Come to Windfall when through with Stedman. I am here, searching for Mom. Could not stop her."

She hated to ask for his help, but why hadn't Michael given her more information? "Others dangerous, too?" Which others? She already knew the pigs presented a menace and that Jon Flynn was a letch, but she doubted Michael meant that. She should have spent the night with Michael and helped with his research. Then she would have known what he found out. She shivered at the thought of another night in the company of the hunky PI. One night of denying her body's urgent requests had been enough.

She wished she carried a gun, even though she didn't believe in them for protection. Roadkill had once labeled her loud voice a deadly weapon. Her backpack held her Buck knife.

Now to find Mom and discover what kind of poop she skated hip deep in today.

Since Mom had vowed never to face down another hog or its output, Feather skirted the hog barn and corral and headed for the more distant outbuildings.

She heard a distinctive, tinkling laugh. Mom. She didn't sound in distress. Feather's ears rang and she realized she'd been clenching her jaw all morning. When she heard her mother's voice, the tension left her.

Rage replaced tension. Another woman's laughter joined her mother's. Where the *hell* had they been? Jeanette Sullivan thought of no one but herself. Feather bit her lip. Not true. Her mother sought Teddy's killer at Windfall, trying to save both her daughters from arrest. She had no idea she was at the hub of an incredibly dangerous hurricane. On the other hand, no one knew Feather hovered close to the truth.

The less her mother knew, the less she could reveal. Feather had a rotten poker face, but the stakes ran higher today than any she'd played. She readied herself for the role of a lifetime.

"Mom, where are you? What's up?"

Thirty-Five

You'll Be the Death of Me

Her mother, Haley and Jon emerged from behind a building. Jon held a piglet, extending it a ways from his body. Her mother, perfectly groomed, wore a pressed denim shirt over a turtleneck and jeans that cost more than her daughter's entire wardrobe, making them definitely not her daughter's jeans.

"Feather, dear, you've finally arrived." She frowned and continued. "I must tell you, that sweatshirt looks as if it's been in the bottom of the laundry basket for weeks and should remain there."

Of course. Mother would no doubt ask Saint Peter for an iron if Feather couldn't figure a way out of this mess. "Busy, Mom. What have you been up to?"

Jeanette raised her voice an octave and squeaked, "This little piggy went wee, wee, wee, and it ran all the way down Jon."

Jon grimaced. "If you say that one more time, you'll be holding the farrow."

Jeanette reached out a hand to caress the tiny animal. "You must admit, it's adorable."

Haley wrinkled her nose. "Adorable, maybe, stinky, absolutely." She gave Feather an assessing look. "I'll run to the house and get a towel for it."

"I'm sure there are some in the barn," Jeanette said. "It's closer." She, too, eyed her daughter. "Feather, come take a look at this little critter. And give me a hug."

Feather smiled and then sniffed in an exaggerated fashion. "Do I want to hug you, Mom? I can't believe you got near the hogs again."

"I'm a sucker for baby anything. Haley told me one of the sows had given birth, so we all went to check on her. This little guy fell off his momma's milk wagon."

Jeanette drew Feather into a close hug and whispered in her ear.

"Play along with me." Louder, she said, "I saw a stack of old towels in the barn yesterday. If Feather comes along to ward off the goat, I'll run get one. Back in no time." She took off at a trot, towing Feather with her.

"Get two," Jon called out. "Or three. We can smother the little whizzer."

Jeanette giggled gaily but raised her pace.

Inside the barn, she headed for an enclosed area in the center. "I expected you sooner, dear. Did you have time to search the house? I stalled them as long as I could."

The less she knows ... "Searching for *you*, Mom. I thought they'd taken you prisoner. I told you to leave."

Jeanette chuckled. "Oh, piffle. I intend to find out what's going on here. We're partners. What did you find? Hurry, we need to get back."

"I found you. Out here, playing with piglets. Didn't you imagine I might be concerned?"

"Concerned? About me? You? Really, Feather, I still have most of my marbles. I'm not an old growth tree or some charismatic fauna. I can take care of myself." She opened the door. "Tack room. I searched it yesterday. Nothing." She went to a shelf and grabbed a few old terry towels. "This should do it." She headed toward the barn entrance. "I'm disappointed you didn't take time to snoop." She paused. "Actually, I don't believe you. You don't want to tell me."

"That's ridiculous. Why would I keep secrets from you?" Feather couldn't hide her sarcasm.

Jeanette stopped and faced her daughter, holding the towels in front of her like a shield. "You think you're keeping me safe. It doesn't work, sweetheart. I know. I kept the secrets surrounding your father's death from you and Roxanne, thinking I was saving you from pain. And now ...."

"Now's not the time to share ancient secrets." Feather gave her mother a fake smile. "Tell me more about the pigs. We're getting near them."

Her mother's mouth twisted into the world's bitterest smile. "We need to talk, dearest. ASAP. How can anything so tiny, so cute, grow up to create such a horrific stench?"

"Vegans may have a point," Feather said.

"Don't start with me. If vegans had their way, we'd be bathing these critters until their dying day. Maybe massaging them."

They rejoined Jon and Haley and handed the towels to Jon. He swaddled the tiny pig in one cloth and used the others as a cushion around it. Feather decided to do some prodding. "I'd hoped to find Peter here. His office caught fire last night."

Haley and Jon nodded, but Jeanette registered shocked. "The sheriff phoned us, looking for him," Jon offered. "I heard your other daughter was caught there earlier," he said to Jeanette, not even trying to hide his smirk.

Jeanette reared back, tucking her head. "Surely you're not accusing my daughter—"

"She left hours earlier," Feather pointed out.

"Lots of ways to start a fire after you leave," Haley said. "I imagine you're skilled at that, being an activist and all."

"Activist and pacifist, not arsonist. I don't believe in violent solutions."

Haley smiled at her. "Sometimes they're the only ones." Her smile didn't make it past her nose to her cold hazel eyes. Feather knew then that Haley had killed Teddy. Now to get the proof. And to get her mother away safely.

They reached the house and filed up the back steps. Jon went first and found the door unlocked. "Surprised you didn't just wait here for us, Feather."

"I checked inside first. The front door's open, too. Figured Mom was back mucking out hogs and I had to save her." She smiled.

"I am perfectly capable of saving myself, dear. But thanks for your concern."

"Charming family." Innocuous words belied by Haley's flat, hard eyes. "Not all of us can count on a rescuer."

Jon returned from the pantry, where he'd found a box for the piglet. "I'll rescue you, anytime, Haley." He waggled his eyebrows at her.

Haley ignored him. She asked Feather, "What do you want with

Peter?"

Thank the universe I came up with my story. "I went by his office early this morning to try to convince him Roxanne meant no harm, and found it in flames. Well, really, by the time I got there, they had it under control." She shuddered. "It was awful." *At least that was no lie.* "Couldn't find him at his house, either."

Haley sneered. "My, my, you have been the busy little detective."

"Only trying to get Roxanne out of trouble."

Jeanette patted Feather's arm. Feather flinched and hoped no one noticed. Only Mom could find the biggest blister from the fire. "You're a good daughter. I need to tell you more often. Jon, what shall we feed this baby? Do I need to go to town for formula?"

Jon laughed. "This is a hog farm. There's special formula for them in the fridge. All it needs is warmed up." He started for the refrigerator, but was interrupted by voices in front of the house, chanting and shouting. Loudest among them came Roadkill's.

Thirty-Six

Secrets Revealed

"Not in my batyard," Roadkill shouted.

"Stop the pollution, stop the killing."

All four occupants of the kitchen hurried to the front of the house. Feather, tight muscles loosening now that her backup had arrived, noticed Jon locked the back door before leaving the kitchen. She also noticed Haley took a quick peek behind her jacket for her purse. She prayed she'd returned it in the same way she'd found it.

Feather stood by the front window and saw her friend Gina marching, carrying a sign bearing the words, "Any blow is a low blow."

Another woman, one Feather recognized as part of the group long opposed to the wind energy plant, held a sign that said, "This place stinks and so does Hancock." A male cohort bore a placard stating, "Bats are people, too."

Feather's eyebrows rose. *Huh?*

"Downwinders unite!" Feather recognized Roadkill's brother Ed Mustard's voice and saw him wielding a small video camera.

The protesters numbered fewer than a dozen, but made up for their small numbers with noise and activity. One wore a bat costume and flapped around the others, darting in and out of the line of marchers.

Roadkill's ice cream truck parked diagonally across the yard, effectively blocking anyone from leaving or entering the parking area. Ed's old Camry, far more scratched and battered than it had been when he drove up from L.A. more than a year ago, sat next to her mother's car. A small pickup sat beside it. A couple of bicycles were leaned against the low stone fence.

"Incredible timing for a protest," Haley said from behind Feather.

Her mother nudged her way beside Feather. She inhaled sharply.

"There's no way for me to get out. You have to get them to move. Now."

"What's your problem, Mom? They're simply stating their opinions."

Jon opened the front door wide. "Be my guest."

Her mother pulled her cell phone from a pocket in her wool jacket. She glanced at it and said, "I need to use the restroom. Feather, please join me."

Haley stood back to make way, smirking. "Aren't we a little past going to the powder room together?"

Jeanette lifted her head and braced her shoulders back. "I have personal family business to discuss with my daughter. Do not forget that my other daughter is in jail. Give us a moment, if you please." Jeanette touched Feather's arm and gave her a quick, urgent stare. Then she swept past Haley, head high, not deigning to comment. Feather followed, hiding a grin. Her mother "swept" better than most royalty.

Once locked inside the bathroom, Jeanette turned to Feather, her eyes filling. "Leave it to Roadkill and that stupid truck to make me face reality." She pulled down her designer jeans and sat on the toilet.

"The reality that you had to pee?"

Her mother smiled through tears. "No, but I did, indeed." She finished and stood and before she flushed, asked, "You need this?"

Feather did and did, astonished that her mother was doing the eco thing by not flushing. "What's going on, Mom?"

"I can't do this."

Feather resisted saying she just had and remained silent, hoping her expression read receptive instead of skeptical. She'd heard so much drama from her mother over the years.

"I told you I got one of those nasty blackmail texts when everyone else did, but you may have noticed I didn't tell you what it said." Her mother rolled her lips together.

Feather raised an eyebrow. "So? Not my business."

"I could just kill Peter Brewer and his big mouth. It had to be him."

"Peter's the blackmailer?"

Her mother shook her head. "No, I'm certain Teddy sent the blackmail messages. But he spent time with Peter, often late at night, when Peter was drinking." She looked out the curtained window, but it faced the back, and Feather assumed there was little to see. "I told you Peter drank too much, I'm sure."

Feather couldn't remember, but she nodded so her mother would continue.

"I don't often confide in others, but once, several years ago, Peter and I were at The Aerie and I had a tiny bit too much to drink and I told him about your father." She chewed her lip and managed a tiny smile. "I seem to get in trouble at that place. Although I'm sure, Chaz was a mere innocent ship, passing in the night."

"Not innocent. I'll tell you later." Feather looked at the door. "What did it matter if you told Peter about our father? He's dead, his reputation doesn't matter."

Jeanette patted Feather's cheek. "You're right, of course. But I had too much pride. I should have told you and Roxanne years ago."

Feather stiffened and tried to hide her wariness. Her high-pitched voice betrayed her. "Told us what?"

Her mother turned away from Feather's glare and gazed out the window. "Your father spent a great deal of time in Central and South America. As a photographer."

"I knew that." *Get on with it.*

"A talented, successful photographer. Who had another family in Ecuador."

"Another family? In Ecuador? I thought he was shooting the Galapagos Islands."

"He was. He did. He also married a woman in Guayaquil and had three children."

"Three children? Girls or boys?" Stupid question, in light of her mother's revelation.

Her mother turned back to Feather and smiled, the bitterness evident. "Two boys and a girl. He hid it all from me."

"Is Dad really dead? Or did he fake it, to stay down there with them?" Feather sounded like a petulant, jealous child, not an adult, yet she couldn't stop herself.

"He's really dead. Remember, I flew down there to get his body. When I came home without it, I told you he wanted to be buried there, where he spent so much time. That was true. He had a plot for the family down there. Figured he would die up here, but ... just in case. And it made Yerina, his wife, happy."

"You wanted to make his *wife* happy?"

"Believe me, honey, Yerina was as shocked as I to learn Martin had another family."

"And you never told us. That was years ago, Mom."

"I was ashamed. I thought I wasn't good enough to keep him."

"What bullshit. He was a philanderer, plain and simple. He took advantage of two innocent women." Unexpected tears flowed down her face.

Jeanette smiled sadly and used a thumb to wipe away a few of Feather's tears. "See. I knew how you'd react: black and white, right and wrong. It will devastate Roxanne, as well. But ... it had to be done. I can't give in to this blackmailer." She bowed her head. "Thank you, Roadkill," she whispered.

"Thank me. I called Roadkill. We needed a distraction out here. I didn't realize how much we needed one. When did you get instructions?" She knew she had to get her mother out of the house, away from Haley, who most likely killed Teddy. But her mother's little bomb had put her into shock.

"Early this morning. Told me to 'stand by' with ten thousand dollars in cash. I already had the cash, from the first text Teddy sent. Today I realized I can't pay. It could go on and on."

A rap sounded on the door. "You two okay in there?" Jon asked. "We have to discuss what to do about that riot out front."

Feather stared at her mother. She saw a beautiful woman who had been living a lie, a woman who chose to keep a dark secret from her daughters and from the world. Jeanette told Feather she'd kept quiet for the sake of her daughters, but Feather wondered how much had been her pride, her damaged confidence. It didn't matter all that much. What mattered was Mom had the courage to stand against the blackmailer and tell the truth today.

Feather threw her arm around her mother's shoulder. "I'm proud of you, Mom. But now we need to leave. Fast. Please don't ask me to explain."

They returned to the front of the house, where Jon stood like a quivering statue at the front window, staring nervously out. "We have to disperse them."

Feather didn't understand his extreme concern. "They're not hurting anyone. Just making a lot of noise. I can ask Roadkill to tone it down, if you want."

"Can you get him to retreat?"

"I doubt it."

Haley rose from her chair, where she'd been tidying things up. *She must be planning on getting out of here soon, but she doesn't seem nervous about the drive being blocked.* "Chill, Jon. He won't be here for hours."

"He who?" Feather asked.

"He who is none of your business," Haley replied, more cleverly than normal.

Jon moved to stand in front of Haley's desk, ignoring Feather and her mother. "I think we should call the sheriff. This is private property."

Haley smiled in good imitation of the Grinch. "You *really* want the cops swarming this place?"

Feather thought a swarm of police a good thing at this moment.

Jeanette chuckled. "Been to Hancock much? There's no swarm of police. If Sheriff Warnock called out all his regular and 'temporary' troops, it might come to five."

Goose bumps rippled down Feather's spine. *Oh, Lord. Did Mom just tell a criminal the police force in these parts is puny? I am definitely not tracking.*

Haley still spoke as if she and Jon were alone. "I repeat, you sure you want five officers of the law wandering around here?"

Jeanette didn't like to be on the fringe of any conversation. "Whyever would you care? Would they find something illegal?"

Feather's fingers curled, as if around her mother's throat and way-too-mouthy mouth. Better yet, she wished she could make her eat her words and that Haley and Jon had not heard them. She whispered into her mother's ear. "One of them could be the blackmailer. Teddy's killer. We've *got* to talk."

Jon and Haley each shot Jeanette intent, suspicious looks.

Jeanette laughed, a tinkly, airheaded laugh that sounded brittle to Feather. Jon's expression relaxed, but Haley's posture remained erect and rigid at her desk.

"That poor little piggy must be starving," Jeanette said. "Jon, will you show me how?"

Jon waved her away. "The bottles are in the fridge. Just heat one up in the microwave."

"Heavens, not the microwave. It kills all the nutrients. I'll find a pan and heat some water." She headed for the kitchen, sending Feather a not-very-surreptitious glance and directing her eyes in a not-very-surreptitious manner in the direction of the kitchen as she left. Sheez. Mom. So not the spy.

Feather remained in the office, hoping to learn why Jon needed to get rid of the demonstrators. Besides, she had nothing she wanted to share with Mom the Spy.

A crash sounded in the kitchen. "Shi-oot. Aach." Her mother's screech of pain impelled Feather to dash to help her. She found her mother standing above the pieces of a bottle, the contents splattered on the linoleum floor. "I burned myself." She rushed to the sink to put her fingers under the tap.

Feather grabbed an ice cube tray from the freezer and handed a couple of cubes to her mother. "Better than the water."

Her mom took the cubes and rubbed them against her fingers. "Who knew it would heat that fast?" She grabbed another bottle from the fridge and stuffed it in the microwave.

"Good thing you didn't burn the poor piggy's widdle throat," Feather said. "Really, Mom, we need to leave. Now."

A high pitched squeal emitted from the box on the counter where Jon had left the pig. Either the petite porker had a great sense of smell or he responded to any presence with a demand for food.

Someone pounded on the back door. Feather saw an enraged Sophia Patton through the window. "Where the hell is Peter

Brewer?" she screeched.

Thirty-Seven
This Little Piggy Squealed

Feather opened the door. The more chaos, the less likely Haley—and Jon, if he also was involved—could cause problems. Sophia, looking more like a banshee than a banker, racketed across the kitchen to Feather. "Someone told me you were looking for the rotten swindler, too."

Feather took a breath, of the calming sort, she hoped. "I'm looking for Peter, along with some answers. Can't say I've found either. Do you have a beef with him?" Talk about a dumb question.

Sophia drew a breath. Alas, it appeared to be for more fuel to her inner fire. "You bet I do. First, the man told me investing in Windfall was a sure thing, a way to make money fast. Then he told me, and I'm not kidding you, that 'sometimes the winds change.' That interest had waned in wind energy. Appears more people than that scruffy crew outside object to the side effects." She inhaled again and rubbed beneath her eyes. "So I asked for my money back. No interest, no harm, no foul, with a U not a W. And what do I hear from him? Zip, nada, goose egg. Next thing I know, I'm getting blackmail texts."

Jeanette reached a hand out to Sophia. "We all got those, dear."

Sophia turned her anger on Jeanette. "But how many of *us* got instructions on where to deliver the cash? This afternoon?" She looked past Jeanette to Haley and Jon. "Brewer's office burned down and no one can find him. He's not home, either. I've got to find him."

Jeanette started to answer but Feather shook her head and spoke loud enough to cover her mother's words. "Have you called the sheriff?"

Sophia's laugh came out bitter and sharp and sad at the same time. "Why bother? I can't pay. Let him, or her, tell my grandmother

I'm a lesbian, married to her so-called roommate."

While Sophia spoke a slim figure entered the now-crowded kitchen from the front offices. "Your grandmother already knows that, dear."

Sophia's pale complexion turned the color of concrete. She pivoted slowly, as if to postpone seeing her grandmother, as if, perhaps, her grandmother might leave. "Grammy?" came out in a tiny voice.

Victoria Douglas, the woman whom Feather had met by the carousel, smiled. "I've had such a time tracking you down, dear. Fortunately Aileen was home and suggested where you might be. I had to park on the road and make my way past those delightful protestors." She wrapped her granddaughter in her arms. "I've been so worried about you, sweetie. You avoided me. I thought your mother had gotten to you."

"She told me you'd disown me. Told me all Americans were intolerant."

"Told you people never change, never learn. Wrong, at least in my case." She cleared her throat. "Maybe we can talk better in private." Jon and Haley had followed the two women into the now-crowded kitchen. Jon looked curious. Haley peered out the back window, at her watch, tapped her foot.

Tears dripped past Sophia's elegant nose but her color had returned. She sniffed. "I still want to talk to that slimy Peter. He's not answering my calls." She turned to Jon. "Can you give me my money back?"

Jon looked at the floor, at the piglet, whose squeals had not diminished, at the stove, but not at Sophia. "Not without the authorization of all the partners."

Sophia's grandmother tugged at the younger woman. "All in good time. Let's go home now. I think your room—wife needs some comforting. And you both can explain to me how money became so gosh-danged important."

Sophia burst into louder sobs. "We're going to have a baby! I want to quit my job."

Her grandmother smiled and patted her arm. "Wonderful news,

dear. Now let's go home. Just smile as we walk by the protesters. They're quite friendly." She turned to Feather and smiled. "So exciting." Sophia's grandmother ushered her out of the kitchen.

Feather realized Roadkill might be wondering about her. In her frantic early-morning call, she'd only told him to bring a crowd and keep them nearby. She hadn't provided details, mostly because she didn't know details.

Feather's mother began feeding the piglet. It quieted, happily sucking. Slurping sounds filled the silence that had taken over the kitchen after Sophia and her grandmother left. Feather found it soothing. The wind must have calmed because she no longer heard the whine of the turbine.

Jon spoke first. "Wonder where Peter went. Lots of folks want to talk to him."

Haley, who had been staring at the back door with an almost vacant, almost—if Feather wasn't imagining it—yearning look on her face, stirred. "Maybe he doesn't want to talk to them. He left and he didn't say anything about his destination. Now, I have work to do." She stomped from the kitchen after glaring at Jon.

If Haley had killed Teddy, if she had taken on the role of blackmailer, her work involved picking up payments from Sophia and from Jeanette. Sophia obviously wasn't coughing up any cash. That left Jeanette, and the blackmailer had to think Feather's mother still planned to pay.

Jon paced between Feather, her mother and the window. "I think we should call the cops. Get them to leave."

Roadkill and his friends had accomplished what Feather had hoped for: making sure she and her mother weren't at the wind farm alone. But she wished Michael were here and that she knew what he'd found out about Jon and Haley. And where was Peter? "I'll talk to him," she said. "But they've got a right to be here."

Her mother shot her an odd look from her chair. "I'll join you when this little piggy is finished."

"Be sure you put him back fast," Jon told her. "Otherwise—"

Jeanette squealed louder than the pig. "Oh, ick! The little bas— cutie peed all over me. It smells gross. And I had him wrapped in a towel."

Jon grinned at her. "Oops. Perils of pig parenting."

Jeanette returned the piglet to its box and began the process of scrubbing up at the kitchen sink. Feather figured she should help her mother but it was more fun watching her suffer, nose wrinkled, hands turning pink from an abundance of hot water and soap.

Haley charged into the kitchen and glowered at Jon. "Chaz phoned. He bought his car. Says he should be back by 2:00 or so. I stalled him by telling him about the view and the wine list at Beverly's in Coeur d'Alene. We gotta get rid of the protesters."

Jon didn't hide his gloating sneer. "Feather offered to talk to them."

Jeanette glided from the sink to Jon and Haley. "Did I hear you mention Chaz? Such a dear, sweet man. We shared a lovely meal last night."

Jon and Haley stared at Jeanette, horror evident on their faces. Haley spoke first. "You met Chaz? Did he know you were a partner here?"

Jeanette giggled. "After I told him. He's the kind of man a person can confide in."

Jon's face mottled, partly pink like the piglet, partly fiery red. "Uh-huh. A real pussycat, our Chaz."

Jeanette narrowed her eyes. "Is that some kind of slang? I assure you our dinner was just that. Dinner."

"He was only describing Chaz's personality," Haley said. "Actually, he's got claws. You want to avoid him in the future." She directed her words to Feather and lost her smile. "You think you can get rid of them?" She jerked her head toward the front of the house.

"I'll try. Come on, Mom, you can give Roadkill a bad time." Feather hoped her voice didn't betray her nervousness. Who was this Chaz Stedman and how did he evoke such fear from Jon, Haley, even Michael? She wanted to tape her mother's mouth shut. She was less a threat before Jon and Haley learned she knew Chaz. That seemed clear. What wasn't clear, was why they feared him. She took hold of her mother's forearm and guided her out of the kitchen.

"Don't drag me, for mercy's sake," Jeanette said. "I am not a sack of beans."

Feather waited until they'd reached the porch to speak. "For heaven's sake, Mom, I begged you to leave when we talked this morning. You wouldn't listen. Michael texted me about Chaz. Told me he was dangerous and that we both should stay away from this place. As usual, your stubborn refusal to think I might have a good idea has thrown us into a pot of trouble. Did you see the looks on their faces?"

Jeanette looked from her daughter to the protesters, most of whom were now seated on the ground or leaning against Roadkill's truck. "You called Roadkill for help. Good idea."

"A compliment for me? Wowza."

"I am proud of you and your capabilities. Especially for being sneaky."

Feather inhaled, held it and let the breath out. Her mother was teasing her and she almost took the hook. "Stick with me, please." She descended the stairs to meet with Roadkill.

"Wait. I've got a text," her mother called.

I so care. Not. Feather continued without pause and suggested that Roadkill and his little band could wait on the highway, out of sight of the farm. "It might take a few minutes to disperse the truly dedicated. I'm going to send them home," he said. "But I'll be here and so will Ed. Call if you need us. And check in with me when you leave."

Feather leaned in and gave him a peck on the cheek. "Thanks, buddy. I owe you."

Roadkill grinned at her. "Believe me, I'll call in that debt."

No doubt. Feather returned to the porch, where her mother sat on a twig chair, staring at her phone. Feather joined her.

"I got a text, telling me where to deliver the money. A park in Sandpoint. At 2:00 p.m. today." She showed her phone to Feather.

"You decided not to pay. But ... the blackmailer doesn't know that. We can call the sheriff and Michael and they can tail him or her."

Her mother smiled. "I have a better plan. I'm going to smoke the blackmailer out."

"Not another fire. Last night was close enough."

Her mother's brows wrinkled. Jeanette Sullivan didn't often allow wrinkles of any sort. "Last night?"

Feather shook her head. The group by Roadkill's truck was disbanding, stacking their signs on the floor of the ice cream truck. "Not important. Let's tell Roadkill to call the sheriff so no one inside will hear." She stood.

Jeanette stood, too. "No. Tell him to expect a call soon from us." She strode into the house before Feather could react.

What ridiculous scheme had her mother dreamed up? Feather went back to Roadkill. "Another blackmail pickup is scheduled. From Mom. Sophia got one, too. Can you let Byron know?"

Roadkill shook his head. "No way. I'm not going near Byron right now. He thinks I broke into Peter's offices and set fire to the place. I'll wait until he calms down, thanks. You can give him a call."

"Please. Ask Ed or Gina. I don't want Jon or Haley to know."

"Sheez. You suspect them and you're in the same house? That's more dangerous than tree sitting. I'll ask Gina. When and where?"

"The Old Ninth Grade Center in Sandpoint, 2:00. I'll let Michael know once I get inside and see what Mom's up to. Thanks."

"Be careful in there. Things have a way of blowing up when you least expect them."

"I'm always careful."

Roadkill smiled. "Uh huh." He nudged the activist who stood next to him, a dedicated guy who went by the name of Shrug, for obvious reasons. Shrug guffawed, which Feather thought entirely inappropriate. Of course she was careful.

Thirty-Eight
Things Couldn't Get Worse

Feather went inside, and finding Jon alone in the front office, told him that the protesters should be leaving soon. She didn't mention that they would regroup at the highway. She wanted Roadkill nearby. Jon walked out to the porch to assure himself they were leaving.

As soon as she tracked her mother down, she'd convince her to leave and go directly to Sheriff Byron Warnock's office. It was obvious Peter wasn't here, or if he was, that he had no intention of being found, so they might as well get out before Chaz returned.

She walked into the kitchen, thinking the piglet was fed more often than she'd been. Her mother sat at the table, Haley across from her.

"Run, Feather! Go for help," her mother yelled.

"Not if you ever want to see your mother alive again," Haley said in a low, menacing tone.

Feather froze. "What's going on?" Her shock erased all creative sentences from her brain.

"I thought you were smarter than your sister and your mother. Guess I was wrong." Haley stood and gestured with the gun she'd hidden under the table. "Up, Jeanette. Let's take a walk. Feather, go into the hall and get my coat and the purse behind it. Don't do anything funny or I'll shoot your mom."

The hallway and front room were empty, Jon still out front. Feather grabbed Haley's jacket and purse and her mother's, as well. She still wore hers. Her backpack was on a kitchen chair.

Back in the kitchen, Haley allowed Feather to give her mother her jacket and to pick up her backpack. "Good job. Now it looks like the two of you are out back, working. Teddy was behind on cleaning the assembly room and sorting inventory." She moved to the back door and gestured with the silencer-equipped handgun. "Out the back door. No sudden moves. Normal pace."

Feather noticed that Haley's hand holding the gun trembled and the woman herself thrummed with nerves, even though her voice sounded steady. She hoped nothing set her off. She followed her mother.

Once they reached the other side of the barn, and were hidden from the house, Haley stopped them. "Give me your purse, and your backpack. Don't try anything cute."

"My bag has the girls' photos. Please let me at least keep them." Jeanette held her bag out.

Haley let out a small breath and glanced at Jeanette. She took Jeanette's purse and looked through it. "Where the hell's the blackmail money you were supposed to have?"

Jeanette's jaw tightened. *Oh, God, Mom. Don't get stubborn now. The woman has a Glock in her hand.* "In my car. Locked in the glove box."

Haley stuffed Jeanette's car keys in her back pocket, kept her cell phone, and returned her purse to Jeanette. "Let's hope you're telling me the truth, old woman."

Jeanette looked more shocked at being called an old woman than she had when Haley aimed her pistol at the women.

Haley tossed their cell phones into the hog corral, followed by Feather's backpack. The hogs hustled over to see what was new in their pen. Pigs are omnivorous and will eat almost anything. If they didn't eat the cell phones, they would chew off parts or bury them. Feather shivered, but from relief, not the chill. At least it didn't look like Haley planned to throw them to the hogs.

Footsteps pounded behind them on the hardened earth pathway. "What are you doing? Haley, have you totally lost it? Chaz will kill us when he gets here."

Haley turned and pointed the handgun at Jon. "I'm not waiting around to experience that. I'm leaving."

"But what are you doing with—"

"Don't try to stop me, Jon. I'm only locking them up so they won't call the cops."

Jon's mouth gaped like a bubble in the hog muck. "You killed Teddy. You took the money Brad gave him. Why?" He started toward her and she raised the gun. "You stole the cash from the safe, too. I thought it was Teddy. I want my money back, you thieving bitch."

"You stole it from Chaz. I deserve it, the way you've treated me. Consider it my salary."

"You can't do this to me." He took another step toward her.

"Don't be more of an idiot than you already are. Turn around and go back to the house, or I'll lock you up with these two."

"No, you wouldn't dare. Haley, put the gun down." He strode toward her, and it looked as if he might grab her gun.

Feather's gaze moved from Haley to Jon. Her eyes were wide, her face pale. He looked ... cocky. Arrogant. As if he knew she wouldn't fight him.

Haley fired the gun and Jon's forward momentum caused him to fall to his knees and then face forward on the ground. Feather's hand hit her chest, as if her body feared her heart would pound its way out. The shocked, horrified look on Jon's face imprinted on her brain like a bad photo, never to be discarded. She moved closer to her mother, clutched her arm.

Jeanette stood, rigid. "Let me go to him," she said, her voice calm.

Haley let the gun fall to her side. "I told him to stop. Why wouldn't he stop?" Her voice trembled. "I have to get away. Things are out of control."

"No one should die face down in the dirt."

Haley didn't want to look at Jon. That was obvious. She focused on Jeanette and Feather. "Go ahead and turn him over."

The two women moved to where Jon had fallen. Feather turned her back to Haley, blocking her view, in case Jon was still, by some miracle, alive. They gently moved him to a supine position. Feather touched his neck, felt a faint pulse. She looked at her mother and saw her tiny nod. When Feather saw Jon's loafers, she gasped. Definitely those she'd seen in Peter's office. Not just a lecher, an arsonist. But still a human being.

Haley moved close to the hog pen, still keeping her eyes on Feather and her mother. "I didn't want to kill Teddy. I didn't want him to die, even if he was a fool. But Jon? He's a monster. He forced me to give him blow jobs all the time. Raped me twice, even though I gave him what he wanted." She grabbed a handful of hog manure and threw it at Jon. It hit his chest. "He always thought he was my boss. Yelled at me, ignored my ideas. But if he would have stopped, I wouldn't have shot him. Why do men think women are stupid?" Another handful of mud and manure hit Jon in the face. Feather took most of it and stuffed it into the wound on Jon's chest, which was still bleeding.

"Ooh, pig shit for a sexist pig," her mother cried. She crawled to the pen and grabbed more manure and dumped it onto Jon. Feather was able to pile that on the wound, as well. She'd have taken her sweatshirt off to cover the wound, but feared Haley would stop her.

The two women stood. Feather wanted to tackle Haley, but a Glock was more powerful than a girl. Haley gestured with her gun. "Walk. Try anything, Feather, and I shoot your mother first."

"What does it matter," Jeanette said. "You're going to kill us, anyway. Sooner or later, we'll die."

Great job, Mom. Get her angry so I don't have time to figure a way out of this. "You have a good defense, if he sexually abused you," Feather offered.

Haley's chuckle revealed despair. "And what defense do I have for killing Teddy?"

Feather hadn't thought this through, obviously. "No one knows for sure you shot him."

Her mother laughed with scorn. "Anyone knows they'll have ballistic evidence linking it to her gun."

"Thanks, Mom. Good thought."

Haley laughed so hard Feather hoped she might drop her pistol. "You two are something. Open mouth, insert foot. Don't make me laugh so hard I pull the trigger."

Feather's mother turned around and gave her daughter an apologetic shrug. "Oops."

"Oops? Oops?" Feather heaved a sigh. "It's okay, Mom. I love you."

"I love you, too, sweetie."

Haley nudged Feather with her gun and Feather jumped ahead, almost colliding with her mother. "Keep walking. Shut up. Get some speed on." She directed them to a gravel drive that led to a large building at the rear of all the outbuildings.

High windows admitted enough light to guide them as Haley hustled them through the building, which held, as far as Feather could tell, more than enough equipment to get the wind farm operational. All they needed were the permits, she guessed. Here was where the investors' money had been spent. So what was illegal about this? Were they growing weed in some other outbuilding? She'd need more time and possibly some sleep to figure all this out, but she worried that time was something they didn't have.

At the wall opposite their entry door, Haley told Feather to open the tall sliding door. They entered another room. The room reeked of moth balls as opposed to the mustiness of the first half of the building and it was dark, only a sliver of light sneaking in through the door. Haley nudged them along the wall until they came to a light switch. "Hit the lights," Haley said.

Feather complied. Fluorescent lights slowly revealed the room's contents. Directly in front of them was a Chevrolet from the 1960s, in pristine condition. Feather gaped. "You said there were 'some old cars' stored here. These aren't just old, they're classic."

Five other vintage automobiles were parked neatly on the carpeted floor. "I barely caught a glimpse before Jon found me. Look. It's an old Plymouth," Jeanette whispered, awe at the old cars overshadowing her fear for the moment. "Why aren't they covered?"

Haley smiled, no doubt amused by her prisoners' interest in the cars. "Better just to dust them often. Sadly, I trusted Teddy to do that."

Her mother moved closer to the Plymouth. "Somebody has a lot of money."

Haley smiled. "Sellers like being paid in cash for these babies. Helps with taxes, I gather."

Feather's gut clenched. "A lot of cash. Stedman's from Canada.

He's … dangerous," she murmured, remembering Michael's text. "That's why there are two documents of incorporation. It's just a clever way to launder drug money. Windfall Works is a sham. Did you ever plan to have a real wind farm?"

"Brad wanted a wind farm. So did the other partners. We might eventually have started up, if Teddy hadn't gotten greedy. But now the bats and eagles don't have to worry. Only you. Head for the far wall. We're going to the office."

Feather and her mother walked slowly, gawking at the cars, Feather hoping to see an escape route.

Haley poked Feather with the gun, hard. She'd bruise, if she lived long enough. "Move it!"

Feather couldn't figure out why Haley would kill them inside one of the wind farm buildings, so perhaps she just meant to tie them up, so she could escape.

They passed a very early Ford Mustang, bright red, beautiful. Jeanette halted. "If you're going to kill me, shoot me now, with this Mustang. I have many fond memories of this car."

Feather wished her mother would stop providing ideas to Haley.

Haley apparently agreed. "Don't tempt me, old woman. Keep walking."

Her mother stomped her foot. "Quit calling me 'old woman.'"

"It's what you are. Now move or I'll shoot your daughter."

Jeanette moved and Feather breathed. She scanned the huge room. Feather had to act before Haley stopped them. If Haley tied them up somewhere, Jon would die before anyone came looking for them or one of them was able to escape and call for help. *If* they could escape.

Along the far wall, peg board hung over a long work bench. A variety of tools hung from the board, but the bench was deep and Feather doubted she could reach anything useful before Haley noticed and shot her or her mother. A rusty tool about a foot in length rested on the workbench. In front of the immaculate, organized tools, the antique sheep shears looked as out of place as a harpoon at a Star Trek convention. Near it lay a fluffy duster for the cars. Weapons, not what Feather hoped to combat Haley and her semi-automatic pistol, but better than trying to tackle the woman empty-handed.

A pristine pale blue Oldsmobile convertible sat at the back of the building, farthest from the office door but next to the workbench. A panel that stretched from the front fender to the rear displayed the model, a Starfire. Feather headed for the convertible as if it had a magnetic field. "Will you look at that? I used to know someone with one of those. I love 'em." She stared at her mother, willing her to join her. "Mom, remember the Olds Fred Willits used to drive in the parade?" *Come on, Mom, play along.*

Her mother angled herself so she was headed to the blue car. "Ah, yes, the memories. Didn't Roxanne ride in that car one year?" She jogged to the door and opened it. "Yes, I remember, all of us got to sit on that luscious leather seat and wave."

Haley followed Jeanette, her face reddening. "Wait! You can't—"

"One last ride, in honor of dear departed Fred." Jeanette lowered herself into the passenger seat and pulled the door closed. From the other side of the car, Feather watched. Haley sighed. She moved to the car door. "For God's sake, you are one stubborn old witch. Get out. Now."

Feather moved as quietly as she could to the bench and grabbed the shears and the duster. She stuffed the duster in the back of her pants beneath her sweatshirt and the shears in the front. If she moved wrong, Haley wouldn't have to kill her.

Her mother slumped in the car seat. "Maybe I shouldn't have sat down. My head ... I don't feel ... I'm not sure I can stand."

Haley jerked the door open and grabbed Jeanette's arm. She dragged her out of the car. Jeanette fell to her knees. Haley yanked at her. "I should just shoot you now," she said. "What a royal pain you two are."

We're going to become much bigger pains inside of a minute. "Let me help her." Feather ran around the back of the car and stood beside her mother. If she knelt she'd become a victim of those shears. "Is there water anywhere?"

Haley snorted. "Water? You're worried about water?"

Feather gave her a steady look. "I thought if I revived her, we wouldn't have to drag her to wherever you plan to dump our bodies." Jeanette moaned and slumped against the car.

"I *told* you I wouldn't kill you. Although you are making it tempting."

"You might claim shooting Jon was self-defense. Not us. Besides, he was a bad guy and so was Teddy. We're innocent women."

Haley smiled at that, a smile with a bitter twist. "The hell you are. You two and your long noses have caused me more trouble than Jon, Teddy and the rest of the partners put together."

Keeping Haley talking might calm her and give Feather the opportunity she needed. Maybe she could also learn something useful. Useful, of course, only if Feather and her mother remained alive. "What about Chaz?"

Every part of Haley tightened—her jaw, her neck, her mouth, her eyes, her voice. "Shut the heck up. No water. She gets up or you drag her."

Feather bent to give her mother's cheeks a light slap. The shears stabbed her breast and she jerked upright. Her mother moaned. She slapped her harder. "Mom. Mom. You have to get up."

Feather pulled her mother up and leaned close. She whispered in her ear. "Get ready. Now or never." Louder, she added, "Walk with me, I'll help."

She grabbed her mother around the shoulders. She stepped backward, as if staggering against the weight, and ran into Haley.

She shoved her mother forward, with luck out of the line of fire, and jerked her right elbow back and up, hard, aiming for Haley's throat or her face. The woman was near Feather's height, so she hit her chin. Haley fell backward with a grunt and shouted, "Shit."

She didn't fire. Feather spun around, snatching the sheep shears from her waistband. The shears snagged on the waist of Feather's jeans and she jerked at them, hard. The shears flew out of her hand and hit the car with a metallic clang. Haley lifted the gun. Feather leapt to the side and pulled the feather duster from behind her. She whacked Haley on her forearm with enough force to break the wooden stick of the feather duster. It may have slowed Haley for a moment. Heck, the woman might die laughing at Feather's efforts to clean up crime. With the broken stub of the duster stick, Feather poked at the tender area inside Haley's elbow.

Haley shrieked. She staggered back.

Her mother had fallen to her knees when Feather shoved, and remained there. Feather gave a second's thought to hoping her mom was okay. Then she saw the gun, and saw Haley plant her feet, ready to fire. She threw the broken duster stick at Haley, distracting her for an instant. Haley fired. Feather heard a metallic ping as the bullet struck the car behind her. Feather had no weapons. In one quick glance she saw the shears on the floor and dove for them as she had all those years scooping for a volleyball.

Her left leg wobbled as she dove for the shears but she ignored it. She spun around, shears now in hand, staying low. Haley smiled, secure in the knowledge that she held a deadly weapon. She waved it at Feather, signaling her to admit defeat. "Drop it," she said.

Then Haley shrieked and staggered forward, falling to one knee. Feather, adrenalin and rage surging too much to concede, charged in low. Haley tumbled over her and dropped the Glock. Feather grabbed the gun, held it in shaking hands.

Jeanette leapt to her feet and pumped her fist in the air. "We did it! We beat the bitch."

Feather shook her head. "We?" Then she saw the duster in her mother's hand.

"I poked her in the back of the knee. That's why she fell." Her mother closed in on her daughter, her arms wide and open for a hug. "You're bleeding. She shot you. Oh my good Lord." Jeanette fell to her knees beside Feather, who gazed numbly at her leg and realized she'd been shot. But the bullet hit that car. Ick. Must have passed through her leg. As soon as she saw the blood, the pain pierced her.

Her mother had already torn off her jeans shirt and pulled her turtleneck over her head. Feather sank weakly to her knees. "We've got to tie her up."

"First things first. You're wounded, young lady." Her mother wrapped her turtleneck around Feather's bleeding thigh, tight but not tourniquet tight, and tied it off with the sleeves. "We have to find a first aid kit. Get help."

"Jon's worse off than we are. We need to help him."

Her mother ignored her and Feather had the comforting thought that things were returning to normal.

Haley groaned.

"Knock her out," Jeanette said, her voice flat and cold. "Or just shoot her."

Feather's eyes widened. Violence did not become her mother. "Tying her up might be an option."

Her mother sighed. "I suppose. But she shot you. You keep an eye on her and I'll check that room she was headed for with us. There might be duct tape or a first aid kit."

Feather scooted slowly and gingerly to the vintage Olds and leaned against the front side panel. She stretched out her injured leg and bent the other in, yoga fashion. She kept the Glock pointed at Haley, even though the woman didn't appear to stir beyond that one groan. The gun weighed heavy in her hands.

When she heard her mother's running steps, she called out to her. "Bring some rags. There ought to be towels on the bench."

"I already got some." Her mother's voice came from beside Feather.

Feather startled and nearly pulled the trigger. "Jeez, Mom. Give me some warning."

"You're losing blood. I'm surprised you haven't fainted."

"I don't faint."

Her mother dropped a stack of folded car towels, and then knelt beside Feather. She held a pair of scissors, duct tape, and a large first aid kit. "Anyone can faint. It's a physical phenomenon, not an emotional event."

Feather jerked her head toward Haley. "Tape her up first. I can wait."

"You're more important."

Feather grinned. "Such sweet words. I *might* faint."

Jeanette's sigh was heavy with drama. She walked to Haley. She wrapped her hands behind her back with duct tape and then taped her legs together. She then wrapped tape between the woman's arms down to her legs, pulling her legs into a bent position behind her.

"Isn't that overkill?"

"Kill? Don't give me any ideas. Wait till you see who's in the office."

Feather did a quick mental inventory and came up with "Peter?"

Her mother nodded. She untied her turtleneck from around Feather's thigh and used the scissors to cut off Feather's jeans leg. She made quick work of bandaging the wound. "You'll need to visit the ER, but let's take care of Jon and get to a phone." She gestured toward the wall. "The one in the office there doesn't work."

Pain merged with sorrow in Feather's brain. "Peter's dead, too? What a nightmare."

Jeanette made a tsking sound. "He's alive. Smells worse than the hogs. I left him trussed up, since we don't know for sure if he's a good guy or a bad 'un."

Jeanette finished her ministrations and helped Feather to her feet. After she recovered from the pain of standing, Feather said, "Let's tape Haley to the workbench. She might come to and be able to crawl away. She's pretty muscular."

"I could do it by myself. It can't be a good idea for you to walk on that leg."

Feather ignored her and began to drag their captor by one leg toward the workbench. Her mother pulled on the other and then used considerable duct tape to tie her to the bench leg.

Feather hobbled away from her mother, aiming for the door they'd come in. She still clutched Haley's handgun. Might as well hand it to the sheriff, so he'd understand why it held Feather's fingerprints as well as Haley's.

Her mother huffed out an exaggerated sigh and followed her, hovering beside her like a head chef watching his sous break eggs.

Beside them the garage door rolled open, the mechanism humming. Brilliant sunlight lasered Feather's eyes. She squinted.

Thirty-Nine

Things Get Worse

Yet another vintage sedan idled outside. As the door glided open, she saw a form return to the driver's side and the car rolled in, rounded fenders and gleaming chrome grill rampant, tires crunching on the gravel, then silent on the carpeted indoor floor. The vehicle stopped.

Feather stilled. Her breath came in small pants. No wonder Haley had been in a rush. This had to be Chaz. If Haley, a killer, was afraid of this man, if Jon's voice quivered when he said his name, she and her mother had better be careful. Very careful. She put a hand out to steady and calm her mother, and possibly herself.

She felt nothing and glanced back where her mother had been a second before. Jeanette strolled toward the car, a saucy tilt to her gait. "Mom," she said in a low voice.

Her mother flipped her hand in Feather's direction, dismissing her. She was either incredibly stupid or incredibly brave. Or perhaps way too confident of her allure.

The car door opened and the man Feather had seen last night got out, smiling. Even though he didn't look threatening, Feather was glad she held a gun behind her back.

Jeanette waltzed close, too close, to the newcomer. "Chaz. How delightful. You must show me your latest purchase."

Feather suddenly recalled that Chaz should be followed shortly by Michael. She let her gaze extend past the antique car. Nothing.

Chaz smiled, looking directly at Feather, but extending his arm to grasp Jeanette's forearm. "Looking for your friend? I'm afraid he's been delayed. The seller was more than happy to drive *my* car north to Bonners Ferry for a small fee." He jerked Jeanette around so her body blocked his. He continued as if chatting about everyday events. "I stopped in the office and walked around back before I moved the car here. Poor Jon. Babbling in his last moments. But no worry. He's in hog heaven now."

Jeanette struggled to free herself. "Let me go, Chaz. Why are you doing this?"

Chaz pulled a knife from his pocket. "Don't make this more uncomfortable than it already is, Jeanette. You and your lovely daughter are far too inquisitive."

"Feather merely came out here to help me. She knows nothing."

Chaz laughed, no joy in the sound. "I'm afraid both of you know far too much. Else why would you have tied the lovely Haley to the workbench?" His gaze flicked for an instant on Haley, who was conscious now but remained eerily silent, her expression watchful.

Feather wondered about his plans for that knife, knowing hers would change if she knew his thoughts. If he intended to cut Haley free, she would have to stop him, because Haley would kill her and her mother in a New York minute. If he intended to hurt her mother, she had to find a way to stop him. Get that knife out of his hands. "You have no clue what the not-so-lovely Haley has been up to. Killing a former employee, shooting your manager Jon, packing all her belongings in preparation for escape." Chaz raised an eyebrow at that last piece of information, but otherwise appeared unmoved. "And for some reason unknown to us, she brought us here and started shooting up your precious cars. Lots of anger in the woman."

Woo hoo! That got a reaction. Dragging Feather's mother along with him, almost idly as if she were luggage, but keeping the knife at her throat, Chaz went to Haley and stood above her.

Haley finally broke her silence. "She's lying. I shot at her when her mother and her attacked me."

"She and her mother," Chaz corrected. "You simply don't learn."

Feather wondered why Haley hadn't told Chaz that Feather held the gun. Apparently she was more afraid of Chaz than of Feather, even when she was holding a gun. Scary thought.

Chaz gripped her mother around the throat and reached down with his knife hand, idly slicing Haley's cheek. The cut was deep and bled immediately. Haley had tucked her head down and Feather realized she'd expected Chaz to cut her throat. Oh, yes, he was a heck of a lot scarier than Feather, even if she'd been holding a machine gun. She had to stop him. What had her idiot mother been thinking? And where, oh where, was Michael? Was he still alive? And Jon?

She stared at her mother, who completely stopped struggling against Chaz. Her face pale, she simply stared back at Feather, as if trying to send a mental message. Feather didn't catch her drift.

Haley mewled in pain but kept talking. "I tell you, they're lying. Peter killed Teddy. I found out and was going to lock him up until you got back. But he had a heart attack. Died. She saw him." She gave a tiny jerk of her head toward Jeanette.

To her credit, Jeanette didn't leave much of a gap. "Yes. Such a shame. But then he carried all that weight in his gut."

Holy crap, Mom. We're not drinking tea together. Okay, my turn. "I thought ... Jon ran after us. Maybe Haley's telling the truth. Not that I believe her." So much more important than a poker game, or even trying to get a logger to back down. Feather prayed they'd at least confused Chaz, slowed his thinking.

Her mother's pale face gave Feather an idea. She wiped her face with her left hand, remembering to keep the gun behind her. "I ... can't stand any longer." She staggered backward, hoping she was near the old Oldsmobile. She was. She slumped sideways against the trunk.

"Stay away from the car," Chaz said.

Thank you, Chaz. "I ... lost ... too much blood," she whispered. She pushed herself away from the trunk, onto her knees, almost around the rear fender, closer to the tire, but not as near as she'd like. As she slumped, she gave her mother a look of appeal. "Mom."

Jeanette cried out, her shriek reverberating in the large building. "My baby." She pounded on Chaz's shoulder. "She's dying, too. Can't you see? Let me go to her."

Chaz chuckled. "You are definitely a drama queen. Hold still or your face will look worse than Haley's. And take a lot longer to heal, at your advanced age."

"Cad. I thought you were a gentleman, last night."

"Your mistake. Good manners don't indicate a kind heart." Chaz looked from the woman trussed on the floor to Feather and then tilted Jeanette the slightest bit away from himself, to see her face. Feather took a breath. Chaz asked in a level tone, "Where's the gun?"

"You're going to kill us. I knew it." Another shriek reached the rooftop. It ended abruptly.

Feather had used her mother's fit, that she hoped was indeed staged, to crawl behind the car and use the shears to pry loose a hubcap.

"No one is coming to your aid, Jeanette. Stop caterwauling. Feather, come out from behind the Olds or your mother dies now."

Feather moaned, hoping it convinced Chaz. Since her leg was bleeding again and the pain stabbed her at even the tiniest movement, she assumed it would. She was convinced. "I ... can't move very fast." She followed it with another groan, this one involuntary as she rose from her knees. She leaned against the Olds' fender for support and placed Haley's gun on the broad blue expanse.

She took a breath and hurled the hubcap at the windshield of Chaz's latest acquisition with all the force she could muster. Apparently the car was built before widespread use of laminated glass. The windshield shattered. Feather snatched up the gun and leaned over the fender to aim. Chaz spun to look for the source of the noise, which sounded gratifyingly like an explosion. He still had a grip on Jeanette, but her mother slumped to her knees.

Feather aimed, praying she was not so weak she'd hit her mother or completely miss Chaz. She'd killed many an aluminum can in her youth. So what if she'd never aimed a gun at a human being? She took a breath, held it, and pulled the trigger. Chaz screamed, high-pitched, the cry of a wounded animal. He staggered backward and clutched his right leg. Weird. Feather would swear her bullet had gone far to the left. She focused again. If only her mother weren't so close to Chaz. Obviously, she was trying to stay out of the line of fire, but Feather had less faith in her shooting ability.

"You bitch!" Chaz shouted and leapt at Jeanette, who scrambled away from him. Feather fired. Chaz fell forward. Her mother kept crawling. Feather fired again, terrified that the monster would rise again, at the same time terrified she had killed him.

She dragged herself around the rear of the Olds and limped to the fallen Chaz. She held the battered shears aloft in her left hand and the Glock in her right, aimed at Chaz. He lay still, but she could see his chest moving. He was alive. Conscious? She wanted the knife he had terrorized her mother with.

Feather didn't want to get too near Chaz, but she couldn't leave him armed. She limped to the workbench and saw a broom leaning against the far end. Why hadn't she grabbed that instead of the feather duster? Sheez. Haley looked up at her. The blood on her cheek had begun to clot, into a shape that looked like a large tear. "I didn't think anyone could kill Chaz," Haley said, awe in her voice.

"He's not dead."

"You ought to kill him. Chaz has a long memory."

Jeanette appeared beside Feather, startling her. "Mom, are you okay? Did he hurt you?"

"It's nothing compared to what we did to him. You go, girl." Her mother raised a hand as if to high five Feather, but lowered it. She looked at Feather's leg, bleeding again after all the action. "We need to get you to a doctor."

Feather so wanted to lie down, to have her mother bring her ginger ale and a cold cloth. "We have to tie up Chaz and find Jon and see if there's anything we can do for Peter." She thought about the best way to incapacitate Chaz, other than cutting his Achilles tendons. "I'm afraid of him, Mom. We both should be," she added, when her mother started to scoff. "We can't leave him anywhere near Haley. I'll hold the gun on him while you find that knife. Use the broom at the end of the workbench to roll him over. Do not get near him if you can push the knife away with the broom stick."

Her mother picked up the broom and walked to Chaz, but only after giving Feather a look. "You worry too much. If he gives us a problem, just shoot him again. Or I'll bite his other leg. I wonder if I need a tetanus shot."

So that's why Chaz had gone after her mom. Feather said nothing. What could you say to a woman who had bitten her captor?

She stood guard while her mother rolled Chaz, who did seem to be unconscious, onto his back. He still held the knife in his right hand. Jeanette started to kick it away. "Use the broom stick. Don't argue, Mom."

Her mother complied, taking a couple of swats with the long stick before the knife skidded across the floor. Feather didn't think she could get up again if she squatted to retrieve the knife. "Bring me the broom, please. I'll use it as a cane. Then you're going to have to truss him up, legs, hands behind his back."

Chaz only moaned when Jeanette tied him up with duct tape. "He's shot in the side and in the leg. I don't think he'll go far."

"Maybe, maybe not. Hand me a leg. We'll tape him to the Olds."

Her mother giggled. "I like it. But we need to hurry. I have to check on Peter. And Jon." She spun Chaz around by clutching both his legs, then handed one foot clad in a designer leather sneaker to Feather. "Keep the gun ready, hon."

Feather realized she would have to walk without the aid of the makeshift cane if she wanted to keep the gun ready. She gritted her teeth and took a breath. "Let's get this over with." She gave her mother the broom.

They dragged Chaz to the Olds. Feather stood guard while Jeanette finished off the roll of tape attaching him to the rear bumper. Chaz was not going anywhere. Jeanette stood and arched her back. "Ugh. No more crawling around. Every part of me hurts."

"Check to see if he has a cell phone." As the fear of Chaz left Feather, it drained her adrenalin as well. She reached for the broom her mother had leaned against the car. She leaned into the wall, her strongest wish to sink to the floor and sleep.

Jeanette checked his pockets and extracted a phone. She dialed 911.

As her mother told the emergency operator their situation, Feather giggled at her absurd report. Two down here, no three, Jeanette corrected. Another shot and thrown into a hog pen. And her daughter shot, as well. Feather told herself she could sleep for two days if she could keep going for a few more minutes. She took a breath. "Mom, let's go see about Jon. There's a chance he's still alive, despite the hogs. Peter will have to wait."

Her mother nodded and moved to Feather's side. "Let's go." Her tone was grim. The women had no idea what they would find outside.

Jeanette shuddered beside Feather. "Remember that Oregon farmer whose hogs ate him?"

"Maybe they were hungrier than these. Hadn't you and Jon and Haley just fed them?"

Jeanette's expression brightened. "Yes. We filled their food bins."

"I searched Peter's office before someone set fire to it and found the original bill of sale for the farm. There's nothing about having to keep the hogs. I think they were doing it to make getting permits harder. Once the farm was working, there'd be more people around and they'd have to relocate the cars. Not what Chaz wanted."

"Scum. To think I invested my money with a drug lord."

"Not to mention ate dinner with one." Feather couldn't resist.

Jeanette gasped. "Do you think I'll be arrested? Serve time?"

The devil in Feather wanted to string her mother's fears out but she couldn't. "You were an innocent victim, Mom." Her mother's tight grasp on her arm loosened.

Jon was not where they'd left him. They went to the hog pen, poised for the worst. Two hogs came to the fence to check out the newcomers. Several more gathered around a water trough.

"Uhhhhh." A moaning, groaning sound came from the pen.

"I am so not going into that pen," Jeanette said. "Maybe if it were you or Roxanne ..."

"Roxanne, for sure," Feather muttered. "There has to be a gate."

"Get over yourself," Jeanette snapped. "I love both my girls." She moved down the fence and found a gate. "Shoot the hogs if they get near me. I am not kidding. And none of your 'power to the pigs-save the animals' crap. If one of them is bleeding, it will draw attention away from Jon."

Feather smiled. "Good thinking. I promise."

Jeanette entered the pen and the two closest hogs came up to her, nudging her legs. She clutched the fence, and made her way to the water trough, a huge round aluminum tank sunk into the ground.

An insulated, thick pipe led to the tank so it could be filled without entering the pen. "Jon, where are you?" She turned back toward Feather. "Bring me that stick. Fast." She climbed up the fence. "And keep the gun handy."

"Bossy much?" Feather put the gun in her jeans and hobbled to her mother, using the broom and the fence to support herself. Her energy drained from her. "Can you see him?" She lifted the broom to the fence and her mother seized it. She wielded it downward, as if mixing cement.

Feather heard running footsteps behind her. She jerked around and found herself pointing the gun at Roadkill and Ed Mustard. They halted, throwing their hands in the air. "Whoa, Feather, it's us," Roadkill said. She lowered the shaking gun.

"The good guys," Ed said. As Roadkill crossed the short distance to Feather and engulfed her in a hug, Ed looked around. "Why is your mother in the hog pen?"

"She's trying to find Jon. Chaz ... shot ...." Feather slumped forward into Roadkill's chest.

Ed raised his voice so Jeanette, surrounded by curious, grunting hogs, could hear him. "Jon's in the house. We called for paramedics."

"Oh my Lord," Jeanette said. "Feather, shoot me. Better, get me out of here." She swatted at a nearby pig with her broom stick and backed toward the fence. "Now!"

Ed and Roadkill helped Jeanette, by now covered in hog muck, back over the fence. "Your timing could have been better," she said, eyeing her ruined clothes and shoes.

Roadkill patted her arm. "We waited a long time before I got worried about you two. No idea what you were up to. By the time we found Jon, he was unconscious. Ed and I were heading out to search the outbuildings."

Forty

Timing is All

Michael arrived, shamefaced at having been duped by Chaz, in time to drive Feather to the hospital in Sandpoint. The ambulances were full. Ed took Jeanette to her B&B to change and clean up.

Jeanette planned to go to Spokane to retrieve Roxanne from the police. "We'll both be by to visit later. Stay in the hospital."

"Pudding!" After assuring her mother that she hadn't fallen into shock, Feather got reassurances from Gina that she would check on the dog and see if she could remain hospitalized for one more day.

Jeanette insisted that both invalids, dog and daughter, recuperate at her home in Sandpoint. Soon to be homeless, Feather agreed. Besides, it might be fun spending time with her mother without a gun pointed at either of them.

At the hospital, Michael explained that Chaz imported heroin from the Far East and distributed most of it to his southern neighbors. Windfall Works and the classic cars served as good conduits for the dirty money he brought in.

If Jon recovered, he would be tried for arson. Feather had confessed to seeing his shoes and legs while in Peter's office the night of the fire. Sheriff Warnock chose to ignore the circumstances of her presence there.

Peter, taken to another room in the hospital suffering from dehydration and his head injury, confessed to embezzling funds from his investors, sending most to assure his disabled daughter had excellent—and costly—treatment in California. He protested ignorance about the wind farm being a cover for Chaz's drug conduit and money laundering. Who knew what prosecutors would decide to pursue?

Michael sat beside Feather's hospital bed while she slept. When she awoke, they talked until, exhausted, she slept again. And awoke again to find him still there with her.

Forty-One

Breaking News

The groundbreaking for Feather's Beds was attended by every soul in Hancock who Feather held dear and quite a few others who previously held her at arm's length. The weather remained blessedly pleasant, even after the three weeks it took for Feather to recuperate and plan the launch of her new enterprise.

In the audience were Roxanne, Roadkill, Gina, Ed Mustard, and Emily Naismith, owner of the land where Feather's Beds would rise. Feather's mother stood in the front row, inappropriately but elegantly attired for the ceremony and party that would follow on tables set up on Gina's front lawn. Sophia and Aileen and Sophia's grandmother Victoria stood a little ways back, arms wrapped around each other, her grandmother's hand resting on Sophia's stomach. Sophia's and Aileen's faces glowed with joy.

Absent, no surprise to Feather, were Brad, Kristin and Jared. At least they'd decided to stay together and in Coeur d'Alene. Possibly one day Kristin would re-institute Feather's visits to Jared, but Feather had decided not to push it. Jared was the child of her heart and her womb, but he belonged with Kristin and Brad.

With Peter, Haley, Jon, and Chaz all awaiting trial, Brad and the other investors had abandoned plans for a wind farm. Sophia, newly retired from the bank, spent hours with a forensics accountant and recouped some of their investment. Selling the equipment also brought in some funds and the investors agreed to set up a trust for Peter's disabled daughter in California.

Not your usual groundbreaking ceremony, this one found Feather seated on her brand new-to-her garden tractor, ready to turn under the first load of clover she'd purchased at a nearby farm.

At some point in the past week, while trying to free her sister and herself from police suspicion, while facing down death, Feather had an epiphany. The dream that provided the name of her bed and breakfast was actually telling her about another kind of bed, a garden bed. She realized that instead of nurturing travelers and their whims, what she really yearned to do was grub about in the dirt and nurture plants. It would take a few years to get organic certification, but Feather's Beds would be producing food next spring.

The same near-death experience had convinced Feather's mother she wanted to support her daughters' dreams regardless of where those dreams took them. Simply because Jeanette thought starting a bed and breakfast was akin to selling yourself into slavery didn't mean she should deny Feather a loan. Her loan got Feather her tractor and a greenhouse.

At Gina's invitation, Feather and Pudding, recovered and accompanied by the silly squirrels, had moved to the foreman's house on Gina's land, so she could be close to her new enterprise.

Feather stood on the running board of her tractor, leaning against the engine block to rest her healing leg. Someone clanged a dinner triangle. Chatter stilled. "Thanks to all of you for coming," Feather began. She shared her hopes for Feather's Beds and gave thanks to her mother, to Gina, and to all the others who'd helped her get settled in her new home. "I've named my new tractor Rocky, in the hopes that he will keep running and keep fighting for a long time." After the laughter subsided, she added, "I owe the idea for the name to my friend Michael, who has decided to move to Hancock and help me with the farm while he applies for teaching jobs."

A few cries of "Hear, hear," broke the silence. Michael turned from where he stood in the front row and took a deep bow.

"Let's dig some dirt." Feather turned the tractor on and began her first formal furrow on her new farm.

The End

Thanks for reading *Foul Wind*. If you enjoyed it, please review it on Amazon or wherever you purchased it. Reviews help other readers find me and like all authors, I love to have new readers find me. If you want to know what's going on in my life and my words, sign up for my periodic newsletter at www.KathyMcIntosh.com.

Acknowledgments

Many thanks to Ben Otto of the Idaho Conservation League for his time and knowledge in helping me understand the pros and cons of wind energy. Thanks also to my daughter Caroline "Frog" Tinker and to Douglas Vaughn Schoellkopf for more facts about birds, bats and wind power. Any technical errors are, of course, mine.

Heartfelt thanks to my critique partner Conda Douglas, who truly gets my humor and knows how to tell great stories, and to my astute editor, Amberly Smith. I'm especially grateful to first readers Cathy Carson and Therese Kissel, whose insights made it a better book.

ABOUT THE AUTHOR

What can I say? I'm addicted—to words. I love the way words sound and the way they look on a page. In addition to creating offbeat adventures for the zany characters in my novels, I write and speak about words and writing. My family transplanted from Idaho to the Sonoran desert a few years ago, gleefully abandoning long johns and snow shovels. Now the scenery has changed from cottonwoods to cactus, with the occasional sighting of javelinas and other extraordinary desert life. I share space with a large, lazy, dog and a husband who most of the time is neither hairy nor lazy. When not enjoying the outdoors or cozied up reading, I love to travel and explore different cultures and cuisines.

Be on the lookout for my next adventure, set in the Sonoran desert. *Cuckoo*'s coming in early 2018.

Find out more at www.KathyMcIntosh.com. Or visit me on Facebook, www.facebook.com/kathymcintoshauthor.

I occasionally peep on Twitter: www.twitter.com/kathymcwrite. May your winds blow fair and friendly.

Mustard's Last Stand

One

Where's the Map?

Ed Mustard figured his life must be a geography lesson. Peaks, valleys, and no topographic map. He slogged on. Up? Down? Who knew? For sure, this jaunt to his ex-wife's wake at the home of his former mother-in-law hit close to bottom.

Time to leave. Past time.

He elbowed toward the street, through the small contingent of reporters. Most accepted his "No comment" reply to their questions and let him pass. Most. Not Con Lawrence, the persistent television anchor whose garlic and gin breath announced his presence before his intrusive question.

"What's the *real* story, Ed? I heard you're leaving Los Angeles. Is it true?"

"Watch out!" The high-pitched, frightened voice of Alexis Margolis, Ed's literary agent, rang out over the din of the paparazzi.

Ed whirled at Alex's cry. Not fast enough to catch the bright yellow plastic jug that sailed at him, striking his shoulder and head. He winced and jerked away from the blow. The jug bounced off his head, its already loose lid popping free. Despite Ed's effort to catch it, the jug fell to the ground in front of him, its gritty gray contents spewing over him and Con Lawrence.

His mother-in-law's distinctive cackle broke the silence that had fallen after Alex's shout. "Here you go. All that's left of the 'incomparable young actress Lise Clanahan.' She's all yours."

The door slammed behind Marliss Clanahan, allowing her return to the remnant of guests celebrating the short frantic life of her famous daughter.

"Oh, gross." Con Lawrence brushed at his clothes and backed

away from Ed.

A trace of a smile came to Ed's mouth. *Hooray. Finally, a way to get rid of pesky reporters.*

Bob Gilman, Ed's lawyer, moved in front of Ed. In his large, dark-skinned hand he held a short-handled whisk broom and a dust pan. "These might help. Keep 'em in my car."

"Of course you do." Ed's smile broadened. Everything about Bob was impeccable—his clothing, his haircut, his car, his home. Count on Bob to have a broom in his trunk.

Ed knelt and swept the ashes of his ex-wife into the plastic mustard jug. He tuned out the clicks and whirs of cameras and the low-pitched murmur of reporters.

Not the way Lise hoped to be remembered.

Into the Unknown, But Not Alone

Ed popped the trunk of his ancient Camry and enjoyed another fleeting smile at the wrinkled noses of his companions. Despite his efforts to clean the car, the trunk retained lingering and not-so-faint odors of the belongings of its previous owners. One of them may have delivered pizza or at least hauled a great many greasy boxes home. Another, like Ed's brother in Idaho, might have collected dead animals—the trunk wafted out an unappetizing metallic odor of dried blood.

"Holy crap." Alex stepped back.

"I don't think so," Bob said. "There's nothing holy about that stench."

"Excuse me," Ed chuckled as he tried to act seriously affronted. "That's my car you're insulting."

Alex widened her incredible green eyes. "Taking a few steps down in lifestyle might be appropriate right now. But this ..." She gestured at the run-down Camry. "What kind of statement is this?"

Ed sighed. "Not a statement. Reality."

"Jesus. The reality is, you've lost your mind. You sold the McMansion, not a bad decision considering it's so incredibly ugly. You hand that screeching witch," she tilted her head back toward the

Clanahan home, "a pile of money she obviously appreciated—not— and you've stopped writing."

"I haven't stopped writing." Ed rearranged the boxes in the trunk to make room for the plastic jug. He slammed the trunk. "Took a break. I'll have the treatment to you soon." He'd promised his agent the narrative version of his next film script weeks earlier. He'd yet to write a word of it. He moved to the driver's door, faced his lawyer and his agent. His friends.

Bob's face held sympathy and concern. "No one could have saved Lise. Stop blaming yourself."

"Nobody else to blame."

"I think it's moronic that you won't tell me where you're going." Even so, Bob walked forward and extended his hand.

Ed grasped Bob's hand and pulled the taller black man into a hug. "Don't know."

Alex crossed her arms. "I'm pissed at you. I'll find another writer and you'll be looking for a new agent if I don't get something in three weeks." She grabbed him in a close hug. "Even so, I love you, sweetie. Take care."

The cremains of Ed's ex-wife stayed in the trunk of the old car for two hours and seventeen minutes. Not that Ed timed it.

Outside Barstow, he pulled off Interstate 15 at a rest stop and extracted an envelope stuffed with state maps from the side pocket.

He'd spoken the truth to Bob. When he left Santa Monica, his only intention was to drive. To escape. Since heading west would be a short drive, he'd turned east. He took freeways to avoid familiar landmarks in the city he'd lived in for nearly a decade. He'd said his goodbyes in a long bike ride the previous week, before he'd sold his beloved road bike and his BMW convertible.

Peering at the California map, Ed decided to take I-40 to Needles, following Route 66 as much as possible. No more signs for Route 66, but he'd look for The Old National Trails highway turn-offs.

After a pit stop, Ed paused at the trunk, opened it and retrieved the yellow plastic jug of ashes. He tightened the lid and put the jug between his laptop case and yet more boxes in the back seat. How was it possible he had enough stuff to fill the Camry? He'd spent the last weeks ridding himself of the baggage and memories of his life since leaving North Idaho.

He settled into the driver's seat. "Don't worry, Lise. I didn't throw away your photos and awards. I knew you'd haunt me if I did." *Not that she didn't, anyway.* "Only gave away your furniture. The thrift shop is planning a special auction."

He took a sip of water now stale and tepid. "I always wanted to follow old Route 66. You killed that idea. No way were you going to stay in ancient, moldy motels in small towns where people might not even recognize you."

No response.

"If you have any objections, best voice them now."

Nothing but the sound of wind-blown gravel and the muffled idling engine of a nearby 18-wheeler.

Ed turned the key. "Could be a long journey."

Kathy McIntosh

Foul Wind

www.ingramcontent.com/pod-product-compliance
Lightning Source LLC
Chambersburg PA
CBHW020438270626
47155CB00022B/632